DEVIL'S ELBOW

ELLE WHITE

To our hearts in vases and our souls in jars, we're sorry.

For those who stood by my side even when the darkness consumed me. To my Aunt Shannon and sister, Meghan. Without your encouragement, I might never have been brave enough to finish.

Preface:

Intently focused on the burning desire to cure me of my affliction. Loneliness has no end in sight, not unless one is willing to offer up their heart so easily. And in doing so, one must prepare themselves for the inevitable heartbreak that will come as a result.

Love is pain, but without love, life seems meaningless. Loneliness is also pain. Instead of being in discomfort from the fullness in our hearts to which love is the sole offender, we are left with emptiness. The lack of love which consumes us so wholly. And how can a heart pump so true with nothing inside? How does it keep us alive?

I'm reminded of dead flowers in a vase. The vase, still full of something that was once so beautiful, it is whole in its existence, being used for its true purpose. Whether the flowers are dead or not, the vase is complete with them inside.

An empty vase is a far more tragic sight. There's no evidence that it's ever been full, so it sits there, barren and transparent. Lonely, empty, hollow. Much too depressing a sight for anyone who's ever been whole before. Because what good is a vase that holds no flowers?

CHAPTER ONE:

I WAS BORN IN A SMALL TOWN in Tennessee known as Hunter's Point. My mother told me that the night I was born, the rain came down with a mighty fury, and it didn't stop for two weeks. My mother said, "Scarlett…I ain't never seen so much rain like on the day you were born. As if the angels themselves were weeping out of sheer jealousy."

But mothers always think their children are beautiful. Really, the only strange thing about the rain on my birthday was that the town flooded, killing three people who were unable to make it to safety. And although flooding isn't that strange of an occurrence where I'm from, three people dying to make room for myself in the world seems like a lot of pressure.

The town in which I was raised is so small and so insignificant that hardly anyone knows we exist at all. Hunter's Point isn't located near a big city. It has nothing to offer an outsider other than the best damn hooch this side of the Appalachians, but that's a home-kept secret. But those people who do know of Hunter's Point, only know about us because of the infamous Rubidoux River that cuts right through town.

The Rubidoux, pronounced (*rooby-doo*), has accounted for twenty-two deaths over the past forty years. Stretching about sixty miles, the Rubidoux does pass through other Tennessee towns, but to them,it's just a river.

The problem Hunter's Point residents face is—despite the name—right outside of city limits are a series of low lying roads and bridges that haven't been maintained the way that one would expect. Roads and bridges that in the midst of a thunderstorm will flood, completely becoming consumed by water.

For example, a girl from the high school was parked beneath one of the bridges one night with her boyfriend on an embankment normally used for fishing. The two had been distracted. So much so that they didn't notice that it had started raining. Or that it had started flooding. But how could one really notice while being under a bridge and being preoccupied?

They managed to make it out before the river carried them away. The car's still down there though, about a few miles up. You can see it when it's low tide. But the problem isn't the 5,000 residents of Hunter's Point necessarily. It's with the hundreds of residents outside of city limits and the obstacles they face in every day life.

There are two roads that cut through or lead to Hunter's Point. One coming from the northern end. The other, coming from the east. This road, known as Y highway, leads to the small community affectionately known to the locals as Devil's Elbow, and during a thunderstorm, the community is inaccessible.

It's because of this that the most infamous story to the locals of Hunter's Point and Devil's Elbow exists. When I was only five years old, we were hit with one of the worst floods we ever saw. The waters of the Rubidoux even managed to reach people living on the point. Schools closed as well as the local businesses.

It wasn't until the flood subsided and phone lines were back up that a thirteen-year-old boy from Devil's Elbow called the local sheriff's office and said that his mother had been murdered two days before. Police swarmed the scene. The mother was found bludgeoned to death in the bedroom. There were two boys. The thirteen-year old who placed the call, and a six-year old who wouldn't speak to anyone.

When police question him, the eldest revealed their father killed her. He then fled, leaving his two sons alone with the body. Because of the flood, the boys couldn't call for help. When the father was found and convicted of murder, he was sentenced to death, although I believe they've yet to execute him. The boys were sent to live with their grandmother a few miles away.

Even though justice had been served, the boys were never the same.

After that incident, the townspeople called for something to be done about the roads leading to Devil's Elbow. They actually made some headway too until another flood drove out the construction crews. It was after this happened that most of the residents of Devil's Elbow moved into Hunter's Point, leaving only a few families to make it on their own in the wake of the terrible floods.

And then it was like the world forgot about them. Almost like we blamed them for their plight. Because who would stay after something like that? Who would choose to live that sort of life? And if the people of Devil's Elbow weren't going to cooperate by abandoning their watery inferno, well then, it was their burden to bare.

It's because of this that when my parents told me we were leaving my childhood home in Hunter's Point to move into a new house in Devil's Elbow, I rebelled. They told me this on the evening of my high school graduation.

They bought a "charming farmhouse off of Y highway." Their dream home. Or so it would be, they said, after all the renovations that needed to take place.

My father had been the only dentist in Hunter's Point for years until my senior year. He brought a partner into his practice. But when my father told me the news about moving to Devil's Elbow, it all made sense. He wanted more time to fix up the house.

I was angry, to say the least. And while we were only moving about eight miles away, the thought of having to leave my childhood home and enter into the secluded community of Devil's Elbow was disconcerting. I remember the summer of my high school graduation was mostly spent moving into the ranch house. It was faded blue, as if it hadn't been repainted in years and the spring downpours washed away its intended color.

The shutters—a darker blue—looked as though they were falling off the house completely. The roof looked as if it would cave in at any given moment. Behind the house was a stable. My parents had no horses.

Either way, while the home had potential, my parents knew nothing of home repair yet spent a good chunk of their life savings on "a charming, 1920s farmhouse off of Y highway" because their only child was moving away to college. At least that's what they told me at our first family dinner in the house.

"We just feel it's the best move for us," my mother said, in her very comforting way.

"Yeah, now that we only have two mouths to feed instead of three," said my father, ever so bluntly. As if it had been funny.

My mother looked at him uncomfortably. "It's just that—we really only ever lived in town for you. To have a social life."

I honestly couldn't believe them and what they'd done. I felt betrayed. As if my objections about the ordeal fell on deaf ears. It was my home they moved out of, even if it had a leaky ceiling. I'd never lived anywhere else.

And what was I supposed to do when I came home for the holidays? Pretend that this new "charming, 1920s farmhouse, completely secluded off of Y highway" was my home? That it meant something to me to be there? That I would lie in my bed and close my eyes and everything would be the same? Because it wouldn't. It didn't smell the same. What once smelled like fresh linens and lavender was replaced with rotting oak and varnish.

I used to hear the light clanging of wind chimes making a lyrically beautiful song. Or even the light drips of water into a bucket when it rained. The sound of my neighbors laughing as they had their guests over a little too late on a Monday night. But it had all been replaced by the old house, creaking and shifting against the wind. A sound that once comforted me now sent chills down my spine because the wind blew differently in Devil's Elbow. It was as if the devil himself were howling.

I hated it there. I hated it there so much that I only returned twice throughout college. Once for Christmas in the first year, an awful occurrence considering my parents hadn't done all the renovations they planned. The second time, for spring break. Though the flooding kept us house bound.

After that, I kind of just decided to stay at school for the remainder of my breaks, through graduation. And post grad. My parents visited me when they could, so I started to not even see the point in going back.

Fast forward a few years and you'll find me working as music journalist still living in New York City. I found a steady job writing music reviews for an online publication, and I gathered quite a bit of followers in my brief time working for the indie music review website. I loved the work. I loved the music. I loved New York. I loved it because it wasn't Tennessee.

I am a music journalist, and the job has perks. Party invitations are a constant, though I attribute this to musicians wanting me to write favorably about them. Some times I feel conflicted, some times I do not. I still get invitations to parties, and people will still love me. Because people like me, we hold their budding career in the palms of our hands.

One night in particular, I attended a release party, and I managed to find myself in a small group of music enthusiasts huddled together on the patio of an upper East Side Apartment.

"Music is something that everyone can relate to," an up and coming songwriter exclaimed, drawing me into the group.

A point most people can relate to, which makes it boring. There's nothing to argue or debate. To me, contribution to a conversation comes with different points of view. And a lot of times up and coming artists will refrain from having a difference in opinion to avoid angering a possible endorser or fan.

I find this to be one of the biggest problems with a lot of artists today. They seem so afraid of being politically correct that they don't challenge the difference of opinions to their work. Or anyone else's work, for that matter. They want everyone to understand. They want everyone to relate in one way or another.

If everyone understood art, then it wouldn't be artistic. If everyone knew the artist's intention, then we'd all do what he or she does. Though I felt no need to mention that point. Not much point in debating with someone who always finds the middle ground.

A man I'd never met before spoke. "Yes, but the idea that everyone should relate is what's mass producing so many wannabe's and putting out terrible music constantly. The idea that there's always someone out there that will like what I do as opposed to actually writing, saying or playing something that can reach into one's soul. I find it lazy and contrived. If you put something out there that everyone can relate to, can we really call it art?"

And here we go, I thought. An opinion worth debating.

"I don't think that's what he's saying," I said, catching the attention of the group. Not because I wanted to defend this new and up coming songwriter. Mostly because I wanted to debate something worth talking about. "I think the point he's making is that music is something that already reaches into one's soul despite having previous knowledge in the art form."

"Yes," the up and comer said, but I ignored and continued.

"With photography, it's helpful to have an understanding of composition and lighting. And with painting, you really must know a thing or two about technique. Sure, you can like a painting, but can you really appreciate the artist if you don't know about the process?"

~~The small crowd that gathered around us laughed, and~~ I successfully caught the attention of the skeptic who smiled at me, intrigued.

"But with music," I continued, "you need know nothing. You don't have to know how to play guitar or write poetry to know what the artist is saying."

"Color me intrigued," the skeptic said. He smiled at me, cheeky. "Please continue."

A maddening characteristic of the artistic types. They always have to have some clever way of speaking their mind. They can never just say "What do you mean?"

"I only mean to make the point that while there are some that can listen to a musician's lyrics and understand what they're saying, music itself holds so much emotion without having to say a word. There are two types of people. The ones who listen to lyrics. And the ones who listen to music. The lyricists are the poetic types. They have the ability to read further into what the artist is saying, perhaps artists themselves. But those affected by the music can tell what the artist is saying based on the sound. Either way is beautiful and relatable."

Along with the skeptic and the songwriter, I'd caught the attention of a new starlet-singer and her guitarist, as well as a manager whose incompetence makes him no better than a manager at a gas station. I felt empowered. Respected for my intelligence as opposed to my looks, something all too common in New York City.

"Take films for example," I continued, "We know based on sound cue's the type of scene we're in for. A fat bass line and shrill violin implies…"

"Horror," the up and coming songwriter commented.

"Right," I said. "But when we hear a harp or a piano, we think more romantic and whimsical. Sound is highly psychological."

And on that note, the up and coming songwriter took over once more in an attempt to further my point, but ~~I tuned him out.~~ I focused on the skeptic who, despite having a date permanently attached to his arm, didn't ever take his eyes away from me. His date narrowed her eyes to me, but he just kept on smiling.

For me, ~~mostly,~~ I knew he wouldn't be the type to call in the morning. I could tell by his cheeky smile and the hateful stare of his date that he'd be the perfect man suited to my needs at the moment. I didn't need a romantic complication in my life. This critic seemed the perfect candidate. Suddenly, my phone rang.

CHAPTER TWO:

I LIKE TO ASSUME THAT I'M LIKE MOST PEOPLE. Not that I don't find myself special or unique in some way, but when it comes to trivial things like ignoring a number I don't recognize, I feel I am completely justified. Phone conversations are awkward enough even when you know the person on the other line. I feel this way about most interactions with strangers, which is very uncommon for someone with my Southern roots. We Southerners tend to be quite friendly.

Fast-forward a few hours and I'd retreated to the hallway with said music skeptic.

I don't know why people romanticize making out against walls. I find it to be uncomfortable, to say the least. And then the idea that someone will walk up and see also ruins it for me. With his lips forced against mine and his tongue wandering aimlessly in my mouth, I was relieved when he pulled away, panting, yet I pretended to be just as excited as he seemed I'm sure he bought it. Most guys do.

"You're so beautiful," he said.

How nice. But my phone distracted me, pulling me away momentarily from the panting, sexually charged paramour pressed against me. I pulled my phone from my purse. The same unknown number. I ignored it again, fearing a possible debt collector. I didn't have time for debt collectors. I had other things on my mind. ~~Sex, mostly.~~

Back at my Manhattan apartment, clothes were strewn all across the floor. Not like it compared to the mess already within the apartment. Boxes labeled "Scarlett's Stuff" written in sharpie took up much of the lining of the bedroom and living room. The walls remained bare and the windows had no type of décor or protection from the sun or the bright lights of the night.

Despite the fact that I'd been drinking and also had carnal relations with a man whose name I can't remember, I somehow managed to awake to the sound of my phone ringing once again.

I ignored the drunken behemoth in bed next to me and reached for my phone on the nightstand. A different number than before but with the same area code as my hometown. I became intrigued.

"Hello?" I answered, groggy and already hung-over. No one spoke, but the person's heavy breathing made me snicker. "Hello?"

"Scarlett?" an unfamiliar man spoke, quiet and raspy.

"Yes?"

The man's voice quivered through the phone, but before I spoke, the call ended. How strange, I thought. I considered calling the number back, but my phone started ringing again. And before I realized the strange number that had called twice before—possible debt collectors—I answered.

"Hello?"

"Hello, we're trying to reach a Scarlett Crawley?"

I sat up and pulled the sheet up around me to maintain my dignity. "This is she…"

I felt numb. As if watching myself in a film instead of living that moment in real life. I understood what was said, though it seemed to be a dream. Or a nightmare. My parents died, and I'd been requested to identify their bodies.

"How'd it happen?" I asked.

A flooding accident. The Rubidoux carried their vehicle away with them inside. Away from Y highway, just like so many before them.

I didn't want to believe what I'd been told. And per the request of the sheriff, I started making travel arrangements to go identify the bodies. The entire time though, I tried convincing myself that none of it had happened.

At an empty La Guardia, I booked a flight into Nashville at around 9am. It took about two hours to arrive in Tennessee, and by the time I secured a rental car, the morning faded into afternoon. With a four-hour drive ahead of me and a hangover from hell, I became all the more resentful of my home state.

On the drive, I kept contemplating the possibility of a giant misunderstanding. I kept thinking about getting back to my parents "charming, 1920s farmhouse," and having dinner with my folks. I called my parents. They never answered. I left voicemails about the sick mix-up the sheriff's office made and for them to call and clear up the whole misunderstanding. But the call never came. Despite this, I remained surprisingly calm even when I arrived at the county coroner's office.

While walking down the long, fluorescent hallway, it still hadn't hit me. I realized the truth when I saw their bodies on the slab. The Rubidoux had washed their car, and their bodies, and their lives away from Devil's Elbow. Even with them knowing about the dangers of flooding on Y Highway, they still attempted to get home from their weekly date night, or so I assumed.

I stood there, staring at their pale, lifeless bodies. It hit me that they were dead, but not that they were gone, if that makes any sense. I stared for the longest time. A knot in the pit of my stomach grew, as if I'd just recently eaten some bad food. A dull, gnawing feeling. A feeling with which I'm familiar, but this time it came out of nowhere and unrelated to having eaten or drank too much.

Although I knew the faces in front of me, dead bodies look so different than what you remember in a person. You see a person with color in their face, brightness in their eyes, and the ability to react. But as familiar as you can be with a person, nothing can prepare you to see them dead. The life gone from their eyes, and no color to their skin. But something even more suspicious than what I assumed to see in dead people kept me wondering…

"Why do they look so…fat?"

The coroner, a man named Jim and a patient of my father, hesitated to speak.

"They drowned, Scarlett. Typically, in drown victims, the bodies tend to bloat…"

"So closed caskets would be most appropriate?" I asked.

My mind left my body and the pod-person version of me answered the questions. So callus and cold as to the fate of my parents. But the gnawing feeling in my stomach kept me grounded, despite how badly I wanted to escape.

"The bloating will decrease. And the mortician can make them look as you remember for an open casket if that's what you decide you want to do."

The coroner continued on about the process, but I never looked away from my father. My entire life I'd seen him as a man who had control of every situation. Anywhere we went, people listened to him. His opinions had value, and was respected and well-liked by everyone he came across.

I found it strange seeing this man who'd been in control of every situation laying on a slab, bloated and pale. Now with no instructions or directions to give. And no guidance to his one and only child.

The knots in my stomach grew. Much like eating bad Mexican food and then taking a shot of bad tequila. Without meaning to seem crude, nausea is nausea, and the similarities between seeing a loved one dead and being on the verge of puking from too much alcohol sort of unnerved me. While the coroner continued on about how I had to visit the local funeral home to make the arrangements, I focused on not vomiting.

"Can you please cover them up now? I've seen enough," I said.

The coroner obliged. I'd confirmed the horrible tragedy that I'd been called to confirm. My parents were dead, killed in a terrible flooding accident out in Devil's Elbow. Case twenty-four and twenty-five in the accidental loss of life due to flooding of the Rubidoux.

~~Even after being covered, I kept my eyes on their bodies.~~

"These are for you. Their personal effects."

I heard him, but it took a while to acknowledge him. I became worried that if I looked away they'd be taken from me. I didn't want to see them dead, but I wanted to be near them. I knew by accepting their belongings, the process of burying them would be hurried along, and I'd never be close to them again.

"Scarlett?"

I looked to Jim. He handed me a plastic bag. Inside, a wallet and a set of keys along with their clothes. I didn't want their clothes.

"The local funeral home is coming to retrieve them in about an hour. You can discuss with them your plans for burial. When you're ready," he said.

I looked inside the bag and pulled out a set of keys. I twirled them in my hand. The keys to the car that had failed them. A sedan, pulled from the river with them still inside.

An assistant of the coroner took my parents' bodies away. I didn't object, though I wanted to. I'd lost all control. I could only do one thing. Bury them.

"Your parents' lawyer has left his card with me. He wants you to give him a call."

I guess I had to do that too. I took the card. But the dull, gnawing feeling in my stomach grew. I looked to where my parents' bodies disappeared into the back of the coroner's office. I'm not sure exactly how I looked to those around me, but I assume I looked awful because the look on Jim's face became concerned.

"Scarlett? Are you all right?"

I felt hot but cold at the same time. And while I swallowed hard to keep the idea of vomiting at bay, my hearing started to fade, and what I could hear, echoed. That gnawing feeling in my stomach rose to my chest causing my heart to pound and my head to begin spinning. My vision, reduced to the size of pinholes. I wanted to puke. Or die. I stood there, contemplating which until the only relief possible came about. Darkness.

Awaking on the floor of the county coroner's office made me realize something. That I'd never suffered a trauma before, mostly. But also that I'd never fainted before. Fainting, if you've never done it, is a very strange occurrence.

It's your body's way of telling you that whatever you're experiencing is too much for you to handle, so in a sense, it puts you in sleep mode. Granted, it's a much more physiological experience than just turning on a sleep switch, but as scary as the experience can be, especially to those who've never done it before, it's actually quite fascinating.

Really, fainting is just your mind saying "okay, we've had enough of this. Time to clock out for a bit." And there you go. In one of the most embarrassing displays of self-preservation imaginable. I wouldn't mind it so much if people could just remain calm when someone faints. But they never can. People care too much. Or at least they pretend to.

"Oh my God, are you all right?" Jim asked while kneeling next to me.

I barely acknowledged him. What a stupid question. Me on the ground next to him, living, breathing, eyes open seemed enough proof that I was fine. My parents are the ones he should have been concerned about. But then again, I guess you can't really ask the dead if they are all right.

I avoided answering Jim's question. More pressing matters kept me distracted. Like me laying on the floor of a morgue and how cold I felt. I get the cold. The bodies have to be kept fresh. But the fluorescent lights made everything look very clinical in an unsettling way. Horror movie clinical. Dark, dingy, green-colored as opposed to the bright white, clean feeling in a normal clinical setting.

I wrinkled my nose at the smell surrounding me. Something similar to copious amounts of bleach but not bleach. Something I'd never smelled before. And the the audible atrocity of an insufficient air circulation system overpowered the sound of my heartbeat in my ears.

The sound being very similar to when you drive down the highway with one window down, and with that accompanies the maddening WAWAS that no person can bare longer than a few seconds. No wonder I fainted. A morgue is a blatant insult to the senses. I had to leave.

In the parking lot, the smell of fresh cut grass and the sound of birds chirping as they flew by calmed me. The sun on my face warmed me. A brief moment of comfort after experiencing the dark, dingy basement of death. The sun being almost too bright that I had to shield my eyes, which normally I hated.

Yet even though my head hurt from smashing it on the floor in my embarrassing display of self-preservation, I welcomed the brightness of the sun. The two locations comparable to night and day, and after having experienced the dark for so long, I never wanted to leave the brightness of the sun again.

By the time I reached Devil's Elbow, however, the sun began to set, coloring the skies in beautiful shades of pink and orange. I drove carefully with both hands on the wheel at ten and two. I never enjoyed driving on Y highway, but it all felt so different now. Like I actually had reason to be afraid. I clenched the wheel as if I would lose control of the vehicle if my grip loosened at all.

While driving over Hickman Bridge—one in a string of bridges leading to my parents' home—the Rubidoux seemed calm. Not threatening at all and almost picturesque when painted against the hellfire sky. I wondered if that's where my parents died. I wondered if my mother made my father stop to take a picture. The view from Hickman Bridge was unlike any other view of the river. It seemed so centered, as if for a moment you were in control of something so utterly and completely uncontrollable.

I can see my mother doing this. "Honey, stop the car—I need a picture!" she'd exclaim excitedly, and my father would oblige, just like he always did. "Darling, look at the river!" she would shout at the sight of the angry beast beneath her feet growing stronger, more violent and more powerful than either of them could anticipate. As if the mere fact that she wanted to capture the beast in a photo was enough for it to take her life.

While I am uncertain of the events leading up to their death, I can imagine it being something along those lines. They had become too cocky. Thought they knew more than the beast of a river. They'd been wrong.

A few miles past Hickman Bridge was the mile-long, dirt driveway leading to my parents' house. Most of the homes in Devil's Elbow have a mile-long driveway leading to the house, mostly because no one wants to live so close to Y Highway.

Y Highway, so crooked and winding that it prevents anyone from going more than fifteen miles an hour. A devil of an elbow, is how it's described. At night, you can't see more than five feet in front of you. No lights or reflectors guide the way through Devil's Elbow. And the ever present danger of deer running out in front of your car makes it all the more dangerous.

I turned onto my parents' dirt driveway. Even though the sun hadn't completely set, the thickness of the woods surrounding the road barely allowed any of her fading light to break through. I turned on my headlights, now driving about five miles an hour as little branches and leaves scraped the sides and hood of my rental car. The sound unnerved me. Not quite like nails on a chalkboard. More like pins on a chalkboard. It didn't help my headache. The car bounced up and down with every pothole or tree root I drove over. It didn't help my nausea.

I finally emerged from the woods and entered a large clearing where the house came into view. Although the sun started to set, a light blue sky remained, almost as if to light the way home.

Not my home. My parents' home. *Their* home was located on about eight acres of land. The land had been cleared out, so really it was just this farmhouse, an open-faced garage to the right, and a dilapidated stable behind.

We only had three neighbors nearby. And when I say neighbors, I mean about a mile away in either direction, separated by the thickness of the woods. I felt completely alone.

I followed the dirt driveway to right in front of the house. It looked the same as I remembered, which left me feeling unimpressed with their progress over the past ten years. I sat staring at the eerie house that with every passing moment seemed as though the darkness were engulfing it completely.

Only when the house appeared to be moving did I notice I'd been sitting in my rental car, staring at the home for nearly an hour. I tore my eyes away and rubbed them. My eyes were playing tricks on me. Like when you stare at your face too long in the mirror and slowly you become a different person.

I didn't want to go inside. The darkness traumatized me, making me feel abandoned with nothing but that house. I became fearful of what going inside could do to me. I didn't fear the memories because I really had none. Not from that house. I feared being a complete stranger in the life my parents built for themselves. I wanted to, needed to leave.

CHAPTER THREE:

DANTE'S LANDING—AND ITS ATTACHED MOTEL—SITS just up the highway from my parents' house. The local watering hole with a very poorly maintained motel. The motel is really only for the residents out in Devil's Elbow who are too drunk to traverse the angry highway home or for the local residents to try to avoid or wait out the floods.

The bar and restaurant portion are raised about five feet off the ground while the motel behind is held up on stilts completely. And remember that hooch I mentioned earlier? Dante owned his own still where he crafted his moonshine and sold to the patrons of his establishment.

I parked my rental car on the far side of the parking lot. Force of habit, I guess. I left my bags in the car, at least for now. I still hadn't decided whether or not I should get a room.

While walking through the gravel parking lot toward the stairs to the entrance, I couldn't help but notice the amount of vehicles present. A bar in the middle of nowhere doesn't seem like the happening spot on a Tuesday night, but you never know with backwoods folks I guess.

I kept my head down mostly. I didn't want to draw any attention to myself. Although it seemed that someone else yelling on the far side of the parking lot—clearly drunk—demanded the attention of everyone outside.

I saw a middle-aged man, shouting to someone standing at the entrance of Dante's.

"I want my money, Frankie! I want my money!" the drunkard yelled while his friend forced him into the passenger side of a faded, blue pickup truck.

A hard scene to ignore, I must admit. And when the friend made his way to the driver's side of the truck, we locked eyes. In an awkward attempt to spare myself from public humiliation for my nosiness, I immediately ducked my head down and ran up the steps leading into Dante's. Playing off that I'd seen that sort of display a dozen times.

I don't really care what anyone else does. I'm a people watcher. I will watch you even when you're not doing something interesting. Just because human interactions fascinate me. You can learn so much about a person by just watching them. More so than hearing them talk. Talk is cheap and overrated. Most people lie anyway, so really, what's the point? To show everyone how smart we think we are.

Back at Dante's, the bar seemed sketchy, dimly lit with mostly neon signs from obscure brand names that only the backwoods can recognize. A small, fluorescent light hung above the one pool table, and a few twinkle lights behind the bar added to the sketchy, cheap atmosphere.

A few tables were scattered about the room, as well as three small booths lining the walls and windows to my right, allowing a perfect view into the parking lot where the faded, blue truck peeled out and onto Y highway.

Good. The man who caught me being nosy left.

Stale cigarette smoke and bug spray cut my breaths short. With that though, a very distinct smell that I can't help but love. I believe you would only be familiar with this smell if you're from a small town. A mixture of grandma's house, cigarette smoke, old wood and rain. Maybe something in the carpets. Or maybe just asbestos.

I made my way to the bar, pretending to ignore those who couldn't help but stare. I didn't blame them. I probably looked rougher than they did at that point.

I pulled back a barstool and scanned the liquor selection, unsure if I really needed to be drinking at all but still coming up with reasons to justify it in my head. While in the midst of the battle between my mind, body, and soul, a middle-aged black man approached me from behind the bar, smiling welcomingly.

Everyone knew Dante. But he didn't know me. If he did, I don't think he'd have approached me smiling so brightly.

"Well, well, well—someone new!" he exclaimed while wiping down the bar and then placing both hands flat on top, as if to make himself appear more friendly. "What brings you to the Landing?"

"Oh, I'm here for the moonshine," I said, matter-of-factly. I actually really hate moonshine—though I know the good stuff from the bad.

Dante laughed. "What you know about my moonshine, little girl?"

"Just that it's the best kept secret in Devil's Elbow," I said.

Once again, Dante laughed. "Shit, you from around here?"

"I am—more towards Hunter's Point."

"So what brings you all the way out here this time of night?" Dante asked, still with his cheeky smile. Again, I didn't blame him. A youngish girl out in the middle of nowhere in a place like Dante's by herself couldn't be up to anything good. But he didn't know my story. And I didn't want him to know.

"Oh, my folks bought a house not too far from here. Couple miles up the road. I'm here visiting, so…"

Dante's face seemed to soften, and I became confused by his sudden change in disposition. He reached beneath the bar and pulled out a mason jar filled with a clear liquid. Ugh, moonshine. He filled a double shot glass and slid it over to me.

"It's on the house, kid," he said while placing the bottle below the bar again. Dante shook his head and walked away after that.

He knew me. I looked around the rest of the bar to the patrons. They pretended not to notice me now, though their conversations fell to whispers. They all new me because they knew my parents. Of course they did. Why wouldn't they?

I chugged the moonshine in front of me. Gagged. Coughed a bit because moonshine is terrible. And then I did the only thing I felt

I could in that moment. I bought an entire bottle of moonshine, a pack of cigarettes, and a room for the night. Screw it, I thought. The day had kicked my ass, but I'd be damned if I allowed an entire bar of backwoods hicks feel sorry for me.

If there's one thing I hate, it's when people feel sorry for me. It is the ultimate insult to one's character. And I don't mean feeling sorry for the person who drops their milk while coming out of the grocery store and it splatters everywhere. While that does suck, you can help those people.

No, I'm talking about feeling sorry for the people beyond helping. Like myself. When all you have to show is feeling sorry for them. Either you can empathize or you can sympathize with them, but that's really all you can do. And people will tell me, you can't blame people for sympathizing. It's in our nature as humans to be compassionate. But is it though? Or is it something we pretend in order to make us believe we're good people?

The empathizers aren't so bad. They're the ones who haven't been through what you've been through. And although their faux emotional turmoil to your plight can be annoying, they mostly leave you alone to grieve because they don't know! And they know it! They're uncomfortable even being near you! Those people, I like.

It's the sympathizers that drive me bat shit crazy. These are the ones who HAVE been through what you're going through. They're the ones who make everything about them. Your dog died but so did theirs like five years ago so they know what you're going through.

This sentiment has not only angered me in more ways than I care to express, but the worst thing about these people is they don't stop to think that in their attempt to be supportive, they're actually being insensitive.

Don't stand with me at an attempt in solidarity—I don't care what you've been through. It helps me not. Also what they don't understand is people's reaction to grief differs so much from person to person. I'll give you an example. My grandpa dies, I could give two shits. Yours dies, you're heartbroken.

People metabolize things differently, even grief. Even pain. Like those people in the bar, feeling sorry for me, how do they know that I'm sad? Why would you just assume I need your sympathy or empathy or whatever the fuck it is? What if I wanted my parents dead? But humanity is so god damn presumptuous about everything. Someone's dog dies, you say aww. No, motherfucker, that dog was an asshole. You don't even know.

The motel room, while very small and dingy, had a bit more comfort than I expected for the price. There was the same grandma's house, stale cigarette smoke, weird carpet smell, which reminded me of something from my childhood. No an instance, necessarily, but more of a time period.

A queen-sized bed sat in the middle of the room with that strange, motel-room patterned blanket. Above me, a ceiling fan that barely held on. As though its last rotation could be at any moment. It didn't do much to circulate the air or cool down the room.

No, the room remained as humid as the outdoors, but I attributed that from being so close to the river. I threw down my bag and walked over to the window. I unhinged the lock and with almost maximum effort, slid the window open. I inhaled deeply before putting a cigarette in my mouth.

I did miss the smell of the country. A nice change from smelling the piss and garbage in New York. I didn't see much outside my window. Once again, I faced the parking lot but from a much higher vantage point. ~~I heard People chit-chatting in the lot below and the sound of tires on gravel as patrons left the bar.~~

The highway split my room and the woods on the far side. I closed my eyes and listened for a moment. I heard crickets. A slight breeze blew through, rustling the trees, and with the wind came the smell of the river. The air, thick and humid with the promise of rain some time soon. I took a drag of my cigarette, but the taste didn't compliment my other senses.

"God dammit, Bill!" a man yelled while exiting the bar beneath me.

Another sense ruined. I looked down at the drunken man, ~~actually~~ annoyed that he disturbed my meditation time. I exhaled my smoke through the screen, right at his small figure as if the smoke would somehow reach him and make him sorry for being obnoxious. But it didn't matter. The moment passed. I no longer fell victim to the hauntingly beautiful and natural occurrences around me. I drew my attention within the motel room.

My moonshine waited patiently on the rounded table in the corner of the room. You know, the same table that comes in every motel room. I scanned the room for a cup. I can't abide drinking from a bottle unless I'm drinking beer. I still fancy myself a lady.

Next to the severely outdated, bulky television, I found an ashtray. I placed my lit cigarette in one of the divots and made my way toward the bathroom. I searched for the light in the darkness of the vanity area.

I flicked it on and watched as the fluorescent light above the vanity flickered a bit, accompanied by the ticking sound that comes with most fluorescent lights. A small, water-stained mirror hung over the pink sink where I located two small cups wrapped in plastic. I glanced in the mirror and pulled the band from my hair, hoping for it to relieve my headache. Perhaps I'd pulled my hair too tight.

I kept the motel room dark to not exacerbate the throbbing in my skull. I grabbed my bottle of moonshine and poured it into one of my little cups. I took a sip. It made me feel sick. That made me angry. So I chugged the moonshine from the cup. I fought to keep it down. It worked, but the physical ordeal angered me even more.

I looked at the bottle in my hands. I didn't want to drink. No matter how much I tried to convince myself that drinking was the thing to do, I just didn't want to.

Suddenly, the writing on the bottle became blurry. I winced, but when I did, something wet hit the hand holding the bottle. Had I started crying?

I squeezed my eyes shut tight. I didn't want to cry. Crying helps you not. The floodgates opened though, but I didn't start crying for my parents. I cried because my body refused to let me drink. And I knew that attempting sleep while sober would be a fool's errand.

I poured another serving into my plastic cup, my hands shaking while I did. And when I brought it to my lips, my stomach turned, and I only cried more.

"God dammit!"

And as if my only other natural reaction was to destroy something, I threw the bottle of moonshine against the wall adjacent to me. The bottle shattered, and I stood there, panting. Defeated by a bottle of liquor.

The next morning, I went into town and speak with the funeral home about my parents' burial arrangements. I scheduled everything for that Saturday. I figured I needed some time before I put them in the ground. After making the arrangements, I had a few hours to kill before meeting with my parents' lawyer.

I decided to eat lunch at a local diner and try to plan a course of action. Something needed to be done—a change needed to be made, now that I'd lost my parents. A strange feeling in the midst of tragedy. Even though I had no affect on the outcome whatsoever, I felt as though I needed to change something in order to prevent further tragedy, as ridiculous as that sounds.

I walked into the diner, which had a bell on the door. All eyes darted to me once again. Sympathetic or empathetic or whatever. Conversations dwindled, faded into whispers. I grew irritated, already over that sort of thing, even if it had only been a day.

An elderly woman in an apron approached me with a menu, smiling sweetly. "Dining in, sweetheart?"

I inhaled deeply, wondering if really I should. I debated just getting my food to go. But the idea made me mad. I did it in the bar to spare myself the embarrassment of getting drunk and emotional.

Now, I just wanted some food. I didn't want to let these people run me out of the diner. Actually, I wanted to make them uncomfortable with my presence.

"Yes. Booth, please."

The waitress smiled and escorted me to a booth at the far end of the restaurant. Clever girl. It would be difficult to make anyone uncomfortable way over there.

"Something to drink?" she asked while placing the menu and utensils on the table.

"Just coffee for now," I said while getting situated.

The waitress walked away and I scanned the diner. Most people went back about their business. Others sent half-hearted smiles my way. I tried to distract myself with my menu. Nothing looked good though. I smelled French fries and burgers from the kitchen.

"Order up!" the cook yelled while ringing the bell, exacerbating the headache I'd had since the previous day.

The sound of fresh meat on the grill sizzled throughout the restaurant accompanied by the smell of burgers. It made me feel sick. I wanted to leave. But I already committed to staying. If I got up and left then, they'd all just look at me thinking "poor dear." The thought enraged me. I had to stay.

The waitress returned with my coffee. I poured my cream and sugar, hoping that my irritability could be attributed to lack of caffeine and not necessarily from the empathetic or sympathetic stares.

"Anything to eat?" she asked while removing a pad from her apron and a pencil from behind her ear.

I couldn't think straight. The sizzling of the grill, silverware scraping on plates, a small child screaming for more ketchup, it all distracted me. "Uh—just a chicken sandwich and some-coleslaw."

"We're out," she said.

"Of chicken?"

"coleslaw."

"Fine, cottage cheese," I said.

"Don't have none."

Jesus Christ. "Fries will be fine, thank you."

The waitress took the menu and scurried away, finally leaving me alone with my coffee. I took a big swig and leaned back in my seat to observe the patrons, something I do best. And I figured that if I kept my gaze on the room, they'd be less likely to stare. A full proof plan.

By the time my food came, the diner had cleared out somewhat. I'd been there long enough that the patrons remaining had accepted me as one of their own, and I felt comfortable enough to attempt to eat.

The sound of the grill died down. I grew accustomed to the smell of fried food. On my third cup of coffee, my headache started to dwindle, but still, my appetite seemed non-existent despite how hungry I felt.

I grabbed the ketchup and mustard and dispersed a large portion of both onto my fries. Great, now I ruined them. Forget the fries, I thought. I didn't even want them to begin with. I picked up my chicken sandwich and examined it before taking a bite. I immediately set it back on the plate, offended by its taste.

I chewed as best I could. The way you chew your food when you really don't want to be eating it at all. Chewing it until it's complete mush and even still you can't seem to produce enough saliva to make it go down. So what do you do? Drink water. Or in my case, coffee.

I winced at the feeling of this lump of mushy food being forced down my throat. I felt my face contort to the awful combination of chicken and coffee. I looked around the room to see if anyone had witnessed the battle inside my mouth. A middle-aged woman smiled at me as we made eye contact. She'd seen the whole thing. How embarrassing.

But my embarrassment with her didn't last long.

The sound of the bell caught my attention. Two men entered the diner. The older one led the way to a booth, chatting up a storm while the younger one followed. The younger one looked in my direction, and we made eye contact. I held his gaze for a moment, trying to figure out where I'd seen him before. Then it hit me. The drunkard and his friend from Dante's the previous night.

I immediately looked away as if I had no idea I'd ever seen them before, ashamed that they would remember my nosiness in the parking lot the night before. When I looked up again, the young man continued to stare, only breaking his gaze after sitting in the booth with his friend. Both men seemed disheveled, but not in an insulting way. In a blue collar worker sort of way.

The older man's back faced me, but his voice dominated the restaurant as he told his younger friend a story, laughing all the while. Something about a drunken escapade. Not suitable diner talk. His friend forced a laugh, though he seemed just as uncomfortable as everyone else by the man's verbal meanderings. We locked eyes again, and I felt my face turn red.

I wanted to pretend to eat, but it seemed so unnatural. Instead, I ran my hands over my face and reached into my bag for my phone, attempting to appear distracted. Out of the corner of my eye though, the man stood and walked toward me.

Oh my god, I thought. He's going to confront me about the parking lot incident. He's going to call me out for my rude behavior the previous night. Southern boys don't care. They'll call you on your shit one-hundred percent of the time.

I panicked, and before he reached me, I stood, threw a twenty on the table, and scurried past him out of the restaurant. I didn't dare look back. Southern people can get so offended when one is impolite. It was something that always bothered me about the South.

On the drive over to the lawyer's office, I kept the windows up and air conditioning on full blast. I don't think anyone ever gets used to humidity. I mean, I guess some people have to. People who live in tropical climates, I assume, are pretty used to humidity.

But in areas like Tennessee, people start getting used to the humidity, then it leaves for months. And while we're shivering to death and snowed in every day during the winter, we some times even dare say we miss the spring. As if we've completely forgotten how miserable the humidity makes us feel. Days like this make me pray for a snowstorm.

I entered the lawyer's office and became disheartened by the state of things. Rather small and poorly maintained, the waiting room failed to give me any sort of confidence in the meeting that was about to take place. Metal chairs lined the wood-paneled walls, and a fluorescent light hung above me, giving off more of a green hue.

A small fan in the corner of the room noisily rotated back and forth, doing a very poor job of cooling me. My eyes fell on an overweight man standing behind a desk, looking rather confused. Sweating profusely, the man looked at me, exasperated.

"Miss Crawley?" he asked in a thick, Southern accent. I smiled. Yes, it's me. I extended my hand to him. "I'm Gordon Brown. Follow me," ~~he said, smiling.~~

He managed to actually seem pleasant while looking the most uncomfortable and miserable I've seen someone in a long time. His face, red, sweaty—his hair a mess, and his labored breaths made it difficult for me to catch my own.

I followed Mr. Brown into a long, skinny hallway. While he attempted to walk next to me, I had to stay a few steps behind in order to make room for the both of us.

"I have to apologize for the inconvenience. Most of the office is out sick, myself having been included until I received word of your parents' accident," he said.

I followed him into a room at the end of the hall. What I could only assume to be his office.

Gordon motioned for me to sit in one of the chairs in front of his desk. I obliged, and he moved around the room, mumbling to himself. It gave me a moment to look around.

His office, a rather depressing sight. Leather bound books lined the metal shelves of a makeshift bookcase, and the walls, made of some sort of vinyl. The light blue carpet was torn in more places than whole. A large, metal desk took up most of the room and housed papers and files, stacked, it seemed, in no particular order.

Another, smaller rotating fan sat on his desk, pointing in my direction so that every few seconds I felt a cool breeze of relief from the scorching hell hole in which we found ourselves. Gordon looked through an aged, metal file cabinet.

I noticed his accreditations on the wall. Nashville School of Law. Not exactly an Ivy League guy. Mr. Brown slammed the file cabinet shut, snapping me out of observation mode. He sat at his desk, holding a sealed envelope out to me as he did.

I hesitated. It seemed a lot thicker than what I'd been expecting.

"Your parents' last will and testament," he said. "They recently updated it too."

A strange thing, I thought. Recently updated. As if they knew they were living on borrowed time. "And…you wanna, like, give me the rundown? I'm not exactly proficient in legal terminology," I said while ripping open the envelope.

"Well, basically it states that all their earthly possessions, every dime they had in the bank is all left to you," Mr. Brown said. "With the money from their life insurance policy, it's safe to say that you'll never have to worry about money again."

As if money ever concerned me. I removed some of the papers from the envelope. I scanned the document, but none of it made sense to me. The lawyer said I get everything, I believed him.

"I need you to sign some documents for me before you leave," he said. He shuffled through a stack of papers. "Here's a list of contacts you might be needing. My number is the first on the list," he said while pointing out his name.

I took the list and glanced at the names. Their lawyer, their accountant, their project manager, a contact number for building permits, etc.

"Hmm…" I said, dismissing the list. "I was actually hoping you could get me in touch with a real estate agent, like, today. I'd like to get the ball rolling on this thing so I can go home," ~~I said~~.

"Real estate agent?" he asked.

"Yes, to sell the house."

Mr. Brown hesitated to speak. "Miss ~~Crawly~~—you may want to take a closer look at your parents' stipulations for you as the owner of the house before you talk to a real estate agent."

"Stipulations? What stipulations?"

"The house can't be sold until all the renovations are complete."

"Excuse me?"

"There's a lot they had planned to do too. All the information is included in the envelope I gave to you."

I ripped open the package again and searched for said information when, finally, I arrived at a to-do list of sorts, plain as day. Everything I needed to do before I could sell that house. That house which I'd labeled the bane of my existence. I was stuck with it. I was stuck with it and a massive to-do list.

"How do they expect me to pay for all of this?" I muttered to myself.

"Why, with the money left for you in the account," Mr. Brown said.

He handed me another packet, one from the bank. Inside, all the account information for my parents as well as a separate account for the home renovations.

My eyes became wide at the sight of nearly two-hundred thousand dollars between both accounts. Two-hundred thousand dollars and a two-million-dollar life insurance policy. Jesus Christ.

CHAPTER FOUR:

ON THE DRIVE BACK TO DEVIL'S ELBOW, I contemplated just leaving town and never turning back. So what if they wanted the house finished? They were dead, incapable of still telling me what to do. I guess technically they weren't telling me what to do. They were kind of just telling me what not to do. I could totally sell the house. Just only after I renovated the damn thing, something that it seemed they had no hurry to finish themselves.

But it was renovations that they decided to pay for, I might add. Really, I just needed to oversee their project until complete and then make money off of it afterward.

I turned onto the long, dirt driveway leading to the house that now belonged to me. A house I never wanted. That old and noisy house freaked me out. It disgusted me. The carpets, fixtures, tiles, paint—all of it was just too awful.

The plumbing, a travesty; we never had hot water. The lights hardly worked, constantly flickering with any bit of rain. And don't even get me started on the water damage. The roof, the ceilings, the carpets—the smell of mold ruling over all other senses.

I stopped my car in front of the house again, but this time I didn't want to look. My resentment got the better of me. I was stuck with it. Stuck with it forever. It had to have been some sick joke my parents concocted. The to-do list, so vast, and the house, so old that something will always need fixing.

I'd been duped. By my own parents. I pushed the car door open and exited the vehicle in order to make my way to the rickety, old porch that was…white-ish blue? The rain having washed away its intended color. The porch swing,-barely surviving,-swung back and forth lightly, making a terrible creaking sound from the rusted chains that hardly held it up anymore.

I reached into my back pocket to remove the house key. The screen door, a dreadful sight with the screen no longer really attached to its frame. The rusted spring screeched when I opened the door, causing me to wince. I stuck the key into the deadbolt. The only thing that looked new on the entire house. I pushed the door open and stood in the doorway.

I entered the threshold, unable to take my eyes from the layout in front of me. Even though the sun remained in the sky, the house stayed dimly lit. I found the light switch and flicked it on, my eyes falling upon the long hallway ahead.

A standard layout. Upon entry, one would enter the foyer and see the long hallway straight ahead leading to the back of the house. To the left, a living room and a set of stairs leading to the sleeping quarters. To the right, dining nook and kitchen area.

It wasn't what I was expecting though. The old hallway of molded walls, damaged floor boards, and low hanging fixtures no longer remained. They'd been replaced by brand new hardwood, newly plastered and painted walls—a nice shade of gray, and new, modernized fixtures. The water damage on the ceiling no longer remained. In fact, no water damage at all.

I entered the living room to my left. Again, new hardwood, walls, and fresh paint and furniture. They maintained the gray theme with complimentary pillows and throw blankets on the sofas and chairs. In the corner of the room, a large bookcase filled with leather bound books. When did we get all those?

The curtains draped over the window were sheer and fell to the ground, sweeping the hardwood with any slight breeze, something my mother had to have wanted. Everything had been updated. Modernized. Not one thing I remember from my childhood home. Strangely, I didn't mind. It all looked quite nice, actually. Something from HGTV.

I walked into the kitchen and dining room area, blown away by the difference. New, white, wooden cabinets and green tile replaced the orange vinyl and linoleum, and stainless steel appliances replaced the severely outdated ones. The dining area had a dark oak table and four chairs, a vase with wilted flowers as the centerpiece.

A dark cloud came over me. As if the sight of the dead flowers snapped me back into reality. Everything in that house belonged to me now. Even the dead flowers. I entered the foyer once more. At the end of the hall in the back of the house, an enclosed porch that faced the stables. Also a new addition.

I approached the stairway leading to the bedrooms. With each step I took, the hardwood creaked beneath my boots. I reached the top of the stairs and flicked on the light to further illuminate the way. While the floors, walls, and ceiling had been replaced, everything remained plain white, clearly undeserving of the same attention as the downstairs. At its best, a clean slate. At its worst, cold and unwelcoming.

I turned to the right and entered the doorway to my parents' room. New furniture replaced the bedroom I knew as a kid. The same bed that I used to run and hide in during a thunderstorm, gone. They'd finished their room by painting the walls a pale blue and adding new furnishings, and new fixtures.

I hoped to feel comforted by entering my parents' bedroom, but I didn't. I'd entered a stranger's room, nothing of my parents left behind. What people had they become? I didn't recognize anything.

I contemplated going in their bathroom, knowing all their personal belongings remained inside as well as in their closet. If I needed comfort, exposing their belongings seemed to be the way to go, but something stopped me. Instead of entering further into the room, dissecting it in an attempt to find my parents somewhere inside, I backed out of the bedroom and closed the door behind me. I would avoid going back in there. For now, at least.

My bedroom hadn't been touched, of course. A while ago, my mother asked me what color I wanted my room. I never gave a response. Mostly because I had no intention of returning for long periods of time, if at all. So she left it white.

My bed from my high school years, a queen-sized, four poster sat directly in front of me as I entered. My same bedspread, dark purple with olive green sheets and pillow cases remained. No curtains in the windows, no pictures on the walls. The same ceiling fan from move-in remained. In the bathroom, a plain, white shower curtain and pale, blue tile.

The room, although plain, managed to give the only bit of comfort from my childhood, and as beautiful as the rest of the house came to be, I grew resentful. I threw down my bag and turned off the light before flinging myself onto my bed and pulling the blankets over my head. I wanted to stay in bed for the rest of my life.

I inhaled deeply, taking in a familiar scent. A scent I hadn't had the privilege of smelling in years. The smell of myself but from a long time ago. And somehow, even after entering my parents' home, the smell of myself is what formed a lump in my throat and caused my eyes to burn.

I felt a heavy, gnawing feeling in my chest. My stomach turned, and despite how hard I fought, a whimper managed to escape my mouth. I clenched my teeth, a nervous tick from childhood. I squeezed my eyes shut, but it only forced my tears outward.

My tears, my pain, my loneliness, it poured out of me, and not even to the memory of my parents. Frustrated, I turned over onto my stomach and buried my face into my pillow in an attempt to hold in my facial secretions, but I only soaked the cloth beneath me.

Even when it became hard to breathe, I didn't adjust myself. I wondered if the sensation was comparable to how my parents felt before they died. We all know what it's like to hold our breath. We've all been under water before just to see how long we can hold ourselves under. Or when we hold our breath while driving under a bridge. Or even in movies when we try to hold our breath for however long the character is deprived of oxygen. It's fun this way. Because we know we can always just breathe again.

But imagine going to take a breath and oxygen doesn't come. I felt light-headed, but I kept my face buried in my pillow, knowing that my parents suffered worse. How they must have been feeling when they went to breathe but only cold, dirty, river water entered their lungs. I could only imagine or attempt to recreate.

People will ask, what would you prefer? Drowning or burning alive? I'd rather burn. And a lot of people find that strange. But with burning, within seconds, the fire damages your nerve endings. You feel nothing within a minute.

People say you pass out before you actually drown due to lack of oxygen, but do you know how long that takes? About five minutes. Five minutes of panic. Five minutes of wanting nothing more than to breathe in, our most basic need as a living thing, but not being able to. Give me pain, give me dismemberment, deformities, anything. But let me breathe. I need to breathe.

I grew tired of this game. I turned my head to the side and breathed deeply. Deep breath after deep breath until my eyes refused to stay open. Despite all the terrible things going through my head, I managed to fall asleep.

The next morning, I helped myself to a cup of tea while sitting out on the new addition to the back of the house. An enclosed back porch with a lovely view of the dilapidated horse stable. On top of having to make it presentable and functional, I had to fix up the garage, the exterior of the home.

It wasn't fair. They knew I had other things going on in New York. Now, I had this heap of land to worry about. A pile of junk that I never wanted to begin with. I didn't even know where to begin.

The large, open field behind the home with each passing minute became clearer as the sun rose to further shine onto another acre of land. It reflected off the fog that settled along the grass, acting as a giant bounce board to brighten everything a little more.

The birds were now awake, and the crickets had yet to fall asleep. They accompanied the eerie, foggy scene with their noisy chatter. A light breeze blew through, rustling through the trees and with it, the smell of the river. All of it belonged to me, and though hardly an insult to the senses, I didn't want any of it.

I moved inside to the dining room with my parents' legal documents and list of instructions sprawled out in front of me. I didn't even know where to begin. I picked up the list of names and numbers that I'd been given. I called the accountant to make sure the funds were available for renovations. Next on the list, the project manager. I didn't really know what she did. After that, building permits. Would I be building anything?

I had no idea what to do.

Next, the contact number for my father's business partner, Doctor Wilson. I guess *my* business partner now since I owned half the practice. I should call, I thought. Or go in for a routine cleaning at least. It had been a while. Later, I thought. Not a pressing matter at the moment, although I'm certain I developed a cavity or two.

Next on the list, Henry King listed with no number or title. It simply said Henry King with an address next to his name. How strange, I thought. Perhaps a contractor for my parents. Or someone to help explain building permits and project managers. I became skeptical. The address listed him as nearby, but I decided to call the project manager first.

"Hi, this is Scarlett Crawly. I'm calling to speak with Shana Forbes?" A brief hold.

"Shana Forbes," she answered. Ugh, I hate when the secretaries don't introduce me.

"Hi, this is Scarlett Crawly. You were the project manager for Jack and Erin Crawley?"

"Scarlett, how nice to hear from you. I'm so sorry for your loss, truly," she said.

"Thanks. Listen, I was calling to kind of...check in, see what needed to be done with the house..." there was a long pause. "I'm sorry, what's your job exactly?" Really the only question I wanted to ask.

"Your parents hired me to oversee the staff and construction crews for them. Seeing as how they didn't know much about this sort of thing..."

"Perfect! Because neither do I." I started pacing around the dining room. I always pace when I'm on the phone. Nervous, I suppose, as talking to people on the phone can be a nuisance.

Shana let out a laugh. "Yes, so it'll be my job to oversee everything to make sure the contractors know what they're doing and how best to do it according to your wishes."

"Well I don't really have any wishes. This is all sort of my parents' thing," ~~I said~~. "But if you could, like, I don't know, gather up the crew and kind of get the ball rolling, that'd be great. I'd like to have all of this done by the end of the summer," I said, thankful for project managers taking all the stress away.

"Well, there is a problem, Miss Crawley." Of course, I thought. "Your parents had yet to write check for continued services to our contractors or myself even, so until you make a payment in full, we won't be able to continue with the renovations."

I rolled my eyes. Jesus, my parents just died and all they want to talk about is money? "Okay, well how much do I owe?"

"Well, you don't owe anything. The construction crews have been paid already for services rendered. But if you wanted to continue down this route, another payment would be needed," ~~she said.~~

"How much?"

"The quote I last gave your parents was..." ~~she paused~~. "Let's see here...sixty-two thousand."

My heart dropped. "What?!" I exclaimed.

"It's a lot of work they will be requiring to finish the home," Shana assured me. I knew nothing of home repairs, but I could buy a new house with that money, albeit a very small house.

"I'm not paying that, are you insane? It's all just...cosmetic, I mean...how?"

"Miss Crawley, might I suggest another route for you if this seems to be something you're just absolutely not interested in doing?"

"You might, yes." I was putting my foot down.

“Your parents hired a private contractor for majority of the work once the fees became too expensive. I believe his name was Henry King?”

I glanced over at the list of names. The ‘no telephone number guy.’ “Uh huh.”

“I’m not exactly sure of his qualifications, but your father certainly liked the work he did. While my crew was the one who brought everything up to code and living standard, Mr. King was the one to finish the floors, walls, painting. He’s very talented and from what I understand, very affordable.”

I grabbed the piece of paper from the table. It was suspicious, him having no phone number listed. “Would you happen to have a phone number for Mr. King?”

“I’m sorry, I don’t,” she said.

You’re useless, Shana. “Great, thanks for your help.” I ended the call.

Henry King’s address. Literally a few miles down the road. But was it rude to just drop in on someone? But how could it be when he had no number? I had to talk to him somehow.

CHAPTER FIVE:

I WENT TO PAY HENRY KING a visit few hours later when late enough in the afternoon. It took two minutes. That's how close this man lived to the house, and I became unnerved. I knew nothing about him. He knew everything about the house.

I pulled onto a narrow, dirt road, similar to the one leading to my parents' house but nowhere near as long. Little branches and leaves scraped the side of my rental car until I pulled into a clearing that revealed a small, shack-like house. His living arrangements didn't instill any confidence in his construction skills.

The house, small with a low hanging roof over the porch. As if the next rainfall would cause it to collapse. There were blankets in the windows instead of curtains. The wood of the house, eaten away by termites, and the water damage left a less than desirable structure. A house that was once white but hadn't been repainted in so long that majority of it was brown.

I put my rental car in park and stepped outside, skeptical. The sort of home the Unabomber would inhabit. The front yard, neglected and mostly long grass and dirt. I ducked under the clothes line while making my way to the porch, passing a large, wooden log and axe.

I swatted at bugs as I walked, the mosquitos running rampant. What a horrible place to live, I thought, contorting my face to the awful state of things the closer I got.

On the porch, a few chairs and old coffee cans filled with hopefully cigarette butts. But before I got the chance to investigate, the screen door swung open so hard that it slammed into the side of the house, startling me.

"Well go on then, you stubborn ass! I don't need your help anyway!" an older man shouted to someone inside the home.

Man, this was a bad idea, I thought.

The man seemed offended by my presence. "What do you want?" he snapped.

Oh God, I recognized him. The drunkard from Dante's. The loud, obnoxious day laborer from the diner. He stood there, dirty and sweaty. And also a little high on something. About early forties, I'd say. His messy hair thinned out in a way that only an older gentleman's hair would and was matted with sweat.

"What's the matter? Cat got your tongue?"

"Funny," I remarked. "Are you Henry King?"

He scoffed before spitting out a bit of chaw in my general direction. A bit had dribbled onto his chin, but he didn't seem to mind, and neither did I. It took everything in me not to laugh.

"Henry!" the man shouted into the dark home behind him. "Someone here to see you!"

Whew, I thought. My father never would have enjoyed that man's company. We waited in awkward silence. "Been in the area long?" I asked.

"My whole life."

I smiled politely and nodded. Really, I couldn't think of anything to say to him and he looked as if it pained him to speak to me.

"Henry!" he shouted over his shoulder.

"I'm comin'!" I heard a voice shout from within, slightly agitated.

"Don't go gettin' him all riled up, now. We got business to attend to later."

I didn't know how to respond to such a request. Was Henry easily riled? It sounded that way, but I suddenly became much more anxious about the meeting. I opened my mouth to speak, but before the words came to me, a young man appeared from the darkness of the doorway, and we immediately made eye contact.

I became embarrassed at the sight of the same man who'd helped his drunken friend at Dante's the night my nosiness got the better of me. The same man from the diner whom I so impolitely rejected conversation with, if that was at all his intention. He seemed confused, and in my panic, I felt the strong urge to run. Realizing how stupid that was, I turned back, smiling. "Hi."

The drunkard spit once more before wiping the remains from his chin. He jumped from the steps and landed next to me. He smelled awful. As if he hadn't taken a shower in days. His friend, however, much less insulting. At least visually.

"You two ladies have fun now," the drunkard said while walking over to the same, run-down pickup truck from the bar.

The man entertained me. He left us, speeding down the dirt road, and for a brief moment, I forgot about the awkward meeting. What a ridiculous person.

I looked back at Henry watching me, in awe, it would seem. "He's lovely."

"What are you doing here?" he asked. I hesitated. An awkward laugh escaped instead of words. "I mean, how'd you…" Henry began.

We were both uncomfortable and confused by one another. Much like how dogs act when they see another, strange dog. Curious as to what the other creature may be. Only their behavior is acceptable. Dogs aren't self aware. I decided to start off slow.

"I just wanted to apologize for the other night," I said, but he still seemed confused. "Dante's? I swear, I wasn't trying to be nosy, I just…"

"That's all right." He spoke in a quiet, raspy, Southern accent. Almost unsure of how to speak at all. Or at least too nervous to speak more than two words at a time. Much different than how he shouted before seeing me at his porch.

"Your friend, he's…he's okay?"

"He's my brother."

"Your brother? You guys don't look alike."

"Is that why you came out here?"

"No. Sorry. I, uh…" I stepped up the first two steps to the porch and extended my hand to him. "I'm Scarlett Crawley. I believe you may have done some work for my parents?"

Henry released my hand and then suddenly became fascinated with his nails. "Yeah. I was sorry to hear about your folks. They were good people."

"Thanks, me too…listen, they left the house…the one you'd been working on? They left it to me, and…well, thing of it is," I laughed uncomfortably. "I'm supposed to finish the renovations, and…well you came highly recommended."

It was difficult to tell his level of interest. He seemed lost, deep in thought about something. He stood at the top of the steps, pondering something.

His hair, like his brother's, disheveled and a little long for my taste, but there was much more of it and it fell to the nape of his neck. A few loose strands hung in light brown wisps over his forehead while other, unruly strands stuck out behind his ears.

His face, although seemingly young, appeared tired. His constant squinting hid his eye color, and his mouth held a permanent pucker or scowl. Although much more an attractive sight than his brother, Henry hadn't shaved in about a week or two. His arms, revealed by a cutoff shirt, were covered in grease along with his hands and his face. His pants, a faded gray color. Dirty and torn at the knees.

"You talk different…than you used to," he said.

"I'm sorry, have we met before?"

He didn't answer. Instead, he turned away from me and walked to the other side of the porch to fetch a pack of cigarettes, and I so badly wanted to ask for one.

I walked onto the porch and closer to him. I managed to peek into one of the old coffee cans while passing, relieved to not see a severed head inside. "Look, I need your help. The contractors my parents originally used are asking for an obscene amount of money, and…I've been told you've worked on the house, so…I won't be able to sell it until the renovations are complete," I said, almost as a way to get him to feel sorry for me.

"You're selling the house?"

"Well yeah. I can't…I can't keep that…there's just no way."

Henry took a drag of his cigarette and exhaled. "Okay."

I smiled. Though his qualifications remained a mystery, it felt nice knowing I had someone to assist in the process. He had to know more than myself. "Fantastic. I'll pay you, obviously. I mean, how much did my parents pay you?"

Henry shook his head.

"What does that mean?" I asked.

"They didn't."

"They didn't pay you? Like…very much, or…?"

"No, at all. Your dad gave me some free dental work, but…"

"Well, oral health is important." So odd. So odd and so completely ridiculous, and I found it difficult finding anything to respond with. "Look, we'll work out all the legalities later. When can you come by the house?"

"Tomorrow."

"Hmm…my parents' funeral is this weekend. We should wait till next week."

Henry shrugged.

"Can you do Monday?" I asked.

He nodded. "Sure."

"Afternoon?"

"Okay."

"Okay, great," I said while turning to leave.

"How'd you know where to find me?" Henry asked, prolonging my escape.

I turned back to him. Another pressing matter that needed discussion. The more I thought about it, the more annoyed I became that his number wasn't listed. "My parents had an address. And that is all." Henry took his last drag from his cigarette and nodded while flicking it into one of the coffee cans. "While we're on the subject, may I have your phone number so I can call if plans change?"

"Yeah…" he said awkwardly while fixing his hands onto the railing of the porch. "I don't have a phone."

"Sorry?" I asked, surprised.

"Don't have a phone. If plans change just leave a note on the door. That's what your dad used to do."

I didn't know what to say so I said nothing in an attempt to remain polite.

"By the way, you should really think about trading that in for a truck…" he said while motioning to my little rental car. "That is if you're going to be staying a while."

I studied the rental and then looked back at him, slightly offended. Did he not know that I grew up in Hunter's Point? My parents had just died because of this incident. Again, I bit my tongue in an attempt to be polite. "Thanks for the advice. I'll look into it."

"Please do," he said before turning away from me and entering the house once more.

What a strange man. He worked for free, didn't own a phone, and he spoke in a series of long pauses and two or three word responses. This was going to be interesting.

I ran errands the rest of the day. I finally made it back to Hunter's Point to meet with the bank and officially take ownership over my parents' accounts. I then stopped into the funeral home to write them a check and finish off the arrangements for Saturday. I decided on a closed-casket ceremony. It seemed the logical thing to do.

I pulled into the parking lot of my father's dental practice. A modest building off of Main Street with only the word DENTIST on the front of the building. I guess it makes sense. It was the only one in town. I became intimidated, knowing that half the practice belonged to me now. What was I supposed to do with it? I knew nothing about dentistry nor did I care. I should go inside and speak with my father's partner, Doctor Wilson, I thought. But the idea of taking in all the sympathetic or empathetic stares shied me away.

When I was a little girl, my father brought me to his office, and I was always treated like a VIP. The dental assistant used to sneak me lollipops and toys from the toy bin. My father gave me cleanings, a job usually reserved for the hygienist. He always played this sick game with me. Claiming that all my teeth were rotting out because I never brushed. As if to coax some kind of confession out of me. It never worked. I was always very good about my teeth.

As a child, I found this entertaining. Not so much as a teenager. In fact, checkups with my father often made me anxious when I as a teenager. Mostly because I'd started smoking. Cigarettes and weed. He never said anything though. He had to have known, but he never mentioned. But the one time I had a cavity, he lectured me for days. Maybe because he didn't want to admit that I'd started smoking. A cavity isn't really something he could ignore.

I felt sick reminiscing about everything. I wouldn't go inside. Not then. Maybe not ever. I could just call.

That night at my parents' house I rummaged through old boxes that had been stashed away in my bedroom closet. I went through my old records and put on The Talking Heads, Remain in Light. My favorite album from my adolescent years, and I became thankful that my parents kept it along with my record player.

I pulled out old picture albums from middle school. Folded up notes between me and my best friends. Friends I'd lost contact with over the years because I never really liked them to begin with. Friendships based on familiarity because we grew up together, but not much else, and if I wanted any shot at a social life, I had to play their game.

I found some of my old cheerleading photos and my Senior Prom photo buried at the bottom of the first box. I threw the cheerleading photo aside. I hated cheerleading. But my mother had cheered at the high school, so I was kind of forced into the whole escapade. A legacy, if you will. Trained since childhood. Gymnastics to start, then dance of all variations—all preparing me for the day that I became a sideline cheerleader at Hunter's Point High School. How pathetic.

I removed my Senior Prom photo. Ten years younger with my high school boyfriend—Quinn—short for Quinlan. The best looking guy in school hands down. Everyone wanted to date him, but he only had eyes for me. Sophomore through Senior year. I believe he won Prom King, actually. No, I wasn't Prom Queen, but I was nominated.

Quinn and I broke up the summer after Senior year. Mostly because of my impending move to New York, and I believe he went to school in Knoxville. We lost touch after a while, and I somehow even forgot he existed.

How does that happen? You're with one person for so long. The first person you kissed, the first person you had sex with, first person to say I love you…and then you forget about them. Perhaps I never loved him. No, I know I never did.

I tossed the photo aside and sighed. I hoped to find something else to scavenge, but nothing seemed appealing, and I'd listened to the same record three times in a row. It was almost midnight, but I wasn't tired.

I grabbed my phone to read through old text messages. Maybe I ignored one and could respond now. Just to talk to someone. I really wanted to talk to someone. But I had no one. I hadn't held on to any meaningful relationships my entire life. The only meaningful relationship I had no longer existed, thanks to the Rubidoux.

I walked onto the front porch and lit a cigarette, pulling my jacket tighter around me after a gust of wind sent chills down my spine. The country, so unnerving at night. Especially when alone.

No lights other than the stars in the sky and the moon, which barely illuminated the field in front of me. The crickets were the only bit of comfort along with the slight rusting of the leaves any time the wind blew.

I took another drag of my cigarette, but the sound of footsteps caught my attention, though it was too dark to see anything.

"Hello?" I called out. As if whomever stalked me might reply with a "hey, what's up?"

My ears played tricks on me, I told myself while taking another drag. But the footsteps got louder, quicker, and closer, causing me to jump back when a small figure approached.

"What the..."

A dog emerged from the darkness of the night and approached the well-lit porch in which I found myself. The dog stopped at the bottom of the steps, panting and wagging its tail. "Shoo..." I snapped while waving my hand at him, but he didn't move. "Get! Go on, get!" I said, but the dog remained.

He moved closer to me, but I backed away. He stopped, still panting, staring at me with that stupid, dopey look on his face. The one dogs give you when they want something. A mangy mutt, is what he looked like. Skinny with a predominately white coat, peppered with gray and black spots.

"I don't want to be friends," I said while taking another drag.

The dog whimpered and then laid on the ground. I kind of felt bad for the guy. Not bad enough to let him inside. I didn't know him.

"Wait here," I said while walking inside.

I made my way into the kitchen and grabbed a bowl from one of the cabinets. I filled it with water from the tap. While waiting for it to fill, I leaned over to look through the screen door. He'd made it up onto the porch now and patiently waited for me at the door.

When I emerged with the water bowl, he stood and wagged his tail. I placed the bowl on the ground, and he immediately drank. Flea ridden thing. I'd done my good deed for the day. When I turned to walk back inside, the dog whimpered. He looked sad.

"Don't start," I said to him, as if we spoke the same language.

I closed the front door and locked it, but it didn't drown out the sounds of the dog crying. Nothing did. He cried while I lay in bed upstairs. I had to put on my headphones just to drown him out.

Now, I don't think I'm a cruel person. I can't be alone in thinking that letting an unfamiliar dog into my house was a recipe for disaster. And I was right to think he'd give up eventually, because the next morning, I didn't see him anywhere.

CHAPTER SIX:

I SPENT THURSDAY cleaning the house as best I could in order to receive guests after the funeral on Saturday. I didn't expect a big turn out considering how far my parents' house was from town, but just in case, I wanted to impress people with my parents' efforts at renovations. Or for those who'd already seen it, not angry about how trashed I'd let it become.

Not so much cleaning as organizing and rearranging. Moving couches, chairs, tables, all in order to fit more people. I wished I had someone to help. Not because I found it to be hard. I found it to be sad. A sad thing to have to do by yourself.

I finally got around to chucking the old, dead flowers from the dining room table, but an empty vase remained. A sight far more depressing than dead flowers in a vase. At least with dead flowers, there's evidence that someone once cared.

I rinsed out the vase and stuck it under the kitchen sink before leaning back to rest on the counter. An uneasy feeling overcame me with the realization of my parents' funeral coming at me in full force. The day after tomorrow, and they'd been six feet under. I'd taken care of everything I could think. Now, I just had to wait to hear back from an old friend of my father's for the last spot of pallbearer.

The house, quiet and made me feel lonely. A loneliness I'd felt since arriving, but the eeriness drove me mad. I didn't even really want to talk to people anymore, but being in their company might make me feel better. The thought that everyone could carry on with their lives, comforted me.

I decided to go to Dante's. I didn't want a drink necessarily, though the prospect of drinking didn't sound too horrible. Really, I just wanted something to do. That's it. Nothing more, nothing less. I grabbed my jacket from the counter and made my way to the exit.

As soon as I walked outside though, the dirty mongrel from the night before caught my attention. "Ugh, what do you want?" I asked while turning to lock the door behind me.

The mutt whimpered. Hard to ignore, especially since he stood between me and my car. "Well, come on then," I said while walking past him to get to my car.

I opened the hatchback for him and he jumped inside. Impressive, I thought. I closed it behind him and climbed into the driver's side, certain that if I left him at Dante's, he'd just wander off and never come back again.

I'm more of a cat person anyway. Cats don't need you. They're so oblivious to your presence that I find it to be endearing. Dogs, on the other hand, are needy. I'm not one for needy behavior.

A few cars scattered throughout the parking lot of Dante's gave me hope that I might find comfort at the bar. Exactly the environment I felt I needed at the moment. A few people, not a big crowd. Small enough to where I could still have some quiet, but active enough to not feel completely alone.

I opened the hatchback and the mutt jumped out. I grabbed a nearby stick and threw it across the parking lot, and he chased it down. Perfect opportunity to duck inside.

I entered the bar, and just like before, I managed to get a few stares from the local patrons. I accounted this for my "new face" mostly. Dante's was a regular spot. A place hardly anyone new would drop in on. I convinced myself that this was the reason for their stares. Not because my parents just died.

I approached the bar, and Dante smiled at me weakly. "Come back for some of that moonshine?" he asked.

God no, I thought. "I'll just take a beer. Whatever's on tap."

"Coming right up," he said while grabbing a glass from beneath the bar.

While waiting for my drink, the old man next to me stared at me. Clearly drunk, I don't think he realized how obvious he was being. I smiled and nodded to the man, who seemed skeptical of my presence.

Dante handed me my drink. I threw him a twenty. "For the next one," I said while grabbing my beer and moving to a booth on the far side of the bar.

I strategically chose the booth closest to the jukebox to better hear the insolent wailing of whatever backwoods, mountain man played. Don't get me wrong, I like mountain music. Simply because it's such a rich part of Southern, American culture.

I can't relate to it, but the twangy sound of the guitar or banjo mixed with the inaudible lyrics—well, inaudible to anyone not from the Appalachians—seemed beautiful to me simply because not everyone can understand. Specific to a very small group of individuals, esoteric and exotic, in a way.

Next to me, a few men played pool. I hadn't played pool in years, but I always enjoyed doing so. I attribute that to my competitive nature. I hated losing.

God, did I want to play. Not with them. I didn't know them. And any attempt I've ever made to meet new people in that sort of setting had always blown up in my face. I'd wait until they were finished.

Two beers later the table had cleared. Eleven o'clock at night, but it gave me enough time to order another drink and practice my pool skills. I exchanged some bills for quarters at the bar. Dante's cleared out somewhat, so not only did I have the pool table to myself, I also had full reign of the jukebox.

However, in an attempt to remain on the patrons' good side, I decided to stick with the theme of the night. Not mountain music, but Southern rock. No self-respecting Southerner hates Southern rock. Always a safe hand to play. Bands like Blackfoot, ZZ Top, Charlie Daniels, and the obvious Lynard Skynard. All of these, safe bets when in a Southern bar.

I racked up and gauged which pool stick I should use before making a decision. After chalking up the end, I lined up the shot. I took my time. I knew the break would distinguish me from a chick playing pool and a chick who plays pool. I pushed the stick between my fingers, back and forth a few times, each time gaining more speed and power until the right moment.

Crack!

The sound of the cue ball smashing into the others echoed throughout the bar. The billiard balls were sent across the table in many different directions. A proud moment for me.

I took a celebratory swig of beer before focusing on where to move next, but the sound of people entering Dante's distracted me. I stood upright and tensed at the sight of Henry and his brother. I much preferred being in the company of unknown patrons.

I locked eyes with Henry and became flustered. I needed to focus again. Only now, I had no strategy. No sign of where to move next. Just a maze of different colored billiard balls strewn across a desert of felt. What was I even doing?

I went for the four, which required a skillful bounce off of the adjacent wall to land it in the left, center pocket. But of course, I glanced back toward Henry and his brother before taking the shot. He watched me, studied me, it would seem.

My face grew hot. I felt like he observed my technique, which I didn't appreciate. I took the shot. I missed. Embarrassed, I grabbed my beer and turned my back to the table…and to Henry.

I heard his brother joking around with Dante. His obnoxiously loud voice and booming laughter echoed throughout the bar. I chugged my beer. Ugh, why do that? It's not like I could leave upon finishing. I just started playing pool. I was stuck sucking at this billiard game while everyone watched.

Anxiety set in. I could just order another beer, I told myself. But then I'd have to go up to the bar and order one, bringing me closer to the cause of my anxiety.

Why was I anxious anyway?

"Scarlett?"

I choked on my beer at Henry's voice. I removed the glass from my lips and wiped my mouth before turning to him. "Hey," I said, very uncouth.

"You here by yourself?" he asked in that quiet, raspy voice.

Such an embarrassing question, I thought. No sense in lying though. "Yep. All by myself."

Henry looked cleaner than last time, although he maintained his squinty eyes even in the dimly lit bar. A slow, exaggerated nod followed my response while he studied the pool table, observing the order of the billiard balls.

"Do you…want to play?" I asked. The only thing I could think to say, really.

Henry considered my offer. His brother watched us intently from across the bar, making me feel even more uncomfortable for even having offered. "Okay," Henry muttered.

Great, now I get to suck in front of somebody for real this time. I handed Henry my pool-stick before grabbing another from the rack. "It's anyone's game at this point. I've yet to make one."

Henry stood over the table, studying the balls. Taking his time, just like a pro. He moved around the table and lined up his shot. He took it, made it in, and then set the precedent for the rest of the game. He was solids, I was stripes.

"You've played this before," I said coolly.

"Once or twice," he said while moving across the table to his next shot. One that he'd clearly already set up by how fast he moved. "I'm more of a darts guy, actually."

"Isn't that just throwing darts at a board, trying to get a bulls-eye?"

He smirked before taking his shot. Another point for him. "There's more to it than that." He moved around the table once more, again having set himself up perfectly for the next shot.

"You're good at this."

He took the shot, made it in, but the cue ball followed behind. Scratch. "Spoke too soon," he said while backing away.

I stood over the table, observing, but not really observing. Making it seem like I was observing. As if I had some sort of plan in my head. I'd go the safe route. The easy way out. A ball that seemed perfectly lined up with the corner pocket. I couldn't miss that shot, I thought. I leaned over the table. The entire time, I felt Henry's eyes burning into me. I took the shot.

A sigh of relief came over me when the ball entered the pocket. Whew, I thought. "That was intense."

Henry chuckled, and I was pleased with myself. With my confidence slowly coming back to me, I began moving around the table like a professional, trying to decide my next move, but the awkward silence distracted me.

"So how long have you been doing construction?" I asked him while leaning over the table to take my next shot. His infamous long pause followed.

Henry shrugged. "Couple years."

I took the shot. I missed. I sighed in defeat while moving out of the way. "How long have you been doing construction for my parents?" I asked.

Henry leaned over the table. "Couple years."

"You don't talk much, do you?" I asked, skeptical of him and his mystery.

Henry took the shot. He made it in, which came as no surprise. "No, I uh…never really did construction until your dad asked for my help."

"Really?"

He nodded. "But I've always been pretty good at fixing things, so…" he shrugged.

"It just came naturally to you."

"I guess you could say that," he said while leaning over the table once more.

I glanced back towards his brother. He seemed resentful. "I don't think your brother likes me very much," I said while moving to grab my beer.

Henry took his next shot. Again, he made it in before standing upright to move to the other side of the table. "Don't take it personal. He don't like anyone."

"What's his name?"

"Max," Henry responded while lining up his next shot.

Max. I'd never seen anyone stare at me the way he did. So hateful without knowing anything about me. I finished my beer and set the empty glass—along with my others—on a vacant bar table next to me.

"That's you," Henry said while approaching me, breaking my train of thought.

"You missed?"

"I did."

A smirk crept across my face as a grabbed my stick and moved toward the pool table. There seemed to be a lot more of my balls left than his. I concentrated hard, but three beers made it difficult to really think about pool. "I don't know what to do," I admitted.

He smirked. "Do what feels right."

"I'm feeling pretty good about the green one," I said while pointing it out with the stick. "What do you think?" I asked.

Henry smirked. "Looks good." Validation obtained. "Did you want another beer?" he asked.

I considered. Contemplated whether or not I should. I'd had three already, and I started to become less anxious yet more demonstrative, which isn't necessarily a good thing. I tend to have an abrasive personality, which tends to shy people away from me.

But for the first time since being home, I started enjoying myself. But Should I be enjoying myself under the circumstances? I thought so. Hell, I'd be laying my parents to rest in a few days, never to see them again. If that doesn't justify having a fourth drink, I don't know what does.

"Sure. Thank you."

He nodded and made his way over to the bar. With him gone, it became easier to focus. I stared at the ball, long and hard as if to telepathically communicate with it in hopes it could understand and just go in the pocket. I took the shot, and for a brief second believed in telepathy because the ball obliged and went into the appropriate pocket.

I cheered to myself, but when I noticed Henry in conversation with his brother, I felt uncomfortable again. Max seemed angry. Henry, uncaring. Had I just caused a problem between the two?

Henry turned his back to Max and ~~made his way back~~ toward me, beer in hand. I watched him, concerned. When he handed me my beer, I couldn't help but ask, "Everything okay?"

"Everything's fine."

"He seems angry."

"Don't worry about him. Did you make it?" he asked.

"I did, so it is still my turn," I said before taking a swig of my fresh beer. "You didn't get one for yourself?"

He shook his head. "I don't drink."

Wow. Impressive. Especially for a young, Southern man. "Good for you," I said. And not in a sarcastic way either.

I wish I didn't need alcohol. It's not the process of drinking that bums me out. It's the hangovers. Every time I drink, I think I've figured it out. Hydrate between beers or cocktails or shots, whatever your poison. It's the obvious thing to do. But alas, we rarely do. Because who wants to pause the game to go chug a glass of water? No one likes commercials. So we man up. And we pay for it the next morning along with promises to never do it again.

"Whoo!" I shouted after making three balls in a row.

"Looks like you might actually win," Henry said.

"Is that so surprising?" I asked through a big, shocked smile.

"No," ~~he said through a slight laugh.~~

I shot him a playful glare before leaning over the table once more. I lined up my shot, took it, and missed. I gasped, and he was smirking while exhaling cigarette smoke.

"You jinxed me."

"Sorry." He put out his cigarette and made his way to the table. I became eager to see what would happen next. I didn't stand a chance, I thought. My only hope at winning was to keep him off the table.

Henry set up his shot when two men entered the bar. They seemed out of place. Well kept and dressed in black. They made their way to Max, and Henry watched them for a bit while putting more chalk on his pool stick. When Max let out an obnoxious laugh, Henry leaned over the table once more to take his shot, making the ball into the pocket.

"I'll be right back." Henry approached them, and I couldn't help but wonder who they were.

I grabbed my beer and sat in one of the nearby barstools when I heard my phone chirp. An email from the last pallbearer for my parents' funeral came through, sending his regrets from California. So without the last pallbearer, I came back to reality.

Henry approached, and I put my phone away, disheartened.

"You okay?" he asked.

"I'm fine. I should actually probably go home. Something just…fell through, and I gotta think about what I'm going to do," I said while grabbing my things.

A long pause followed. "Let me take you home."

I hesitated. "No, you have people waiting on you…"

"They're not waiting for me."

A kind gesture as I'd been drinking, though I considered just grabbing a room for the night.

"Scarlett," he spoke, snapping me from my thoughts.

"What about my car?"

He looked toward the parking lot, pondering something. "Here, give me your keys." I did as he asked. "Come on," he said, and I felt his hand on the small of my back as he escorted me toward the exit of the bar.

"Henry!" Max yelled as we walked.

"I'll be right back."

"We got friends here!" Max yelled.

"I'll be right back! Damn," he said while opening the door for me. The loudest I'd ever heard him project his voice.

Outside, the mangy mutt greeted us. The one I'd completely forgotten about while playing pool. The dog stood from his spot at the bottom of the steps and wagged his tail.

"Who's your friend?" Henry asked.

"He's no friend of mine."

The dog became excited, doing a little dance back and forth on his paws, wagging his tail, and even started barking. Henry approached him. He kneeled down to pet him, and the dog started licking his face.

"He sure thinks he is," Henry said.

"He doesn't have a collar. Just a stray. Some mangy mutt."

"He's a Catahoula," he said. "A friendly one."

"A what?"

"Louisiana huntin' dog."

"He's a long way from home," I snickered. Henry ignored, clearly not entertained at my attempts at humor.

Kind of cute, I guess, Henry petting the dog. But the idea of petting a dog that had probably never been bathed, had its shots, most likely covered in fleas, kept me away from him. The dog panted, excited with his tongue hanging out of his mouth, and for a moment, it seemed like he smiled at me.

Henry stood. "Do you need anything out of your car?"

I shook my head and Henry led the way to the truck. "Come on, dog," I said while passing the mutt.

I climbed into the passenger seat while Henry opened the bed to allow the dog inside. He whistled to him, and through the rearview, I watched the exchange between man and beast. Two dirty, dingy guys bonding over a mutual respect and understanding of where the other exists in the world.

I became distracted on the drive back to my parents' house. Tired mostly, thanks to the beer, but stressed from everything coming my way in full force with no way to slow any of it down. And for the first time in a long time, I wished for a companion to hold my hand.

"You feel okay?" Henry asked in his quiet, raspy voice.

I watched the trees whizzing past us as we drove. "Yeah, I'm just tired. Stressed."

Henry remained quiet. He seemed so focused on the road. So focused on getting us to our destination safely. No doubt on alert for rogue deer that might dart across the highway at any moment. I felt safe with him driving though. You know those people you just trust automatically? Without any reason, really. Just the way in which they carry themselves, I guess.

"How long did you know my parents?" I asked.

Another long pause. "A long time."

"Even before you started working for them?"

"I knew of them, yeah."

I didn't know if I should ask, but without any other options, I became desperate, and a possible solution sat next to me, going out of his way to make sure the daughter of people he used to care about got home safely.

"I have a favor to ask you," I said. An awkward favor, one that could make anyone feel uncomfortable. "The last pallbearer can't make it on Saturday. I need six per casket. I only have eleven now."

Another long pause made me anxious to ask, and it seemed as though he wouldn't respond until I did. Despite the obviousness of the situation, and I'm unsure if the hesitation could be considered polite or the opposite.

"Would you…be willing to step in and carry the…? I mean, you've known them for a long time, so…"

"Sure."

"Really?" I asked, somewhat surprised. Although how does one really say no to that? Oh yeah, by saying they can't make it like the previous one had done.

"I'd be honored."

I said nothing but gave an approving nod. His response made me feel all warm inside, touched by his kindness. I wanted to remain strong, but it proved to be difficult in a moment like that. Especially because of the alcohol. I felt that at any moment, any act of kindness no matter how small, would send me into a fit of tears.

We arrived at my parents' house and Henry climbed out of the truck and walked to the bed to let the dog out of the back. I climbed out and shut the door behind, the old, empty house waiting patiently for me to enter. I didn't want to go inside.

Henry approached with the dog at his side. "You should really consider keeping him," he said. "He could be some good company."

"I'll think about it."

Henry took my keys from his pocket and removed the house keys before handing them to me. "I'll drop your car off later," he said.

"Thanks for the ride. It was nice of you."

He nodded, though it seemed there was something he wanted to say. "Have a good night, Scarlett." Guess not.

And with that, he made his way back to his truck, leaving me and the dog to our own company. I looked down at the mutt, staring up at me, panting. When I approached the porch, he remained seated, as if waiting for me to invite him inside. ~~I turned back to him.~~

"Well come on then," I said, and as soon as I opened the door, he bolted ~~inside.~~ through the doorway

I didn't really want to let the dog inside, but Henry made a good point. As lonely as I felt, any company seemed better than no company at all. Especially in my drunken state. I went upstairs and flung myself onto my bed. The dog followed. He sat at the edge, expectedly. I patted his head, which he must have taken as an invitation to climb up.

"No," I said, pushing him away. "Off."

The dog obliged. He did a few circles on the floor next to me before laying down completely. I kind of felt safe with him there even if I didn't want to cuddle, and when I awoke the next morning, he remained on the floor, next to my bed. I guess I needed to get dog food for the poor mutt.

CHAPTER SEVEN:

SATURDAY CAME TOO FAST. After spending the morning cleaning whatever I'd put off the previous days, the time came to get ready for the funeral. I stood in front of my full length mirror, trying to determine the appropriateness of my dress for my parents' funeral.

While it seemed conservative enough, it came down to just above my knees and hugged me tighter than I expected. With a low cut back, I started to second guess the thing. I guess that's what I get for grabbing my dress from Winter Formal Junior year.

I pulled my hair into a loose bun and put on these knockoff pearl earrings I found at the local supermarket. Yes, I said supermarket. Gotta love small towns. I put on a bit of mascara and a light colored lipstick. The best I could do given the circumstances.

The drive to Hunter's Point seemed to take forever, but I didn't mind. I considered not even going. Would anyone really say anything if I didn't? The only two people whose opinions I ever cared about were dead.

The gray storm clouds prevented the sun from making an appearance that day, overcast with the promise of rain some time soon. It seemed appropriate for such an occasion. No sign of rain yet though, and the Rubidoux remained dormant for now.

I hoped and prayed for rain during the funeral so my retreat to my parents' house would be solo. But a truly dreadful thing would be if it started raining while everyone was there. Then I'd be stuck with them.

When I arrived at the funeral home, a crowd of people already gathered in the parking lot. They broke off into scattered, smaller groups throughout while others made their way into the funeral home.

My heart pounded. I didn't know how to navigate something like that. What was I to do when someone told me they were sorry for my loss? Say thank you? For what, exactly, am I thankful for? That you're sorry?

I contemplated leaving and coming back right before the service. That way, I could avoid awkward conversation. Before making the decision though, people in the crowd already started noticing me. The orphan sitting in her car, staring at all of them, terrified. A sacrifice to the wolves, it seemed.

I tried to ignore them while walking to the entrance, and when I entered the funeral home, it was as if I parted the red sea of mourners. They all ceased their conversation, or so it seemed. One by one, they moved aside to allow me through.

They felt sorry for me. I lost both my parents in one night and expected nothing less from. But as quickly as I dismissed their empathetic or sympathetic stares, that's how quickly I forgot about them completely when I saw two caskets at the front of the viewing room.

I stopped dead in my tracks, and those around me seemed to disappear. I became afraid to enter. Like when you know your parents got your report card so you don't want to face them. Strange how those emotions are so similar.

My heart fell into my stomach. A knot in the pit of me grew. I walked toward them, the last time I ever would. And even though they were out of sight, hidden by their closed caskets, I felt their presence. They stood at their appropriate casket, waiting for only me to come and bid them farewell.

I never took my eyes from their caskets, wondering who might need me closer. My mother, most likely. Her memorial photo I'd chosen painted her in a much different light than I remember. A photo of her from college before she had me. She seemed so young.

I placed my hand on her casket. The sleek, polished wood beneath my fingers held a barrier between me and her. I'd always been closer to my father. We were more alike. But for some reason, in that moment, I wanted her.

I brought my hands to the lid of the casket and attempted to open it, but someone put their arm around me, stopping me completely. "You don't want to do that, Miss..." a man said.

The funeral director gave me a weak smile and escorted me to my seat at the front of the room. The guests started crowding inside, and I felt scrutinized for my little episode. When I went to breathe the air seemed to get stuck in my throat, and I whimpered.

Throughout the ceremony, I remained distant. Staring off into nothing, not really hearing anything about my parents. Occasionally, someone in the crowd would cry, breaking me of my train of thought. But it didn't take long to get lost once again. A form of self-preservation, I felt. If I had been present, I'd cry as well. I didn't want to do that. Not in front of all those people. Although I'm sure it's what they expected.

When I heard the priest say my name, I came back to the moment. I stood and made my way to the podium. I'd forgotten about this part. People wanted to hear from the remaining family member. Their only child. What a sick thing, I thought. You all want to know how I'm feeling? How I'm grieving? Why, so you can feel better?

The familiar faces in the crowd waited for me to speak, though words failed me. I needed to express my appreciation for all their love and support. I locked eyes with Henry, leaning against one of the walls in the back of the room, dawned in a black suit. Something I wouldn't have guessed he owned.

I took a deep breath and searched for the inspiration from my mother's casket. "Thank you all for coming," I began. "I know it would have meant a lot to my parents, having you all here...I, uh...just wanted to say that..."

No thoughts or inspiration came to me. What an awful thing to have to admit to a whole room of people. But maybe I just needed to see her again. I had to see her again before putting her in the ground.

"I'm sorry, I have to…" I walked out from behind the podium and approached my mother's casket. I felt all the eyes of the crowd burning into my back, and when I lifted the lid, even chatter. I became frozen at my mother's dead, lifeless body. No longer bloated, but still very much dead. I felt a knot form in my stomach. A lump in my throat swelled, and my eyes burned.

"Oh god," I muttered to myself. I closed the casket. My head felt fuzzy, and as I staggered, I felt the support of two men grab onto me to escort me out of the room.

I heard people in the crowd cry, some even gasped, but two men brought to an empty room in order to regain some composure. Jesus Christ, my parents were dead, and I only had minutes to calm myself before leaving for the burial. I needed to build up a wall, disappear in my head for the remainder of the service. I needed to lose myself in my mind.

I stood in front of the funeral home as the pallbearers carried their caskets to their appropriate hearses. A few people close to my parents stood next to me, offering support in case I fainted. But I remained distant from them, from everything happening around me. I convinced myself that none of it really happened. I managed to numb myself, hardly even acknowledging that the pallbearers carried my parents and not just some wooden boxes.

I broke free of my trance when the time came for burial, just to say goodbye once more. I knew in the moment I saw them lowered into the ground next to each other that they were gone for good. I don't believe in Heaven or Hell. I don't believe in the after life. I knew that in this world, all of us were alone. Completely and utterly alone.

The thought consumed my mind when back at my parents' house despite people surrounding me. I greeted everyone who entered, mostly in an attempt to avoid conversation for the rest of the afternoon. Still, the occasional busy bodies had to know about my life the past ten years. I kept my answers short. One word responses, mostly. And the question I kept getting was…

"What does a music critic do exactly?"

Good question. Even I don't know what I'm doing half the time.

I broke free from the social atrocity that requires congregation after a funeral, but with no alcohol in sight—a decision I started to regret—food became my saving grace. Lots and lots of food. I piled pasta salad, potato salad, bread rolls, deli meats, cheeses, all sky high on my plate at least three times in hopes the food ran out. If the food ran out, I assumed people to follow.

Guests scattered ~~about~~ in every which way. On the front porch, enclosed porch, kitchen, living room, foyer, dining room…not upstairs though. I kept upstairs off limits. And when people weren't patting me, hugging me, squeezing me, sticking their noses in my life, they were commenting on how great the house looked.

"Scarlett!" I heard someone shout while walking away from the food table with my fourth plate. With my fork in my mouth, I turned to see who the hell would shout so excitedly at such an occasion.

A woman with blonde hair pulled back into a curled ponytail, wearing a tight, black dress and a toddler in tow approached me, smiling. Before removing the fork from my mouth, she pulled me into the tightest bear hug I never wanted, pressing against my already full belly. While mid hug, I locked eyes with the toddler. Who was this child and its mother?

The woman finally released me, allowing me to remove the fork from my mouth. "Hey, how are you?" I asked.

"Well I am just so sad for you and yours," she said.

"I appreciate that. Who's this?" I asked, feigning excitement to seeing a toddler at such a dreary occasion. Social etiquette and whatnot.

"This is Robert Junior, ~~or RJ as we call him.~~"

"Robert junior," I said while filtering out every name of every person I'd gone to high school with. Finally, the names became clear. Robert Cavanaugh and his long-time girlfriend Katherine, Kate for short.

Actually, Kate and I never really talked much. Her boyfriend, Robert, had been good friends with my ex, Quinn, although I'm pretty sure Quinn and Kate had hooked up at some point. Not while we were together. Well, maybe. Anyway, Robert hailed from one of the richest families in Hunter's Point, his father being one of the only physicians in town.

"Wow, Kate…" I said. "You married Robert Cavanaugh?"

She nodded, wearing the world's biggest, fakest smile. "Six years now!" she said while holding out an atrociously large diamond ring. I wanted a ring that big. Bitch.

"So where is hubby?" I asked.

"Stuck at the office, I'm afraid. He sends his regards."

"Tell him I said thanks," I said while shoveling food into my mouth. I didn't really care if she told him. I doubt he sent his regards at all. Not that Robert and I hadn't gotten along in school. I dumped his best friend quite brutally after graduation.

"God, this potato salad is the best," I said in an attempt to show that I had better things going on, giving me an excuse to move along.

"Oh my God, Scarlett…"

A petite red head approach me. I knew exactly who that was. Our old prom queen herself, and actually someone I rather enjoyed throughout high school. Ella had been a member of student counsel, and the reason people liked her so much was because she never got involved in drama. That includes not dating anyone either, although I attribute that to her father being a pastor.

"Ella," I said, impressed. She hadn't aged a day. Though she seemed not to care that I was impressed with her because she immediately pulled me into a hug.

"I can't believe this happened, I don't…I don't even know what to say," she said. I heard her voice crack. Tears seemed inevitable, and I patted her back in an attempt to comfort her.

Ella released me, partially. “It’s just…I always remember sleepovers at your house in Hunter’s Point, and your parents would always set up the tent in the living room with the television inside…and we’d watch scary movies…” she’d started ~~really~~ crying.

“Yeah, I know,” I said.

“They were such good people,” she sobbed.

I didn’t know what else to do. So I handed her my plate. She took it, grateful. “Thank you. I’m starving,” she said while shoveling food into her mouth.

Ella had become a teacher at the local elementary school. Unmarried, had no children, and thought the idea of New York was just ghastly. Which, I can’t really blame her. Most everyone I spoke to in Hunter’s Point didn’t seem very interested in the big city life. Too different, I suppose.

New York was different for me as well, but that’s why I liked it so much. In New York City, no one judges you. No one questions your decisions. They don’t hold against you that you’ve been out drinking every night of the week. They don’t care if you skip church on Sundays. They don’t even care if you die. Which is perfect. People care too much in the South. It’s smothering.

“Here, let me hold him,” Ella said while reaching for RJ. “You are so cute!” she exclaimed after Kate had released him into her grasp. “Isn’t he cute?” Ella asked.

“He’s a cutie…” I began.

“Scarlett?” Jesus Christ. I turned to the sound of my name, stunned at the sight of who called out to me. Like staring into my past.

“Oh my God, Quinn!” I said while opening my arms for a hug. He pretty much looked exactly the same only his auburn hair was longer, combed to the side and had a well maintained, short beard. His eyes, just as fiery an amber, and his smile, just as warm and comforting as I remember.

He gave me a tight embrace ~~before pulling back, smirking.~~ “Hey kid.”

"What are you doing here?" I asked, excited. I'm not sure where the excitement came from. Probably because we were close for so long. The only real friend I ever had, and I preferred seeing his face over all others.

"I moved back here," he said.

"When?"

"About four years ago," he said, proud.

I became confused. "Why?"

Quinn smiled ~~and exchanged glances with Ella and Kate.~~ "Well, I was offered a job, so I took it. And I missed home."

I laughed. How ridiculous. "What job?"

Quinn diverted his eyes to the ground and cleared his throat. "Dentistry," he muttered.

What an odd thing to say, and the news perplexed me. Quinn had never shown interest in Dentistry. I'm pretty sure he wanted to be, like, an athletic trainer…I don't know. But dentistry seemed so far off and disturbing. Mostly because…

"Isn't there only one dental practice here?" I asked. Quinn opened his mouth to speak, but hesitated. "Oh God, you work at my father's practice, don't you?" ~~I asked.~~

He exhaled. "Your dad never said anything?"

I shook my head. I dunno, maybe. It's possible. "So wait…you, like, kind of work for me, don't you?"

Quinn laughed uncomfortably. "For now."

"Huh." I grabbed my plate back from Ella and ~~started walking~~ away, all while shoving food into my mouth. Stress eating, I discovered. Something I used to do a lot of in my youth. For some reason the news of Quinn being a dentist working in my father's…MY practice, really bothered me.

I walked into the kitchen and threw my plate into the sink. My mouth, still full of food. I'd bitten off more than I could chew. That's not a euphemism, I really did. I felt sick and anxious that I was going to choke to death in a room full of people.

With so much food in my mouth, it became difficult to chew, and I took deep, labored breaths through my nose. What a sight, I'm sure. Before I could get any of it down, Doctor Wilson approached.

"Scarlett?"

I nodded while holding my finger up to the man's face, letting him know I needed a second, and he waited patiently while I chewed my food like a mad man and swallowed in portions.

"Sorry," I said, still with food hidden in my cheeks.

"That's all right, take your time," he said.

I extended my hand to him. "Hey Doctor Wilson. I've been meaning to come by the office, just…haven't really had time."

"Oh no, take your time, Scarlett. I understand what you're going through." Great. A sympathizer. "But while I'm here, I wanted to give you something," he said.

I picked food from my teeth with my tongue. Quite the uncomfortable experience, talking to a dentist with food in your teeth. Almost like he'd fixate on it, wondering if you noticed you had food in your teeth.

Dr. Wilson handed me a folded up piece of paper. "What is this?" I asked.

"The amount I'm prepared to pay in order to buy you out," he said. "There's no reason for you to stay with the practice now. I promise you, I'll take good care of it for you. And the amount there is well within reason…"

I tuned him out, offended that he actually came to me on the day of my parents' funeral to offer to buy me out. And while I knew selling anyway would be the best thing, the fact that I hadn't been the one to mention it really irritated me. Worse than that, it actually made me feel sick. Or maybe that was the food. Oh God, I'd eaten way too much.

"Doctor Wilson, let me just stop you right there," I interrupted. "While I appreciate you coming out and showing your support, I hope you can understand when I say that this is neither the time or the place to be dealing with such matters, so would you please excuse me so I can go throw up?"

Doctor Wilson's eyes narrowed ~~and his lips pursed.~~ It seemed I'd offended him, though he nodded. "Well, the offer stands. I'll be waiting to hear from you. When you're ready."

[I watched as he walked away, astounded at the nerve of him. Asshole.]

I stuck my finger deep into my throat until my fingernail clipped the fleshy, wet mucous membrane that lined the back of my esophagus. When I felt the urge to vomit, I held my finger in place. One, two, three…and then I vomited into my bathroom toilet. I'd done this before. No, not to lose weight. Because I have a tendency to eat too much or drink too much when I'm stressed. And as horrible as vomiting feels in the moment, it certainly is worth it when you feel like you're no longer going to pop or the room is no longer spinning.

I felt safe in the seclusion of my upstairs bathroom. Free to vomit as much as I pleased without the rest of the congregation downstairs being able to judge me.

I stuck my finger into my throat once more. But as soon as round two left my mouth and landed in the toilet, a knock came to the opened, bathroom door. Quinn. Well, I guess that's all for now. I flushed the toilet and hung my head in defeat.

"You okay?" he asked.

"Don't look at me, I'm gross."

I heard Quinn laugh, and when I felt his presence grow closer, I looked up at him. He grabbed a wash rag from the towel rack and wet it under the bathroom sink. He handed it to me, and I wiped my face and mouth.

"Had a few drinks?" he ~~asked while kneeling~~ [kneeled] down next to me.

I scoffed. "I wish. Too much food."

"Well some things never change," he said, smiling coolly.

You don't know me. Well, actually he did. And I hated that after all those years, he still knew me so well. I forced a smile and wiped my mouth once more, and I could tell he wanted to say something.

"I saw you talking to Doctor Wilson."

"Well, he is my business partner now," I muttered, annoyed at the thought.

"Did he ask you about selling?"

"He did."

Quinn paused. Whatever he wanted to say, it proved to be difficult. "Are you going to?"

I groaned. Not this conversation again. Though Quinn had every right to know what I planned on doing with the business as my employee. Though hardly the time for me to make that announcement.

I knew not selling would be pretty stupid, but a part of me felt horrible to entertain the idea at the moment. Selling the house, selling the practice. Getting rid of all the evidence that my parents ever existed? I wanted to puke again.

I saw someone appear in the doorway, and when I locked eyes with Henry, a feeling of relief overcame me. A distraction from the question that I really didn't want to answer. Even better, a question I didn't know the answer to.

Henry sort of hesitated. "Sorry, I was…"

"There's a bathroom downstairs for guests," Quinn snipped.

I rolled my eyes. "He knows where the bathrooms are."

Henry stared at me for a moment while I remained sitting on the ground next to the toilet. "You okay, Scarlett?" he asked.

"Can you give us a minute?" Quinn snapped.

Awkward.

"Quinn, will you do me a favor and let the guests know I'd like them to leave now? I'm tired, and it's going to start raining soon anyway," I said. "But, like…nicer than that."

I said it in a way that made Quinn feel needed and appreciated in the moment. Almost like a co-host, mostly just so he'd do what I asked. If I acted wounded and incapable of seeing anyone, he'd be more inclined.

Quinn gave me a weak smile and nodded before standing. He pushed past Henry to exit the room completely.

"Sorry about him," I said.

"It's okay. Me and him have never really seen eye to eye."

I used the toilet as a crutch to stand to my feet. I adjusted my dress and made my way to my vanity where I'd stuck a bottle of mouthwash in the medicine cabinet.

"Do you need anything?" Henry asked.

"I'm fine, thank you," I said before taking a swig from the bottle. I rinsed my mouth and spit the mouthwash into the sink and wiped my face and hands with the rag Quinn gave me. "How do you know Quinn?"

A long pause, as usual, and then he shook his head and shrugged. Clearly it didn't matter. Most likely through my father, I assumed.

"Listen, I…I wanted to thank you for today," I said while leaning in the door frame. "It meant a lot that you did that…" Henry opened his mouth to speak, but I continued. "I mean, I'm sure lots of people would have, but…it was nice knowing that someone who actually knew my mother was there to…carry her."

Henry nodded. "I was happy to do it."

I gave him a polite smile and then moved past him to my bedroom window that overlooked the dilapidated horse stable. The pressure of this very big home renovation started weighing down on me, and I remained unsure of where to begin or where to draw inspiration. Sure, my parents had a list. A list that to me was more like guidelines.

If I was going to spend all the money left to me into this house, I would make it how I thought it should look. Not because I wanted to keep it for myself. Simply because I felt the need to have some sort of control in my life now that everything had gone to shit.

"I'll leave you to it then. Just wanted to come check on you before I left."

"Thank you, Henry."

I heard the door close. I needed to come up with a plan. And to do some research. Granted, I wouldn't be the one building anything, I felt it was necessary to at least brush up on my handyman skills, or whatever you'd call it.

The sun started to set by the time all the guests left. Quinn offered to stay and clean, but I declined. I needed time to reflect, but he would only leave with the promise of having dinner together at some point. I agreed.

CHAPTER EIGHT:

I GATHERED TRASH into a large, industrial sized garbage bag. I tied it up and threw it onto the porch to be dealt with later. Once finished, I moved the furniture back to its original place. But nothing looked right. I started rearranging things accordingly. It still didn't feel right. I convinced myself the lower level needed a good scrubbing.

I grabbed some gloves, all purpose cleaner, and a rag. I scrubbed every table, counter, chair…anything that anyone touched. I'm not OCD or anything, but I felt the integrity of my parents' home had been compromised in some way. ~~Like the guests dirtied it up.~~

In one afternoon and by twenty people, any remaining sign that my parents lived there seemed to be scrubbed away. I guess technically, I scrubbed them away. I realized the floors needed to be cleaned as well.

I swept the entire lower level. I let Dog back in at that point, and he kept trying to attack the broom with every sweep, though I ignored. I remained focused on all the dust on the floor. After sweeping the rooms three different times, I snapped.

"You're the reason the floors are so dusty!" I yelled to Dog.

He looked at me questioningly. I put him on the back porch to keep out of the way, choosing to endure his cries for freedom from his generously spacious crate.

Still, the dust wouldn't come up all the way. I grabbed the mop and bucket to do things the old fashioned way. But that didn't do it either. A scrub brush should suffice. But after about an hour on my hands and knees, I gave up and threw my gloves and brush into the bucket.

I positioned the furniture in a way that I liked. But something still wasn't right. The house looked great. But it didn't smell right. I'd used too many chemicals. I opened the living room windows, but as sweet as the night air smelled, my problem remained.

I made coffee, hoping to overpower the chemicals with that sweet aroma. But that didn't do it either. Air freshener didn't do the trick. Something was wrong. Horribly wrong. I needed to go into the last place I wanted. Perhaps it was the only way.

I passed by the back porch while making my way to the stairwell, ignoring the cries from Dog to be let inside. I made my way up the stairs and turned to the right instead of going left into my room. I hesitated. Just a room, nothing more, nothing less.

I opened the door and stood in the doorway for a moment before reaching for the light switch. My parents' room hadn't been touched, of course. It was a tomb. I considered not going inside, but smells from downstairs drove me insane. I entered the room and immediately made my way to the bathroom. I opened the medicine cabinet and stared at my mother's perfume for a while before grabbing it from the shelf and exiting the room completely. No point in going back in there any time soon.

I moved around the living room, spraying a generous amount of my mother's perfume in the air. The same perfume she wore for as long as I could remember. When finished, I took a step back. I examined the room then closed my eyes and took a deep breath. I inhaled her. The smell of her. But the air got caught in my throat. It burned. Then my eyes burned. I'd sprayed too much, I thought.

None of this was right.

I started panting. My face became hot. Angry tears poured out of my eyes. My heart started pounding. Nothing I did could make it right. I screamed in aggravation and threw my mother's perfume bottle to the ground, shattering it and sending perfume everywhere.

But I wasn't finished. In a fit of rage, I pulled the books from the shelf. I threw the blankets and cushions from the sofa. I threw one of the lights from the end table into the wall, completely destroying the bulb and sending a bolt of blue light from the base of the lamp.

Finally, I grabbed a family photo from the end table and threw it at the window, sending it straight through the glass at the top of the pane. I stopped, gasping and staring at the mess I made. But all I could do was fall to my knees and cry.

None of it felt right because I tried so desperately to make it feel like home. Home, somewhere I needed so badly at that moment. But nothing in that house made me feel at home. Not the furniture or decorations. Not the sounds, not the smells. Not even the scent of my mother could make it feel like home to me.

I wailed for the first time since hearing my parents had died. I wailed as loud as possible, and Dog, as a sign of solidarity, howled. I wanted my mom and my dad. I needed their comfort. I wanted them to pick me up and tell me that everything was going to be okay, even if I knew they'd lie to protect me. Because I knew better.

Nothing was going to be okay.

"You said Dog did this?" Henry asked when he came over that Monday. He examined the hole in the window, confused.

I nodded. "Yep."

"And he did…all this?" he asked while motioning to the state of the living room.

"Mhmm." Henry seemed skeptical. "Well, there was…a mouse."

"A mouse." He repeated.

"Yeah, a tiny, little…garden mouse, and Dog just lost his shit."

"A garden mouse."

Henry looked at Dog sitting in the entryway with his tongue hanging out, panting. Completely oblivious that I put the blame on him. Stupid mutt. Henry turned back to the window to measure the length, I narrowed my eyes at Dog, as if to warn him not to say anything. I knew he wouldn't. I could trust him.

"Why'd you decide to name him Dog anyway?" Henry asked while measuring the width of the pane.

"I didn't see the point in giving him a real name. He'll be dead in a few years anyway," I said, though he seemed to understand as he tilted his head to the side and groaned a bit, and I sort of felt guilty. What a strange dog.

Henry put away his measuring tape. "I need to go to the hardware store to get something to board this up with for now. It'll probably take a couple days before the glass gets in," he said. "Interested?"

"In going to town?"

Henry nodded.

I contemplated, unsure if I wanted to be in public just yet. Then again, the sight of the mess I made in the living, depressed me. I knew I had to clean it, but I didn't want to do it then.

"Why not," I said while throwing my hands to the side as if to show a certain level of disinterest. I didn't want to come off as desperate for friends.

We climbed into Henry's truck with Dog in the bed and started to make our way into town. The clouds still blocked the sun's appearance, though the rain had yet to arrive. Any day now, I thought.

I felt suffocated by the thick, muggy air. Spring needed to be over. Not because I welcomed the summer. Summers in Tennessee were miserable. But there wasn't as much rain, and no rain in Devil's Elbow makes for a happy community.

Henry remained quiet on the drive to town. I kept looking at him, trying to think of something to talk about, but talking to him made me nervous. Not because I had a crush on him or anything. Mostly because Henry was the type of person who didn't really speak unless he had something to say. I didn't picture him the type to partake in small talk.

And while I relished the idea of having no social obligation whatsoever, Henry and I had yet to reach a level of comfort where complete silence is acceptable.

"What kind of music do you listen to?" I asked while turning on the radio. Henry shrugged while tightening his grip on the steering wheel. "Seriously?"

"I don't know. Whatever's on the radio, I guess," he said quietly.

Awkward pause. "You know I work in the music industry."

He nodded. "I know."

"How?" I asked, intrigued.

"Your parents told me," he muttered.

"My parents talked to you about me?"

He did a double take, seeming unnerved about my inquiry. "Does that bother you?" I shook my head. It really didn't, though I felt disadvantaged. "They said you write…music reviews for new bands. Something like that."

I smirked. "Something like that."

Another long pause. "Do you like it?" he asked.

"When people agree with me," I said, coolly, and Henry smirked. "I don't know, I'm very opinionated so the job is easy for me. But even when I have to give a negative review, it's not necessarily because I don't like them. Just that either what they're doing has been done before or that…they haven't really found their voice yet. Still, it's admirable, and there's always an essence of beauty in music whether you like it or not. It's how someone is feeling. Something they've been through that they now want to share with the world." Henry continually looked at me as I spoke, listening although I'm not sure really understanding. "What do you think?" I asked.

Henry shrugged. "I dunno…I always kind of thought music was for people who couldn't stand to be alone."

"What's so wrong with that?"

Again, he shrugged though I became impressed that I even got a response out of him. And while I absolutely couldn't get on board with with his opinion, I appreciated that he put in the effort.

For my sake. "Have you ever thought about writing your own music?" he asked.

"No. Well yes, but…no. Not really." He did a double take. "Spit it out." I knew he wanted to say something.

"I dunno, it just seems to me, like…if you're gonna spend your time critiquing other people's music…maybe you should try it first."

I scoffed. He wasn't wrong, but that drove me crazy.

"What do you know?" I spat.

Truth is, I had written songs before. I even knew how to play the guitar and the piano. What I lacked were the vocals. Me, tone deaf and all, and I found it to be a sick, cosmic joke. What kind of a God would bless me with such a lyrical soul but with no vocal ability whatsoever? A rather sensitive subject for me, but one I'd never reveal to Henry.

We reached city limits, and I knew we would be driving by my old high school. When we passed, a strange feeling came over me. Not the same melancholy I'd felt the entire time since being home. Instead, a sort of happiness in the familiarity of it all. For the first time, I felt comforted by something.

"God, it's so weird being back," I said while looking at the school parking lot where me and my friends hung out after school to avoid going home. "And nothing's changed."

"A lot's changed."

He pulled into the hardware store parking lot. Suddenly, I became very curious about his past. I really knew nothing about him other than the fact that he knew my parents for a while, but they'd kind of been neighbors for ten years.

Henry parked the truck and I climbed out to make my way to the bed to let Dog out. Immediately, he took off running toward an open field to our left.

"I'm gonna run to the electronics store real quick. I'll meet you back here," I said as Henry made his way into the hardware store.

The electronics store. A family owned business with nothing of value. Or perhaps the fact that I had so much nice stuff in my apartment back home made me kind of a snob. Top of the line speakers, headphones, sound system. All gifts from my parents. An investment into my career, is what I told them. I didn't feel bad either despite the thousands of dollars they spent. I went to school on a scholarship, so really, it was just them paying their dues.

"Is this all you have?" I asked while looking at the cellphones in the glass case.

"We were supposed to get some of those real fancy ones in, but the boss decided there weren't enough people who would buy them."

"The fancy ones. You mean smart phones?"

"I guess."

What the…never mind. I really should be more tolerant considering this was my home town. You'd be surprised at how many communities throughout this great country are still living decades behind as far as technology goes. But I didn't need a smartphone necessarily. I needed a phone. One to withstand being knocked around, battered, and bruised.

"What about that one?" I asked.

The kid removed a small flip phone. "It's twenty-two fifty," he said.

"For that lil thing?"

"It is a phone…" he said, confused.

"It's hardly a phone. Whatever, I'll take it."

"All of our phones are prepaid, so how many minutes do you want?" I sighed, frustrated.

I walked back outside with my purchase in hand and saw Dog still running around like a mad man in the open field across from me. I wish I had his energy. It had only been about thirty minutes since we left, but I grew tired already. I made my way to the hardware store, but Henry exited soon after.

"Get everything you need, dear?" I asked.

"It'll have to do," he said while putting his supplies in the bed of the truck. "Glass'll be in tomorrow. I'll swing back by and pick it up." Henry whistled for Dog, who came running.

"By the way, I got you this," I said while tossing the small, black cell phone at him. He caught it and studied the thing, skeptically. "Don't worry, it's prepaid. In case I need to get a hold of you. I saved my number in there too in case you need to call me."

He didn't say anything while placing the phone in his pocket. He opened the bed of the truck to allow Dog entry when he arrived, and with that, we headed back to Devil's Elbow.

We were quiet on the drive home. My mind raced about everything I needed to do. All I really wanted to do was sleep for years, but I didn't have that luxury. What with the mess in the living room, the home renovations, and now I felt as though I struck a nerve with Henry.

"What did you mean when you said a lot has changed?" I asked. "I mean...there's the obvious things, of course, but...everything seems to be carrying on like it always has."

Henry glanced at me, his expression almost challenging in a way, though difficult to really interpret through his squinting and permanent scowl. "You wouldn't know. You've been gone so long," he muttered.

"So tell me."

"It's not like we had the same life, Scarlett."

"I know, but...it seemed like I really hit a nerve back at the hardware store," I said while we pulled into my driveway. Henry didn't respond, and this time, he didn't even look at me as if considering what to say. I became annoyed. "Oh, what? We can't talk about you?"

"I didn't say that..."

"No, but you clam up every time the subject comes up."

Again, no response. He stopped the truck in front of the house, but I think he knew I had more on my mind. He turned off the truck and hung his head, as if waiting for me to lash out at him. Like he'd seen that sort of thing a million times.

And as much as I didn't want to play that role, my annoyance got the best of me. "This isn't fair. We're going to be working together, you really need to open up."

"About what?" he asked.

"Anything. You know…everything about me. I know nothing about you. Or your parents, where you've been, even how old you are…" His narrowed eyes and tight lips shushed me.

"I'm twenty-nine," he grumbled and then flung his door open to step outside, slamming it shut behind him. Leaving me in awe.

Maybe Max had been trying to tell me something when he said not to get Henry riled up. Clearly a lot easier to do than I had anticipated, which made no sense to me. He seemed so calm, understanding, and patient until now.

I gave Henry his space while he boarded up the window. I sat on the enclosed back porch, lost in a trance. Deciding on the best course of action for the stables and how I wanted them to look. My parents never talked about that sort of thing with me.

"Window's boarded," Henry said while walking onto the porch.

"Thank you." I walked toward the screen surrounding the porch. "Come here," I beckoned.

When I felt him next to me, I opened myself up to him more. Body language is a very powerful tool, especially when it comes to men. It's not really in what you say to them. Men are creatures of sight. What they see is a driving force. What they want to see. By opening my body up to him, I was saying I need your advice, or I value your opinion. "I'm thinking…gray stone for the foundation. White wood with green trim. We could fit…four, maybe five stalls in there?" I asked.

Henry tipped his head to the stables. "More than that, if you want. That whole structure has to come down."

I was confused. "The whole thing? We can't just…build off of it?"

Henry shook his head. "Nah, the structure's not sound enough. We could use some of those old bricks to rebuild the foundation, but other than that…" he motioned his hand across the window as if to bulldoze the stable with his fingers.

"When can we start?" I asked, anxious to get the ball rolling.

He thought for a moment. "We need to get the building permits. All the supplies."

"A crew," I added. He looked at me, concerned. "Don't act so surprised, I'm not going to be the one out there building with you like my dad." I smiled at him. "You can choose whoever you want. They'll be working for you." Henry nodded. "I'll pay you five-hundred a week, three for your crew. To start. If I like what I see, I'll pay more. You and your crew," I said before turning away to go into the house.

And just like that, it was as if our little spat never happened.

We spent the remainder of the afternoon talking about all the things I wanted done, and Henry took notes. He took long pauses in between my words, considering everything I said before coming up with a plan in order to get it done. He started sketching the exterior of the stables and then an interior version to show me, and after a few attempts to get it down, we decided on the design.

Henry said he needed to draw up a more technical design for the purposes of running electricity, but I started to lose interest at that point. And my mind went to my parents. I started to wonder what they planned for the stables, and an overwhelming sense of guilt came over me for never even having asked Henry what they wanted. What they talked about as far as renovations went.

"You all right?" Henry asked.

"I'm fine, I just…thought of something." I went off into my world again while drumming my fingers on the dining room table. I'm not so sure I even wanted to know what they planned to do. Maybe it would make me reconsider what I wanted.

"Nothing's official yet, Scarlett. If you think of something else, we can make that happen."

I smiled at his willingness to oblige me. "No, I was just…am I way off base here?" I asked.

He hesitated to speak, and when I saw his eyes soften, I knew he understood what I meant. An extraordinary thing considering the two of us hardly even knew each other. "No, you're not. This all sounds…really great."

"Do you think they would have liked it?"

He nodded. "Yeah, I do."

That's all I needed to hear from him. I felt confident that if Henry approved, my parents would as well. I appreciated his support, and for the first time in a while, I felt as though someone genuinely cared about my struggle.

CHAPTER NINE:

THE NEXT COUPLE OF WEEKS, we spent our time finalizing the plans for the renovations of the stables. Henry took the time to explain things to me I didn't understand like building permits and legal documents for the workers. He was very helpful every step of the way, though he left me to work out the budget. Something so completely and utterly boring, I felt the need to shoot myself in the face. But Henry picked out his crew, purchased supplies, and assisted me on the blueprints for the stables.

We decided on a stone base with a wood lining, six stalls, and a storage space on the superior potion of the stable with a sturdy, built-in ladder. Henry did all the technical planning for the purpose of running electricity and even came up with a clever drainage system to prevent water damage to the roof, which would be aluminum but painted green to match the trim.

I ended up spending more than I'd hoped, but I found comfort in that more money spent would increase the value of the home. And within a month's time, primary construction started.

I watched the destruction of the previous foundation in awe from my back porch with Henry next to me, supervising. His friend, Joe, attached chains to the pillars of the foundation, and by use of his truck, just yanked the whole thing down. As if it were all too easy.

"Wow," I said as the structure collapsed. I smiled at Henry, probably bigger than I smiled in months. I don't know what it is about destruction that makes me happy. Or anyone else, really.

We all enjoy watching buildings being demolished. Well, I guess only when it's a planned destruction. Otherwise it's depressing. But perhaps this viewing became more about moving on in a way. Like when people say "out with the old, in with the new."

"What do we do with all that junk?" I asked.

"Recycle it," Henry said. "Max is picking up a truck right now. He should be here soon."

I rolled my eyes and made my way into the house. "I can't believe you brought your brother into this," I said while walking into the kitchen, and Henry followed.

"He's a hard worker. He knows what he's doing."

"Water?" I offered while grabbing a bottle from the fridge. Henry declined. "I get that. I just find it difficult to be paying someone I know hates me."

Henry shook his head. "He doesn't hate you."

"Oh yeah?" I asked before taking a drink.

"And even if he did, it wouldn't matter. You won't be dealing with him." I found little comfort in his words. Max didn't even know me. I wondered about potential problems with him and my parents. Perhaps his hatred was misplaced. "Well I'm gonna head back out there," Henry said.

"I'll be here."

He left me with Dog. Dog, who so patiently awaited a treat, which I usually give while in the kitchen. "No. You're getting fat." He put his paw on my leg and whined. "Don't look at me like that, fatty." He whined again and placed his paw back on the ground. "Go on, get…get outside with the men, you mangy mutt," I said, ushering him to the back door.

Dog bolted towards Henry who pet him for a bit. I started to wonder about Dog in New York. It seemed inconvenient to have a dog his size in the city. Maybe I could leave him with Henry?

Ugh, the thought of New York weighed on me. While I'd been in touch with my landlord and came up with a way to continue paying rent, the idea of not having worked in almost a month followed me around like a dark cloud.

Not because I needed the money, I had plenty of money from my parents. The thing about music critics is you have to keep working in order to gather followers. And new music is always coming out. I'd yet to check my email since returning home. Perhaps it was time?

The doorbell rang though. What a strange sound, I thought. It took me a moment to make the connection though because Henry would always just walk inside.

I opened the front door, expecting to see a delivery man, but instead I saw Kate and Ella. They were smiling, holding on to bottles of wine and grocery bags. Son of a bitch.

"Heyyy…" I said, forcing a smile.

"Oh my God, she forgot," Kate said.

Forgot what? "I didn't forget…girls' day…"

"Why do you look so confused?" Ella asked.

Ella and I remained in contact since the funeral. And I may or may not have agreed to plans at some point. I just expected it to be later. Way later. Like I'd be back in New York later. But I was being rude. I opened the door further and stepped aside.

"Why aren't you at work?" I asked Ella. Kate didn't work.

"It's Saturday."

A perfect out. "Oh…you see, I thought it was Friday, so…" I closed the door behind them. Now I felt bad that Henry and all his guys were working on a Saturday.

The two followed me into the kitchen and I looked out the window to the crew, now looking for signs of disgruntled workers. They seemed happy to be working on a Saturday, just as anyone would be.

"Scarlett, white or red?" Kate asked.

"Red," I muttered. I mean, they were being paid. And people work on Saturday all the time. It's not like it's God's day.

Kate handed me my glass, breaking me from my thought. It was only noon. Don't get me wrong, I'm not above day drinking. It sort of added to the guilt of having laborers in my backyard though. Beer would have been a nice gesture. I'm awful.

"What's with all the trucks outside?" Ella asked while removing snacks from a grocery bag. Wine and munchies. This was going to be bad.

"I have some workers here."

"No kidding," Kate said and then hurried to the window. "Oh, how I love me some hot, dirty, Southern men."

Ew, I thought. Some people, when they've been around something so long, grow tired of it while others embrace it as the only life they've ever known and they only life they'll ever want. Kate was the latter, clearly.

"Hey, you're married," Ella stated while throwing a bag of chips at Kate.

Ooooh, barbeque flavored.

"Don't start," Kate said. "Robert has the kid, today is for me. I need this," Kate said.

We all have that one friend who "needs this." She's the one in the group who got married and had kids too young. The one who was never able to enjoy her youth. The one who when finally has a night to herself forces you to drink copious amounts of alcohol as if you're also making up for lost time. The one who will catcall any decent looking man that passes.

We sat on the back porch, drinking our wine and ogling the help. With my mouth full of potato chips, Ella took it upon herself to show me some new app on her phone. I feigned interest. In the background, country music blared from the junk truck.

"He's cute," Kate said, catching our attention.

She pointed to a man named Eli throwing bits of old wood into the back of the truck. Five men made up Henry's crew, including Max. Six if you count Henry himself. Eli—who I assumed to be the youngest due to his lack of facial hair or any type of stress lines that begin to appear in one's late twenties—had a reputation in Devil's Elbow for being the promiscuous type. He had a sweet, baby doll face and dirty blonde hair. A master of using his charm to get the local girls in bed with him.

"That's Eli," I said. "I think he's like…twenty-three? Twenty-four, maybe?"

"Too young for me," Kate said. Ella rolled her eyes, and I smirked. "What about that one?" Kate asked.

I tipped my head to a man with a beard and a baseball cap. "That's Joe," I said. "He's married. With kids."

"Nope," Kate said, as if these men were viable options for her.

The crew started to notice us as well. Three women sitting on the back porch, watching them, checking them out, really. When Henry continually looked over at us, I became embarrassed. I had nothing to do with the charade. Though Kate continued to wave at them any time one looked over to us.

"How you ladies doing this afternoon?" Eli shouted.

"Just fine," Kate shouted back.

"It's hot out here, ain't it?" Eli said, and Kate fanned her face.

Eli removed his shirt, revealing a chiseled six pack that glistened in the sun. I mean, even I had to admit that the boy looked good.

"Oh no," Ella exclaimed while covering her face.

Eli flexed. "We don't want none of that, little boy," Kate said flirtatiously.

Eli kind of stretched a bit to flex his muscles better, and my face grew hot. He laughed and tucked his shirt into his jeans, knowing all too well what he'd done. All right, I see the allure of Southern men.

I looked away, embarrassed, but then locked eyes with Henry. He didn't seem amused. I stared at him for a while before breaking my gaze to finish my glass of wine.

I caught eyes with Max, who'd also been staring at me. His disapproval, much more noticeable than his brother's by way of scoffing and turning away from me. As if I'd been the one egging on the young Casanova.

"Get back to work, Eli," Henry said.

"Sorry ladies, show's over!" Eli shouted.

I started to wonder why Ella seemed so disinterested in the men. She was texting. Perhaps she had a boyfriend and just didn't like talking about him.

"Who are you texting?" Kate asked.

"Stop, Kate," she warned.

"I know who you're texting," Kate laughed, but when Ella shot her a pointed look, Kate stiffened up and sipped her wine.

"What?" I asked.

"Nothing," Ella said.

I became confused, but also uninterested. The two of them had something they didn't want me knowing, which suited me fine. I hadn't been home in years.

"What about him?" Kate asked.

"Nate?" I asked. Nate remained somewhat of a mystery. Seemingly attractive, Nate had mostly kept quiet throughout the process. He looked a little older than us, but seemed pretty fit and well-mannered.

Really, the only other options for her were Max, Henry, and a middle-aged man named Wade. Wade and Max seemed one in the same. Friends, no doubt. Not really Kate's type. Not really anyone's type, to be honest. But then I started to wonder why Henry—the more attractive one, in my opinion—had yet to be mentioned.

"What about Henry?" I asked. "He's a nice guy…" I looked to them and they were both staring at me strangely. As if I had an extra limb growing out of my head or something. "What?"

"Henry?" Ella asked.

"He's cute. Kind of on the quiet side, but…"

"Nah, he's damaged goods," Kate said and sipped her wine.

"Damaged goods?" I asked.

Kate lowered her glass. "Yeah, you know…they look good but far too much baggage. Like you know something has to be wrong with them."

"Kate, come on," Ella said.

Kate's opinions about Henry surprised me. I never considered the possibility of Henry being damaged in some way because he seemed so well-adjusted. Definitely far too quiet for my liking. But I hardly knew anything about him, and frankly, his outburst a few weeks ago deterred my interest. Though the prospect of Henry having imperfections, I found alluring.

I watched him with a newfound appreciation, knowing that Henry had more to him than he led on. Those are my favorite kinds of people. The ones who are damaged in some way but feel no purpose in mentioning it. They are unaffected by sympathy or empathy. They just want to be left alone. Perhaps he and I had more in common than I thought.

"Scarlett, more wine?" Kate asked.

I shook my head. They'd worn out their welcome.

Within a month's time, Henry's crew finished the foundation of the stable, underlying frame and stone base included. The stables, now an easier sight to imagine in a completed state. I walked through the foundation, staring at all the hard work from the crew, impressed with their efforts. I ran my hands along the wooden support beams.

"This looks great," I said to Henry. "Sturdy."

"Yeah, they did great work."

"Well don't short-change yourself, mister foreman," I said and entered one of the stalls.

"I figure we can start working on the roof in about a week or so," he said.

I turned to him. "And then?"

"Finish the interior…the stalls, windows, running wires for electricity…we'll finish with the paint," he said, and I felt a grin spread across my face. "I know you're excited about the paint. It has to wait."

"No, I get it. Don't let me spoil the process." I said, holding my hands up in retreat. Though, the only fun part about renovations is picking out color palettes and fixtures.

I walked around the structure, staring at every nook and cranny, taken with the capability of a person when given a task. Henry's work, impossible for me to do, though I imagine he felt the same about my job. Mostly because of lack of interest. Still, the things he managed to do for the stables thus far definitely put me at ease for the remainder of the project.

"So next is the garage?" I asked.

"Yeah. Then the exterior of the house…have you thought about what color?"

"White. With green shutters," I said.

"What is it with you and white and green?"

I shrugged. My phone rang. I looked at the screen and immediately became irritated. I pushed ignore. "Ugh, stop calling me."

"Everything all right?" Henry asked.

"No, it's…Doctor Wilson. My dad's old partner. He just can't let go of the fact that I'm not ready to sell," I said. Henry was quiet for a moment. "What?" I asked.

He shrugged. "Don't let him pressure you into selling if that's not what you want to do."

"It is…I mean, there's no point in keeping the practice. And he's offering a lot of money…"

"Money isn't everything, Scarlett."

I scoffed. "You don't live in New York," I said while deleting the voicemail. I considered for a moment. Selling proved to be much more difficult than I imagined, though the reasons remained unclear. My father's practice, for one, but that couldn't be the only reason. Of one thing I was certain; ~~and~~ selling felt wrong. "I'm just…not ready. You know?" I asked.

Henry nodded, a sympathetic look in his eyes.

"Scarlett?" Quinn approached in a button up shirt and a pair of slacks. Although smiling, he seemed confused, to which we could relate. "You forgot about dinner, didn't you?" Quinn asked.

"Oh shit," I said while running past him toward the house. "Two minutes!"

CHAPTER TEN:

I'VE NEVER BEEN VERY GOOD at keeping plans or even remembering that I've made them. I've always been the type of person where I'll agree to something, thinking it's forever away, and then when the time comes, I'm ill-prepared.

I agreed to go to dinner with Quinn a few weeks earlier in order to catch up but only at his persistence. Though my troubles flooded my mind, and even remembering the day of the week proved to be difficult. Could he really blame me? Still, a text would have been nice.

"I texted you before I left…you didn't get it?" Quinn asked as I entered the kitchen.

"Ugh, I did…I must have just forgotten to read it," I said. I put on my earrings and gathered my belongings in the kitchen, but the sound of Dog growling distracted me. "Dog, shut up."

"You live around here or something?" Quinn asked Henry, who was going through his toolbox on the dining room table.

"Couple miles up the road."

"All right," I said after grabbing my bag. "Shall we?"

Quinn gave me a strange look. He leaned in closer. "You're just gonna leave him here?" he whispered, though I'm certain Henry heard judging by the smirk on his face while he dug into his toolbox.

"I always leave him here. It's fine." I made my way to front door. "He's fixing my faucet," I said, smiling to Henry as I passed. Quinn followed closely behind. Before exiting completely, I stopped and leaned back in the doorway. "Henry, can you feed Dog before you leave?"

"Yep," he said while tossing something back into the toolbox.

"Thanks."

"When did you get a dog?" Quinn asked.

Before exiting the house, Henry spoke. "Scarlett?"

“Yes?” I waited for him to speak. He seemed concerned about something—troubled in some way, but he hesitated and then glanced at Quinn. “Everything okay?” I asked.

“Just, uh…be careful out there. Weather forecast said it might rain, so…I wouldn’t want you to get stuck out in the Point.”

Quinn chuckled, but I smiled politely to Henry. “Thanks, Henry. We’ll be careful.”

We started to leave again. “And if it starts raining, just give me a call. I’ll come out there and pick you up,” Henry said.

I started to realize where his concern came from in that moment, and it made me feel sick. I some times forgot that I wasn’t the only one to lose my parents—Henry having been friends with them for years. Perhaps their death traumatized him as well.

I felt the amusement on my face fade, and my eyes grew tender. “Thank you, Henry. I’ll call you if I need you.” After that, Quinn ushered me out the door.

Quinn spent the drive to Hunter’s Point talking about everything he’d done since high school, which seemed to be a lot. Originally, he’d gone to school to study sports medicine, but when he realized how much he hated it, he ended up moving back to Hunter’s Point for a bit. And at the influence of my father, which he stressed more than enough, he decided to become a dentist.

Since graduating dental school, Quinn took off on humanitarian missions to places like Ethiopia and Fiji. After that, my father offered him a job. “I love it,” he said at dinner, the conversation having yet to change.

“That’s great, I’m glad you found something you love.”

“So what about you? I only really know what your dad told me,” he said.

I shook my head. “I’m sure that’s really all there is to it.”

“Come on, tell me about it. What’s New York like?” he asked, leaning back in his chair, smirking that ever-so-handsome smirk with his perfect teeth. Teeth only a dentist would have.

I figured I could indulge him. “Well…New York is big. And dirty. Far too many people in close proximity at all times. It smells bad. I love it.”

Quinn laughed. “What’s not to like?”

“Mostly I like it because it’s so different than here,” I said.

“Yeah, you never really did fit in here, did you? Strange considering you’re from here.”

“It’s weird, huh?”

Quinn’s smile disappeared. He leaned forward and lowered his head, his demeanor suddenly becoming very serious. “Let me ask you something…have you given any thought to what you’re going to do with the practice?” God, not this again. “It’s just that…Doctor Wilson won’t shut up about it. He says you won’t return his calls.”

“Is that why you asked me here? To convince to me sell?”

Quinn expression softened. “God no. Scarlett, I wanted to see you. I care about you.”

“I don’t know what I’m going to do. And frankly, I’m tired of thinking about it. I don’t mean to be rude, and I know you have reason to be…excited or anxious or whatever you are, but…I need time.”

He nodded. “I understand.” There was a long pause. “Let me ask you something else. Is something going on between you and Henry?”

What a strange question, I thought. “Not at all. Why?”

Quinn shrugged. “I know your parents liked him, but…I mean he was a pallbearer at their funeral, and now he’s at your house. Alone…”

“He’s fixing my shower.”

Quinn winced. “And you trust him? Alone in your house?”

“What, are you jealous?” I asked.

He smirked. “No. I just want you to be careful is all.”

“Henry’s harmless, you have nothing to worry about,” I said. “He’s just…” I hardly knew Henry, and I found it difficult to explain to Quinn why I trusted him. A well-placed concern, but my perception of people had yet to raise any suspicion about Henry. "He's really just kind of…"

"We don't have to talk about it," Quinn said.

I smiled, relieved. "Yeah, I don't…I don't know. But I trust him."

When the waiter brought us our food, I stared at the plate in front of me. My appetite had yet to really return though. Stress eating is a very different thing. That's not about wanting to eat. That's about trying to focus on something else.

"Let's make a toast," Quinn said while holding up his wine glass. Making a toast seemed a bit odd. What were we toasting to? Dining in Hunter's Point at a two star Italian and BBQ restaurant? Still, I love alcohol and hardly ever turned down the opportunity. I grabbed my glass. "To old friends," he continued.

"Old friends." Our glasses clanked and I took a big swig.

The ride home, Quinn and I reminisced about the good old times back in high school. Good times that I'd faked more than anything, but conversing with an old friend made me feel nostalgic. Even the stories that I chose to forget, Quinn made them enjoyable to remember. Like the time I got hit in the face with a football during cheer practice and had a black eye for two weeks.

"You were so mad at Devin for throwing it, you didn't speak to him for months," Quinn laughed, and I couldn't help but chuckle.

"Well yeah, he ruined Winter Formal for me. Douchebag."

Quinn had yet to stop laughing. "I know, he spent the whole dance trying to get you to forgive him, but you were so brutal. I think he even cried."

"No he didn't."

"No, I think he did in the bathroom. He was drunk, but…"

"So dumb." There was a long pause. "Didn't he die?"

"Car accident." Oh my God, how depressing is this town?

We pulled up in front of the house. Henry left the lights on for me, something I constantly reminded him to do. I hated coming home to a dark house. Although he found it to be a waste of energy, he did it anyway.

"Would you like to come in for a drink?" I asked.

"Um..." Quinn looked up at the house and then at me. "I think I should probably head home. It's getting late, and I have to work tomorrow," he said in a light-hearted manner. As if work pained him, but him having an excuse not to come inside was a relief.

His response surprised me. I thought Quinn had ulterior motives for our evening, but this proved to be untrue. "Oh..." was all I could manage to say.

"But this was fun. We should do it again some time."

I smiled at him, nodding in agreement. "Well, drive safe."

"Good night, Scarlett."

Rejection is one of the worst emotions imaginable next to jealousy. And loneliness. I felt empty. Depressed. I wanted more than anything to be back in my New York apartment. That's the great thing about New York. You can be completely alone but still never feel alone. Life continues to move in a fast pace around you, despite you being stunted by your emotional turmoil. It's soothing in a way. Knowing that you're not the center of the universe.

Devil's Elbow, a completely different story. I felt alone most of the time. The only sign of life in the house, and in that, I felt like the world was mine. But not in the way one would want. Like in the midst of the apocalypse, you were the sole survivor. A very empty, lonely, dissatisfied feeling.

I opened the door to the home and immediately dropped my purse on the ground. At twenty-eight years old, I owned a house in the middle of nowhere and completely by myself. Not the life I wanted. Not a life anyone my age deserved.

I walked into the living room and sat on the couch, defeated by the events that were currently taking place in my life. I contemplated how to spend the rest of my evening. Sleeping was out of the question. I had too much on my mind. Like being stuck somewhere I never wanted. How Quinn rejected my invitation to come inside, his reasons unclear. Perhaps to be a gentleman? It seemed out of character.

Maybe because he was a doctor he felt the need to act a certain way. Follow a code of ethics or something, I'm not sure. Or maybe because I owned half the practice and he answered to me. The boss. The thought made me sick. I would sell the practice, I decided. Just another task on my never-ending to-do list. Another thing keeping me in Devil's Elbow.

I looked around the empty living room, trying to imagine my parents spending their evenings there—what they did to pass the time. Surely nothing of interest to me. Still young and exciting, I had so much to live for. Or so I tried to convince myself.

Strange how one, small mistake can change an entire life. Not any mistake of my own. I did everything right, everything I planned. Yet I still felt so unsatisfied and so utterly alone. An unfairness forced upon me by life. Funny how people can hold so much weight in another's life. You can do everything according to plan, live the life you've always wanted, but someone else makes one, small mistake and your life is ruined forever. At least that's how it seemed.

I took a deep breath. I felt my eyes burn. I hated my parents. I hated them for being so selfish, and in feeling that way, I felt guilty. What right did I have when I still had air in my lungs and blood pumping through my veins? Though despite that, I felt dead inside.

I found no enjoyment in anything since they died. Even music. I found no comfort in it anymore, not having listened, really listened since returning home. Not my home. My parents' home.

A record player sat untouched in the corner of the room. A Christmas gift I got for my parents two years ago. I doubt they ever used it.

I decided to put on a record. Something of my parents' in an attempt to feel something from them. Even if it had been years since they listened—they weren't the musical type. But I felt as though I'd be closer to them if I listened to one of their records.

I grabbed a random album and placed it on the player. The silence, broken with the sweet sound of a whimsical guitar.

I grabbed a family portrait we'd taken before I moved to New York from the bookshelf. Ten years ago, but it felt longer. We looked happy. I'd been faking. Something that made me feel even worse. To my parents, that portrait probably meant a lot. To me, a forced ritual to commemorate the fact that I had a family. Nothing I thought needed celebrating.

How well I faked living even at a young age started to scare me. Far removed from anyone that mattered—my parents especially. I wondered what led to my dissatisfaction. Some people are so content with their existence even if it means nothing to anyone else. Others, we're tortured in that we always think we're made for bigger and better things. Delusions of grandeur, though a mild form.

A teardrop fell onto the glass. I wiped it away, but a runny nose followed shortly after. My chest tightened and the lump in my throat grew. I tried to swallow it, but my attempts were futile. My floodgates, they opened.

"Scarlett?"

I dropped the picture frame at the sound of Henry's voice, shattering the glass on the ground. He stood in the entrance of the living room with Dog at his side, and I started to feel foolish.

I kneeled down to clean up the mess I'd made, hiding my face as best I could from him. "What are you still doing here?" I asked, bewildered and somewhat embarrassed. I felt Dog's wet nose followed by his tongue on my face. "Off," I commanded.

I heard Henry approach. He kneeled down next to me and grabbed on to my hands to keep me from touching the broken glass. His gesture being far too kind to avoid eye contact.

His eyes, sympathetic. Or empathetic. Whichever. When he released me and started picking up the broken glass, I diverted my attention to his hands. He was so careful. So gentle as to not cause injury. A strange sight, Henry being gentle with his hands. The hands that worked so hard to keep food on the table.

"I always liked this picture of you," he said. He stared at the photo, as if remembering that girl from so long ago. The same girl kneeling next to him only not as transparent. Almost what you expect someone to be—what you want them to be versus how they really are.

His words confused me. The two of us hardly knew each other. Had my parents talked about me often? Was it the sort of thing where my father boasted about me? Had Henry known so much more about me than he led on?

"Henry…"

"Dog kept crying any time I tried to leave. I felt bad."

Dog rested on the rug, despondent, it seemed. Almost as if he wanted to comfort me but knew I would never allow such an act of kindness from him.

Henry gathered the glass and stood, using the frame as a tray.

"My parents, they…they were always trying to take pictures of everything. As if every moment were some major event that it would be a crime not to," I said. "I wish I would have been more cooperative. I think it meant a lot to them when I was." My words, more of a confession than anything.

"You thought you had more time."

He wasn't wrong. We always think we have more time, almost an infinite amount despite our impending doom.

Henry exited the room, leaving me alone with Dog. He picked his head up, seeming hopeful. Sweet mutt. Sadly, the company of my mangy mutt did nothing to comfort me in that moment. I wanted the company of another person. A human being capable of comprehending what I was feeling.

I restarted the first song. It was soothing. When Henry walked back into the room, he set the photo back on the bookshelf only without the broken glass. "We'll get you a new frame tomorrow."

"Thank you."

We were quiet for a moment. "I should probably head out. It's getting late…"

"Don't…" I became impressed with his patience. He seemed so willing to give me what I needed in that moment no matter what it was. "Don't leave just yet. I don't want to be alone."

He nodded. "Okay." We both had something we wanted to say, but the two of us were still so unfamiliar with one another. "Do you wanna talk?" he asked quietly.

I shook my head. Henry remained a mystery, shut off from the world and the people around him. Because of this, the idea of being close to someone seemed to unnerve him. I walked closer to him, and when within arms reach, we stared into each other's eyes. Me, desperate for attention. Him, terrified to give it.

"Dance with me," I whispered.

I leaned into him and placed my head on his shoulder, and he inhaled deeply. I felt his other hand drape loosely around my waist. He'd obliged, and the two of us swayed to the music.

Henry remained tense beneath me. I placed my head on his chest. I could feel his heart pounding. I felt guilty for forcing him to comfort me, but I needed him in that moment. Not him necessarily, but someone. Someone who could have been anyone, it didn't matter to me. I closed my eyes and continued to sway to the music, pulling Henry along with me.

"Am I making you uncomfortable?" I asked.

"No," he said quietly.

I brought my free hand around the back of his neck and felt him lower his head. He rested the side of his face against my forehead. I felt him becoming less tense as we moved. The small, insignificant movement made my chest tighten. The lump in my throat caused me to choke up, yet I managed to stifle a whimper.

I found his kindness to be moving, mostly because I knew he danced for me. Because he knew I needed him in that moment. No, not him. Anyone.

I squeezed my eyes shut and another tear fell onto his shirt. The tear, so tiny and minuscule I expected it to go unnoticed. But then I sniffled.

"Are you okay?" he asked.

My face grew hot. My despair, aching to be released on someone. I opened my eyes and adjusted my head on his chest. The way you do when you've been stagnant for so long that you can't feel anything anymore. "I just feel so alone, Henry. And I'm so tired of feeling alone."

"You're not alone, Scarlett."

I nodded. "I am. I have been my whole life. It's as if I'm completely incapable of being satisfied with anything, so I keep looking for something…I keep leaving people behind. And now the only two people who grounded me are gone." I sniffled again and buried my face into his neck. "Now I'm just afraid I'm going to float away forever. Do you ever feel that way?"

"No…" he said. As if he could only wish to float away someday. "But I understand why you do."

"Will you help me?" I asked.

He exhaled. "Yes."

"You will?"

He swallowed hard. "I'll do anything for you, Scarlett. All you have to do is ask."

I picked my head up to look at him. His eyes narrowed, and his brow furrowed. He concentrated on me intently, waiting for me to request something of him. "Kiss me," I whispered.

He hesitated, and I became nervous about possible rejection again. He brought his hand to my chin and lifted my face a bit to stare into my eyes. We stayed like that for what felt like forever, and the anticipation nearly killed me. I leaned into him a bit, and my lips brushed against his.

"Scarlett," he whispered.

I placed a light kiss on his soft lips, but he barely reciprocated. His breath on my lips sent chills down my body though, and I wanted to be closer to him. "Henry, tell me you want me," I said, and the desperation in my own voice made me loathe myself. I felt weak—something I attributed to Quinn's rejection just moments before.

Henry brought his hand to the side of my face and studied me for a moment. I wished to know what went through his mind. "I want you, Scarlett."

I hardly believed him. But when he pressed his lips onto mine, I knew he cared. My hand remained in his, and he squeezed onto it tightly. I parted my lips slightly and brushed my tongue against his upper lip. He exhaled heavily through the kiss.

I felt his tongue against mine, warm and soft. The perfect amount of tenderness and force. Gentle yet passionate. My core tightened. I wanted nothing more than to pull him onto the couch on top of me to further his attempts at comfort.

Dog whimpered from behind, and Henry pulled his lips away. I tried to kiss him again, but he turned his head. His eyes were shut tight. I felt embarrassed. Sure, he'd given me what I wanted, but at what cost? He regretted kissing me, that much I could tell.

"I have to go," he said.

"Henry…"

"Please…please don't ask me to stay."

I wanted him to stay. And if I asked, I'm certain he would. Though I felt conflicted for forcing that upon him. Despite him saying he would do anything for me, there has to be a point where I draw the line.

"I'm sorry," he said and then exited the living room, leaving me alone with Dog.

CHAPTER ELEVEN:

THE NEXT MORNING, Dog jumped on the bed and curled up next to me. He started whining, pawing at my arm to wake me. I heard thunder. I rolled over in bed to look out the window. It started raining at some point during the night. I climbed out of bed and went to look at the stable below, soaked and getting wetter. No crew in sight.

My phone buzzed. A text from Henry saying that the crew couldn't make it out because of the weather. The next day, the same text. Followed by the next. The rain, ever present for an entire week sent my crew packing, retreating into their homes for shelter. Every morning, the same text message from Henry postponing construction.

Dog and I, imprisoned in my parents' house with only each other for comfort.

The time had come for me to check my email. Over two-hundred messages. Mostly from colleagues checking in to see how things were. The others, unsolicited messages from up and coming artists wanting a review. I considered. A nice distraction, perhaps.

I spent the rest of the day listening to unsolicited music. Mostly garbage, and I only gave about thirty seconds per song, though the occasional tune caught my ear. A punk band from New Jersey, a folk trio from upstate New York, and even a young female from the city focusing on rhythm and blues, though her recording sounded much too amateur for a review.

I wrote some notes about the songs. A summary of my thoughts, more or less. As interested as I became with the two acts, my circumstances prevented me from really diving in to write any reviews. I tend to watch the artists perform beforehand. So I passed along the punk band and folk trio to one of my colleagues with my notes. Really, the best I could do for them.

By the next morning, the rain stopped. Still, everything seemed quiet. As if civilization remained hidden away from the traumatic rainfall. Henry's text came, once again postponing construction. With the river still at its peak and most of the roads being inaccessible, having the crew work seemed impractical.

That evening, I went to Dante's despite the roads being less than desirable. The idea of seeing Henry made me anxious after he rejected me, but my loneliness got the better of me.

With only a few vehicles present in the lot, I became confident that the chances of running in to Henry were slim. Not even a drinker, I had more right to be there than he.

At least that is what I told myself when I entered Dante's. Once again, the patrons seemed surprised to see me, though I blamed the weather.

Dante's smelled even stranger than usual. The water from the leaky ceiling had managed to soak through the carpet, and the stale cigarette smoke and humidity did nothing to compliment the scent. The windows were cracked open and the old, fixed unit air conditioner did a poor job of cooling the room.

Dante smiled at me skeptically. "Is it safe for you to be out here little lady?"

I shrugged. "Figured I'd stop in for a drink."

"Well just remember, we have rooms available if you need."

Dante filled a beer mug and slid it over to me, and I felt accepted. One of his regulars now. Once again, I found a lone booth in the corner of the bar and made myself cozy, unsure of how long I'd be there without any other obligations dragging me away. A welcomed feeling.

By six o' clock, I'd had four beers, and my reasons to stay started to dwindle. The idea of being at my parents' house,-a far more depressing thought,-made me consider grabbing one more beer for the road. But Dog being all alone left me with a guilty conscience.

Eli,-the young member of Henry's crew,-entered the bar and made his way to Dante, and a feeling of dread came over me. I often feel uncertain of how I should act when seeing an acquaintance, though we were hardly even that. He worked for me, the two of us hardly ever having a conversation before other than the occasional greeting.

Eli looked over in my direction and smiled. "Scarlett!"

It seemed he thought we were better acquainted than I. I forced a smile and waved. Eli grabbed his beer and made his way over to me, taking the seat across from me. Without an invitation. Southern boys.

"What are you doing out and about?" Eli asked.

"Drinking," I said, holding up my beer.

"Yeah, same. It's about time too. I've been stranded at home for days."

"Me too."

"Yeah, Henry was saying it was too bad over by your place to keep working."

I scoffed. "He wouldn't know."

"What, are you guys in a fight or something?" Eli asked.

I took a swig of beer to appear cavalier. As if mention of Henry didn't unnerve me. "No. Why, did he say something?" Eli shook his head. Good because there was nothing to say. Nothing at all awkward had taken place between the two of us. I felt like the longer I was there though, the better my chances of running into Henry. "I should be going," I said and stood.

Eli stood. "Well, hang on…stay and have a beer."

"I've had like four."

"Just one more. Come on, what else do you have to do?"

I had nothing else to do. I would just go home and talk to Dog. A depressing thought, not because I felt his company lacked any sort of comfort. But some times it's fun to talk to someone who can respond. I looked to Dante and nodded. One more beer.

Three beers later, and I became tipsy. The place cleared out a bit, so Eli and I dominated the jukebox, and surprisingly, he had good taste in music. Not the type I expected someone from Devil's Elbow to be interested in at all.

We spent our time exchanging hilarious and crazy stories, like the time he'd gambled all his money away in a casino in New Orleans and had to hitchhike home. Or the time I ran from the cops while at a house party in Newark. Even though I'd been of legal age to drink at the time.

For someone of his means, Eli traveled a lot. He managed to make it out to Nashville, Atlanta, New Orleans, even New York. "I didn't like it," he said.

"Of course you didn't, you're Southern."

"You're Southern!" he shouted.

"I'm not really though. Like I was born here, but I'm not from here."

"That makes no sense, woman."

I laughed and hung my head in amused embarrassment. My blurred vision and hot face made it difficult to pretend to be sober. And no matter how hard I tried, the volume of my voice seemed uncontrollable.

"So tell me, what's your favorite movie?" Eli asked. I shrugged. "Oh, come on," he said.

"It's really hard to say. I feel like if someone can narrow their favorite movie, band, ice cream down to one, they haven't experienced enough." It had gone over his head. Tone it down, Scarlett. "But I have always been quite partial to horror films. George A. Romero is one of my favorites," I said.

"Huh, well I love Lock, Stock and Two Smokin' Barrels."

"You would."

Max entered the bar, accompanied by two men I'd never seen. When he looked at me, I started feeling sick. I certainly had way too much to drink, and the sight of Max only brought me back to reality. Seeing someone I know hates me is hard, but being drunk as well made me start feeling emotional and judged for being there with the young Casanova.

"Ugh…I really should be going," I said.

"Already?" Eli asked.

I walked stiffly to the door. "Scarlett!" Eli yelled.

Please don't follow me, please don't follow me.

I walked outside and felt relieved when the cold, evening air hit my face. I walked down the steps, gripping the railing for support as I did. But my drunkenness got the better of me, and my ankle rolled, sending me to the ground.

"Aww shit," I said at the feeling of wet gravel stuck to my palms.

"Scarlett!" Eli yelled. He ran over to me and assisted me to my feet. "You all right?"

"I'm fine, I just…lost my balance."

"Let me give you a ride home."

I hardly trusted Eli. Not like I trusted Henry. Older and much more responsible, Henry would not have encouraged me to keep drinking. The young and reckless Eli hardly instilled any confidence that I'd make it home unscathed. Decisions, decisions. I had to make a decision. "I think I'm just gonna rent a room for the night."

"Don't be stupid, I can give you a ride. It's not far."

Eli's truck, bigger and newer than Henry's. Probably safer too. And the idea of Dog spending the entire night alone, wondering where I ran off to weighed on me. "Fine."

Eli smiled and assisted me to his truck, though I felt the gesture to be unnecessary. I still had the ability to walk, albeit not as well as when sober.

He opened the passenger side door and I climbed inside. While Eli moved around to the driver's side, I saw Max exit the bar. He stared at us, a cigarette hanging from his mouth. A strange thing that someone would endure the humidity for a smoke. Dante's welcomed smokers.

His stare sent chills down my spine, so cold and unwelcoming that I began to wonder if anyone actually enjoyed being in his company.

When we arrived safely at my parents' house, I felt relieved. Relieved and tired. I wanted nothing more than to climb into bed and sleep until the following afternoon. I wondered if the weather would be kind enough to allow construction to continue. Or if I would be greeted by another disappointing text message from Henry.

Dog picked his head up from the porch, anxiously awaiting my return. Sweet mutt.

"Thanks for the ride," I said while reaching for the door handle.

"Hang on," Eli said while grabbing my arm. Red flag. He smiled at me and then released my arm to turn up his stereo. "I want you to listen to this song," he said. As if I'd care about anything HE came across.

Some run of the mill rock song. Not a bad song, but not groundbreaking. Not a song worth prolonging my departure. But Eli banged his head and sang along with the lyrics, much more taken with the unoriginality of the lyrics than myself.

I should have got a room for the night. "Okay, well…I'm tired…"

"Well, wait a second," he said, and I sighed, exasperated. "Did you like the song?"

"It was fine."

"You know, I always thought music was the best way to let out aggression. You know what I mean?" he asked.

"It certainly can be used for that."

"You're really pretty, you know that?"

Oh God. Barf. "I'm gonna go."

"Hang on a second," he said while grabbing my arm again. I became unnerved. "Jesus Scarlett, what's your hurry?"

"I'm tired," I groaned.

"Yeah, well…I gave you a ride home…"

"So?"

Eli scoffed. "So…let me kiss you."

"Oh my God, does that actually work?" I asked.

"Come on," he said and leaned into me.

"Eli…" I pushed him away. "Look, I appreciate the ride, but this is never going to happen."

"Why are you being like that?" he snapped.

"Being like what?" I retorted defensively.

"One kiss, come on," he said and started pulling me closer.

"Get off…" I demanded and opened the door. My heart started pounding though when Eli maintained a firm grasp. I started fighting harder, but he jerked me in closer and brought his face to mine.

I scratched his face, thankful for not having cut my nails in a few weeks. He hollered and released me, and I fell from the truck and hit the ground, hard, knocking the wind out of me.

"That fucking hurt!" he yelled. Visible scratches along his cheek started bleeding. When he touched his face, he smeared blood along his cheek and onto his fingers. "Bitch..."

Before he could reach me, Dog jumped in front of me and started barking and growling. I became amused at Eli's nervous expression, knowing he'd have to go through Dog to get to me.

"Shut up!" Eli yelled.

"Careful now, he bites," I warned. I lied. He can't even catch a bird.

Eli withdrew into the driver's seat. "Screw this," he said and sped off so quickly that the passenger side door slammed shut.

I sighed and rested my head on the wet grass, perplexed by the situation having been escalated so quickly. How Eli ever thought the two of us had any chance of ever hooking up amused me, though his insistence was far from entertaining. A kid like that, not appealing at all, and I started to wonder what all the girls in Devil's Elbow saw in him.

Dog's big tongue on my face comforted me, a feeling I don't typically enjoy. "Good boy," I said, patting his head to show my appreciation. My sweet mutt. Loyal as they come.

I allowed Dog to sleep in my bed with me that night, something I never used to allow. But he earned a bit more affection that night, and I never realized how much I enjoyed that sweet mutt's company until then. Henry had been right about Dog—I found him to be great company. But not only that, I felt safe and secure with him next to me. As if some higher power sent him to be by my side during my time of grief.

Lord knows no one else assumed that role, so why not a dog? But even with Dog at my side, I had trouble falling asleep that night. The paranoid part of my brain kept thinking that Eli might return to do something awful. Like egg the house. And even though I had Dog at my side to protect me, I felt tempted to call Henry and tell him what happened. Just to see if Eli would be capable of such a thing.

Actually, if I'm being honest with myself, I just wanted to talk to Henry. But I refrained from calling him, knowing that nothing good would come from him knowing about Eli. And also, the idea that he'd blame me for getting drunk and getting myself into that position made me want to puke up all the alcohol I consumed. It's something my dad would have done.

"Scarlett, you really should be more careful. Scarlett, you really shouldn't drink so much. Oh, Scarlett, why do you hang around the type of people who will try and take advantage of you?" Yep. That's my father.

CHAPTER TWELVE:

THE NEXT MORNING, I awoke to the sound of a buzz saw. It had been so long since I'd heard the sound of the crew. Really, only a week, but it felt longer. Though my hangover came at me in full force when I opened my eyes, and I loathed the idea of hearing workers all day.

My head throbbed. I groaned and rolled onto my back, but the buzz saw echoed throughout my brain. I remembered Eli the night before. I became angry at the thought of him being outside, working. Like nothing had happened.

I walked out onto the porch and Dog bolted out from behind, immediately making his way to Henry. Uncaring of my haggard appearance, I focused my attention on the men. Though my eyesight was blurry and strained from the sun, I saw no sign of Eli.

Henry started petting Dog while in conversation with Max. I hesitated. I remembered Max from the previous night too. The two looked over at me, and I made my way to them.

"Where's Eli?" I asked.

The two exchanged an awkward glance before Max dismissed himself from my presence.

"He quit. Last night," Henry said.

A surprising yet pleasing bit of information. I folded my arms and nodded my head. I'd taught him a lesson and he'd learned. Serves him right. "Good," I said. "I was going to fire him this morning anyway."

"What happened?" Henry asked.

"Nothing for you to worry about." I didn't need his judgments.

The stables seemed to be coming along quite nicely even though construction had been postponed for a week. A silver lining in the dark cloud surrounding me.

I felt Henry's eyes on me and then I remembered our kiss. Yikes. I wondered if he felt as awkward as I did. I looked at him, studying him to try and find any shred of remorse or discomfort from me being next to him. But I noticed that his knuckles were cut and swollen. Freshly inflicted wounds.

I winced. “What happened to your hand?”

He looked at his knuckles and shook his head. “It’s nothing.”

“It looks painful,” I said. “Come with me.”

In the kitchen, I grabbed a bag of peas from the freezer and tossed them to Henry. My parents kept a first aid kit in one of the cabinets.

“Thanks,” he said while placing them on his knuckles.

“So what’d you do? Get into a bar fight with the local riff-raff?” I asked while pulling out a chair at the dining room table. I motioned for Henry to sit next to me.

“Something like that,” he muttered.

“You don’t really seem the type to be gettin’ in fights.”

Henry shrugged. “It really just depends, I guess.”

I went through our supplies. Anti-bacterial for the cuts, gauze, and a bandage to wrap his knuckles. “Depends on what?” I asked as I placed the gauze on the table.

“Circumstances.”

I removed the vegetables to better examine his wounds. With a large Q-tip smeared with bactine, I started cleaning his cuts. “What were the circumstances?”

“Someone forgot their place,” he said. “Tried to take something that wasn’t theirs.”

“Something of yours?” I asked. Henry’s expression softened. As if to somehow say the two of us were okay without having to say a word. I looked back at his knuckles and continued to clean the wounds. “You shouldn’t let other people rile you up so much. You’ll end up getting hurt. Exhibit A,” I said while lifting his hand.

Henry smiled weakly. I set the Q-tip aside and placed the gauze over his wounds and then started wrapping his hand with the bandage.

"Look, I uh…I wanted to apologize for what happened the other night…"

"Scarlett…" he began.

"Please, let me finish," I said while looking up at him. He remained quiet. I started wrapping his hand again. "I just…I don't know; I feel…comforted by you in some way. I know that sounds weird because we hardly know each other. But I feel like you…get it? Whatever IT is."

He nodded. "I do.".

I looked at him after finishing with his hand wrap, and for the first time, his pale blue eyes were unmistakable. I never paid attention before, and he constantly squinted. Though his squinty eyes became piercing, concentrated. Puckered lips, now reserved. As if trying to hold in a secret. Something he desperately wanted to say but never did. I released his hand.

"You okay?" he asked.

I never realized how much I enjoyed watching his lips move when he spoke. Mostly because speaking for him seemed rare, so when the time came for him to say something, I wanted to pay close attention.

"Scarlett?" He reached his hand out to mine. His hands, rough from working all the time, but so gentle in the way he touched me. I looked at his arms, muscular, though I never took the time to notice. Not a big guy, but not small either. He had a nice build to him and was broad. I snapped back into the moment, confused by my sudden intense reaction to him.

"I'm sorry, I just…thought of something," I said, flustered. "My car. I have to go get my car from Dante's." I stood.

"I can give you a ride," he said while standing.

"No, stay here. You have work to do, and…I could use the exercise. So could Dog," I opened the back door for the mutt to enter, anxiously awaiting our attention.

"Be careful," Henry said. "Roads are still pretty slick."

"You too. With your wounded hand. Come on, Dog," I mumbled while making my way to the front door, whistling for my companion to follow.

I walked along the side of the highway with Dog at my side. The air, muggy and thick. The smell of the Rubidoux, overbearing. If I stood still and made no noise, I could even hear the vengeful waters raging.

The gravel beneath my feet had a very distinct smell. The way pavement smells right after or before a rainfall. A smell I'd grown to like, actually.

A truck whizzed past and snapped me from my sensory observations, kicking up water as it did.

The sun had reached its peak by the time we made it to Dante's. Beaming down on us, the sun started to soak up the water that remained. I approached my car, ignoring a few patrons in the parking lot. Dog jumped inside the car, but the feeling of someone watching me put me on alert. I saw Eli talking with one of his friends, both glaring at me. Along with the scratches on his face, I noticed his right eye was blackened, beaten to a pulp.

I kept staring at him through my rearview mirror as I left the parking lot. Had Henry done that to him? It seemed suspicious, though I thought it best not to ask. Such matters were better left unattended. If anything, knowing had the potential of making me feel worse about myself.

I drove carefully on Y highway. The Rubidoux, angry and ferocious about having to return to its docile state. As if it and the sun were constantly at odds with one another. I was unsure how the other bridges would fair against the angry beast that was the Rubidoux. After passing Hickman bridge though, I felt confident about an uneventful journey into town. Unless it started raining again, of course.

Still in a pair of shorts and a t-shirt when I pulled into the parking lot of the dental office, I felt empowered. Much like the rich business owners who come and check in every once in a while, but they'll always be wearing a pair of blue jeans and a white t-shirt. They have nothing to prove. It's their business. Those people, I like.

I left Dog outside to run around. I trusted him not to do anything stupid. As soon as I entered the dental office, all eyes fell on me. Even a few of the patients waiting to be seen stared at me. In the worst kind of way. Sympathetic. Or empathetic.

The front desk receptionist smiled. "Scarlett…"

I became distracted by two men installing cameras in the waiting area.

"Scarlett, what are you doing here?" Quinn asked, perplexed. He approached from the back hallway of the practice, his face seeming concerned.

"What's with the cameras?" I asked.

I felt Quinn's hand on the small of my back. He ushered me quickly into the back hallway. "Extra security."

"Well yeah, but why?" I asked.

Quinn looked around the hall, cautious. As if trying to avoid someone. He ushered me into one of the exam rooms and closed the door behind us.

"Quinn, why are there cameras in the waiting room?" I asked.

He seemed worried, but he shook his head. "There's been a string of robberies in the area. Just taking some extra precautions."

"And nobody thought to tell me this was happening?" I asked.

"We're not concerned about it. Who would rob a dental office?"

His response perplexed me. "People looking to score drugs, Quinn. And high-priced medical equipment…"

"What are you doing here?" he asked.

I didn't even feel the need to remind him of the fact that I owned half the place and that technically, I was his boss. I bit my tongue. Which is really hard for me to do. "I came to talk to Doctor Wilson…"

"About selling?" he asked, anxious.

"Yes."

"You're going to sell?" Quinn asked.

I opened my mouth to speak, but the response made me feel guilty. "Why does that bother you so much? Doctor Wilson knows what he's doing, and my involvement only complicates things…"

Quinn moved closer to me, silencing me. "You can't do that, Scarlett."

"Why?"

"Look…I didn't want to tell you. You have so much on your plate already, but…Doctor Wilson has been in contact with these guys from Nashville who are interested in buying the business."

"So…?"

"Scarlett, they would change everything. It's a major corporation. So whatever Doctor Wilson is paying you for your half, he's going to make triple that amount when he sells to them."

"But why would some major dental practice want to buy us out?" I asked.

"No competition in the area, I suppose. I don't really know the details."

It was a sneaky move, having me sell my father's practice for chump change while he made triple the amount. But Doctor Wilson had nothing to do with opening the practice, and I felt annoyed that he found himself more deserving than I.

"Why are you telling me this?" I asked.

"Because…because I care about you."

Bullshit. "You're lying." I knew Quinn. I knew when he lied. Mostly because his eyes became wide and he'd stare straight into mine, as if proving his sincerity by becoming bug-eyed.

"I'm not…"

"Quinn, tell me the truth. Why are you telling me this?"

He considered. "I…I do care what happens to the practice. Your dad was a huge influence on me and my career, but…"

I was getting irritated with his hesitation. "Oh, for God's sake just spit it out," I snapped.

"I'm trying," he said. "Look, I've been fighting this whole deal since the beginning. Doctor Wilson hates me for it and anyone else who opposes him. Almost like he wants to get rid of us for being loyal to your father."

My expression softened. "He's going to fire you, isn't he?"

Quinn nodded. "And anyone else who isn't on board with the deal. As of right now though, he can't terminate an employee without your permission."

"Jesus Christ." I found the news to be disconcerting. With people's careers on the line, the idea of selling became much more complicated.

"I know, it's a lot to take in," he said.

"No shit."

"Just promise me…promise me you'll reconsider. Don't do anything right now. Doctor Wilson, he…he doesn't want you to know any of this. And I'm sorry for throwing all of this at you. I know it's the last thing you needed…"

"No, Quinn…I appreciate your loyalty. "Thank you."

"Come on. Let's get you out of here before Doctor Wilson sees," he said while opening the door to the exam room.

In the waiting room, Quinn remained on edge, fearful Doctor Wilson might see the two of us conversing. "Will you please call me? Any time. For anything…if you need to talk through some of this or whatever," he asked,

"I will. Thanks again."

The two of us hugged, and I exited the practice quickly. With my anger boiling up inside me, I became convinced that if I saw Doctor Wilson, I'd attack him. His betrayal to my family sickened me and further complicated my position. What once seemed like an understandable request, now seemed corrupted and blinded by greed. He wanted to sell my father's practice to get rich, leaving me with pennies. Bastard.

I felt Dog's wet nose rub against the palm of my hand, begging me to pet him, as if he knew something bothered me. He always knew, the perceptive little mutt. But my mind remained distant, contemplating what I needed to do.

If I cared for having a clean conscience, the practice needed to stay in my hands. But being a business owner—a business I knew nothing about—weighed on me, and I became concerned that as partial owner, I'd do more damage than good.

But perhaps further monetary gains could persuade me. The idea of hard-balling Doctor Wilson into a bigger cut seemed tempting. Surely my father never thought I planned on running his business for him some day.

I remained so lost in my mind that I hardly noticed someone approaching me as I walked through the parking lot. "Scarlett?"

Ella stood before me, exasperated. "Ella, hi…"

"What are you doing here?" she asked.

"Um…checking in. Seeing how the business is going," I said. There seemed to be something bothering her too. "Getting your teeth cleaned?"

She laughed, uncomfortable. "No, I was, uh…just…I've been having tooth pain."

I hate when people go out of their way to talk to me but clearly have nothing important to say. Or maybe she did but refrained. "Well, I gotta head home. I have a construction crew there, so…"

"Okay," she said, though she looked as if she had something to say. I gave her a moment to decide. Nothing.

"Take care, Ella," I said while getting in my car. I heard her say something else as I began to shut the door, but her voice made me stop. "What's that?"

"I said, you too."

I forced yet another smile and shut my door. "That was fucking awkward."

While driving along main street, I saw a local deli, one that hadn't been there throughout my youth. I decided to pick up a few sandwiches for the crew—a medium sized platter of assorted sandwiches, of course grabbing one for myself. Perhaps my kind gesture would motivate them to work faster.

I got into the car and set the platter of sandwiches in the passenger seat, but something felt off. It seemed as though I forgot something. Something that I needed to do? I took a bite out of the sandwich and thought for a moment. What was I forgetting?

"Oh my God!"

I pulled into the dental parking lot and saw Dog sitting on the sidewalk, perking up immediately. He started whining and wagging his tail, excited and completely without judgment.

"Baby, I'm so sorry! Come here!"

I felt awful. I gave him my sandwich. He forgave me.

I returned home with the sandwiches, and the crew seemed grateful. Except for Max. He refused to eat, saying he had a big breakfast or some crap like that. Whatever. I loathed him as well, so really the two of us had sort of an unspoken bond. We both despised each other therefore never had to speak to one another. I love unspoken bonds like that.

"Everything all right?" Henry asked as I leaned on the back of his truck bed.

I've never been good at hiding my emotions. Not like the master himself, who happened to be standing right next to me, asking if everything was all right. "Everything is totally and completely screwed up," I said. "But…I'm hangin' in there. Sandwiches make the heart grow fonder." Ugh, I gave mine to Dog.

~~Henry chuckled, and the sound surprised me. I never heard him laugh before.~~

I looked back at the stables, observing the workers and all they were doing. They were almost finished, which meant they would start on the house soon, bringing me closer to New York.

With summer fast approaching and the rainfall being less violent in those months, I became confident I'd be home before fall.

"Hey, I've been meaning to talk to you," Henry said.

Uh oh, I thought. "What's up?"

"We won't be able to make it out on Friday."

I became concerned. "Is it going to rain?"

"It's not supposed to," he said. "I dunno, you never know I guess. No, I have something I promised I'd do…it's kinda important."

I didn't want to pry, though the idea of him taking the day off when they just started working again, annoyed me. I got the feeling Henry wasn't really asking though. Sure, he worked for me, but I often felt he agreed as a favor to my parents. A friend of theirs, and suddenly the kiss we shared became much more awkward.

Also, I kind of always saw him as more of a business partner, working with me to decide on a course of action for the house, and I valued his opinion. I wanted his respect. Not like my other business partner.

Ah, business partners. I became irritated again at the thought of Doctor Wilson trying to pull a fast one on me. The shit. Surely he knew Quinn had every intention of telling me when push came to shove, which is exactly what seemed to be happening.

"Scarlett?" Henry spoke, snapping me back into reality.

"Yeah, sure…whatever you need. Listen, I've got to go," I said while making my way back to the house. "Do you think the stables will be done by the end of the month? I want to start looking for an agent."

Henry shielded his eyes from the sun, taking a long pause before nodding.

I gave him a thumbs up. When I entered the house, I started digging through the drawers. I found Doctor Wilson's business card stashed away. Calling the practice directly seemed suspicious, risky even if Quinn found out.

I waited impatiently for him to answer. "Hello?" I'd forgotten how to speak. "Hello?" he said again.

I cleared my throat. "Doctor Wilson, it's Scarlett. Look, we need to talk."

CHAPTER THIRTEEN:

DOCTOR WILSON AND I PLANNED a business dinner for the following evening. He knew nothing of Quinn's confession because I refused to deny myself the satisfaction of seeing the surprise on his face.

While getting dressed the evening of the dinner meeting, I noticed that Dog kept whining. Something he did a lot when he knew I'd be leaving, but that evening in particular seemed suspicious. Like he knew what I had planned and judged me. Paranoia is strange.

I did feel somewhat guilty about not telling Quinn. He specifically asked me to talk to him before speaking with Doctor Wilson, though I felt I was completely justified in wanting to meet with my business partner. All drama and politics aside, a dinner meeting with my business partner seemed harmless.

When I arrived at the restaurant, Doctor Wilson was already there in a pair of slacks, shirt, and tie. "Scarlett," he said with a smile and kissed my cheek.

I wanted to punch him, though I remained pleasant for the time being. The two of us sat across from each other. What an unattractive man, I thought. My father's age, but hardly any of his white hair remained. He looked much older than my father too, or perhaps my father looked young for his age. Maybe he came off as vile because I already hated him. I always had. So did my mother.

"What are you having?" he asked.

"A glass of cabernet would be great," I said while grabbing my menu. The waiter approached, and he ordered my drink for me. Something older men often do.

I stared at the food options, but my non-existent appetite made me content with just wine.

The waiter returned with my drink shortly after. "Are you ready to order?" he asked.

"No, we're not ready," I said while setting the menu aside.

"I'll come back and check on you in a few minutes," ~~he said.~~

"Thank you." I lifted my glass to my lips. The dryness of the wine made my cheeks tingle. I love that about cabernet. It gets me right in the cheeks every time.

"So, what is it that I can do for you, Scarlett? Clearly you have something on your mind."

His drink, a double of what I assumed to be whisky. Neat. An older man's drink. While I typically find this drink choice to be attractive in a man, with him I found it revolting.

"Let's just get right down to it, then," ~~I said.~~ I leaned closer to him. "This deal you've got going on with the big corporation from Nashville?"

He looked down at his drink. "Quinn?"

"Doesn't matter," I said. "I want in." Doctor Wilson chortled and then took a sip of his whisky. "You seem surprised."

"Well, it certainly isn't how I saw this conversation going." He studied me for a moment. "Why?" he asked.

"Why? Because I can't stand the idea of you selling my father's practice, a practice that he built from the ground up, mind you, and then making off with three times what I'm making."

"So, it's money."

"Don't judge me. You're the last person in the world who has any right to do so."

Doctor Wilson smirked. "I'll give them a call. See what I can do."

I scoffed. "Don't be selfish. Just give me half of what you're making."

A faint, condescending smile and nothing else. "I'll see what I can do." Asshole.

"I have another request," I said and then laughed. "More like a stipulation."

"Which is?"

"You can't fire Quinn. Or anyone else for that matter."

He scoffed, the idea seeming absurd. “That decision won’t be up to me anymore. It’ll be up to the buyers who stays and who goes,” he said in a patronizing manner.

“Make it so they can’t.”

His eyes narrowed and lips pursed. “Scarlett…I respect that you’re finally willing to discuss the future of the practice, but Doctor Holmes is…incompetent, to say the least. He’s a danger to the patients and to the practice.”

As badly as I wanted to defend Quinn, I bit my tongue. “Listen, I’ve told you what I want. If you can’t make this happen, then I won’t be selling. And you’ll be left with nothing but a dentist’s salary until the day you die or until I can find a reason to get rid of you.”

“I own half the practice. There’s no getting rid of me,” ~~he reminded.~~

“So you say.” I made sure to finish my wine before taking my leave. “I think we’re finished here,” I said and the two of us stood to shake hands.

“I think so,” ~~he said.~~

“Think about my offer. See what you can do. I’ll be awaiting your call.” I started to walk away but then doubled back. “You got this, right?” I asked while motioning to the drinks.

“Drive safe, Scarlett.”

I smiled and gave him a thumbs up before exiting the restaurant. When I did, the cool, night air hit my face. I took a deep breath, now feeling as though I could. Though I handled myself well, the entire time I wanted to puke.

While the guilt of selling my father’s practice still haunted me, I managed to breathe a little better knowing I negotiated the job security of Quinn and the other employees. I felt invigorated. Powerful. As if no one could touch me or my amazing bargaining skills. Doctor Wilson would have to abide. He had no other choice, really.

I returned to my parents' house to find the screen door had fallen off one of its hinges. What a wonderful thing to see upon returning to my living quarters. Another thing on the list of things that needed to be fixed. I tried to lift it back into place, but the door fell off completely, making a loud bang as it hit the porch.

"Son of a..."

I leaned it against the side of the house. My inheritance in all its glory. A house, falling apart and a dental practice, desperately being pursued by a rival company. Thanks mom. Thanks dad.

I entered the house, annoyed. Dog approached from the back, walking slowly. His tail was lowered. He didn't seem to be too happy to see me upon my return, which was strange for him.

"Hey buddy."

He made his way to the back porch. I understand that Dog is a dog, but I felt rejected by him in that moment. It seemed as if he'd only come to greet me just to be certain that no one broke in. The thought made me bitter. Feeling loved and wanted is the reason people have dogs. Like that quote "be the person your dog thinks you are." I guess I'd become so transparent that even Dog saw through me.

The next morning, I pulled Henry from stable duty to fix the screen door. It drove me insane seeing the screen propped up against the side of the house. I watched him examining the door while I stood on the front porch, drinking coffee. It was too early.

"The hinges are rusted," he said.

"Can you fix it?" I asked, monotone...not really in the moment yet.

He looked at me. "Yeah, I can fix it. You need new hinges though."

"So you can't fix it right now."

"Nah. You need new hinges."

"I heard you the first time," I said, cranky.

Henry chuckled and pulled a screwdriver from his belt. "Not a morning person, are you?" he asked while removing the hinges.

"No, I love mornings. It's repetition I don't like."

A car pulled on to the gravel road leading to the front of the house. I felt my muscles tighten and my heart drop into my stomach. It was Quinn exiting the car, and he looked displeased. "Ah, shit," I muttered.

"What?" Henry asked.

I sat my mug on the railing of the porch and made my way down the porch steps to greet him. I tightened my sweater around me as a cold chill shot up my spine at his expression.

"You're selling the practice?" he accused.

"Quinn, I…"

"You said you'd talk to me first," he snapped.

He stopped within inches of me but didn't lower his tone. I knew he'd be upset, and words of comfort failed me.

"It's not that simple, Quinn. And how do you even know about that?" I asked.

"Kate and Robert saw you at dinner with Doctor Wilson last night. So I asked him about it…you certainly made his day, I'll tell you that."

Ugh, Kate and Robert. Busy bodies. "Please, don't bully me into something I don't want to do…" I said while turning away. I felt his hand on my wrist though, keeping me in place.

Henry made his way to the top of the porch steps, watching us the entire time. He stood proud, body opened up to us, waiting for a sign that I needed his help. But I shook my head.

"Scarlett," Quinn said sternly. "You owe me an explanation. You wouldn't even have known about the deal if it weren't for me."

He released my hand. "Quinn…this is what's best. For me and for the practice. I can't run a business from New York…"

"What about me, huh? What about the people that work for you?" he asked, his tone becoming louder.

"Keep your voice down," I said delicately. I didn't want Henry to know the gritty details of what I'd done. Henry, the only person left who even sort of liked me.

“What were you thinking?” Quinn asked.

I hesitated. “You wouldn’t understand, Quinn…it’s complicated.”

“Help me understand.”

“Look…nothing is official yet. I only made that deal with the assurance that you and everyone else gets to keep their job,” ~~I said.~~

“It doesn’t work that way, Scarlett! You actually trust them?” I thought for a moment. “Sure, in the beginning they might play along. It’s only a matter of time before they come up with an excuse to fire us.”

I contemplated. It seemed a real possibility, which left me even more perplexed about my decisions for the practice. “You can be a dentist anywhere, Quinn! It’s not like this is the end all be all,” I snapped. He was fuming. His eyes were glossy, his face was red. He was tense. I could tell he wanted to say something awful. But would he? Would he even dare? I dismissed him before he could. “We’re done here,” I said. “We’ll talk when you’re less volatile.”

“Your parents would be ashamed of you.”

His words seemed to stab into my soul. Before I even had the opportunity to restrain myself, I felt a sting across my palm followed by a burning sensation after I made contact with his face. My hand tingled. I hit him hard.

The force knocked him to the side a bit. He walked a few steps away from me, running his hands over his face in an attempt to compose himself.

I watched him, angry, offended…I wanted to hit him again. But when he turned to me, tears running down his face, I started regretting what I did. My anger overpowered the will to apologize, however, and I turned away from him to make my way to the house.

“I’m getting married, Scarlett…”

The news was stunning, to say the least. I whipped around to look at him. To make sure I heard him correctly. I held my breath, afraid any sound I made would disrupt his reiteration, which I clearly needed.

"I'm getting married…to Ella," he cried. "I can't leave Hunter's Point. She has her whole life here. And mine too. Please, don't do this to us…"

Words failed me. Instead of speaking, I walked toward the house, passing Henry as I did. His kept his head down, as if fearing the wrath of my hand against him next. I walked inside and slammed the door shut behind me.

It made so much sense now. Why Ella acted strange the other day. I'm sure I made her uncomfortable, but on top of that, I held the fate of their marriage in the palm of my hand.

I started pacing around the living room, my mind racing. Selling just became so much more complicated than I ever anticipated.

I heard the front door open and then slam shut. Henry appeared in the doorway, looking rather disgruntled, breaking me of my train of thought.

"Don't start," I snapped.

"Jesus, Scarlett…"

"Henry…I'm getting it from all angles, I don't need this from you," I said while trying to exit the living room, but he blocked my path.

I looked into his eyes and he stared into mine, challenging me in some way. He hadn't been afraid of me, I thought. He merely averted his eyes out of respect for Quinn.

"Were you gonna tell me?" he asked.

"Why? Why would I? This has nothing to do with you. It's none of your business."

"Is this what your dad would have wanted?" he asked.

Again, I felt the annoying twitching in my hand, but I refrained from violence. Henry wouldn't take that from me. I already knew. Instead, I clenched my jaw in an attempt to hold in the rising aggression building in my stomach.

"Why can't you just take my side?!" I yelled and then shoved him instead. I moved past him and started walking down the hallway, but he followed.

"It's kind of hard to do when you don't tell me what's going on. You want to sell, you don't want to sell, you're selling anyway…Jesus, do you even know what you want?"

I turned to face him, and he came to a halt, practically running into me as he did. "If I don't make this deal then Doctor Wilson will be making off with three times as much as me. And I can't run the business from New York, Henry!"

"So leave New York."

I scoffed. "Leave New York? Leave my entire life behind for this?"

"Your life is here, Scarlett. This moment, right now, you're living it."

"I don't want it!" I shouted.

"You don't have a choice!" he yelled, and I cowered. "I know you never wanted this, but it happened. And now, whether you like it or not, people are depending on you. Their jobs, their lives are depending on you and the decisions you make! So stop being so selfish." He pushed past me and exited ~~the house.~~ through the back

His words paralyzed me. I'd never heard Henry yell like that before. I surely never expected him to speak to me that way. I looked like the bad guy, the only reason being the pathetic display Quinn put on in the front yard.

My parents just died, and I felt like losing all control. I wondered if I started to lose steam on the whole parents being dead excuse. Even still, I did what I felt I had to, what I thought to be right. And unless I'm an inherently bad person, the decision couldn't be all that horrible.

I wanted to cry, but not because of sadness. Because of anger. I felt as though the world turned against me. Hell, even Doctor Wilson—the epitome of shady—found the deal to be in poor taste. I felt as though people projected their ideas of how they thought I should be. How I should mourn the loss of my parents.

I felt the anger boiling inside of me, spilling over until I took my aggression out on a nearby vase. I threw it to the back door, smashing it, screaming loudly as I did. As if Henry were still there and my intended target. But he'd left. My anger, aggression, my tantrum went unnoticed. In moments like this, if you don't allow people to see how you're feeling, they assume you feel nothing at all.

I don't know which is worse. Being hateful or being indifferent to pain.

Sleeping proved to be difficult that night. My mind raced with the events of the day. I'd set out to have a clear conscience, did what I felt needed to be done for myself and the people who worked for me, but I remained the villain. They say the road to hell is paved with good intentions, but I only just started to understand that concept.

I thought about Quinn and Ella and how shocking the news of their pending nuptials was. How long had that been going on? Had they always had a thing for each other? And then the argument between Henry and myself. A thought that made me sick to my stomach.

I rolled onto my side. I saw Dog laying on the floor. He normally slept with me. "Come here, buddy," I said, but he remained still. No head perk or tail wag. Even my dog seemed disappointed in me. "Dog…" I begged.

He slowly stood and ducked his head under my hand. Moments later, he jumped onto my bed with me. As disappointed as Dog seemed, he knew his owner needed his affection. He started licking my hand and then set his paw on my leg, crying a bit. I wish I understood him. Perhaps his words were quite wise. Or perhaps just "I need to pee." Sweet, stupid mutt.

CHAPTER FOURTEEN:

THE NEXT MORNING, HENRY AND HIS CREW hadn't shown. It was overcast but the rain had yet to make an appearance. A knot grew in my stomach. Had Henry really been so angry with me that he put off construction? The roof needed to go up—now seemed the worst time for a petty grudge to slow us down.

I waited for about an hour, but Henry never showed. So I called him. Straight to voicemail. I became bitter. I'd got him that phone to reach him when I needed, not so he could ignore me.

I showered and put on some clothes. A sundress and a pair of boots. I wanted to appear sweet and innocent, something generally very hard for me to do. I pulled my hair up into a messy bun and put on some makeup to hide the dark circles under my eyes.

I brought Dog with me. For some reason, I felt I needed the emotional support. I pulled into the dirt driveway leading to Henry's. The small, dilapidated home came into view. Max sat on the porch, and I became tense, knowing that pleasantries tended to fall by the wayside between us.

"Come on, Dog," I said and opened the door.

With Henry nowhere in sight, my interaction with Max seemed unavoidable.

"What do you want?" he snapped.

And it begins. I sighed and stopped just shy of the porch steps. "Is Henry here?"

"Is he expecting you?" Max asked.

I scoffed. "No, but…"

"Damn, woman. You just decide to show up without him even knowing? What if he was busy gettin' laid right now?"

"Well, unless it's a prostitute charging by the hour, I could give a shit."

"You better watch yourself, little girl."

"Where's Henry?" I asked, unaffected by any sort of warning he would give.

Max spit a bit of chaw off the porch. “He’s not here.”

I narrowed my eyes. “I feel like you’re lying.”

“You can come in and check if you like.”

The house, not a place I ever desired to enter. Hell, I don’t even think it was structurally sound. “I’m good. So where is he?”

“If he didn’t tell you then he didn’t want you to know.”

I kept my cool, unsure of Max’s capabilities in a fit of rage. While sniffing around the yard, Dog managed to ease my anger. That whole “be the person your dog thinks you are” thing again, I guess.

“Look,” I began. “I know you don’t like me. You probably think I’m a bad influence or something on your brother, I get it…” Max scoffed. “But this is really important. I wouldn’t even have come here if I didn’t absolutely need to see him.”

Max considered. He spat again. “I’m only telling you because you need to be reminded of your place. Where you stand with him.”

I didn’t care. Whatever. “All right…”

“He’s over at the Miller place. Off of Tuttle.”

“Thanks a lot,” I said. I whistled for Dog to follow, but, Max spoke again.

“I should warn you…that Miller girl’s got a jealous streak in her. You might wanna watch yourself.”

I didn’t know what he meant by that, but Max’s warnings often held no weight. Hardly any truth behind them. The Miller girl meant nothing to me nor did her involvement with Henry, whatever it may be. I figured he might still be angry with me, but his anger is a poor excuse to not show up for work. It’s not how the world works, and the longer we delayed finishing the stables, the longer I’d be in Devil’s Elbow.

It took about five minutes to reach the Miller house from Henry’s. I reached Tuttle Road and turned onto the gravel pathway leading to the home. The dirty driveway, shaded by trees and the thickness of their leaves. I started feeling anxious about showing up to someone's house unannounced and not even looking for the owners. While I felt my reasons were justified, Southerners are big on manners.

An old, ranch style house came into view along with Henry's truck and another. I saw Henry and an older gentleman loading a couch onto the back of a truck. With them, an older woman and a young girl, early twenties maybe.

The Millers, I assumed. It looked as though Henry agreed to help people move on a day I expected him to be working.

Henry shook hands with the older gentlemen. Afterward, he and his wife climbed into the truck, smiling and waving to me as they did. I returned a half-hearted wave, but I fixated on Henry and the young Miller girl. The two hugged. They seemed intimate. Perhaps what Max warned me about.

I debated just leaving after witnessing the tender moment, but I locked eyes with Henry. No escaping now. Instead, I exited the car with Dog, though I lingered by my vehicle until I knew their goodbyes were finished. Such an awkward situation, disturbing goodbyes.

The girl placed a kiss on Henry's cheek and the two separated. They said something to one another, and when she approached her parents' truck, she gave me a strange look. The kind of look you give someone when you've heard of them but haven't heard anything good.

I hesitated to approach Henry, forcing a weak smile at the girl as we passed, but Dog at my side gave me the courage to continue along.

"What are you doing here?" Henry asked when I came closer.

"Looking for you," I said. I looked over my shoulder to the Miller's truck as they started pulling away. "Sorry, I didn't mean to interrupt your goodbyes…"

"Yeah, you did." Henry lit a cigarette.

Awkward.

"Well…I didn't know that's what you were doing here." The girl leaned her head out the window to watch us. She seemed upset about something. "Girlfriend?" I asked while folding my arms and leaning on his truck.

Henry moved next to me. "Ex."

"How long?"

He took a drag of his cigarette. "How long what?"

"How long were you guys together?" I asked.

"Couple years," he muttered.

Interesting, I thought. Although I remained uncertain of the reason behind Max's warning. She seemed…sweet. "Why did you guys break up?"

"Scarlett, why don't you just say what you came out here to say?"

I hesitated. "Well…you didn't come to work, so…"

"I told you I needed Friday off."

I'd completely forgotten. Embarrassed, I hung my head and covered my face. "Ugh, it's Friday." I removed my hands. "I'm so sorry, you did tell me. I just…been losing track of the days. Everything seems to be blurring together."

"You all right?" he asked after a long pause.

He seemed genuinely concerned. I nodded. "Yeah, I'm okay. Are…are we okay?" I asked, somewhat afraid of the answer.

"We're good."

"Because you seemed really…mad at me yesterday, and…"

"We're fine, Scarlett. I just wish you would have talked to me. You seem like you need someone to talk to."

I hesitated. "I do…but I don't know if you're the right person. I mean, if you knew half the shit that went through my head at any given moment, you would despise me."

He shook his head. "Nah, I wouldn't."

"That's sweet of you to say," I said, unconvinced.

Henry finished his cigarette and flicked it into the yard. "What are you doing the rest of the day?"

I shook my head. “I don’t know. I haven’t given it much thought.”

“Come on. I want to show you something.”

Oh, an adventure. Henry walked toward the forest and I hesitated to follow. Dawned in a dress, the forest seemed a foolish idea. But when Henry stopped and turned to me, asking me “You comin’?” I conceded and whistled for Dog to follow

The three of us walked through the forest, Henry leading the way, me in the middle, and Dog trailing behind. I pushed tiny leaves and their branches out of my way, reacting as if it were poison ivy. Too much time passed since my last visit to the woods, something I used to love as a child, but as an adult, lost all its allure.

I smacked the mosquitos off my leg and ungracefully jumped over small rocks and fallen branches in my way. Far from my element, though I found the scent of the woods refreshing. So refreshing and a nice change from the urine soaked streets of New York.

“So…are you gonna answer my question?” I asked.

“What question?”

“Why did you and…what was her name?”

He hesitated. “Ally.”

“Ally. Why did you and Ally break up?” I asked.

“Irreconcilable differences,” he said~~, careful not to reveal too much~~.

“Did you love her?” I asked after a long pause. Henry stopped walking and turned to look at me, as if considering something.

“I thought I could.” He shrugged. “But after a while…she started talking about marriage and kids, and…I never even considered it with her. I started to feel like I was leading her on.”

“Were you?”

He nodded and continued walking. I wanted to know more about his relationship with Ally, but it seemed painful for him to talk about, and I remained unsure of when to stop with Henry. And even though I hadn't known her personally, I started feeling sorry for Ally.

We walked together in silence for a bit, and I searched the furthest corners of my brain for something to say.

"You probably think I'm awful now, don't you?" he asked.

His question surprised me. Henry didn't seem the type that needed affirmation. "Not at all. Relationships are hard, you know…it's like you always have to take the other person into consideration, you can never really say or do the things you want to…it's all just one, big, complicated mess that I'd rather not take part in," I said.

He was quiet for a moment. "Nah, I think It's only hard if you're with the wrong person."

I snickered. "Is there a right person?"

"I think so."

How ridiculous. I stopped walking, somewhat put-off by his ideas of love and romance. It seemed so optimistic and naïve, a strange thing coming from Henry. "So you believe that there's one person out there for everyone?" I asked, catching his full attention. "One right person that unless you find them you're doomed to a life of loneliness and sadness?"

He shrugged. "Well, when you put it like that…"

"How would you put it?" I asked.

"You'll always find them, Scarlett. It's just a matter of whether or not you choose to notice them." He shrugged and continued along the way. "It's a nice thought."

"It's a scary thought."

After pushing through a few more trees and killing off a few more mosquitos, we entered a small clearing, and I heard the river nearby.

Henry pointed to a small, abandoned shack on the opposite side of the meadow. The scene, beautiful and somewhat eerie. Something seemed off, and it sent chills down my spine. The overcast did nothing to paint it in a better light. On a sunny day, I imagined the scene to be picturesque.

"What is this place?" I asked.

"Crybaby Hollow."

"Crybaby Hollow?" I winced. "Jeez, what's the story there?"

Henry smirked. "Come on."

"I don't know if I want to."

"You scared?" he asked while walking into the clearing toward the small shack.

I hesitated. The long, unruly grass tickled my legs. The trees in the surrounding area seemed rotted, decayed despite it being spring. All around us, the smell of the river and rotting wood, and the sound of katydids buried inside the brush. Not complimentary to the senses, but not a blatant insult either. Beautiful in that nature took its course in someone's home.

"Watch for snakes," Henry said.

Yuck. I hate nature. I ran to catch up to Henry, picking my feet up high as I did. A copperhead bite might ruin the afternoon.

Dog darted toward a group of birds, not catching any, of course. I smiled at his efforts though. He seemed so happy when running around with no purpose.

"So, the story goes…there was a young couple living out here…forever ago. I don't even think it was called Devil's Elbow yet. Anyway, the wife was pregnant, and one night while waiting for her husband to come home, it started raining pretty bad."

A knot grew in my stomach. "I don't like where this is going."

"Yeah, you can guess what happened," Henry said. "Husband's body washed up a few miles down couple days later."

"Oh my God," I said, disgusted.

"So, the pregnant wife in her depression one night…stood out on the balcony of the house. And because the river was so high at that point, the water had reached the foundation. She threw herself into the river…killing herself and her unborn child."

A chill shot up my spine. The hairs on my body become erect. "Jesus." I looked at the house as we approached. Such a depressing story.

"Yeah, well they call it Crybaby Hollow because…they say if you come out here at night, you can hear the sound of the woman crying out for her husband and her baby."

"That's terrifying. Why are we here?" I asked. We stopped in front of the house, and I became anxious someone might sprint out toward us.

The shack, very unwelcoming. If anything, it seemed to be telling us to leave. A strange thing about old buildings. They talk to you, but only if you care to listen.

Henry walked up the steps, and when he reached the top, he turned back to me. "It's only an urban legend, Scarlett," he said.

His reassurance helped somewhat, but I remained uneasy about the prospect of entering. Staying outside by myself, though, made me anxious as well, and Dog remained distracted by the birds taunting him when he got too close.

I entered the house after Henry. The smell of rotting wood and mold became much stronger as I entered. The small structure, empty, abandoned, and forgotten. Upon entry, we found ourselves in a somewhat spacious room with missing glass on the windows and an empty doorway leading to the back porch. The only source of light in the shack.

To our left, what looked like a kitchen, separated from the living room by a counter. And to the right of the living room, a smaller room which I assumed to be a bedroom. Two windows with broken glass existed inside, but not much else. Not even a bathroom.

Henry motioned for me to follow him. When we walked onto the back porch, my eyes immediately fell onto the river ahead of us, slightly blocked by a few trees, but visible. The back porch, held up by stilts. Below us, rocks, fallen branches, and leaves paved the way to the river bank.

The drop seemed to be about fifteen feet, but a nasty fall for anyone to take. The faded color and sogginess of the rocks, branches, and ground below made apparent that when the river was particularly volatile, it would rise up and engulf the landscape.

"Wow," I said while moving closer to the railing. Old slabs of wood that barely seemed to be holding on.

"I used to come up here as a kid. We'd dare each other to go inside," Henry said.

"Did you?"

He laughed. "Nah, I was always too afraid."

"You don't seem afraid now."

He shrugged. "I dunno. I guess as you get older, you just start…putting that stuff behind you. Like…video games or something."

"Hmm…when I was a child, I thought like a child. But when I became a man, I put away childish things."

"You read the bible?" he asked.

"Is that where that's from?" I asked coolly.

Henry smirked. I moved past him to get closer to the railing. The river seemed so content with its existence. Either completely unaware or completely unscathed at how much pain it had caused over the years. And while the tide remained low and the river tame for the time being, it still seemed to be so hateful in its existence. As if it were mocking us, daring us to get close. The giant leviathan waiting to take on another opponent and to claim another life, destroying the lives of those who knew her.

I gripped the railing. With the rotting, splintering wood beneath my palms, I looked to the ground below us and wondered if such a fall would cause instant death. I suppose it would depend on how one landed.

"Careful," Henry said. "It's not structurally sound."

"Do you ever think of what it would be like to die?" I asked. "They say your brain continues to work up to seven minutes after your heart's stopped beating. Do you think those seven minutes are squandered on terror? Or spent blissfully, reminiscing about life?"

"I don't know," he said.

I swallowed hard. Tears formed in my eyes, causing them to burn. "I wonder what my parents thought...what they were thinking before they died. Do you think they thought of me?" I started to push on the railing. The wood cracked, and felt it give beneath my hands.

"Scarlett..."

My heart fell into my stomach at the feeling of Henry's arm around my waist. He spun me around so fast, holding me away from the railing that fell to the ground below. After a moment, Henry released me, allowing me to back away and lean on the house for support.

My heart pounded. Not from my fear of falling. From my fear of someone catching me.

Henry leaned over the side to look over the edge. He turned to look at me, breathing heavily. Clearly more shaken up by the events than myself. "You all right?" he asked. I nodded. "Scarlett..." he said while bringing his hand to my chin to force me to look into his eyes.

"I'm fine, Henry."

He exhaled heavily and moved his hand to the back of my head to pull me into a half-hearted hug. I felt his heart pounding against me. "Come on," he said quietly.

Henry released me and entered the shack, but I stood there for a moment, deep in thought. I could have fallen. I should have fallen. But Henry refused to let me. Something inside of him made him feel he needed to protect me. Perhaps a debt that he felt he owed my parents. Or perhaps something much greater.

I pushed myself off the side of the house and entered. Greeted by darkness once more, I stopped in the doorway and stared at Henry. He waited for me to follow.

"Scarlett?"

"I don't want to leave yet."

He stared at me, waiting for me to speak. Or to act in some way. I stopped inches away from him and stared into his pale, blue eyes. Eyes that seemed to be filled with some kind of love or desire. Or perhaps my own love and desire projecting onto him.

I brought my hands to his chest. His muscles were tense beneath them. I started unbuttoning his shirt, moving into him while I did. And when I kissed his chest as I revealed his flesh with each button, Henry breathed in deeply.

Halfway down his shirt, though, he brought his hands to my waist and pushed me back. "Don't, Scarlett…"

"Why?"

"Because you don't know what you're doing."

I nodded. "Yes, I do." I ran my hands up his chest, his neck, his face, and through his hair before bringing my lips closer to his, but he pulled his head back.

"No, you don't. You couldn't," he said in his quiet, raspy voice.

"Kiss me, Henry."

I felt his breath on my lips. And when I leaned into him again, he didn't pull away. Our lips collided, and I felt his tongue enter my mouth. A wonderful feeling, comforting yet foreign in the tenderness of him. He inhaled deeply through the kiss, breathing me in while his hands pulled my waist into him.

I felt him grab my ass, lifting my dress slightly. But then he released me and brought his hands to my arms to pull them off of him. "Scarlett…"

I became concerned. "What's wrong?"

Henry sighed. "I can't do this."

His response made me feel awkward, to say the least. "You don't…?" He hesitated to speak, but my embarrassment got the better of me. I felt my cheeks become hot. "I'm so embarrassed," I muttered.

"Scarlett…"

"I'm…sorry, Henry, I…" Words failed me. Unsure of how to navigate such a humiliating rejection, I thought it best to leave. But Henry brought his arm around my waist and pulled me back into him.

"You have nothing to be embarrassed about," he said.

I hardly found comfort in his words. I wanted to run away and hide my face forever, but Henry still held onto me. So I buried my face in his chest and groaned.

"I don't want you to regret me, Scarlett."

I picked my head up. His eyes narrowed while concentrating on me intently. But his words confounded me. His only reason for not wanting to continue being that he thought I would regret my decision. How innocent he must think I am, I thought. Though I felt no need to clarify. If Henry wanted to see me as innocent, then by all means. His skewed perception of me did nothing to weaken my desire for him.

I shook my head. "I won't regret you."

"You could?" he suggested.

I considered. "No…"

Henry's lips crashed onto mine. Passionate, firm, full of desire. An aching need having been released into me, and I became weakened by his scent and the taste of his mouth. I wanted him. Henry had an affect on me that very few people in their life get to experience. A very innate, animalistic, sexual reaction.

I wanted him in the most biological way possible. A physiological reaction animals have when they find a suitable mate, though not for the purposes of reproduction. I needed to be freed in some way. Freed from the loneliness, aggression, self-doubt. Whatever the case, I thought Henry to be the cure to my affliction.

"We shouldn't be doing this," he whispered against my lips.

Again, he confounded me. I'd never met a man so eager yet so restrained. "Why?" I asked.

Henry sighed, exasperated. "I dunno…your parents, they trusted me, and…shit, I feel like I'm taking advantage of you. You're…traumatized, and…"

I'd never seen him so out of sorts. "Shush," I whispered and placed a light kiss on his lips. "Baby," I whispered, soothing. I pushed his hair out of his eyes, and in them, the desire for me to continue, but also a vulnerability I never thought capable. "Henry, I want you to fuck me."

He exhaled. "Jesus, Scarlett…"

"Don't you want me?" I asked, innocent.

Henry bit his lip and nodded. "Yeah. I want you so bad, I…I always have…"

I kissed him, hard. The exchange, just as passionate and eager as before, only Henry held me tight against his body and grinded himself against me. He awakened a hunger in me, a strong desire that I didn't think possible during my time of grief and turmoil. His lips, soft but forceful. He devoured me.

My skin grew hot and my heart pounded. I started feeling light-headed, weak in the knees even. I moaned through the kiss, but it seemed that small, insignificant sound drove Henry over the edge. He forced me back into the wall and brought his hand to my thigh, lifting it around him while he grinded himself against me.

"Henry," I gasped.

Henry dropped my leg and immediately lifted my dress. He pulled down my underwear, and I balanced myself on him to step out of them completely. He stuck them inside his pocket, one of the sexier things I've witnessed in my life. I didn't give my underwear to him, he took them. A trophy of sorts.

My anticipation became overwhelming, and I started panting while Henry unbuckled his belt and pants. I became flushed, though so did he. The two of us, completely consumed by our desires, and I began to wonder what took us so long.

He grabbed onto my thigh, once more lifting it around him. He guided himself to me. I felt him pressed against me, causing my grip on his shoulders to tighten. He teased me for a moment—it was maddening. And when I felt the head of his erection enter me, I quivered.

It felt as though my heart skipped a beat and my breath caught in my throat. I kissed him again, but he continued to taunt me. As if to say "this is all you get."

"Henry," I begged.

And that's when he thrust himself deep inside me. He groaned, and I whimpered in pain. I wrapped my arms around his neck, and he lifted me completely into his arms. He held still for a moment. The force of him thrusting inside me felt like an electric current throughout my body, sending a wave of heat from between my legs to my outer extremities.

"You okay?" he asked.

I nodded. He crashed his lips onto mine once more. I felt him pull back before thrusting into me again, smashing my back into the wall as he did. I moaned, though as good as he felt, our position complicated things. He held me awkwardly against a dirty wall. Though strong enough to hold me, the actions strained both of us. Clunky and uncomfortable, something had to change.

Henry slammed into me two more times before placing me back on the ground, defeated by our awkward positioning. The two of us, panting, beaten, but not ready to give up just yet. He pulled out of me. "Come here," he said.

He bent me over the counter and lifted my dress above me. The surface beneath me, dirty, disgusting…nothing I wanted my face pressed against. But when I felt Henry enter me again, I threw my head back and whined in ecstasy.

I felt his hands on my hips, his fingers digging into my flesh. He pulled back and then crashed into me again, using my hips as leverage.

"Harder," I begged, and he obliged. I whined with every thrust.

He released my hips and planted his hands on the counter on either side of me, leaning over me to fuck me. Comforting me while being hovered over me. Protective, in a way, and I knew nothing would happen to me with him so close.

A moan escaped his mouth. Such a beautifully haunting sound, I thought. One I'd never forget. I felt his hand around my neck. He pulled my head back and leaned into my ear. I loved the smell of him. I loved everything about him in that moment—everything he did to me.

He reached his free hand between my legs to rub me, causing my body to flinch, satisfying every part of me. He pulled my head back further, paralyzing me. Like grabbing a cat between their shoulder blades. With his face next to mine, he started kissing my cheek, sloppily, licking and even biting.

"You like this? You like when I do this to you?" he asked, panting.

"I love it," I moaned.

He bent me over the counter once more. His hand remained between my thighs, rubbing me while dominating me. He grabbed one of my breasts and leaned over me, moaning more frequently. He was close.

"Tell me you love me, Scarlett," he begged.

"I fucking love you." In that moment, far from a lie.

He grabbed onto my hips again, digging his fingers into my skin once more. He thrust inside me, cried out in pleasure, and then held me in place for a moment. He moved in and out of me a few more times and then held himself inside of me again before loosening his grip. The two of us remained in place until he leaned over me to kiss my back before resting his head on me.

"I'm sorry," he said.

"Don't be." Even though I hadn't climaxed, the torrid exchange between the two of us would not soon be forgotten. He, the type of man I'd only wished to ever conquer. Normally so reserved and quiet, but I saw him differently now. After witnessing him in his most shameful and vulnerable state, my affections toward him only grew. I loved what he did. All the dirty, dark, grimy parts of it.

Henry removed himself from inside me. I stood upright and pulled my dress down to cover myself. I turned to him, backing away from me. He buttoned his pants and did up his belt, his face still flushed. I leaned against the counter, watching him, grinning.

Unsure of what went through his mind, though I felt confident that he felt no remorse. Not yet at least. His eyes, tender as a smirk spread across his face. Though I noticed the rain through the windows behind him, and my heart dropped into my stomach.

"When did it start raining?"

Henry looked over his shoulder. "I guess when we were…" I immediately ran for the front door. "Scarlett?" Henry called.

I ran onto the front porch. I searched the field for Dog, but he was nowhere in sight. "Dog?" I ran down the steps and entered the rain, immediately becoming soaked. "Dog!" I screamed. Henry exited. "Where is he?" I asked, panicked.

"Dog!" Henry shouted. He whistled loudly. "Come here, boy!"

I waited for any sign of Dog. I held my breath, afraid that the sound alone would make it difficult to hear his cry for help. My obscured vision from the rain had my eyes darting around the field, desperately searching for my mutt. But when Dog sprinted out from the tree line, scattering another flock of birds from his path, I sighed in relief. He ran to me, blissfully happy.

"See, he's fine," Henry said. "Come on, let's get out of here."

CHAPTER FIFTEEN:

WE WALKED BACK TO THE MILLER'S IN SILENCE, miserable about the conditions in which we found ourselves. Soaked and uncomfortable, though my discomfort came more from the silence between us. Because of his silence and his insistence to walk ahead of me a few paces, I started to feel somewhat ashamed. Like he had a sort of foresight into the future, knowing our indiscretions would result in awkwardness. Or perhaps hindsight.

It also didn't help that he still had my underwear, and I felt even more vulnerable as a result. I couldn't ask for them back though—too awkward. Probably as awkward as he felt holding them hostage in his pocket. God, how I wished to know what went through his head.

Henry followed me back to my parents' house. We gave a half-hearted goodbye and then went our separate ways. Being in each other's company proved to be too awkward.

I immediately took a shower. Having been covered in rain water, dirt from the shack, and Henry's sweat, I became disgusted with myself. By the time I dried off and dressed myself in my comfortable clothes, the rain stopped and I became hopeful that the weekend would be dry enough to continue construction on Monday.

Monday came too slow, having been confined to the house all weekend. I awoke to the sound of the crew out back. I felt Dog perk up and start licking my face, letting me know that he needed to go outside. When I walked onto the back porch to let him out, I saw that the crew started working on the roof. In no time, the stables would be complete.

I noticed that they were down a person. Max. Before I could even ask about him, my phone rang. I felt my heart drop into my stomach when I saw *Dad Work* on the screen.

"Hello?"

"Scarlett, it's Quinn. We need you to come in to the office," he said, melancholy.

They never needed me to come. "Everything all right?"

"There's something you should see," he said.

I arrived at the practice about an hour later and saw a repairman replacing the front window. Inside, a hygienist cleaned broken glass from the floor. Before I could ask what happened, Quinn exited from the back to escort me to my father's old office, and much to my displeasure, security screens covered his desk.

Two police officers, along with Quinn, accompanied me in the room. I recognized one of the officers instantly. A man named Keith that I knew from school. The two of us familiar with one another from Varsity Club. He'd been a baseball player. Even though the two of us knew each other, Keith still referred to me as Miss Crawley, which made me feel uneasy.

Quinn pulled back my father's chair for me to sit while he worked on bringing up the recording. I glanced around the office. A photo of me and my mother still remained on my father's desk, along with all of his degrees and awards.

"So, it happened last night," Quinn spoke.

Quinn pressed play and scooted closer to me to see the screen better. The angle of the camera pointed to the front door. The wide lens captured the plated glass along with a portion of the road from outside.

A few cars passed, but nothing suspicious. But a few seconds later, a man wearing all black appeared in frame. He looked inside the window, backed away a bit, and then threw what looked like a large brick directly at the glass.

"Jesus," I muttered.

The glass didn't break on the first attempt, but the mysterious man refused to stop his efforts. He picked up the brick and threw it again, using his body for leverage as he almost fell into the window. The glass shattered.

I became angry but never looked away from the screen. While the man's face remained hidden by a hooded jacket, I could sense something very familiar in the way he moved. He seemed drunk. I watched the man stagger backwards, bury his face in his hands, and then run out of frame.

Quinn stopped the recording and looked at me. "Scarlett..."

"What'd Doctor Wilson say?" I asked.

Keith cleared his throat. "He insisted we talk to you. He says he has no idea who the man is nor does he know anyone who would commit such an act of vandalism."

"You expect me to believe he has no enemies?" I scoffed.

"Ma'am," Keith continued.

"Does this have anything to do with the robberies?" I asked.

"It doesn't seem like it. Nothing has been reported missing."

My mind started racing. I tried to think of anyone who could do such a thing. I rewound the recording and watched the way the man moved again, searching my brain for any type of connection when the answer came to me, clear as day.

"Ma'am?" Keith began. "Do you know anyone who would want to hurt you in some way? Someone with a grudge?"

I sighed and shook my head. "No, I don't. It looks like some drunk bastard to me," I said while grabbing my purse. Quinn stood next to me, but I avoided eye contact with him. We had yet to bury the hatchet, and now seemed an inappropriate time for amends. Especially since I had bigger fish to fry.

"Let me know if you find anything out," I said.

"You'll be sure to do the same? We take this sort of thing pretty serious around here, Miss Crawley," Keith said.

"Trust me, so do I. Very seriously and very personally. Y'all have a good day."

My heart started pounding. A wave of heat overcame me, but I somehow managed to keep my cool while exiting the dental office. Even on the drive home, screaming, shouting, crying—what I really wanted to do—seemed pointless. I needed to remain in control.

Whatever problems someone had with me, my father's practice was sacred.

Henry and his crew were taking their lunch break when I returned. I took a few deep breaths and made my way to Henry, careful not to reveal too much. His involvement would only exacerbate things. When I approached, all the men seemed to fall silent.

"Henry…" I said.

Henry leaned on his truck but stood upright when he saw me. "Scarlett…"

"Where's Max?"

He seemed confused. "He said he wasn't feeling well. He stayed home today…"

A convenient story considering the situation. If I'd just vandalized someone's business, I also would not want to see them any time soon. I walked back to my car, hell-bent on revenge.

"Everything all right?" Henry called after me.

I waved my hand to him and got into my car, driven by anger and my need for answers. Certain of Max being the one to vandalize the practice, but why? I knew he never liked me, but it all seemed a bit extreme. My animosity toward the disrespect that I felt inflicted upon my father gave me the courage to confront him, though I almost preferred if he just spit in my face than do what I was certain he'd done.

I pulled up in front of the poorly maintained home. As I approached the steps, Max kicked the screen door open and exited, beer in hand and looking rather pleased with himself.

"Well hey there, Miss Scarlett. What brings you 'round these parts?" he asked. Miss Scarlett. Miss. Twice in one day, and I wasn't a fan.

"You seem well," I said while folding my arms.

"That why you came here? Catch me playin' hooky?"

"Why'd you do it?"

Max shrugged. He took a swig of beer. "Felt like taking the day off."

"Not that, dipshit. I could care less about you coming to work."

"Well, then I'm confused," he said smugly.

"Vandalism is a felony in these parts, Max. That window is going to cost over a thousand dollars to replace."

Max laughed. "I have no idea what you're talking about."

"Cut the shit," I snapped. "I know it was you. What I want to know is, why?"

"I feel like my lawyer should be present for these accusations."

I scoffed. "You can't afford a lawyer."

Max scowled. I'd crossed the line, but none of that mattered. He needed to answer for disrespect to my father. "You ain't got no proof."

"Security cameras tell a different story," I said, knowing full and well that the evidence hardly painted a clear enough picture to convict. Nothing wrong with bluffing a little bit. And when Max's face turned white, I knew I'd hit a bulls-eye.

"Where are the cops then?" he asked through a smirk.

"I told them I didn't want to press charges. Out of respect for Henry."

And as if by saying his name alone triggered his hatred, Max threw his beer across the yard and shouted in anger. Though I'm certain he wanted to hit me.

He walked toward me, and as much as I wanted to cower beneath him, I held my head high, daring him to do something. "Let's talk about Henry for a second," he said.

"Is that what this is about? He fucked me, and now you're bitter? What're you, jealous?"

Max pointed his finger in my face causing me to flinch, but I held my ground. "You don't know what you're doing to him. Too caught up in your own shit, in your own world to even realize. Just as selfish as you've always been," he snapped.

"You don't know me."

"Stay away from Henry, Scarlett. That boy's got enough problems to deal with. He don't need you screwing with his head."

I sneered. "Nah, he's a good guy. I think I'll keep him. But it's mostly just to piss you off," I said. Though it had nothing to do with Max. I cared for Henry, and under any other circumstance, I would have admitted that to Max. My anger overpowered me though, and I walked back to my car.

"You're playing with fire, little girl!" Max shouted to me.

I stopped dead in my tracks. When people say those sorts of things it's because they underestimate me. They don't know what I'm capable of. I turned back to him, slowly. Daring him to test me.

"I am the fire." I felt a few raindrops hit my flesh. The rain finally decided to make an appearance.

I pulled my car door open to climb inside, my face hot, my heart pounding. But when I felt Max's hand grab my forearm, I turned to face him, ready for a fight. Ready to defend myself if necessary.

"You think this is a game?! You think you can just walk all over him and then leave him heartbroken?!" Max shouted in my face.

I attempted to pull away, but he wouldn't let go. "Get off!"

"Not this time, Scarlett. I swear, if you hurt him I will fucking kill you."

I waited for him to follow up on his threat because I knew it was empty. Max shoved me away and started backing up, shaking from his rage.

The sound of a truck pulling onto the gravel road sent chills down my spine. Henry had returned home at the most inopportune moment. And in the most unscrupulous form of manipulation, I screamed, fell to my knees, and began bawling.

I covered my face until I felt the tears falling, screaming, wailing the entire time.

"What are you doing?" Max asked.

I heard the truck door slam. "Scarlett!" Henry called. I heard him running toward me. He dropped down next to me, and grabbed on to me, and I bawled into his neck.

"Henry!" I cried.

"What happened?" he asked, his voice bleeding with concern.

"She's faking it," Max said.

"Max, he…he vandalized the practice, and…and when I came over to find out why, he…he threatened to kill me if I told anyone. And if I didn't leave you alone…" I said through forced pants and tears, all while squeezing on to Henry. I pulled back to look into his eyes. It seemed the information pained him.

Henry looked to Max. "Why?" he asked, his voice cracking.

"Oh, she's crazy. Don't listen to her!"

I shook my head, crying even harder. "I swear, look…" I said and held my arm out to him. Fresh handprints Max inflicted seconds before. "He grabbed me and threatened to kill me if I didn't leave you alone," I cried.

"Scarlett…" he said while bringing his hand to my face.

"I don't want to leave you alone. I care about you, Henry…I do," I cried.

"Henry…" Max said, almost like he wanted to cry. "You're not actually buying this."

Henry released me and stood. I stifled my cries to watch the scene. Max crossed the line attacking my father's practice. I had no desire to send him to jail and have Henry angry with me, but I felt he deserved some form of punishment. Especially when he threatened my life.

"You grab her?" Henry asked.

Max was quiet for a moment. "You steppin' to me, boy?"

"What are you doing, Max?" Henry asked, almost begging.

The two seemed to share a tender moment. Brother amongst brother. Until Max pointed to me. "She needs to learn her place!"

"Her place? What about yours?" Henry snapped and shoved him.

"You shouldn't have told him, Henry," I said.

Henry turned to look at me, the events clearly weighing on him. "I didn't tell him anything." His response stunned me.

"He didn't have to! I saw it on his face when he came home that night," Max snapped.

And in that moment, not only did I feel completely ridiculous for the scene in which I'd escalated so quickly, but I felt cheated. A broken window at my father's practice all because of a hunch.

But then I realized I had the same amount of evidence to coax a half-hearted confession out of Max. Neither of us really knew if the other party were guilty, yet somehow we were convinced.

"Wait, so...all of this was based on a hunch you had?" I asked.

A child screamed in the distance, and Henry and Max took off running. I followed behind, running through the woods, dodging and jumping over fallen branches in the way, guided by the sound of a child's screams.

"It's coming from over here!" Max yelled.

When we emerged from the forest, we found ourselves on the banks of the Rubidoux. A narrower portion than most, but the tide was higher than normal, and the current seemed stronger than when at rest. On the edge, a little girl cried. She looked at us, face red and tear-streaked.

"Help! My dog!" she said while pointing to an embankment in the middle of the river.

My eyes fell upon a Labrador puppy, moving around frantically, as if contemplating whether or not he should attempt swimming back to shore.

My heart sank into my stomach. I thought of Dog. For a little girl or a puppy, the river was too strong an opponent. But perhaps for an adult, an easy journey to make.

I took a step into the water, my body immediately becoming rigid from the cold. Even though I'd been wearing jeans, I felt as though a million pins and needles stuck into my flesh. Only when the water reached my knees did I hear Henry yell.

"Scarlett, come back!"

The murky water made it difficult to find a safe route. I held my arms up, trying to keep myself dry as possible, but the water hit my stomach, stealing my breath away.

"Scarlett!" Henry yelled again, but his voice was fading.

The Labrador, barking and whining for help, but only now did I hear him. I sort of tripped over the rise in land when I reached the embankment but caught myself before reaching out to the dog.

"Come on," I said.

He moved back and forth, still debating whether or not is was such a good idea. With no time for his games though, I planted my feet firmly into the ground. I grabbed onto the dog's collar and pulled him into me. Heavier than I expected, and he became rigid in my arms.

I looked upstream, panicked at the sight of branches and other debris floating near us. I took big steps, but without the use of my hands for balance, walking proved to be difficult. The stiffness of the dog only made things worse, and when we almost made it back to shore, he started whining and trying to break free.

"Stop!" I shouted.

But with a wriggling mutt and unforeseen rocks on the river's bottom, I slipped and dropped under the water. I grabbed onto his collar, praying that he wouldn't slip out.

My hand scraped the rocks on the bottom of the river. Everything fell silent in those moments. I tried to stop myself from being dragged away from the current, but despite my efforts, I felt the time had come for me to meet my maker.

Someone grabbed onto my collar. They pulled me upward until I could take a deep breath of the sweet, sweet air I'd been denied moments before.

"I got ya," Max said while pulling me to my feet.

"The dog," I coughed.

He grabbed onto the puppy and pulled him to shore, allowing me to make my way back on my own. Henry greeted me in the water at knee level. He grabbed on to me and pulled me back to land.

Max set the dog on the ground, and he greeted the little girl by jumping on her and licking her face. It warmed my heart, reminding me of my sweet mutt.

"Thank you!" the little girl cried.

"Go on, get on home," Max said.

She disappeared into the woods with the dog at her side as she held onto his collar. I smiled, knowing that the little girl would still have a lifelong friend because of my bravery. I pulled my hair up into a bun to keep it from dripping—not like it mattered.

"What a day," I began.

"Jesus, Scarlett…" Henry snapped.

"What?"

"What the hell's the matter with you?" he yelled.

His anger stunned me. "He needed help, Henry!"

"He's a dog! He's not worth your life!" he shouted.

I stepped up to him. Challenging him in return. "What if it had been Dog?"

"People die out there, Scarlett! Your parents died in that river! Maybe next time you should think about that before you go off tryin' to be a hero."

I felt my anger boiling up inside me. As if I somehow forgot the reason my parents died. I screamed and shoved Henry. "Asshole! How dare you throw that in my face?"

"You need to start using your head before you get someone killed," Max said.

"Oh yeah, let's all just gang up on Scarlett…she can take it, right?" I snapped.

"Scarlett…" Henry began.

"No. It's always the fucking same. Everybody wants a piece of me, everybody's got something to say, judgments to throw, well I'm sick of it!" I shouted. I grabbed a rock and chucked it at both of them, missing them completely.

"You judge me so harshly, but have either of you stopped to look in the mirror lately? I'm trying to keep things together, I'm trying to…hold myself together, do right by me so I don't…lose sight of absolutely everything…" I started to panic. I brought my hand to my head and took deep breaths in an attempt to calm myself. "I don't know what I'm doing," I said, more to myself than to them.

Henry stepped toward me, but I backed away. "Scarlett, please…"

"No, Henry…you just stay away from me," I ordered.

Henry seemed to be more trouble than I anticipated. I needed to get out of there. Even though I'd been outside, I felt claustrophobic.

CHAPTER SIXTEEN:

THAT NIGHT I LAY AWAKE IN BED, troubled by the events of the day. I felt as though I had everything yet nothing at the same time. I felt empty, something I'd felt my whole life. I'd spent my time trying to fill the void, chasing after dreams I'd long desired since being a child. But even after having all of that, I was still empty inside. Lonely despite constantly being found in crowds of people. And now with my parents being gone, the loneliness only grew inside of me, devouring me from within.

I'd put on a mask. Something it seemed people preferred. But when I started feeling like I was suffocating, I came out for air and those around me ran for cover. As if the mere sight of my real self was something too awful for anyone to acknowledge.

People like me, we're expected to hide ourselves away. Pretend to be something we're not. We can't be driven by emotion, it must be by logic and reason. We can't be honest about how we feel. Far too many people become resentful.

Mostly because they themselves are too afraid to show the demons within. We all have them, but some of us are more in tune with our dark side. Or perhaps our demons are much more violent, breaking free despite our deepest efforts to keep them locked away. I didn't know how much longer I could hold on to mine.

And that's really what the day had been. Me, unable to hold on my mask anymore. And even though saving that little girl's dog seemed like a valiant act, the reactions from my peers further convinced me that it's not what I did that was wrong. It's who I was that was wrong.

You can do something completely selfless for someone, but if people don't like you, they'll always find a reason for why it's wrong. And that's how villains are made.

And as much as we don't like the title of villain, really, we should be flattered at the concept that we were born to fill such an important role. Without villains, there would be no heroes. But without heroes, there would still be villains. We are the superior species. Perhaps a form of evolution, bred into darkness in order to further enhance our abilities and see different shades of the world and of humankind. I couldn't please the world and all the people therein. I could only please myself.

A knock at the front door snapped me out of my train of thought. Dog growled, and I ran my hand along his coat to soothe him. Past nine, so nothing good could come of whomever stood on my front porch.

I ascended the steps in a pair of boyshorts and a t-shirt, certain that whoever was there had been mistaken when they came knocking. I opened the door, immediately greeted by the rainfall and Henry standing in my doorway, soaked He seemed discontent.

"Henry?" I asked, less than thrilled to see him standing there.

"Scarlett..."

"What are you doing here?" I asked.

He hesitated. "I'm sorry, Scarlett...I shouldn't have said those things about your parents. It's just...when I saw you go under, I..." He took a step toward me, but I stepped back. He seemed pained by my reaction. "And I'm sorry about Max...and what he did."

"It's fine. I'm not pressing charges."

"You should," he said, confounding me.

"You want your brother to go to jail?"

Henry looked as if he wanted to say something, but some force unbeknownst to myself kept him quiet. I'd never seen him so ready to talk yet not be able to. As if a different person stood in front of me, trying to find the way in which Henry would speak.

"Henry?" I turned on the porch light. His right eye, bruised with a cut over his brow. "Oh my god," I said, unimpressed.

"It's nothing, Scarlett."

"Yeah, it's always nothing, isn't it?"

"Don't. What happens between me and Max is none of your business. Just like what happens between us is none of his business."

"Great, are we done here?" I asked while closing the door, but Henry stopped it. He walked inside, sending me back. "Henry…"

He pulled me into him, embracing me tightly. His heart pounded against me, and he breathed heavily against my face. "Forgive me?"

I nodded, though completely put off by his behavior.

But I thought about people running away when my mask falls off. Judging his true face seemed unfair. Perhaps revealing himself to me proved he trusted me in some way. And maybe that's really what Henry was. An emotional mess. Damaged goods, as Kate said. Something he seemed far better at hiding than me.

He crashed his lips onto mine so forcefully that my head flung back. "Henry…" I said while attempting to pull away, but he grabbed the back of my head and pressed his mouth onto mine again. His tongue brushed against my lips.

"Open your mouth," he whispered against me, though I refused. He gripped my hair, pulling my head back slightly. "Open your mouth, Scarlett," he said. I did, and he stuck his tongue inside, deepening the kiss.

I inhaled him. His scent drove me insane, triggering that animalistic part of me. Not cologne, not deodorant or any sort of after-shave, but *his* scent. A scent that only he possessed, one that made me melt even after a slight detection.

The taste of him, intoxicating. As he exhaled through the kiss, I inhaled him, envious of the air that had been inside of him—the very thing keeping him alive and in my arms. Yet as much as I wanted him, I remained uncertain about him being the aggressor.

I pushed his shoulder, but he gripped my wrist and brought my hand to his erection. He let out a quivering breath and then lowered me on to the stairs.

He climbed on top of me, moving between my legs. He grabbed on to one of my hands, pinning it down onto the steps. It was painful, the stairs beneath me, but Henry kept me in place. My pain had no affect on him, something strangely arousing. His hand moved up my shirt and grabbed onto one of my breasts, and I writhed beneath him.

"Henry…"

He stuck his fingers inside me, and I arched my back in pleasure. "You're so wet, Scarlett," he panted against my face.

A secret not worthy of keeping. As much as I tried to play the victim in that moment, I wanted him to continue. Further proving my sexual deviancy to the man on top of me.

He lifted my shirt and kissed my abdomen, moving upward until he revealed my chest. He hesitated, admiring me beneath him. He grabbed my breasts again and soon replaced his hand with his mouth.

His tongue on my nipples made me squeal. I thrust my chest upward, further presenting myself to him, something he seemed to enjoy. He moaned and continued pleasuring me in that way, neglecting neither side of me.

I felt his hands undo his jeans. He rested his forehead on my chest for a moment, breathing heavily against me. He whimpered. "I want you so bad, Scarlett."

He pulled my underwear aside. No teasing this time. No warning, and no easing into the situation. With one mighty thrust, Henry entered inside of me completely, causing me to scream out in pain while he moaned in pleasure.

"Ow!" I whined, but he ignored.

Intense pain throughout my body caused me to hit his shoulder. He grabbed my hands and pinned them to the steps. His mouth devoured mine again, choking my screams with his tongue.

He thrust into me a second time. Then a third and a fourth. He fucked me hard, his animalistic side having completely taken over. Oh, he felt so good. And with him grinding against me, hitting that perfect spot of me, I started to seize with pleasure.

"Henry," I moaned.

He released my wrists, and I grabbed his waist to pull him into me, his hips grinding into me with every advance. Jesus, he was going to make me come.

His face hovered over mine, now completely focused on me, knowing that I had completely surrendered to him.

I quivered, shaking beneath him at the feeling of his pelvic bone grinding against me in that perfect spot—becoming more tender and vulnerable with each movement. And then an explosion of sheer pleasure moving from between my legs and outward to my body. My core muscles tightened, pelvic muscles contracted against him.

"Fuck, baby…" he moaned.

I dug my nails into his shoulders, causing him to wince. My body became one with his—consumed by him, inflicted with such a deep appreciation and love for him. I screamed in pleasure, but his mouth consumed me once more.

I wrapped my arms around his neck, never wanting to let go. Holding on for dear life. But I started to fear him. I started to fear everything he could make me feel for him and what he could do to destroy me.

His breaths became shaky. "I'm gonna come," he whispered against my lips. He thrust into me two more times and then held himself deep inside of me, a booming groan escaping from his mouth.

I looked up at him, scared, defeated by him yet completely lost in him. In his eyes, I saw a wild animal having been freed from its cage. Something all too familiar with each time I looked into a mirror.

Perhaps Henry had also been bred into darkness and he struggled to keep his demons at bay. I found the thought alluring as I longed for a companion. A demon to accompany my own. But almost as soon as I noticed his demons staring back at me, Henry's eyes softened. He pulled out of me and buttoned himself away.

"Scarlett, I…" he panted.

He backed away to the door, and I sat up slowly, in awe of him. He seemed terrified, though he hesitated to leave. And when he exited, he slammed the door shut behind him. I wanted him to come back, but my cowardice kept me from calling out to him.

Dog forced his head beneath my hand, and he whimpered.

My efforts to sleep seemed futile. I wasted the night tossing and turning, thinking about everything that happened that day. But mostly, I thought of Henry. Something in him terrified me yet drew me further into him. What had been a harmless attraction grew into a deep desire and curiosity for him.

He always seemed to shy away from the world, hiding his true self from everyone, and in one moment of weakness, destroyed the mask he wore. A beautiful thing. I identified with him, noticed a kindred spirit. Someone who knew what true pain and loneliness felt like. Someone aching to be freed.

I finally managed to drift asleep once the sky became light blue, but my dreams brought me no peace from the thoughts that kept me awake. I dreamt of Henry.

Dog growling woke me. He jumped from my bed and ran out of the bedroom, barking. I became frozen. And when Dog fell silent, I became concerned.

As I descended the stairs, I was cautious. I looked over the railing toward the hallway. There, Henry kneeled beside Dog, petting and shushing him. "Henry?"

My presence startled him. He stood, seeming ashamed. "I tried not to wake you. I just needed to grab some tools," he said, tipping his head to the toolbox at his feet.

I shook my head. "It's okay, I was…barely asleep. You're not working today, are you?"

"I have some things to do inside the stables. But I don't want to have to put off construction much longer. I'd like to get it done for you. So you can go home. To New York."

I walked further down the steps, studying him. Trying to find some sort of reasoning behind his eyes. "Is that what you want? Me to leave?"

He hesitated. "I want what's best for you. Whatever it is, I don't think you'll find it here."

His words hurt. He diverted his eyes to the ground, as if looking at me pained him. "Scarlett, I'm so, so sorry about what I did last night…"

My heart went out to him. I knew what it felt like to regret something. I carried that burden with me constantly. "It's fine, Henry…"

"No, it's not," he said sternly. "It's not fine, Scarlett. I…I lost control, and…I hate myself for what I did to you, and I swear...it'll never happen again. I'll never do that to you again."

I felt conflicted. If Henry only knew that he consumed my mind after what happened, that I developed a strong desire to be closer to him, he might not feel so regretful. But admitting that to him terrified me. Admitting that I liked what he did to me, it seemed so depraved. And what sort of floodgates could open as a result?

Henry fiddled with his gloves. "Please say something," he begged.

I moved closer to him. To somehow show that I still needed him. "I still trust you, Henry. You didn't lose that because of what happened."

"I don't want you to be afraid of me. I'd never hurt you, Scarlett. You know that, don't you?" he asked, his voice shaking.

"I'm not afraid of you," I said to ease his guilty conscience. I lied. I feared him more than any other man. I feared the things he made me feel for him.

He hesitated. "Well, I should get to it."

"Okay. Be careful out there," I said as he grabbed his toolbox.

Henry seemed touched by my concern. "Yeah, I will."

He walked outside, and I started feeling heavy. I wanted to reach out to him, pull him in closer to let him know I cared. But as much as I didn't want him to run away from me, I remained uncertain of his reaction to being pulled back in to me.

CHAPTER SEVENTEEN:

OVER THE NEXT COUPLE OF WEEKS, Henry and his crew worked around the clock. They came out earlier, left later, worked through the adverse weather. I tried to pay more for their efforts, but Henry declined. Saying that they needed to make up for lost time.

Max resigned completely, which suited me just fine. But being down a man, the others struggled to pick up the slack.

They seemed to be in good spirits though, driven by some sort of factor that remained a mystery, and by the time May rolled around, they finished the stables.

The gray, stone foundation complimented the white, wooden exterior perfectly. The shutters and roof were a dark, forest green. Inside the stables, six stalls were built along with storage space above and inside of the stalls. I didn't know much about horses, but if I had any, I would be proud to keep them there.

With the excellent turnout of the stables, I became excited to see what Henry could do with the exterior of the home. I started to resent the house less and less, and even tried to become more involved in the renovations when I could.

Henry refused to let me build anything though. Too dangerous, he said. But I started to clear out the garage for them so they had more room. Boxes, bicycles, a bunch of junk that for some reason my parents decided to keep, I had to go through it all. I had to decide what to throw away and what to put in storage.

Though I became a bit distracted.

"My old cheerleading uniform. I wonder if it still fits."

"Try it on," Henry said from the ladder behind me.

I contemplated. "No. Because if it doesn't fit, I'm gonna be depressed." Nate and Henry chuckled, and I set the uniform aside.

I dug deeper into the box and pulled out my varsity letters from cheerleading. Beneath them, an old photo from Junior year cheerleading. I looked so young.

"Wow," I muttered.

"What?" Henry asked, interrupting his conversation with Nate.

"Nothing, just…I looked so different in high school," I said.

"We all did," Nate said.

"I can't believe I actually wore my hair like that. That stupid red ribbon in my hair, every day. God, I looked like such a freak."

"Nah, you didn't," Henry said.

I looked over my shoulder to him, skeptical. "How would you know?" I asked. He and Nate exchanged awkward glances. "What?"

Henry shrugged. "I've seen pictures of you."

"Hmm," I mumbled while turning back to the boxes in front of me. "Oh wow, my old yearbook from…Junior year?" I opened the book.

"Hey Scarlett…" Henry spoke and jumped from the ladder.

"Huh?" I muttered while flipping through the yearbook.

"You wanna come into town with me? I gotta pick up some more paint for the house."

I became confused by his invitation. The last time Henry made an effort to spend time with me was at Crybaby Hollow weeks ago. But his invitation pleased me. I wanted to be closer to him.

"Sure," I said. I tossed the yearbook back into the box and stood to exit the garage.

Henry lingered for a bit, discussing something with Nate, and I waited impatiently for him at his truck. "Come on, slow poke!"

We arrived at the hardware store, and Henry immediately went to the cashier. I turned down the paint aisle, really the only thing about hardware stores that can be entertaining for most women. Colors.

Tools, wood, measuring tape…that stuff is boring. But colors can never be boring. I like to envision my dream house and which color palette I would use.

I stopped in front of the many different shades of orange and grabbed a burnt orange swatch from the wall. The color fascinated me, but on an entire wall? Perhaps a bit too tawdry.

I replaced the orange and continued along until I reached purple. I love purple. It's so classy and regal. I grabbed a plum purple from the wall and held it up, admiring it in all its beauty. What a wonderful shade.

"Hey…" Henry said. He stopped next to me.

"What do you think?" I asked while handing him the swatch.

He seemed unimpressed. "For what?"

"For upstairs. I'm getting sick of the white."

He shook his head. "Nah," he said while replacing it on the wall. "It's too girly."

"Well, I'm a girl, so…"

"Yeah, but your buyers might not be." He started scanning the wall, stopping in front of the blues. "You need something more gender neutral."

"Since when is blue gender neutral?"

He ignored and grabbed a sample. "This would go well with the gray downstairs."

A navy blue color. Very pretty and classic. I envisioned the color covering the walls. "You like this one?" I asked.

He shrugged. "Doesn't matter what I like. Do you like it?"

"I do like it. I think I'll get it," I said. I considered. "What do you think, like…a gallon?"

Henry smirked. "Nah, I'll take care of all this. Anything else you wanted to look at?"

I contemplated, smirking sheepishly at him. "Well, now that you mention it." I grabbed Henry's hand and drug him down the aisle to the bathroom care section.

There it stood, setting itself apart from everything around by the sheer master of its crafted structure. A beautiful, vintage, claw foot tub. I gasped at the sight.

"Oh, it's even more beautiful in person," I said.

I released Henry's hand and started to move around, observing every detail. The exterior base along with the claws, copper and distressed. The inside of the tub, white with its faucet located on the middle lining of the tub as opposed to either end. Spacious enough to where three people could easily fit inside.

"This?" Henry asked.

"You don't love it? I saw it in the monthly catalogue, and I almost died. Who would have thought something so beautiful would make its way to Hunter's Point?"

"It's really…something," he said.

"You hate it."

"I don't hate it. It's just…it's very gaudy."

"It's perfect," I swooned.

"For you, sure." I waited for his approval. "I don't know, Scar…it doesn't go with the bathroom. You'd have to change everything."

"What, not up to the challenge?" I asked.

He bit his lip, concentrating hard. Though he decided not to speak his mind. Something that drove me insane. I became fearful that the reason he wouldn't want to redo my bathroom had more to do with him wanting me gone than putting in extra work.

He looked at the price tag. "It's three thousand dollars."

"I really want it."

"I know you do. But honey, you gotta think about what the buyer would want."

He called me honey. A good sign. I considered. Henry made a valid point, but I knew that if I sold the house AND the practice, I might never see him again. And although the two of us were hardly involved enough to the point where a life altering decision might be swayed, perhaps I could prolong the process for a bit.

I shrugged. "Maybe I won't sell."

"What?" he asked.

“I dunno…it might be kind of nice having the house. In case I need to get away from New York for a few days.” I anxiously awaited his response.

He considered. “I could look after it for you while you’re in the city?”

“Then it’s decided. We’re getting the tub.”

Henry nodded. “Well all right then. Come on, let’s go checkout,” he said and waited for me to walk beside him.

“Does this mean I can get the purple paint now?” I asked.

Henry scoffed. “Nah.”

Back at the house, Henry and I approached the garage, but I noticed that all the boxes were packed and set aside, all labeled accordingly.

“What’s going on here?” I asked.

Nate and Wade waited for some sort of guidance from Henry. “We thought we’d take care of it for you, Miss Scarlett. You shouldn’t be troubling yourself with all that,” Nate said.

“And we needed more space,” Wade said.

“Okay…you guys really didn’t have to do that…” I began.

“I can load them in the truck for you,” Henry spoke. “Take ‘em out to storage so you don’t have to.”

I became suspicious. “What’s going on?”

“Nothing,” Henry said. He brought his hand to my back and escorted me out of the garage. “I just don’t want you to feel like you have to go through all that stuff before you’re ready. I know you still have reservations about your parents’ room.”

As thoughtful as his response seemed, I hardly believed him. Still, he had a good point. While I’d only started going through my old things from high school, the idea of coming across my parents’ old belongings unnerved me.

“Okay. That’s really sweet of you, Henry.”

“Come on. Let’s go get you started on your arts and crafts project.”

Henry had bought painting tape, new brushes, rollers, roller trays…pretty much everything I needed. We started in my bedroom, and he helped me move the furniture and cover it with plastic. He then explained the purpose of paint primer, which disheartened me. I wanted to see paint on the walls, but Henry shut down the idea of painting without a primer.

So for the rest of the evening, I spent my time priming all of the walls in my bedroom and upstairs hallway. I stayed out of my parents' room though.

The next day, I started painting. The navy blue proved to be a fantastic choice. It suited the hardwood and crown molding perfectly. By noon, I finished the first wall. I stood back to admire, pleased with my efforts. I felt Dog's wet nose against my thigh.

"Whatcha think?" I asked, and Dog barked. "Yeah, I like it too."

I started on the next wall, but painting gets boring really fast. I started becoming lazy with my strokes, and when Henry came in to check on me, he laughed.

"What?" I asked.

"Scarlett…you have to keep the same stroke or else it won't look right."

"But my arms are tired," I whined.

"Why aren't you using the roller?" he asked, tipping his head to the roller in the tray.

"I don't like the roller. It's hard."

He grabbed onto the roller and soaked it in paint, like a true professional. He handed it to me, but I hesitated. "It's too big."

He chuckled. "You'll get done a lot faster, I promise." I took it, though far from pleased with the preferred method of painting. "Come here."

Henry escorted me to the haphazardly painted wall. He moved behind me and reached his arms around me to grab the hand that held the roller. He started guided my hand up and down with the appropriate amount of pressure and quickness of strokes.

"See, it's not that hard. Just keep it up and down. Don't change it from side to side."

I became focused on his touch, his body pressed against my back. Weeks had passed since being so close to one another, and I missed the feeling of him.

Our faces were inches apart. Henry stopped moving our hands and stared into my eyes. In them, desire. I started to lean into him, but he released me and moved to my side.

He studied my paint stained legs and chuckled. "You're all blue."

I became frustrated with his attempts to distance himself from me, though I remained comforted by his presence. Unsure of how to navigate the two emotions, I smeared fresh, blue paint along his cheek.

His eyes became wide. "Why?" he asked.

I laughed. "Now you're blue too."

His smile faded, but a look of appreciation in his eyes remained. A thoughtful, thankful expression. Or perhaps what I projected onto him.

Henry wiped his face. "Well, I should get back out there."

"Henry..." I said. While he had to leave at that moment, I liked the idea of spending time with him. Just the two of us. "Do you wanna hang out later?"

He hesitated to answer.

I laughed, cavalier. "I could clearly use your help in here. We could order pizza and have a painting party?" I offered.

"Nah, I can't," he said. "I got plans with Max later."

I became embarrassed. That rejection thing again—hard to handle. "Oh. Yeah, it's Friday night. Of course you have something planned."

"It's not like that, Scarlett..."

"No, no...it's fine. Just...still having trouble keeping track of the days." I said. "How are you and Max?"

"We're fine. Things are good," he said.

I nodded. "Good. I'm glad."

"Well, I should..." he tipped his head to the door.

"Yeah, go, go...get outta here." He exited the bedroom, and I felt heavy. Unsure of how to continue, I felt it best to withdraw my efforts for a connection. Henry seemed like he wanted to just be friends.

I looked down at Dog, staring up at me. "Don't look at me like that."

The next day, Henry seemed so much more distant and more tired than usual. I attributed that to the crazy evening with Max, even though Henry has an aversion to alcohol. He seemed bothered by something though. He remained cordial, but avoided speaking to me unless he had to. I started wondering if it had something to do with my invitation the previous night.

And when I noticed the amount of time he spent on his phone, texting and talking to persons unknown, I knew Henry had some sort of crisis. I refused to ask though. As much as I wished for him to open up, I felt it best to leave him alone.

CHAPTER EIGHTEEN:

I MADE A TRIP TO HUNTER'S POINT that afternoon to grab a bite to eat. Really just to get away from the house. I became disheartened every time I saw Henry. I felt rejected by him, though far from angry. Silly, I guess. Silly for ever having thought the two of us made any sense whatsoever. We lived completely different lives.

I tried to force myself back into the mindset I had the first time we slept together. I expected nothing from him after our sordid tryst at Crybaby Hollow, which is exactly what I needed to expect now. Nothing other than his friendship. Hell, even that proved to be difficult.

I stopped at a local café, a new addition to Hunter's Point. Well, new to me. It looked trendy and out of place, though comforting in that it reminded me of the restaurants in the East Village of New York. While sitting on the patio, I actually smiled at the idea of going back to New York, something that hadn't been on my mind as of late.

Perhaps because my life seemed so much less complicated in New York. Though constantly working, the hardest decision I ever made came down to which venue needed my attention at the time.

I became nostalgic thinking about the long nights spent in dive bars, listening to indie bands perform. My favorite method of finding new artists.

Those bands, passionate and driven by their love of music. They never cared what anyone wrote about them. They had something to say. A burning desire needing to be fulfilled through music, and that mentality is what made writing about them so pleasurable. I never felt conflicted in what to say simply because to them, it never mattered.

No thirst for fame or fortune, so long as they kept a roof over their heads and their guitars regularly restrung, they remained content in their existence. I envied them. Wanted to be like them. Live the life of a struggling artist. It seemed so romantic.

"Scarlett?"

My meal and thoughtful trance, disrupted by the sound of my own name. Ella stood before me. Behind her, Kate with her child—a bitter look upon her face.

"Ella," I nodded.

"I'll be out front," Kate said.

I groaned at the thought of my violence toward Quinn spreading like wildfire amongst the old gang.

"How are you?" Ella asked.

I shrugged. "Fine, I guess."

Ella sat next to me. "I wanted to apologize for how you found out. About me and Quinn."

What a strange thing to say. "That's okay, you don't have to apologize…"

"No, I do," she continued. "I didn't want to tell you, and I should have. It's just that…you and Quinn dated for so long, and…"

"Like ten years ago." It seems that the performance of my youth had been so well delivered that the idea of denying my "feelings" for Quinn seemed petty.

"I know, but still. We grew up together, all of us knew each other in high school. I want you to know that nothing ever happened between us while you two were together."

"Oh, for Christ's…"

"It wasn't until he came back from Dental school. The two of us went out for drinks to catch up, and…I mean these things just happen though. You know?"

It seemed like some sort of confession, though hardly necessary. Ella seemed to be feeling guilty for some reason though, and I thought it rude to deny her the opportunity to make herself feel better.

"No, I don't…I don't really know. But you two seem happy," I said. Though I realized I actually had yet to see them together.

"Which is what I wanted to talk to you about," she said.

Here we go. "You want to know if I'm actually selling the practice."

"I don't mean to pry…"

I sighed. The idea of the practice made me sick. Henry did a good job of distracting me, it seemed, because I realized in that moment that I had yet to hear from Doctor Wilson about my proposal. A good thing, I convinced myself. Circumstances changed the day I found out Quinn and Ella were getting married.

"I haven't decided on anything yet, but I promise when I do…you and Quinn will be the first to know. Not like last time."

Ella stood. "I didn't mean to upset you, Scarlett."

I sighed. "It's not you I'm upset with."

She hesitated. "I'm here if you need help with anything."

Her words comforted me in some strange way. Though hardly intrigued by her offer of help, she seemed genuine. A kindness that I felt had only been genuine from one other person since returning to Devil's Elbow. Henry.

The next few days, Henry spent his time gutting my bathroom with Nate to make room for the claw foot tub. Which only left the shower in my parents' bathroom. I settled for monkey baths in my bathroom sink.

Finally, the day came.

I stood in the doorway, staring at the tub in admiration. A marvelous sight, and even though it seemed out of place with the rest of the house, I became confident that Henry would make it work somehow.

Henry moved it into position. "What do you think?" ~~he asked.~~

"I love it."

"Yeah?" he asked, skeptical.

"I really, really do." An excited squeal escaped my lips. I hit Henry's chest playfully as I passed him. A passing "thank you" for all the hard work of giving me my dream tub. "Oh my God, it's huge!" I exclaimed.

A little too large for the bathroom, but I found it difficult to regret the decision. I grabbed onto the side of the tub and stepped inside to really determine how much space I had for any further ablutions.

"We gotta fix the floors where the old one used to be," he said. "You happy?" ~~he asked~~.

"Am I ever!" I stretched my legs out and leaned back, pleased. I waved him over. "Come on in, the water's fine."

He smirked. "I'm good."

His apprehension, I refused to tolerate. I put time in trying to convince him that a claw foot tub was the way to go, and the time came to prove it to him. I snapped my fingers and pointed to the other side of the tub. "Get over here."

Henry hung his head, defeated. Unable to decline my offer anymore, he climbed into the tub. He lowered himself in the opposite side of me. I made room for his legs, and when seated, he nodded. "It's pretty big."

"It's actually pretty comfortable too," I said. Silence followed, but not an awkward one. An appreciative, taking it all in kind of silence. "I could stay in here all day."

"I imagine you'd get pretty bored," he said.

"Are you bored?" I asked, surprised.

He smirked "No."

I nodded. "You know what we could use right about now?" ~~I asked~~.

"What's that?"

"A joint."

Henry smiled. He reached into his shirt pocket and pulled out a small, somewhat crooked joint. My eyes widened as he held it up, offering it to me. Not an uncommon thing, someone having weed on them in our small community.

"I didn't know you smoked pot," I said.

“I don’t usually. Max gave it to me this morning, asked me to hold on to it for him,” he said. He put the joint in his mouth and removed a lighter from his pocket.

“Is he gonna get mad that you smoked it?” I asked.

Henry took a few puffs. “Nah, I’ll just tell him I lost it,” he said with a mouth full of smoke. He handed it to me.

I examined the thing. I didn’t really trust Max and the ways he chose to get lit. “It doesn’t have, like…crystal meth in it, right?”

Henry coughed a bit. “What’s that supposed to mean?”

I shrugged. It smelled fine. I took a long drag, holding the smoke in for a bit. When I saw Henry watching me, I couldn’t stifle a laugh. “Stop watching me,” I said through coughs and laughter.

“Does it make you feel insecure?”

“Little bit, yeah…” I said. I took another drag and handed it back to him.

“I’m actually surprised you smoke,” he said.

“Oh, that’s the only thing that got me through school. And it helps with my job too.”

I already started to feel the affects. The last time I smoked months before my parents died, and it seemed my tolerance faded. My head became fuzzy and I could feel my face settling into a permanent smile.

“How does it help with your job?” Henry asked and blew a smoke ring. He passed the joint back to me.

“Well, it kind of opens your mind. Makes things easier to interpret,” I said. “Like a form of meditation, you become calm. And you’re able to just sit there and listen…and you can listen for hours and not even realize because…your mind has become one with the music.”

He started smirking at me.

“What?” I asked.

“You’re just really passionate about what you do. I like it.”

I studied him. Henry always maintained a level of mystery, something that unnerved me, though I grew envious of his cool nature. I wanted to be more like him. Quiet, soft-spoken.

"What are you passionate about?" He shrugged. "Construction?" I asked sarcastically.

He laughed. "Get outta here," he mumbled.

I held the joint out to him. He reached for it, but I pulled away. "Hold on, I'm swimming over to you," ~~I said.~~

I began to crawl over to him. The high had taken effect, throwing me off balance and giving me the sensation of being in water. I positioned myself next to him and leaned my head on his shoulder, thankful for him being there to anchor me.

"Does this bother you?" I asked.

He shook his head. "No."

"Good. I like being close to you." He handed me the joint and I studied the end. It was halfway gone already. "Do you know how to give a shotgun?"

"Mhmm," he said and reached for the joint.

I handed it to him. He blew the ash off the end and placed the lit end inside of his mouth. When he did, I leaned in to him. He blew gently, and I inhaled as much as my lungs could take. I pulled away, satisfied with the amount of smoke.

Henry removed the joint from his mouth and flipped it around to take another drag. But the shotgun had done it for me. I exhaled slowly, coughing as the smoke trail became faint.

I felt removed from myself, but in a good way. I leaned my head on his shoulder again and stared out the bathroom window. The clouds seemed to change shapes and take the form of many different creatures and creations.

I felt Henry take another drag. He exhaled and the smoke engulfed me, causing me to close my eyes and breathe deeply once more.

"I'm so high," I said. Henry put out the joint in a nearby candle. "Are you high?"

"Little bit," he said.

I smiled. I rested my head on his chest, and he brought his arm around me. Loosely draped at first, but moments later he pulled me in closer. I listened to his heartbeat for a while. What an extraordinary thing to hear.

I looked to his hand resting on the side of the tub. "One of my friends in New York taught me how to give a palm reading."

"Oh yeah?" he asked, feigning interest.

I nodded. I grabbed his hand and turned it over to look at his palm. His hands, dirty from working all day, and a buildup of callus surrounded the base of his fingers. I examined the lines in his hand. I ran my index finger along them.

"This right here?" I began.

"Uh huh"

"This is your life line. It says you are going to live a very long, healthy life. Filled with joy and happiness."

"Does it really say that?" he asked.

I shrugged. "I dunno, I'm high. It looks like it."

He snickered. "You're a clown."

I focused on another line on his hand. "This one here, this is your head line. And it says…" I brought his hand closer to my face. "It says that you're sensitive to other people. You're compassionate." I smiled and looked up at him. "Awww…"

He laughed and turned his head away from me, as if I'd embarrassed him. "What does yours say?" he asked.

I smiled. "Mine's depressing, you don't want to know mine." He grabbed onto my hand and turned it over to reveal my palm. "Well…okay, see there? My life line's all screwed up."

He looked closer. "No, it's not."

"Yeah…long life filled with sadness, illness, loneliness…" he gripped my hand, and even though I'd been joking, his grasp somehow made me feel better.

"Nah. It looks like mine."

The whites of his eyes, somewhat red from the marijuana, though it managed to make the blue pop even more than usual.

Henry placed a gentle kiss on my lips, pleasantly surprising me. His distance as of late led me to believe he just wanted to be friends. "I'm sorry, I..." he began.

I shook my head. "Don't apologize. Unless you're not going to do it again."

Henry hesitated. And when he kissed me again, I opened my mouth for him without him having to ask this time. His tongue against mine, so soft and tender. His kiss bared his soul. He touched the side of my face, inhaling me deeply. As our kiss intensified, his breathing became deeper, heavier. His heart pounded beneath my palm.

I ran my hand down his chest and over his stomach, his muscles tightening as I did. And when I started rubbing him—already somewhat hard—Henry quivered. He stopped kissing me and closed his eyes, becoming lost in the feeling.

"Do you want me to stop?" I whispered to him.

Henry swallowed hard and shook his head. "No. Don't stop."

I kissed his cheek and then his neck. And when I stopped touching him, he opened his eyes to look at me. I began to mount him, and he seemed intrigued.

He brought his hands to my waist when I lowered my body onto his, and when I started grinding myself on top of him, he moaned.

"Jesus, what are you doing to me?" he whispered.

I smiled. Hopefully something good. Henry pulled me down further onto him. He grabbed my ass and forced my hips to grind against him harder, faster. He started to thrust his hips upward onto me, his excitement and pleasure growing with each passing second.

"Does that feel good?" I asked.

"Yeah," he moaned.

"What do you want, Henry? Tell me what you want me to do to you."

Henry exhaled heavily against my face. "Tell me you love me."

"I love you." But the words sounded strange coming out of my mouth. The last time I said those words so genuinely, I said them to my parents. Even that felt forever ago.

His grip on me tightened, and his body became tense beneath me. He seemed concentrated. His upward thrusts became more violent, and he started grunting with each move. He'd taken control of me, moving my hips on top of him.

"Talk dirty to me, Scarlett."

I wanted to please him, but I lacked the inspiration. I have absolutely talked dirty before, but only during sexual exchanges with men I never cared for. And the inspiration came in the heat of the moment. I never saw Henry as the type to enjoy a trash talking partner though, so I never even considered. My mind raced, trying to find something tailored to him as a person.

"I liked what you did to me on the stairs that night," I moaned, and Henry's eyes opened. They seemed to soften at my words—some sort of shock and tenderness inside of them.

"You did?" he panted.

I bit my lip and nodded. "I touched myself to the thought of you that night," I said while leaning my face closer to his.

He let out a quivering breath. "Scarlett…"

"I want you to do it again," I whispered and then ran my tongue over his lips.

"Fuck, Scarlett…" Henry became rigid, holding me in place on top of him as he winced in pleasure. He stopped breathing for a moment and then let out a booming groan. His hips moved upward against me a few more times and then stopped, his breath catching in his throat. He brought his hands to my face. They were shaking.

"Did you come?" I asked

He let out an exasperated sigh. "Yeah," he said, his voice cracking. "I'm sorry," he whispered against my lips.

"Don't be sorry. I love making you come." He stared at me, seemingly taken aback. As if hardly able to comprehend the idea.

"You're so beautiful," he whispered.

I became confused in that moment. Normally, I hate hearing that sort of talk from a sexual partner. I find it unnecessary and contrived. But when Henry said it, I felt touched. I realized that I wanted to hear those things from him. He had never complimented me so genuinely before. Hell, he'd never called me beautiful before. A nice thing to hear. Especially since I felt anything but beautiful lately.

I kissed his lips and rested my head on his chest. He ran his fingers through my hair and kissed my forehead. We sat like that for a while in silence, allowing ourselves to come down from the high. But then his phone rang, ripping me out of my dreamlike state.

I sat up to let him get to it, but he sighed and ignored the call.

"Who was that?" I asked.

"It's nobody."

Still true to his mystery, and I became irritated that he felt the need to keep secrets from me. Henry placed the phone back into his pocket and pulled me back onto his chest. The two of us were quiet for a while. But when I picked up my head and started looking around the bathroom, Henry spoke.

"What?" he asked.

"I think I want hardwood in here now," I said, now finally able to visualize the bathroom in a completed state.

"Jesus woman."

CHAPTER NINETEEN:

I FIGURED THINGS WOULD CHANGE between Henry and I after what happened in the bathtub. I thought he would start to open up to me. Perhaps even start making more of an effort to spend time with me. I figured the moment we shared in the tub proved that I wanted him around, and that when I opened up to him and told him I enjoyed what he did to me on the stairs, he would welcome me into him with open arms.

But he never did. Henry went back to being withdrawn and distracted, and I started feeling embarrassed about sharing my dirty secret with him. It seemed as though he enjoyed hearing those things in the moment but then judged me for it afterward. Because who could ever take a girl like me seriously?

Henry and his crew managed to finish repairs on the garage and begin repairs on the exterior of the house. He finished my bathroom too, which turned out to be absolutely amazing. Hardwood floors, dark blue walls… but an onset of thunderstorms finally sent them packing one afternoon. Though Henry continued to find reasons to come to the house during the thunderstorms, he remained withdrawn.

He fixed the swing on the front porch, finally replaced the screen on the front door, and even helped me finish painting the upstairs, something I gave up on for a few days. I decided that I would hire someone to paint next time I decided to renovate something.

But as Henry ran out of things to fix, his visits became fewer and fewer, leaving me alone with Dog in our watery inferno.

I spent my time listening to music, trying my best to get back into the critic mindset, though I found no comfort in the songs.

I started to not even trust my own judgment. I listened to songs from new artists on repeat, but inspiration never came to me. One musician in particular was good…I think. But even when I tried to summarize my thoughts in order to pass him along, I contradicted myself. I praised his lyrics but bashed his guitar skills. I complimented his chosen genre, but complained that he didn't have the right voice for it. And by the time I finished the outline, even I didn't know if I recommended him or not.

For the first time ever, I lacked courage in my convictions, which is a terrible, terrible thing for a critic. Perhaps the reason being that I knew it wouldn't be me writing the article. Or perhaps my mind had become so polluted with things so far removed from my New York life. I really should go home, I thought. The longer I went without writing, the harder it would be to maintain a following.

I closed my laptop. My only comfort were a few bands and musicians promised to me exclusively, but even they seemed antsy. Dog put his paw on my leg and whimpered. I felt awful about leaving the poor mutt behind, but New York didn't seem the place for him.

The next morning, I awoke to the sun shining bright and not a single rain cloud in the sky. A wonderful sight after having been locked up at my parents' house for what felt like months. And while I knew the roads were most likely dangerous, I needed some fresh air. Dog wagged his tail when I sat up.

"Let's take a walk."

The two of us walked along the side of the highway. The grass, the roads, everything around us, wet. But the smell of wet pavement mixed with the scent of the forest and river refreshed me in some way. Perhaps my true Southern decided to return. It had been so long since I cared for the smell of nature.

Though the mosquitos were unrelenting. I swatted one from my leg and continued along the road with Dog by my side. While the sun shined, the air remained muggy. Another rainfall would soon come.

A truck passed us, kicking water up from the puddles on the side of the road. A comforting thing to see, the world returning to normal. As we started nearing Dante's, my phone rang, and when I saw *Doctor Wilson* on the screen, I became anxious.

"Hello?" I answered.

"Scarlett, it's Doctor Wilson..." Duh. "I wanted to call and let you know that I heard back from the buyers."

My heart started racing. I tried to think of a way to tell him that my proposal was made under the wrong circumstances. That I hadn't been thinking clearly at the time of our dinner meeting. I tried to think of how to tell him that I needed more time.

"What'd they say?"

Doctor Wilson sighed. "They rejected your proposal. It seems they only want to pay the agreed upon amount, and with two owners to deal with, they're worried things could get messy."

I felt my heart skip a beat, but a smile spread across my face. It perplexed me, my reaction. Though it became obvious in that moment that having the practice made me happy. Something I never thought possible.

"Scarlett?"

I tried to hide a snicker. "I'm here."

"I'm still willing to buy you out. I've even decided to raise the price a bit."

"How kind."

"I want this process to be easy on you. I know how much the practice means to you."

I hesitated. But the thought of even accepting weighed me down, ruining the excitement I felt from still being an owner. Not an owner necessarily, but the practice still being in the hands of people who cared for my father. "I, uh..."

"Scarlett?"

I cleared my throat. "I'm sorry, I...I'm not gonna sell."

He scoffed. "I'm sorry?"

I felt confident in my answer, though I remained unsure of where the confidence came from. A business owner, me? A business I knew nothing about, but none of that seemed to matter at the moment. I wanted to keep the practice, not even for myself. For those who loved my father and worked hard for him for so long. The thought made me laugh.

"I'm not selling," I said, confident.

A long pause. "Scarlett, you know nothing about the business…your involvement would only complicate things."

A thought that I spent time considering already. "Maybe I don't have to be involved. Maybe I could just…be there as financial support, I mean…my parents left me a lot of money, and…"

"It's not practical. You lack the experience and business education to run a practice, Scarlett."

How foolish he made me feel. As if I were incapable, too stupid to handle the weight of being a business owner. "Look, I'm not selling," I said firmly. "You can try and bully me all you want, but this…this is the right decision."

"You're making a mistake."

I scoffed. I considered. "I don't think I am…"

Dog barked and took off running across the street toward the parking lot of Dante's, almost triggering a wild panic from me. "Dog!" I yelled, though he made it to the parking lot unscathed. Stupid mutt.

"I'm not certain I'm willing to take on the burden of an inexperienced partner," Doctor Wilson said, but I became distracted by Dog running to greet Henry as he approached the entrance of Dante's with Ally at his side, her arm around his waist.

I felt sick. Jealous, really, though unfamiliar in that I never felt jealousy in a relationship. Even though Henry and I weren't in a relationship necessarily, I felt entitled to him. A horrible revelation, but true all the same. I felt betrayed that he allowed me to open myself up to him just to be off gallivanting with other women. His ex being the the other woman. Or perhaps the other woman was me.

"Scarlett?" Doctor Wilson spoke

I hesitated, my thoughts disturbed. "Look, uh…you're free to give up your half if you wish. I'm…not selling…I don't think…"

"You don't think?" Doctor Wilson asked.

My thoughts confused me. Henry kneeled down to pet Dog. "No, I…I know." The exchange between Dog and Henry only made me more upset. I felt betrayed by my mutt.

"Scarlett…"

"I have to go." I ended the call.

I jogged across the street to Dante's to retrieve my mutt. To remind him where his loyalties should lie, but Henry stood at the sight of me, seeming perplexed. Guilty of something. I started feeling very uncomfortable when Ally gave me a pointed look and moved into Henry's back, though I tried to play it off.

"Come on, Dog…" I grabbed his collar.

"Scarlett?"

I felt like I needed to say something. Be civil or some shit like that, but it proved to be difficult. Words failed me. The sight of Ally—who I thought moved away—gripping on to Henry's shirt, beckoning him to enter Dante's with her, disturbed me.

Perhaps the reason Henry seemed so distracted the past few weeks had more to do with another girl than I originally wanted to believe. "Sorry, I…Dog just took off running," I muttered.

Henry's expression softened, but Ally continued to glare.

I felt embarrassed and angry. So embarrassed that I wanted to cry and so angry I wanted to hit him, but I had no right. Hell, she had more right to him than myself, though the thought did nothing to ease me.

I started pulling Dog away, having to use more force as he fought to stay with Henry. "Dog, stop," I pleaded.

My eyes started to burn, which angered me even more. Never in my life have I cried for a man, the exception being my father. "Dog…" I begged and put all my weight into pulling him away from Henry and Ally.

"Scarlett, please…"

I felt his hands on me, something that made the floodgates open. Without a second thought, I hit him. I smacked his face, not nearly as hard as I hit Quinn, but hard enough to stun him and myself.

"Oh my God," Ally gasped.

Shit, I thought. Henry won't take that from me, and I started feeling even more embarrassed and vulnerable at the possibilities in which he would put me in my place. But he didn't say anything. He seemed hurt, surprised, though not one shred of malice upon his face.

I needed to leave. With or without Dog. If he wanted to stay with Henry so bad, fine. I released his collar and walked away.

"Scarlett!" Henry called, but I refused to face him.

I ran back across the street and started heading home. Only when I reached the edge of my parents' property did I notice Dog at my side.

That evening, I sat in my empty tub smoking a cigarette and drinking a glass of wine. I felt depressed and lonely. Something I felt a lot since my parents' death, but those feelings seemed to dominate me less and less with Henry's presence in my life.

I felt he understood me and my pain. I thought he saw beauty in it, and even though he started distancing himself recently, I felt comforted by him. I thought maybe the two of us just tiptoed around our feelings. Me, unsure of how to pull him in. Him, waiting for me to figure it out in some way.

Though seeing him with Ally convinced me the reason for his withdraw had everything to do with her.

Dog whimpered from beside the tub, but I remained distant from him. Traitor.

Henry called. I ignored. He called again, and as much as I didn't want to act like a child, the thought of talking to him after I hit him unnerved me. I felt ashamed for hitting him despite all the reasons I convinced myself he deserved it. Hitting Quinn, that's one thing. Henry? I started to wonder why I felt the need to strike when pushed too far. Not a very adult thing to do.

Someone knocking at the front door sent my heart into my throat and Dog out of the bathroom, barking. I debated not even answering, though it seemed ridiculous. Much like me ignoring Henry's phone calls. It felt immature to ignore his presence completely.

I went downstairs and opened the front door. Henry stood before me, solemn.

"Why haven't you been answering my calls?" he muttered.

I felt foolish even speaking to him. My actions toward him proved that he hurt me, but having to verbally admit something like that made me feel weak. He made me feel weak. In all the good ways as well as the bad.

"I didn't want to talk to you," I said, insecure.

Henry's expression softened. He leaned on the doorframe. "Can I come in?"

I considered saying no. But at the insistence of Dog, I pulled the door open and stepped aside, and Henry entered.

In the living room, I sat on the couch while Henry stood on the other side of the room, arms folded while leaning against one of the walls. The only bit of happiness present being from Dog, panting and looking back and forth between us.

"I'm sorry I hit you," I muttered.

Henry shrugged. "Did it make you feel better?"

I winced. "No," I whined. "It made me feel awful."

Henry snickered, the bastard, and I shot him a pointed glare. "I'm sorry," he said and attempted to maintain a serious demeanor. "It's just nice. You showing some humility."

His words angered me. "You deserved it."

He seemed confused. "So you're apologizing…for what?"

Clever man, though I felt no need to clarify. I started picking at my nails, trying to appear distracted in some way. Trying to think of something to say, really. But the thought of Ally dominated my mind. "I thought…Ally moved."

"To Hunter's Point," he said.

"You guys…back together?" I asked.

He hesitated. "Would it bother you if we were?"

Involuntary facial spasms ensued. I felt my face contort into something awful. The same face babies make when trying to convince themselves they want to cry. I stood and walked toward the exit of the living room, angered by his callus behavior when I so clearly needed comfort. "Whatever, I don't care…"

Henry moved, blocking my escape route. He grabbed my waist and pulled me into him. ~~As much as I wanted to push him away, his scent and his touch proved to be too difficult to ignore.~~ "Stop," he said when my breath quivered. "We're just friends, Scarlett."

I pushed him off of me. Sure, I believed they were friends. But JUST friends? Not with the way she touched him. Not with the way he became unnerved by the sight of me. True, Henry and I were "just friends" as well, and I had no right to demand answers of him. But I hated seeing him with her. Friends or not, the idea of him carrying on with another girl hurt me in more ways than one.

I started feeling unworthy of his love. I felt belittled by him, rejected in some way. I resented him for making me feel so weak when I always prided myself on having a spine and the ability to never really need anyone.

Henry reached for me again, but I pushed his hands away. He sighed. "Scarlett…"

"I fell for you, Henry. You didn't catch me this time."

His eyes softened. He seemed surprised by what I said though, his pale blue eyes darting to the ground, searching the furthest corners of his mind for something to say. He hesitated to reach for me, but I pulled back again. "Baby," he began, seeming insecure in his words and vulnerable in the way he moved. "You just…you just haven't gotten to me yet is all."

Unsure of what to say or how to respond, I kept my mouth shut. Henry crossed the room to sit on the couch. He hung his head. He ran his hands over his face and inhaled deeply. "I didn't know you felt that way, Scarlett. How could I? You never said anything, I…never knew what you were thinking…"

"I told you that day in front of Max that I cared," I snapped.

"Hell, I care about a lot of people. I care about Ally, but it doesn't mean I want to be with her. Do you wanna be with me?" he asked, timid.

I hesitated. He noticed.

Henry pointed to me. "That hesitation right there…scares the hell outta me."

I did want to be with him. More than I ever wanted to be with any man. My shameful desires for him grew into something much stronger, much greater than I ever anticipated. Though I became confounded by the thought. A few months ago, my career and my life in New York seemed the only thing worthy of my time.

But things changed, and now the only thing I wanted sat on the couch in front of me, waiting for me to say that I wanted him. A truly terrifying situation to find myself because if I asked for him, I became convinced he'd give himself to me, though what would that mean for me? For my career, my life in New York?

Henry stood, ripping me from my thoughts. "I'll come by tomorrow. Take a look at the windows for you. Looks like you got water comin' in," he said and then walked past me to exit the living room, though the sight of him leaving sent a panic through me.

If I let him leave, I might not ever have the chance to pull him back into me. "Henry!" I called, and he turned back to me so fast, a sort of eagerness in his eyes. I hadn't come up with a plan. I hit the buzzer for fear I'd lose my turn without even knowing the answer. "I, uh…"

"Is it really so hard for you to say how you feel, Scarlett?"

I scoffed. "You're one to talk." Henry, unimpressed, started to leave again. "Wait…" I grabbed on to him. I pushed him back into the wall, and before he could speak, I forced my lips onto his. The only solution I had. The only answer I knew to be true. I wanted to kiss him.

Henry returned my affections. He pulled me into him. Our kiss deepened. We devoured each other, inhaled each other, held on to each other for dear life. His heart pounded against me when I hugged him tighter. His scent triggered that fire inside of me, the one burning so bright that it signaled him, letting him know that I needed him with me. But then he tried to pull away.

"Please, stop" he whispered, but I held him tight. Even though it seemed it pained him to have me so close.

"Henry…"

He brought his hand to the side of my face and caressed my cheek with his thumb. In his eyes, love and devotion. Though fear dominated him. "You can't keep doing this to me, Scarlett," he whined. "I want more."

I hesitated. "I want more too."

He seemed skeptical. He pulled back a bit, studying me. Looking for the fault in my words. "I want to believe you."

"Let me prove it to you," I whispered and kissed his lips.

He barely kissed me back. Still unconvinced by my words, I could see hesitation in his eyes. An unshakable doubt that made him want to run for the hills, though the prospect of me giving more seemed far too alluring for him to leave.

"How you gonna prove it to me?" he asked.

A difficult question, ~~though~~ one that couldn't be answered by my words. Telling him wouldn't be enough, and I think he knew. I kissed him again. "Stay with me," I whispered against his lips. He considered, but my lips hovering over his proved to be too difficult for him to resist. He kissed me, deeply.

His kiss, so tender yet eager and passionate. I doubt he ever kissed anyone so intimately before. I knew I never had. And kissing him in that moment seemed so much different than the other kisses we shared. Henry became mine in that moment, and I, his. No will to fight it anymore, and the kiss held no secrets between the two of us. I loved him. I loved his tenderness, his protectiveness, his devotion. Everything he managed to reveal to me in one, simple act.

We retreated to my room. Unable to fight our desires any longer—something we'd done too much of, and knowing that I would no longer have to made me all the more eager to claim him in that moment. I started unbuttoning his shirt, and Henry watched me, consumed with me. And when I pulled his shirt off, revealing his chest to me, I kissed his flesh. I kissed him softly, slowly—taking my time as now it seemed we had all the time in the world to worship each other. No hurry. Just love and appreciation.

I ran my hands down his chest. So beautiful the way he stood in front of me, succumbing to me, trusting me so. My love for him became overwhelming, and it started to frighten me. But when Henry brought his hand to the back of my neck and placed a tender kiss on my forehead, I knew I had nothing to fear.

His kiss said so much.

I love you.

I'd never hurt you.

I'm yours forever.

I raised my arms above my head, allowing Henry to pull my shirt off of me. And when he threw it aside, I unhooked my bra and let it fall to the floor. My turn to be vulnerable, but Henry's tender and appreciative gaze only empowered me. He looked at me as though he'd never seen anything so beautiful before. I moved into him again, pressing my body into his while wrapping my arms around him. His bare chest against mine, and I wanted to hold him like that forever.

His fingers ran down my back, gently, slowly. It seemed as though he would be content standing there, just holding me forever. But I grew eager to be even closer to him. I needed to be. When I pulled Henry down onto the bed, he crawled on top of me slowly. The moment, so unlike our past sexual experiences. Before, we fucked, and I'm not ashamed to admit it. But Henry taught me something that evening. What making love is—a concept I never really understood.

I always thought making love was just a term people used to appear less crass. But the way we touched each other, kissed each other, took small pauses to just hold each other for a moment. Yes, I'm certain that's what making love is supposed to be.

Henry pulled my jeans off of me, revealing my naked body to him completely. He threw them aside and ran his fingers down my stomach. Gentle and tantalizing. He leaned over me again, placing small, tender kisses along my thighs, moving upward between my legs, my hips, my stomach, and my body began to shake.

I watched him the entire time, and when he made his way back up to my lips, our mouths collided. I became eager to be closer to him, knowing I wouldn't be satisfied until I had him completely.

I ran my fingers down his stomach to unbutton his jeans, and Henry watched me. He seemed so much more calm than myself, and I started to envy his demeanor. And while Henry had certainly been the more vulnerable between the two of us on more than one occasion, it was a nice change of pace. Perhaps a new precedent for our new relationship.

I started to pull his jeans down, but Henry took over. Removing them completely, freeing himself from his binds, and I stared at him in admiration.

An Adonis to me. Built to perfection. Every detail of his body, so perfectly constructed and so specific a form that I started to wonder how I could have gone so long without having him as my own. Or perhaps I loved him so immensely that he soon became everything I ever wanted. The only thing I ever needed.

The evening turned out to be the most intimate, erotic experience of my life. Henry worked his way inside of me, taking it slowly—so unlike our previous sexual encounters. Instead of violently thrusting hips, he moved rhythmically, a gentle easing in and out of me, his breath quivering against my face.

He filled me completely, in all the ways a person would expect to be whole. Henry satisfied me in more ways than I ever thought possible. My body ached for him, skin ablaze from the feeling of his body moving against mine, pleasuring me from so deep within that I started to feel weak with every advance. My heart pounded, and every time Henry kissed me, my heart fluttered.

"Scarlett, I love you," he panted against my lips.

My sweet Henry. If only he knew how much love I had in my heart for him. Words can't even express. He started shaking beneath his own weight, but the two of us, so connected, so in sync with one another that we knew exactly what we wanted. And I wanted to be on him.

Henry leaned back onto his knees and grabbed onto my hands, pulling me up onto him as he did. I wrapped my arms and legs around him and started grinding myself onto him, stimulating that perfect spot of me. And when Henry moaned, my body shivered.

"Henry," I panted.

He held me against him, cupping my ass to guide me on him. And when his hips started moving upward to meet my advances, I knew it was only a matter of time before I came. I started panting, moaning more and more frequently. The feeling of him so deep inside of me, stimulating a part of me that I didn't even know existed, made me want to cry.

I felt my core muscles tighten, that perfect spot in between my legs became more and more tender. An aching desire, begging to be released built up inside of me. I became tense, completely focused on my movements, knowing that at any moment, all of that love and appreciation would be released onto him.

He brought his hand to my face, forcing me to look into his pale, blue eyes. "You gonna come?" he panted.

I nodded and brought my hands to his shoulders to stabilize myself and to further intensify where he reached me so deep within. I leaned back, arching my back to thrust my hips into the perfect position on top of him.

"Baby…" I whined. It was happening.

Henry grabbed my waist and sat further upward to thrust into me, a bit more violently than before, but it directly led to the explosion of pleasure, desire, appreciation—all of it coming out of me in full force.

"Oh God," I moaned.

"I'm so close, Scarlett," he quivered, but I became lost in the euphoria of my own orgasm. Henry lowered me onto the bed to continue his advances, moaning, whining, and I knew he hadn't been able to hold himself back anymore.

Though always a gentleman, he continued to move his hips into me, deeply and slowly until I stopped seizing against him. Even if it looked painful for him. He did it for me though.

Henry hovered over me, panting, sweating, face red, very similar to myself. The two of us, so appreciative and in love with one another. I caressed his cheek with my thumb and pushed the sweaty, unruly strands of hair from his forehead.

"Tell me you love me, Scarlett," he whispered.

I smiled. "I love you, Henry King."

CHAPTER TWENTY:

I LOVE YOU, HENRY KING. No truer words have been spoken. I loved him with all my heart, and now I knew I had no reason to hide it from him. The next morning, Henry woke me by kissing my cheek gently.

"Wake up," he whispered.

I smiled at the feeling of his lips on my face, so tender and loving. But when I opened my eyes, I realized the sun had yet to appear. The clock read five in the morning, and I became confused. I can't remember a time I awoke so early.

I rolled into him and groaned. "Why?" I asked, my voice raspy.

Henry chuckled. "I wanna show you something."

He kissed me again and got out of bed. I couldn't resist rolling over and burying my face in his pillow, not wanting to deny my intemperance to his scent.

Henry stood and pulled his jeans up, and I wanted nothing more than to pull him back to bed with me. Indulge myself in the aching desire I had for him. He looked at me and smirked. "Get up."

Henry took me to the bluffs in Hunter's Point. A series of cliffs that overlooked the town, and in the perfect spot, you can see the river. We stopped for coffee along the way, and by the time we made it to his chosen vantage point, the sky turned light blue.

He backed his truck toward the edge of the cliff—far enough away so falling would be of very little concern. He opened his truck bed and the two of us sat, staring down at the town.

The spot in which he chose to watch the sunrise allowed us to see bits and pieces of The Rubidoux through the thickness of the forest in the distance. From that high up, it seemed as though we dominated the land—the beast of the river included. It had been a while since I felt so powerful.

"I've been here before," I said and took a sip of coffee.

Henry wrapped a blanket around me and pulled me in closer. "Yeah?" he asked.

I nodded. "Me and my friends used to come up here and get stoned after school. We figured it was the safest place."

Henry snickered. "A bunch of high kids standing on a cliff. I see what you mean."

I couldn't stifle a laugh. "No, like—the cops wouldn't show."

"I get ya."

"I think there's still…a peacock farm around here. Aaaahaaah!"

Henry laughed. "What are you doing?"

"Just wait. Aaaahaaaah!" I yelled.

Seconds later, the sound of peacocks returning my call in the distance made me laugh hysterically. "I don't know why that's so funny!" I said through fits of laughter.

Henry chuckled. "You're a clown."

I sighed, breaking myself of my amusement. "I totally forgot about this place."

The wind blew and I inhaled deeply to capture all the scents the morning and nature had to offer. But when Henry started scooting into the back of the truck bed, I became distracted. He positioned himself against the cab and sprawled his legs out, reaching for me as he did. I crawled back to him. I leaned into him, and he wrapped his arms around me.

"You okay?" I asked. He nodded. "You seem tense."

"Yeah, I, uh…kinda have a fear of heights."

I picked my head up. "Then why are we here?"

He shrugged. "It's not so bad if I stay away from the edge. Just keep looking outward. The edge is what freaks me out. But it's a nice view. Especially when the sun comes up."

I never knew that about him. There seemed to be a lot of things that I didn't know about Henry, and I became intrigued in that moment. "Tell me something else about you," I said.

"Like what?"

I shrugged. "What did you want to be when you were a kid?"

He kissed my forehead. "Mmm…I wanted to be a firefighter when I was a kid."

Awwww. "What changed?"

He shrugged. "I dunno. Just grew into a different person, I guess. Civil engineering kinda became the goal after I finished school."

A civil engineer. Something I imagine Henry would excel at. "You have to go to college for that."

He nodded. "I know. I still want to go to college, just…" he paused.

"What?" I asked.

"It's expensive."

I laughed. "Yes, it is."

"Yeah, I can imagine how much your parents spent on your education. You got a master's degree, right?"

I scoffed. Presume much? "Yeah, I do. But my parents didn't pay for my school."

He pulled back to study me, seemingly confused. "No?"

"My dear boy, haven't you ever heard of scholarships? They didn't spend a dime, not when I could get in-state tuition here in Tennessee."

"Huh. I never knew that."

"But maybe that's something you should think about. A scholarship. And then there's financial aid…"

"Will you help me figure all that stuff out?" he asked.

A monumental moment for the two of us, and I almost thought I heard him wrong. Henry never asked me for help before. With anything. Ever. It was always me needing his help with something, and I started feeling appreciated for my knowledge and experience in the matter. I became thrilled at the prospect of helping him achieve something he always wanted.

"Yeah, I'll help you!" I said, a little too excited.

He smiled. "Yeah?"

I sighed, disappearing into a dream-like state. "Think of it now. A civil engineer and a journalist. We're gonna be rich."

Henry laughed and pulled me in tighter. He kissed my forehead, and I became fixated on the sun breaking over the forest in the distance. The colors in the sky becoming beautiful shades of pink and orange. Rain seemed a distant memory, and each day carrying on to summer, it would become non-existent until the following spring.

"Tell me something else about you," I said.

"Uh…like what?"

I shrugged. "What do your parents do?"

He hesitated and inhaled deeply. "Uh…my mom died when I was just a kid. My dad…I don't know the guy, so…my grandma's the one who raised me. But she died when I was sixteen."

"How did she die?" I asked delicately.

"Heart attack."

"Not your grandma, your mom."

He sighed and shook his head. "That's a story for another time."

His response only intrigued me, though I knew better than to ask. Clearly a painful subject for him, and I could only imagine how I would feel if someone pried about my parents' death before I trusted them enough to tell them.

The thought of my parents weighed on me. I started feeling guilty for my moment of elation with Henry. They only died three months ago, yet it seemed like I already put it behind me. When I thought of them, I missed them. But I started to wonder why they were no longer front and center in my mind.

"You okay?" he asked.

I nodded. "Just thinking about my parents. It doesn't really feel like they're gone. Like, I know they are, but…I hardly ever saw them to begin with. Not since moving to New York. I think that I feel guilty about that, but also…relieved. I mean, I could only imagine how traumatized I would be if I spent every day with them."

"I think you're just trying to protect yourself, Scarlett. Almost like…if you allowed yourself to really feel the pain then you wouldn't survive."

"You don't think I would?" I asked, offended.

"Nah, I mean, like…when something painful happens, we sorta try and block it out. I think because it would overwhelm us if we really allowed ourselves to feel it. Like taking pain pills or somethin', only…maybe on a subconscious level. I dunno."

I became impressed with him but also confused. I never knew him to be so thoughtful or knowledgeable about the world. I started to wonder what sort of pain he went through. The sort of traumatizing experience he had to make him think that way. Damaged goods, as Kate described him.

Henry took me home after watching the sunrise together. He had some work to do for an elderly couple in Hunter's Point, which suited me just fine because I needed more sleep. I hoped he wouldn't make a habit of going on early morning adventures.

While climbing out of his truck though, it seemed the two of us remained unsure of how to be with each other now, and I hesitated to turn back and kiss him. "So, should we, like…?"

"Can I come over tonight?" he asked.

The insecurity in his voice and on his face made me smile. I nodded. "Yeah, you can come over." I scooted into him and kissed his lips, to which he seemed very grateful. With his hand on my face, Henry kissed me softly, gently.

"I could get used to this," he whispered against my lips.

I smirked. "Me too."

Henry smiled and pecked my lips. "Now go on, get on up to bed. Lord knows you want to."

He wasn't wrong. I needed sleep. We said our goodbyes, and I climbed out of his truck. I watched him as he drove away, and once his truck disappeared into the brush of the forest, I started to feel heavy. Not because he left. Because I knew he planned to come back.

I've never been any good at relationships. And even though I knew without a doubt that I loved Henry, I started to question if I rushed into a commitment just to appease him. So I wouldn't lose him. Usually, the courtship lasts a lot longer and hardly progresses to anything serious. But we were already telling each other we loved each other, and I thought myself to be in no position for anything serious. Not with New York calling my name.

I slept that whole afternoon, terrified of waking up and feeling the need to sit Henry down and have a conversation. Terrified of having to tell him that he'd been right to be afraid of jumping into something with me, and that we needed to end things. End things before they even really began.

God, I hated myself. But when my phone started ringing, I knew I had to face him. "Hello?"

He laughed. "Did you just wake up?"

How embarrassing. "No…"

"Are you hungry?"

"Yes."

Henry decided to stop by Dante's and grab some food to go, but the anxiety I felt while waiting for him became overbearing. Mostly I feared that when I saw him, I'd know for sure our relationship was doomed for failure. That even despite how much I loved him, I knew we could never work. Not with me returning to New York. Something I wished we talked about before deciding to be exclusive.

But when Henry arrived and I opened the front door to greet him, all those thoughts fled my mind. And I was left with nothing but sheer happiness and joy at even the sight of him smirking at me.

Oh, how foolish I'd been to even think I had it in me to break things off with him. My sweet Henry.

"You gonna let me in?" he asked through a chuckle.

I stepped aside and pulled the door open for him, but before he got too far into the foyer, I grabbed his hand and pulled him into me. I wanted to kiss him. I needed to feel those butterflies again. And with his lips pressed against mine, I fell into him all over again.

In bed together that night, Henry held me close. I tried to initiate sex—something I felt he wanted—but he said he just wanted to hold me for a while. And while holding me, he talked to me like he never had before. He opened up to me about his feelings. About the things he always felt to afraid to show me or tell me.

"I always wanted to tell you how I felt. I just never knew how you'd react to that sort of thing. You don't really seem the type to enjoy hearing those things."

"Usually, I'm not. But it's different with you. I just feel so comfortable around you. Like I could tell you anything in the world."

"Me too, baby," he said and then kissed my head.

We remained silent for a moment, and I started to wonder how long he felt that way about me. Even though Henry started opening up to me, his mystery remained an unsolvable puzzle to me. Something I never wrapped my brain around, though I envied him for his enigmatic nature. The two of us, complete opposites.

"How long have you known?" I asked.

"Known what?"

"That you loved me," I muttered. It sounded stupid coming out of my mouth.

He hesitated, and I turned onto my back to try and decipher his mystery once more. He smiled slightly and pushed a few strands of hair from my face. "Since the first time I saw you."

I had to turn away from him to hide the fact that he made me want to cry with how sweet I found his response. Though I hardly thought he actually loved me at first sight, knowing that he had such strong feelings for me since day one made me feel wretched for only just realizing in the past couple weeks how much I cared for him.

I grew anxious at the thought of him asking me the same question. How awful it must sound that it took me so long to realize. But Henry never asked. Maybe he knew. Maybe his mystery allowed him to see the transparency in others.

"You know, when you went out on that date with Quinn, I almost lost it," he said through a chuckle.

"It wasn't a date."

"Sure looked that way to me. You looked sexy as hell. But the idea of you carrying on with him again just…hell, I almost outed myself right then and there."

A revelation in my eyes. "That's what all that worrying was about." I laughed. "I should have known." Henry laughed and buried his face in my neck, as if embarrassed. But his words triggered something inside of me. "How…did you know I dated Quinn?"

I rolled over and looked up at him, but Henry shook his head. "Nah, your dad used to talk about him when he was going to school for dentistry. He mentioned the two of you."

Of course, I thought. "Yeah, we dated for a long time. But I never really liked him. We were friends, sure, but…I never loved him. Not really, anyway."

"No?" Henry asked. He seemed pleased. "Have you ever been in love before?"

I shook my head. "I don't think so. You?"

"Yeah, once. But I don't really feel like talking about that. I'm here with you. That's all that matters to me."

A mystery love to add to his mystery. Fine, I thought. I hardly wanted to hear about the first girl Henry ever loved. Because it became so blatantly obvious in that moment that none of that mattered—just like he said. He was there with me, loving me. Only me.

"Are you scared, Henry?"

He kissed my shoulder. "Some times."

I turned into him again, and he hovered over me, looking deep into my eyes. He seemed confident in his response. "Of us?"

He hesitated, but then nodded. "Yeah. But I try not to think about all that stuff. All the things that freak me out, there ain't no good in thinking about them."

"I know you're right, I just…I haven't been in a relationship for so long. I'm not even sure how they really work anymore. It's just always been so much easier to be friends, and…"

"Don't think that way. We are friends, Scarlett. We'll always be friends first."

"I know, but…"

"You put too much pressure on yourself, Scar. And the last thing I want to be in your life is another source of stress. Us being together, it really doesn't have to be so complicated. We're friends, and…we love each other. And we're here for each other, right?"

A smirk started to spread across my face, and Henry smiled. He shook me. "Right?" he asked.

"Yes."

"Okay then. Stop stressing out about little things."

But me returning to New York at some point seemed far from being a little obstacle for the two of us. The only comfort I found in Henry's words—we'll always be friends first.

He leaned closer to me and placed a kiss on my lips, his hand moving to the side of my face as he did. I grabbed onto his hand and turned it over to study his palm, but when his fingers interlocked mine, I became focused on the state of them being together.

His hands, so much bigger and worn than mine. My hand looked delicate, fragile in his grasp. "Your hands are so small," he laughed.

"No, yours are just big."

"Bigger than yours, which doesn't seem that hard to pull off."

"You know what they say about big hands, right?"

He sighed. "Uh…big gloves?"

I laughed. "Yes, baby."

I had more fun with Henry that night just laying there, talking with him about absolutely nothing. And when he fell asleep, I admired him. Admired how beautiful he looked to me, admired his strength, his sunny disposition. Damaged my ass, I thought. Kate had him all wrong, and the thought escaped my mind completely over the next couple of weeks though. Henry seemed far from damaged. Actually, one of the more well-adjusted men I ever had the pleasure to be with. Nothing phased him. He always had a solution for everything. And not just when it came to the house either.

Though I grew frustrated with the constant repairs needing to be done. Small things like loose floorboards, leaking windows, the water heater. But Henry always fixed those things for me. I suspect he even started fixing things before I noticed because things stopped breaking after a while. At least it seemed that way.

But aside from the home repairs, Henry always knew what I needed at every second. Whether I needed food, comfort, to be left alone. I hardly ever had to say those things to him, he just knew. He brought me flowers every week. Told me I was beautiful every day. Always said how lucky he felt to have someone like me.

I took Henry's words seriously—about him wanting to believe me when I told him I wanted more. So every day, I did everything I could to prove to him he made the right decision in taking a chance with me. Whether I made him dinner, cuddled up with him after he had a long day of work, massage him when he grew sore.

I told him I loved him every day because I think he needed to hear it. I told him that he was my best friend, that I trusted him, felt safe with him. And I never, ever turned him down when he needed a bit more affection. Just like he never turned me down. Mostly because any mention of it got me ready to go within seconds. Hell, even just kissing him got me going.

I loved making love to him. Henry always seemed so appreciative every time. The way he looked at me, it seemed as though he'd been waiting an eternity to touch me even if it had only been a few hours. He would look upon my naked body in wonderment. Like it was the first time all over again.

I loved him. I loved pleasuring him. I loved the way his eyes grew tender anytime I touched him. I loved how gentle his hands were—hands that work so hard to keep food on the table. I loved the way he moaned, the way his abdomen would tremble beneath my lips when I went down on him. I loved the way he begged for me with only his eyes. And the way he said "I love you." As if it were always some kind of confession that he'd been keeping inside much too long.

He soon became the anchor I needed to keep my feet on the ground. The only thing to keep me from floating away, forever becoming lost in my own darkness. The darkness that I used to revel in because I thought it made me unique. A quality I thought the two of us shared. But after being with him—sublimely happy with him, I realized that perhaps we weren't meant to traverse the darkness together. Perhaps we were meant to save each other from it.

My insecurities about the relationship never faded. Complications on the horizon were impossible to avoid. Like me having to return to New York when they finished the house. Or what to do about my career—something that became increasingly difficult to focus on. Because all I ever wanted to do, was be with Henry.

"Baby!" I screamed and jumped into his arms, interrupting his conversation with Nate.

Henry seemed all too thrilled to hold on to me, my legs wrapped around him. He kissed me, smiling widely through the exchange. "Good morning," he said in his quiet, raspy voice.

"Good morning," I cooed and kissed him again. He tasted like mint. I ran my hands through his hair, inhaling him deeply. "Mmmm…you want some coffee?"

"Nah, I'm good." Again, he kissed me and placed me back on the ground. "What do you think?" he asked, tipping his head to the fresh coat of paint on the side of the house.

"I love it."

"Yeah?" he asked while pulling me into him again. I nodded, grinning widely. He kissed my forehead. "Why don't you go put some pants on. Your ass is hangin' out your shorts."

I chuckled. "What, you don't like it?"

He smirked. "Nah, I do. I think the guys probably like it too."

Gross. I obliged, and Henry affectionately smacked my ass as I left the men to their work. Though it was the first time I started feeling anxious about the progress of the house. In the beginning, I felt as though the crew moved too slow. That I'd be stuck in Devil's Elbow for an eternity, never able to shake myself of my burdens that my parents forced upon me.

Now it seemed they moved too fast, and I became fearful of the decision that lay ahead. Decisions about the house, about the practice, my life in New York. My Henry.

A long distance relationship seemed too absurd, though I'd be willing if it's what Henry wanted. We never spoke about it though. The conversation never came up, and I started to wonder if he preferred it that way. Though we couldn't avoid it forever.

In the kitchen, I fell into a trance while brewing myself a pot of coffee. I welcomed the sweet aroma as it seemed to carry promises of a fresh, new day. A day full of possibilities, good things to happen between Henry and I. Even him being outside painting, made me feel comforted and happy.

Dog started barking from outside, and when I leaned over to glance out the window, Quinn's car stopped in front of the house. Shit, I thought. The last time we spoke was the day I found out Max vandalized the practice, and even then it was all business and awkward as hell. I never apologized for hitting him, but he never apologized for his shitty comment about my parents. So I became suspicious of him being there.

I opened the door before he had a chance to knock, but his vulnerable expression made me retreat my pointed glare. “Quinn?”

“Hey Scarlett,” he mumbled. “The house looks great.”

I nodded. “Everything all right?”

He hesitated, but a smirk crept across his face, though he did seem ashamed for his amusement. “Can we talk inside for a moment?”

Curious. I pushed the door open for him to enter.

The two of us sat at the dining room table with coffee in silence for a moment. I studied him, trying to figure him out. He seemed enlightened in some way. In a happier mood than usual. He smiled and touched the petals of the bouquet of flowers Henry brought me the day before. A beautiful assortment of wild flowers sitting proudly in the vase that had been empty since returning home.

“These are nice,” ~~he said~~.

“Is there something you wanted to say?” I asked.

Quinn’s smile faded. He paused for a moment, seeming uncomfortable. I don’t think I ever witnessed someone being so entertained yet disturbed at the same time. “I heard about you…deciding to keep the practice.”

“Of course you did.”

“I wanted to say thank you,” he said. “I know you had reservations about being a business owner, but…I think its what your dad would want.”

I sighed. Surely something else plagued his mind. He could have sent a messenger to say thank you. “Well, I’m going to do my best. Probably just offer financial support because I don’t know what I’m doing. But you have something else on your mind, don’t you?”

Quinn shifted in his seat and sighed. He hung his head. "Doctor Wilson wants you to buy him out," he said. "I guess…he doesn't want to deal with the hassle of having an—sorry to say—an inexperienced business partner."

"How much does he want?" I asked.

"Two-fifty."

Jesus Christ. "A quarter of a million dollars, fuck my life."

"You don't have to do it, Scarlett. But, I wouldn't count on him being any help to the practice if you don't give him what he wants."

"No shit."

Though I never relished the idea of being in business with Doctor Wilson, I had the comfort of an experienced business man. Someone who knew everything about not only the business, but years of experience in dentistry as well.

And then the idea of having to pay a quarter of a million dollars to get rid of him made me sick, though the only reason I considered was because I knew Quinn had a point. The lingering possibility that Doctor Wilson would not only be uncooperative, but that he even might go as far as trying to run us into the ground, made me consider paying him the ungodly amount. To which I might not be so helpful as an investor to the practice.

CHAPTER TWENTY-ONE:

THAT EVENING, HENRY AND I SOAKED in my beautiful claw foot tub together. A moment of relaxation needed after his hard day of work and my hard day of being myself. We lit a few candles, giving the room a nice, warm, romantic glow. We sat across from each other, and in between us, Henry set up my father's old chess set on the soap rack.

My father taught me to play chess years ago, though years ago was the last time I played. Henry seemed familiar enough with the game, but the two of us hardly paid any attention. Really, just sort of blindly moving pieces and stealing each other's when necessary. No strategy involved. At least not for me.

"He wants me to pay two-hundred and fifty thousand to buy him out," I said while moving my knight.

"Jesus," Henry muttered. He considered his next move. "You got that kind of money?"

I sighed. "Not really."

I did have the money. I inherited two million dollars from my parents' life insurance, but that money remained untouched, stashed away with hardly any intentions of being spent unless push came to shove. To me, it was blood money.

I stole his rook and tossed the piece aside. "I have to pay him though. If I don't, I really believe he's going to do something shady. Something to ruin the practice."

"He sounds like a real asshole."

I laughed. "That's putting it mildly." Henry moved his knight along the board, but my mind remained distant. Not focused on the game at all. "Maybe I should just sell."

"Nah. You're doing the right thing."

"But what am I going to do as the sole owner of a dental practice? I don't know anything about business or…dentistry."

"So you learn," he said while leaning back in the tub. His eyes intently focused on me and a cool smirk spreading across his face. I loved looking at him in candlelight. The way the flames danced upon his face, lighting him just enough to detect the perfections of his form. "You're smart. I imagine you'll catch on pretty quickly."

His compliment touched me, though it hardly made me feel any better about the decisions I had to make. I groaned. "I don't know how I'm supposed to run the business from New York."

"New York?" he asked. I moved my rook.

My eyes grew tender. I never liked talking about that with Henry, but I had no other options. "I have to go back at some point. If I pay Doctor Wilson that money, I…need to start working again. It'll only be a matter of time before I'm broke. And the longer I'm out of work, the harder it'll be to get back into it."

"What about profits from the practice?" he asked.

I scoffed. "Profits, what profits? A dental office in a small town isn't exactly a booming business. It's gonna take up most the profits just to maintain the place. And hire a new dentist. At least with my dad, he knew about business. Hell, he could run that place on his own."

Henry averted his eyes to the chess board. They became concentrated. "You should just ask Quinn to sign a power of attorney. At least for now while you figure out what you're gonna do." He moved his knight to steal my rook.

I considered. While not a terrible idea, it still didn't resolve the financial problems I faced after paying Doctor Wilson. I tried to focus back on the moment, not wanting to squander any second I had with Henry on the things that plagued my mind.

I moved my bishop to get his king in check.

Henry chuckled. "Scarlett…you can't do that."

"Why not?" I asked, studying the board.

"The bishop can only move diagonal," he said.

I scoffed. "You're just saying that so I don't steal your king."

Henry laughed. "Baby, it's the rules."

Lies. Or perhaps not. Either way, chess lost all its allure, if it ever had any to begin with. I bulldozed his king into the water with my bishop. "There, sort that out."

Henry stared at me, his smirk fading from his face. "I'll take care of you, Scarlett. You know that, don't you?"

If only, I thought. True, I believed Henry to take care of me emotionally, spiritually, physically, but financially? I was more inclined to take care of him, though I became stubborn. The idea of spending any dime of my parents' life insurance money made me sick. But with my financial gains dwindling since the renovations, it seemed I would soon be out of options. Unless I returned to work. But then I'd be away from Henry.

"You ready to dry off and go to bed?" I asked.

"You tired?"

I grinned and shook my head. "No."

A wry smile spread across his face.

Henry did well to distract me for the remainder of the evening, but the next morning, my mind raced with any and all options I had. Upon looking at my father and Doctor Wilson's partnership agreement, I realized that most of the responsibility fell on Doctor Wilson—no doubt because my father wanted to retire soon.

I suggested to him that I just take on his burden. That I assume the role in which my father hired him to carry out—assuming all responsibilities and liabilities therein. But he refused. And he managed to point out that because the partnership agreement had been between him and my father—it didn't apply to our partnership.

I chastised myself for not seeking a lawyer early on. Even though at the time, I had every intention of selling, it would have behooved me to renegotiate the terms of the partnership. By the way

Doctor Wilson acted, I knew it wouldn't be possible to simply dissolve the partnership. I had to pay him. Not a quarter of a million dollars, I thought.

So I hired an evaluation consultant. His job proved vital in determining the business worth and projected profits. Basically anything Doctor Wilson would be walking away from. And upon finishing the evaluation, my consultant told me that a quarter of a million dollars seemed reasonable enough. That he could actually ask for ~~me~~ more if he wanted.

I told Henry everything. I kept him informed, mostly because I felt like I started losing all control. And even though he had no words of wisdom—nothing could be done—Henry remained supportive. He tried convincing me that money meant nothing, and all that mattered was getting Doctor Wilson out of the picture.

Easy for him to say. He wasn't the one writing a check for a quarter of a million dollars. A quarter of a million dollars being taken from the sanctity of my parents' life insurance policy. My heart broke at the thought.

On top of those expenses, I hired an acquisitions lawyer to assure Doctor Wilson would play fair. Nothing shady between the two of us, and once I paid him, he'd be gone for good—unable to claim any sort of success or finances from the business. By the time everything was said and done, I felt broken.

"Henry," I called while stepping off the porch. Dog bolted out from between my legs, almost knocking me over in the process.

The house, almost complete, and a few months ago I never would have dreamt of pulling him away from his work at such a crucial time. "You okay?" he asked

"I need you to come with me," I said.

Henry glanced at the house, considering for a moment. His crew, continuing to work despite my attempts to pull their boss away. "You going to meet the lawyer?"

I nodded and folded my arms. "I have to sign the paperwork. And write the check to Doctor Wilson. I need you there with me."

He nodded. "All right. Gimme a second, let me talk to Joe."

Henry and I entered the practice, and I became vulnerable. The first time ever in my life I entered the practice and didn't feel empowered. I hesitated to even enter the back. I avoided Quinn and the receptionist's thoughtful gazes. I wanted to appear strong to them—though I felt anything but strong.

Henry grabbed my hand. "Come on," he said.

In Doctor Wilson's office, the lawyer went over the terms of the dissolved partnership. Basically, Doctor Wilson had no claim to anything. No possibility of return, no further financial obligations either. On top of that, he couldn't be held responsible for anything. Even if something happened during his time as boss. Something he included, and I felt sick at the possibility of him keeping something from me.

The two of us signed. Now, I had to write the check.

I hesitated. My pen started shaking over the signature line.

"Everything all right?" Doctor Wilson asked, though not in a comforting way. In a condescending, humored way.

I wanted to cry. Though Henry's tender eyes kept me from doing so. He seemed concerned. I felt his hand on my back. "You don't have to do this, Scar."

"Yes, she does," Doctor Wilson said.

Henry ignored. He brought his hand to my face. "I love you no matter what. I'll be here no matter what, sweetheart."

The only encouragement I needed. I signed the check—begrudgingly—and handed it over to Doctor Wilson. Though I'd be lying if I said I didn't hold on a bit longer, hoping the thing would just tear in half from our game of tug o' war.

I released it though, and a smug smile spread across Doctor Wilson's face. "Good girl."

"Don't do that to her," Henry muttered. "You got what you wanted, so just keep your comments to yourself and get out."

Though Henry's defense of my dignity impressed me, Doctor Wilson seemed unaffected. He smiled and stood from behind his desk. My desk now, I guess. "Very well." He extended his hand to me. "Pleasure doing business with you." While clenching my hand, Doctor Wilson glanced to Henry—clearly put off by him being there.

"You can do better, Scarlett. I'm sure your father would have thought so."

Henry stood, scooting his chair back while he did, and I assumed the role of emotional support in that moment. I grabbed onto his arm and pulled him down, though he kept his eyes on Doctor Wilson, ready to attack if he felt the need to continue with his insults.

"Doctor Wilson, please leave now," I said, exasperated.

The doctor smiled and nodded. He exited the room with the lawyer, leaving Henry and I in awkward silence, unsure of how we should comfort each other.

That evening, Henry retired to his house, which seemed odd. The two of us had practically been inseparable since we became a couple, and I started to wonder if his want to spend the evening alone had more to do with what Doctor Wilson said than just wanting to go to bed early. Even though I had my own problems to worry about, my mind fixated on Henry.

I tried calling him, but he never answered.

I decided to go see him. As much as I tried giving him his space, I couldn't rest until I knew things were fine between us. Again, I brought Dog with me for moral support. In case I had a run-in with Max, I wanted him there.

I pulled into the small clearing in front of Henry's, the only light illuminating the dark forest surrounding me and the shack was the porch light. There, Henry sat, smoking a cigarette. Max, nowhere in sight along with Henry's truck.

I let Dog jump over me to start sniffing around the yard, and when I exited the vehicle, I noticed that Henry looked despondent. "Hey," I said while walking up the porch steps.

"You look nice," he said quietly.

I put a little effort into my appearance. A dress and some makeup, though my hair remained a wavy mess. Still, I liked to look pretty for him whenever I could. Especially when I knew something bothered him.

"Thank you," I said and took the seat next to him. An old, splintered stool, hardly comfortable on my bare legs. "Are you okay?"

Henry nodded and flicked his cigarette into one of the butt cans. "Just thinking about some things," he muttered.

"Me?" I asked, nervous to hear his answer.

He stared at me for a moment. "Yeah, baby. I'm always thinking about you."

I hardly found it to be a good sign though. When someone says they're thinking about you, but they appear sad, it doesn't give much promise to their train of thought.

"I'm sorry for just showing up. I tried calling you, but…"

Henry shook his head. "Yeah, my phone's inside. And you don't have to be sorry, you're always welcome here."

Dog continued to sniff around the yard, occasionally stiffening up at the sound of something within the woods. "Everything all right?" Henry asked.

"Yeah, I was just…worried about you."

"Worried about me?" he asked.

He knew what I meant, but Henry tried to be strong in every situation. Something that I used to find admirable, but now I found it unnecessary. "You seemed…bothered by what Doctor Wilson said earlier. You know I don't care what he thinks, right?"

Henry shook his head. “It’s not that. I don’t care about his opinion of us.”

“So…what?”

He sighed and hung his head. “I dunno, Scar. What he said about your dad, it got me thinkin’. Got me wonderin’ if your parents would have wanted you to be with me. A poor man from Devil’s Elbow, hell—I don’t think I’d want my daughter with someone like me.”

“That’s stupid. My parents, they…loved you…”

“You wouldn’t know. They never even talked about me to you before. Maybe to them, I was just some blue collar worker. Hired help or some shit like that.”

The mention of my parents saddened me, and I started to wonder what they would think about everything. About the practice and about Henry. But none of it mattered. I shrugged and shook my head, my eyes burning from tears fighting to break free.

“They’re gone, Henry. And I miss them every day, but…I also know that they would want me to be happy.”

“They’d want you to be taken care of too…”

I scoffed. “So…what then? You’re breaking up with me?”

He seemed taken aback by my words. “What? Nah, I just…I got nothing to offer you…”

I stood, silencing him. I grabbed onto his hand, and he watched me, confused. “I only want you, Henry. Nothing else.”

He hung his head. He wasn’t convinced. I brought his hand to my lips and kissed his fingertips gently, and he looked up at me. He ran his thumb over my lips, and in his eyes, I saw unconditional love. And fear.

I leaned over and kissed his lips. Soft and sweet, though it seemed he felt undeserving of my kisses. He held back, something out of character for him as of late. I ran my tongue over his lips, but he barely reciprocated any sort of passion.

Dog remained at the tree line, still sniffing about, completely unaware of our actions. I climbed on top of Henry, straddling him, pushing him back into his seat while I pressed my lips onto his again. He opened his mouth for me, and I welcome the taste of him. He tasted so sweet to me. I inhaled his breath as he exhaled through the kiss. And when I grinded myself on top of him, Henry quivered.

"You know I care about you," I whispered against his lips.

He swallowed hard and nodded. "I know you do. I'm just scared you're gonna wake up some day and realize you deserve better."

I shook my head and kissed his forehead. How he could ever think such a thing was beyond me. But I'd excited him too much in that moment. He brought his hand to the back of my head and forced my lips back onto his.

Finally, his passion broke through. He grabbed a fistful of my hair and held my mouth against his, his tongue running against mine, warm, wet, messy, intoxicating. His other hand moved up my thigh, and when he reached my backside, he pulled his lips away from me to look down at me, straddling him.

"Jesus Christ," he quivered. "You're not wearing underwear, are you?"

I shook my head. "No."

He panted against my face. His cheeks turned red, his eyes hazy. "Fuck me, Scarlett," he said, desperate, and I wanted to. I wanted to show him that I loved him, that I found him to be the perfect man to me. I needed to prove to him that what Doctor Wilson said had no affect on me whatsoever. That I would love him no matter what.

I undid his jeans, freeing him from them. And when Henry entered inside me, a booming groan exited his mouth. He held me close while I rode him. Held on as tight as he could. It seemed as though he hadn't relieved himself in a few days because within a few minutes, he couldn't control the sound of his pleasure. "Scarlett..." he panted. "You drive me crazy."

I ran my fingers through his hair and grabbed a fistful to pull his head back. I devoured him, everything he had to give me. I wanted every part of him forever. The feeling of him so deep inside of me sent a wave of heat through my body and made my heart race.

The excitement I felt while being so connected to him, so intimate with him—it never changed. Never faded, never dulled over time. Each time with him seemed like the first all over again, and he did well to make me feel desired.

I grabbed onto the back of his chair for leverage while crashing my body onto his, his hands guiding me up and down on him while he threw his head back and moaned loudly. I buried my face into his neck. That scent of his, it tormented me, and I never felt I had enough of him. Our bodies pressed together, rubbing together, us panting against one another—both of us radiating heat. We became unclean—tainted by our own desires.

"Scarlett..." he panted.

My lips hovered over his. "Henry, I love you."

And only moments after that, he came.

"Oh...oh, baby..." he moaned and buried his head into my chest, breathing heavily against my breasts. He held me in place for a while maintaining a firm grip on my ass until he had enough strength to pick his head up and kiss me. "Stay with me," he whispered.

His request, I found somewhat surprising. Henry never suggested we stay at his house. I never even went inside before, but the longing in his eyes, the vulnerability inside of him—needing comfort and reassurance that I wanted to be with him—I agreed.

His house—just as I expected—was a dump, through no fault of his own. We entered into the living room. Wood paneled walls and brown, shag carpet did nothing to welcome us, and the couch along with an arm chair was tattered and torn. The coffee table, faded and worn with beer cans scattered about and an ashtray full of cigarette butts. A small, boxed television rested on a makeshift entertainment stand, and a lamp on an end table gave the room a dull, yellow glow.

"Sorry about the mess. Max never cleans up after himself."

"Where is Max?" I asked.

"Oh, he's just…out with some friends," he muttered and grabbed my hand to pull me down a hallway to our left.

The rest of the house remained dark, something that suited me just fine. I hated seeing the way my Henry lived. Almost in poverty, it seemed. He opened a door at the end of the hallway, and we entered his bedroom.

Much neater than the living room, and the smell was alluring. It smelled like him, but with a hint of air freshener. The obscure kinds that never really smell like their label. Like "Summer Breeze" or "Fresh Rain," or some crap like that. Still, I found the smell enjoyable.

Henry's room, nowhere near the size of my own. Small and claustrophobic, the same wood paneling and shag carpet in the living room. His bed, much smaller than mine as well, though neatly made with a solid, blue comforter. No headboard. Just a mattress on a frame, and two pillows that were so thin, they could hardly be considered as such.

I sat on the edge of his bed. Henry removed his shirt and tossed it aside before pulling out one of the drawers on an old dresser in the corner of the room. The dresser had scrapes and scratches along the wood, and a few of the drawers were missing entirely.

"Do you want something to change into?" he asked.

I shook my head. "I'll just sleep naked."

Henry smirked. "Well, I got no problems with that."

He started to put on a clean shirt, but I reached my hands for him. "No," I whined. I pulled him closer to me. "Sleep naked with me."

He leaned over the bed and kissed me. "Okay," he whispered.

I pulled Henry onto the bed with me, and for a moment, it seemed as though he forgot all about Doctor Wilson's rude comment about him.

The sound of thunder disturbed our tender moment though, and I sat upward.

"What?" Henry asked.

"Dog's still outside."

The two of us laughed at our irresponsibility. I guess MY irresponsibility, but I got up and made my way out to the front porch.

"Dog!" I yelled while pushing the rusty screen door open, once again entering into the humid, spring night. The porch light gave a slight glow to the land before me, but the forest lining remained dark. "Dog! Come here, boy!" I called.

I stepped off the porch and searched the area as best I could, keeping quiet for a moment to hear which part of the yard he might be sniffing around. Though I heard nothing. Just the sound of wind rusting the trees and crickets buried within the forest.

I became concerned. The sound of the rusty, screen door assured me Henry came to the rescue. I shrugged and shook my head to him, and he became fixated on the darkness before us, his eyes narrowing while attempting to find my mutt.

"Dog!" he yelled and then whistled with the ferocity of a rebel yell.

We heard nothing, but the wind blew harder. Another crash of thunder in the distance made me feel uneasy. "Dog!" I yelled and made my way to the trees.

"Scarlett!" Henry yelled.

I pushed through the trees and walked further into the darkness of the forest. My eyes started to adjust to the darkness within, though I only managed to see about a foot in front of me in either direction. “Dog!” I yelled.

The rusting of leaves and crunching footsteps coming up behind me kept me in place, knowing that Henry could be useful in that situation. Henry grabbed on to me. “What’re you doing?” he asked.

“Do you have a flashlight?”

Henry sighed. “Scarlett, it’s the middle of the night. You can’t just go wandering through the woods…”

“Dog’s out there,” I snapped.

“Yeah, and he was a stray before you found him.”

I knew searching for Dog without Henry’s help would be futile. The woods, an unfamiliar place to me, and Henry seemed discontent with the idea. “He’ll be fine, he’s probably just chasing after a coon or something.”

“There’s a storm coming, Henry,” I whined.

“Baby, listen to me,” he said while pulling me into him. “It’s too dark to be out here; we’re too close to the river. Dog’s smart, he ain’t gonna go get himself killed…”

“Oh my God…”

“I said he’s not. Come on, let’s just go wait for him on the porch. If he’s not back by morning, I’ll take you into the damn woods myself and we’ll find him.”

As much as I hated the idea of leaving my mutt out in the woods to fend for himself, Henry had a point. The forest, although a sight to be admired during the day, presented dangers and obstacles unseen at night. Coyotes, snakes, the river. I hated the idea of Dog being out there alone. But he had been a stray before finding me. The only comfort I had.

Henry brought out a blanket from inside, knowing I found it difficult to just retire to bed with Dog being gone. The two of us huddled together—not for warmth—but for comfort. He rested his head on my shoulder, but I kept a watchful eye out for my mutt, counting the seconds between each crash of thunder to try and determine how long we had before the rainfall. Surely one of the last before summer.

CHAPTER TWENTY-TWO:

THE NEXT MORNING, DOG HADN'T RETURNED. The rain had yet to make an appearance, but the mugginess of the morning air led me to believe that it would only be a matter of time.

Henry did as he promised an escorted me through the woods, looking for any sign of my mutt. The second time I'd been in the woods in a dress with no underwear, and I chastised myself for my reckless lifestyle and poor decisions.

We walked through the forest, quiet and careful, pausing to listen closer to any sound we heard. Though the more we walked, the closer we got to the river. I could smell it, I could hear it, I could almost taste it, and I grew concerned that my poor mutt might have fallen victim to it at some point in the night.

"Dog!" Henry yelled and then whistled. "Come here, boy!"

We waited impatiently. The sound of a stick snapping in the distance sent my heart into my throat, but Dog never revealed himself. I grew disheartened. Henry approached me from behind and brought his hand to my waist.

"Come on," he said.

We continued to walk. I no longer recognized the area around us, but Henry led the way, confident in his ability to navigate the woods. He'd grown up in those woods, and I assumed it was the same as him navigating in his own house.

We trudged through the forest for about an hour, but Henry continually looking up at the sky. "It's gonna start raining soon," he said. "We should head back."

"Not without Dog," I muttered while pushing past him.

"He might be back at your parents," Henry said.

I considered. But when I heard the sound of a dog barking in the distance, I knew it was him. I took off running. "Dog!" I yelled, hopeful. Perhaps he'd hear and meet me halfway.

"Scarlett!" Henry called.

I ran as fast as I could, fearing every second that he might be in some sort of distress. The sound of his barks became louder. I jumped over rocks, logs, pushed leaves out of the way—impressed with my own ability to navigate during such a stressful situation.

I emerged from the woods and entered a clearing. The sound of the dog barking intensified, and when my eyes fell on a Rottweiler, chained to a post and out for blood, I jumped back. "Shit!" I cursed at the sight of the thing jumping at me.

It hadn't been Dog. It hadn't been my mutt at all. I wanted to cry at the sight of the angry beast chained to his post. A post that looked as if it wouldn't hold much longer.

A trailer sat before me, one that looked rusted, almost completely caved in. The sound of a staticky radio playing gospel music slightly detectable over the dog's hateful barking.

Though far from hunting season, a buck suspended upside down with his innards spilling onto the ground made me highly skeptical of the people residing in the trailer. The smell, awful. The poor animal baking in the heat, giving off something putrid—the sort of smell one would only associate with something evil.

"Scarlett!" Henry yelled as he ran up behind me. He grabbed my arm. "You can't just go runnin' off like that..."

The door to the trailer kicked open, and a middle-aged man exited, pointing a shotgun at us. I became paralyzed at the sight. Never in my life had I ever had a gun pointed at me, and I wasn't sure how to navigate the situation.

Henry pulled me back and stepped in front of me, but it didn't do much to ease my fear.

"Y'all are trespassing!" the man yelled while stepping down to level ground.

"She didn't know," Henry said.

The man approached, hate in his eyes. He kept his shotgun pointed at us, ready to blow our heads off at any wrong move. Henry held his hands up in retreat, and I clenched his shirt. I always knew

Devil's Elbow had questionable inhabitants, but it all seemed a bit extreme.

"All right, take it easy. We're leaving. Come on, Scarlett…"

With the Rottweiler's incessant barking though, I found it difficult to put my own mutt aside. Perhaps the man had seen him at some point.

"Ask him about Dog," I muttered.

"What?" Henry asked, stunned.

I pleaded with him without having to say a word. Surely the man wouldn't shoot because of a question, I thought.

Henry considered. "Have you seen a Catahoula Cur wanderin' about?" he asked.

"I ain't seen nothin'," the man spat, his shotgun still pointing directly at us. "Now go on, get!" he yelled and spit a bit of chaw, though it seemed he'd had enough of his dog's barking. "Shut it!" he hollered and kicked the dog, causing the hound of hell to whimper and cower beneath him.

"What's all that racket!" a woman from inside the trailer yelled. The door swung open once more, and the middle-aged woman appeared in the doorway, a bloodied apron draped around her. I felt the urge to vomit at the sight, though I attempted to maintain a friendly demeanor.

Even without a shotgun in tow, the woman's hateful stare seemed almost a scarier thing than the twelve gauge in the man's hand. She looked at me like she'd never seen such a sight before. Like I was scum, beneath her class. "You," she said. "What're you doin' here?"

I hesitated. "I'm just looking for my dog…"

"I know what you're doin' here," she spat, and when she moved toward me, I cowered behind Henry. "We will not fall victim to your evil ploy. God is strong with us, and because of him, we cannot be tempted."

"Tempted?" I asked.

"I see the devil in your eyes, girl. I can smell him on you. You're one of his," she spat.

"A whore of Satan," the man said, stunning me.

Henry started walking me back to the forest lining, keeping himself in front of me the entire time. The couple watched us, and I became terrified that they would sacrifice me to God. God damn bible thumpers. And why was Henry so innocent?

"You better watch yourself, boy. Satan disguises himself as an angel of the light," the man said as we reached the forest lining, not far enough away to turn our backs to them yet.

"Do not let your heart turn to her ways or stray into her paths. Many are the victims she has brought down; her slain are a mighty throng!" the woman yelled.

"Scarlett, go," Henry said, and I entered the forest once again.

Once out of their sight, the two of us started running. We ran for what felt like forever, fearing that the backwoods couple might come to kill us. No one would ever know in Devil's Elbow. Not until it was too late.

When we reached the bank of the river, I felt relieved. The first time I ever felt such a thing when coming face to face with my parents' killer. I stopped running and leaned over to catch my breath, my heart racing from the events.

"You all right?" Henry asked.

I waved my hand at him. "I'm good," I said through heavy breaths. I stood upright and brought my arms above my head—trying to open my lungs a bit. "Jesus, what was that?"

"Backwoods folks." Henry hardly seemed phased by all the running as he waited for me to catch my breath.

"Why did they call me a whore?" I asked.

Henry shrugged. "Those kinds of people, they think any woman who isn't covered from head to toe is a whore. I wouldn't take it personally." Henry hung his head and sighed. "Look, I'm sorry I didn't say nothin' back there when they said that…"

I scoffed. "That man had a shotgun pointed at you. I would have smacked you upside the head if you felt the need to defend my honor back there."

Henry chuckled. Though hardly the occasion for laughter, I smiled at the sight of him finding humor in our misfortunate afternoon. I felt raindrops on my face. The sight of the river suddenly had no comfort whatsoever, and I knew that if the rain continued, by the end of the day, the river would rise up and engulf the land, something far more evil and sinister than the bible thumping couple in which we encountered.

"Come on, let's get out of here."

By the time we made it back to Henry's the rain stopped—a teaser for the brutal storm ahead as rain clouds remained in the sky. We had yet to find Dog, a more terrifying realization knowing that the storm would hit.

When we walked into the clearing, Henry's truck came into view, along with Max exiting the vehicle, glaring at me. "Henry!" he called while walking toward the house. "You ready?"

Henry waved. "Yeah, just…gimme a sec."

Ready for what? Henry turned to me, his eyes concerned. "Look, I'm going out of town tonight," he said, stunning me.

I hesitated. "Going out of town? Where are you going?"

"Max asked me to come with him to meet some friends. I told him I would."

Again, I hesitated, confused by the situation. Henry never mentioned it last night. And while I'm not the controlling type, his horrible timing annoyed me. "But…Dog's still out there…"

"He knows his way home, Scarlett. Trust me, he'll come back when he's ready."

I had nothing to say. I felt angry, though unsure if I had reason to be—actually—so I kept my mouth shut. But keeping my displeasure hidden from my face proved to be a fool's errand.

Henry moved into me and brought his hand to my face. "Hey…I don't know if I'll be home tomorrow. If the storm hits, we won't be able to make it back until the roads clear."

"So don't go," I said quietly. Though I sounded pathetic, and I resented him for bringing out the "clingy girlfriend" in me.

"I have to, baby." He moved his hands to my waist. "Look, go on home. Take a nice, hot bath. I'll stop by before we head out. Bring you supplies for the storm."

I remained displeased, though I nodded. Henry kissed my forehead and pulled me into a tight hug, breathing me in deeply as he did. "I'll see you in a bit."

When I returned home, Dog was nowhere in sight. I walked around the house, calling for him, checking the stables and garage for him, but he never appeared. I ~~started to~~ fear for his safety, but Henry's words remained front and center. "He'll come home when he's ready," I told myself. "He was a stray, he'll be fine."

Henry did as he said, and thirty minutes later showed up on my doorstep with a case of water and a bag full of canned food—just in case, he said. Also in the bag, a flashlight, matches, a can of lighter fluid, and a small, heart-shaped box of chocolates.

"I feel awful about leaving you right now," he said while holding me against him.

"I'll be fine," I assured while running my fingers through his hair.

Henry buried his face in my neck, breathing me in deeply, and I started to wonder if he found my scent to be just as addicting as I found his. "I'm gonna call you tonight. You gonna answer?" he asked.

I nodded. "Unless I'm asleep."

Henry chuckled. “Well, wake your ass up, woman,” he said while gripping my backside. I laughed, and he pulled back a bit to look into my eyes. He pushed a bit of hair from my face to better admire me. “My god, you’re so beautiful.”

“Hmmm…just remember what you’re leaving behind,” I said as a jest. Though Henry’s smile faded and he pressed his lips into mine. He kissed me tenderly, holding on to me tight as he did, and I could feel him shaking.

“I love you so much, Scarlett. You know I’ll do anything for you, right?”

I nodded. “I know.”

Outside, Max honked the horn, ruining our perfect moment—his intention, I’m sure, and Henry left me shortly after.

I stood in the kitchen, leaning on one of the counters, deep in thought. Once again, I found myself confined to my home—alone. Completely and utterly alone, something I hadn’t felt since Henry and I started seeing each other. Now with Henry gone and Dog missing, I realized that my depression and anxieties had never really gone away. They just kind of hid away for a bit—distracted by the love I felt for my two mangy boys.

It started raining that night. A mighty downpour, and I knew Henry wouldn’t be home for the next few days.

I became all the more concerned for my mutt. I stood on the porch every hour, calling out to him, but the sound of the rain and thunder overpowered my voice. And I knew that only miles away, The Rubidoux was on a war path, possibly seeking the innocent life of a dog. The thought destroyed me.

I tried to distract myself with small projects around the house. I went through family photo albums and replaced all the pictures of me throughout the home with photos of my parents. I felt it only appropriate. Their dream home nearly finished, the house became a monument to them of sorts. Something far too sacred to sell, despite me having considered after buying the entire practice.

Ugh, the practice weighed on me. I needed to speak with Quinn. I needed to come up with a plan—a course of action. Though the rain would keep me from my duties as owner for the time being. Perhaps not a completely horrible thing.

I grew tired at around ten in the evening, but before retreating to bed, I stood on the porch again and yelled for Dog. The thought of him being caught in the storm broke my heart. I stood out there, at odds with the storm, trying to raise my voice over the sound for nearly thirty minutes. Dog never showed.

That night while laying in bed, I started to cry. Something awful happened, I knew it had. I wanted my dog, and I wanted Henry. Both felt so far away. Henry called that night, but the conversation was short. He asked about Dog, and when I told him he had yet to return, Henry did his best to comfort me.

He told me he loved me, but he seemed discontent. Distant in the way he spoke, almost cold. It seemed something bothered him, though he never said anything.

"Are you having a good time?"

"Nah, not really."

He kept his answers short, his voice lowered. I started to become suspicious, but he ended the conversation before I mustered the courage to ask. Said he'd call me tomorrow to check in and keep me posted about when he'd be coming home.

It rained for two days. I spent the entire time worrying about Dog. I continued to call out to him from the porch, but he never showed. The day it stopped raining, I went looking for him on foot in the forest. A terrifying experience, one that seemed pointless without Henry being there to guide me through.

I walked slowly, cautious of anything I might come in contact with, and I listened carefully, only calling out for Dog every so often when I stopped to scan the area.

Every time I called for him, a moment of relief came over me. Like I knew he would come running out from the trees with each effort I made. But he never did.

For nearly an hour, I walked through the forest, searching for my mutt. The trees and leaves around me, dripping with water from the violent rain fall the day before. The ground, muddy and thick with fallen leaves and branches. The sound and smell of the river, ever-present. I emerged from the tree line and my gaze fell upon the waters of the Rubidoux.

The rushing waters devoured the river bank. Fallen branches moved past me quickly as the water carried them downstream. The water, murky, brown. I imagined Dog being carried away by the current, just like my parents had been. The thought made me anxious, and I could no longer face the beast.

That night, I sat on the back porch, chain smoking, staring out into the darkness of my land. Every second, I spent in anticipation—waiting for my mutt to just come running out of the woods, barking happily, oblivious to how worried he made me. But a black cloud formed over me, and if I became truly honest with myself, I knew Dog was gone.

My phone rang. Henry.

"Hello?" I answered.

"Hey you," he said in his quiet, raspy voice.

Just the sound of his voice made me want to cry. I needed him. "Henry," I cried.

"What's wrong?" he asked.

Tears burned my eyes. I tried to keep them inside—I didn't want to ruin his time—but the fear of never seeing my mutt again forced the floodgates open. "Dog's still…still not back," I cried, my voice quivering, hands shaking as I attempted to hold onto a cigarette.

"Shit," he cursed away from the phone. "All right. I'll be home in the morning."

CHAPTER TWENTY-THREE:

HENRY SHOWED UP WITH MAX at eight o' clock the next morning. A strange sight, Max standing by Henry's truck, waiting for him. Though he seemed discontent to be there, and I didn't blame him. I wondered about Henry's reasoning myself.

"Max knows the woods better than I do. If anyone can find Dog, it's him."

"Why's he helping anyway?" I asked.

"Because I asked him to." Max leaned on Henry's truck bed, glaring at us, his bottom lip protruding from the amount of chaw. "You gonna be all right?" Henry asked.

I became confused. "I'm coming with you…"

He shook his head. "Nah, you need to get some sleep. You look like you haven't slept in days," he said. He wasn't wrong. Though my confidence in Max and Henry dwindled after seeing how tired they both looked as well.

I wanted to ask him what happened when he went out of town. He seemed burdened for some reason, not for my poor mutt. No, Henry didn't seem concerned at all about Dog. Simply appeasing me and my needs by going to look for him.

Sleep seemed to be the best option at that point, so when Henry and Max left I took some cough medicine to knock me out. Sleep proved to be difficult without, if the past two days were any indication. I found no comfort in sleep. My dreams haunted me, and seemed a bit more realistic than most.

I dreamt of the river. I dreamt that I was swimming against the current, but my efforts were useless. The river, so much stronger an opponent, and despite how hard I fought, it kept pushing me downstream. I heard Dog barking, but I couldn't see him. The water seemed so real—so cold that it felt like a million pins and needles stabbed into me.

And then I was pulled under. I don't know what from—perhaps the current or the undertow, but I screamed. I inhaled water, choking myself. And when I gasped for air, I awoke to the sound. I shot upward in bed, panting, coughing. Terrified of my dream but relieved to know that's all it had been. A horrible dream.

The clock read 9 o' clock pm. I grabbed my phone. No missed calls, no text messages. I started to become concerned for Henry, and when I called—straight to voicemail. I felt sick, groggy. The cough medicine put me to sleep but left me with a nasty hangover.

Perhaps I just needed more sleep, but someone knocking on my front door ripped me out of bed quicker than I ever thought possible—especially with wobbly legs.

I opened the door, and Henry stood before me. Though seeing him relieved me, his solemn expression led me to believe something terrible happened.

I hesitated. "Everything okay?" Henry said nothing, and I became even more concerned. I folded my arms, unsure of what to do with my hands or even how to react. "Where's…where's Dog?" I asked.

Henry averted his eyes to the ground. He reached into his back pocket to reveal Dog's collar to me. Though the sight disheartened me, a bit of hope still remained. Perhaps it just got snagged on a tree or something.

"Well…where did you find it?" I asked.

Henry sighed. "Next to the river," he muttered.

I forgot how to breathe in that moment. I tried to convince myself that it just fell off, but the expression on Henry's face seemed too forlorn for me to believe my own thoughts. He handed me Dog's collar, and I studied the thing. Damp, dirty, the thick fabric, frayed and torn. A bit of mud remained on his nametag.

"Scarlett…"

I entered the house, and Henry followed behind. I walked into the kitchen and placed Dog's collar on the counter. I looked to his food bowls. Empty because he hadn't been home.

"Scarlett?" Henry spoke again.

"I, uh…I need to take a shower."

He hesitated. "Your shower's gone, Scarlett. Remember? We took it out to make room for the tub."

I remembered. "My parents' shower then," I said, now feeling like I could deal with anything. Because how much further could I fall?

I felt Henry grab my hand. "Come on," he said and started leading the way upstairs.

We stopped outside of my parents' bedroom, and Henry turned to look at me, as if to ask if this was really what I wanted. I nodded without him having to ask, and Henry opened the bedroom door. He grabbed my hand and pulled me through the dark room and into the bathroom. He closed the door behind us, and only then, turned on the light.

My eyes fell on my own reflection. My hair, a complete mess. My eyes, swollen, and my face, pale. I looked horrid, and I started to wonder if that's how I'd look for the rest of my life. Because my will to put any effort into my appearance faded the day my parents died.

Henry turned on the shower, but I became distracted with the assembly of my parents' personal hygiene products on the vanity counter top. I reached for my mother's face cream. I removed the lid to the lotion, took a small amount onto my finger, and rubbed some on my face. The smell immediately made me sick, but not because I didn't enjoy it. Because it reminded me so much of her. I closed the lid and replaced the lotion back on the counter.

I reached for my father's aftershave, but I knew the smell of him as well had the potential to only make things worse.

I closed my eyes and felt my face contort into something awful. My chest grew tight and my eyes burned. I could still smell my mother. The scent of her—something I hadn't smelled since right after the funeral, overwhelmed me. Before I could exit the room for a bit of relief, my knees buckled and I fell to the ground, sobbing.

"Scarlett," Henry gasped. He grabbed onto me and pulled me into him.

I wrapped my arms around him, burying my face in his neck, bawling the entire time. "I want my mom," I cried. She had a way of making me feel better. I needed her to comfort me about Dog. She always knew exactly what to say.

"I know," Henry said, soothing.

"Henry," I sobbed.

"I'm here, Scarlett…I'm here…"

I felt like losing all control, and just when I thought things couldn't get any worse, I became lightheaded. I started panting, hyperventilating, causing my vision to become blurred. My heart felt like exploding out of my chest, beating harder, faster, and quite irregular.

"Henry…I can't…I can't breathe…" I gasped, panicking more and more. This is what dying must feel like, I thought.

"Shush," Henry whispered. "You're having a panic attack." He grabbed a cloth from the bathroom counter, maintaining contact with me the entire time.

He soaked the cloth and placed it over my forehead and then lowered me back onto the floor. Henry's calm demeanor soothed me. Like he knew something I didn't, unfazed by my death happening before him. Perhaps he knew more about death than myself. Perhaps he knew that this wasn't death.

A had a feeling of impeding demise despite Henry's comforts though. He lay down next to me. He pressed his face against my cheek and wrapped his arm around my abdomen. He kissed my cheek. "It's okay. It's okay, it'll pass."

My breathing started to slow, allowing me to finally take deeper breaths. Shortly after, my heartbeat slowed as well, and the lightheadedness started to fade. Yet I still felt distressed. Broken. I never had a panic attack before now. I started to wonder whether or not Henry suffered from them. He seemed to know exactly what to do when mine hit.

The two of us rested on the cold tile, Henry holding me the entire time. We said nothing. Nothing needed to be said. His company alone sufficed. I started to wonder what he thought of me, completely vulnerable and pathetic.

My breathing finally returned to normal, but I suddenly felt very tired, exhausted from my rapid breaths and grogginess from the cough medicine. "I want to go to bed," I said.

Henry kissed my cheek again. "Okay," he said. "Come on."

The next morning, I awoke alone in my bed. No Dog. No Henry. I immediately felt the urge to cry. Alone again, it seemed. The hole in my heart felt much bigger than before. I felt it grow when my parents died, and now the absence of Dog ripped it open further.

The reminder of my parents really being gone, it felt like a retractor kept my heart open, bleeding out into the rest of my body. Poisoning me and leaving me feeling empty.

For the first time since being with Henry, I wanted to go back to New York. To no fault of his own—Henry wasn't the one I wanted to get away from. I wanted to get away from Devil's Elbow. From the Rubidoux. The beast of a river that now claimed three lives ~~which~~ I cherished.

I heard the faucet being turned on in the bathroom, and I sat up in bed. Henry leaned over the tub, reaching his hand under the rushing water. He looked at me and stood. Asking me to come to him without having to say a word.

I stood next to the tub and in front of Henry. I held my arms up and allowed him to remove my shirt. I reached behind my back to unhook my bra and let it fall to the floor. I pulled my shorts down, and Henry offered his arms to me for balance as I stepped out of them. He guided me to the tub and assisted while I lowered myself into a seated position.

"Is it too hot?" he asked.

I shook my head. "It's perfect."

"Do you need anything?" he asked.

"A cigarette?"

Henry exited the bathroom, leaving me alone in the tub. I started running my hands along the surface of the water, causing ripples to move inward and greet my body. The ripples reminded me of the waves of the ocean. And the current of the river.

I was reminded of my dream. Of how terrifyingly realistic it seemed. I became unnerved. I removed my hand from the water and brought it to my face, turning my head away in an attempt to keep my tears at bay. But when Henry returned, the urge to cry disappeared.

He handed me a cigarette. I put it in my mouth and he lit it for me, and I took a drag. It soothed me, giving me a bit of a head rush, making me feel somewhat high. But when Henry stood, I became concerned. "Don't leave me."

Henry shook his head. "I won't."

He opened the bathroom window and lit his cigarette, staring outside as he did. I wondered what he thought about in that moment. I took another drag of my cigarette. "Did you sleep okay?" he asked.

"For a bit. I dunno, I was kind of afraid to sleep. I had an awful nightmare yesterday while you were out looking for Dog."

"It's no wonder you're having bad dreams after all the shit you've been through."

"I can't believe how real it felt," I said, more to myself than him.

Henry exhaled a cloud of smoke. "Yeah, I've had dreams like that before."

"About drowning?" I asked.

He shook his head. "About falling, mostly. And my mom."

I put out my cigarette in the tub and set the butt aside before grabbing the washcloth from the tub's edge. I submerged it underwater and grabbed a bar of soap from the rack next to me. I started washing my face, my neck, my arms, my chest. I noticed that Henry started watching me. Though when I looked up at him, he diverted his eyes to the ground. His attempt to maintain a gentlemanly demeanor, endearing but unnecessary.

"You can watch me, Henry. I don't mind." He looked at me again but said nothing. I smiled and rinsed the rag. I held it out to him. "Will you do my back for me?"

Henry flicked his cigarette out the window and approached me. He kneeled down next to the tub and took the rag. He dipped it into the water and rung it out while I leaned forward, making it easier for him to reach me.

I felt his hand on my shoulder. Gently, he pressed the rag against my skin, starting at my shoulder and slowly moved in between my shoulder blades. It felt good. Like a massage.

I closed my eyes and exhaled. Something about having your back scrubbed is so soothing. "Do you think Dog is in a better place?" I asked.

"He's not dead, Scarlett." he said while dipping the rag into the water once more and started scrubbing the middle of my back.

"But you don't know."

Henry remained quiet for a moment. I felt him bring the rag into the water to reach my lower back. "Try not to think about it."

Easier said than done. I started to ponder the meaning of a dog's life. People say they aren't self aware. That they're unable to comprehend the world around them as we do. But one thing I was certain of, they understood fear. And the idea of him being afraid, wondering where I was, killed me.

"They say animals don't have souls. That they don't go to heaven or hell. So I guess it's a stretch to hope my parents could look after me for him in heaven."

"Do you believe in heaven?" he asked.

"No, not really. But for their sake, I hope it's real. It's hard to imagine them just no longer existing," I said, knowing that heaven very well might not exist—or life after death full stop. But the strange thing is, you can go your whole life without believing, but once you lose someone you love, you start to consider the possibilities.

Perhaps as a form of self-preservation. It's our fatal flaw as humans, being self-aware. Being able to comprehend such things. A terrible burden to bare, and I started to long for the ignorance of dogs.

Henry handed me the rag, and I watched him stand. "Are you hungry?" I shook my head. "You have to eat," he said. I knew he was right, but I had a tendency to overeat in moments of stress. And with too much food while my stomach was in knots, thinking about the fate of my poor mutt, vomiting seemed like a certainty. Something I didn't want to trouble Henry with. He'd already been babysitting me all night.

"I'm gonna go make you something to eat," he said. "You gonna be all right for a bit?"

As unappealing as food sounded, Henry made up his mind about me eating. Arguing seemed futile. I nodded.

Henry exited the bathroom. I slowly lowered myself further into the tub until water surrounded my ears, cutting off all sound around me except for the sound of my own heartbeat. I stayed there for a moment, staring up at the ceiling.

I held my breath and submerged my head beneath the water, and for the first time in a long time, I felt free to let out my anger and aggression. I screamed, knowing that the water would only muffle the sounds of my cries.

Fascinating how one can emit such a powerful, gut-wrenching expression of emotion and yet no one can hear. Like the water washes us away completely. Washes away our tears, muffles our cries…erases who we are.

That night, Henry and I lie in bed together. He held me close to him, my back pressed into his abdomen. He ran his fingers through my hair, kissing me intermittently, but my thoughts were elsewhere. I wanted to leave Devil's Elbow after what happened to Dog. The pain, the loss—all of it proved to be too much.

"I want to leave, Henry. I want to get out of here. This place, it's so…I feel like it's killing me," I said, and he kissed my cheek.

His body pressed against me and his breath on my cheek kept me warm, comforting me in the only way he knew how. "Where do you want to go?" he asked.

I shrugged. "I dunno. Canada, maybe."

Henry hugged me tighter. He buried his face into my neck and inhaled deeply. "I'll go wherever you want. Don't matter to me. I just wanna be with you."

A strange thought, one I never even considered. He seemed so willing to take off with me, leave his home and his brother behind. Or maybe he thought it to be a game. The sort of game people play when they have no way of ever escaping their lives, so they fantasize about leaving. Dream about where they would go, what they would do.

"You would just…leave your whole life behind for me?" I asked.

"You're my life, Scarlett," he whispered and kissed me again.

The words paralyzed me. I became confused, somewhat put-off by the idea. True, I loved Henry. I loved him with all my heart, but I never thought about our future, not seriously. And now when presented with the idea of leaving, he never even considered saying no to me. Even though I hadn't asked him to come.

"I love you so much," he said. "I'll go anywhere with you. We can…get married, have a baby. I'll get you another dog, if you want."

My skin crawled at the thought of children, and I started to wonder if Henry said these things to comfort me. Thinking that it's something women like to hear. As much as I cared for him, the two of us had only been together for a month. It all seemed so sudden.

Perhaps our age needed to be taken into consideration. Henry was nearing thirty, and my twenty-ninth birthday was right around the corner. Maybe Henry felt as though his window of opportunity to settle down and have kids grew smaller by the day. Something that never crossed my mind.

"Scarlett?"

I hesitated. "No, I don't…want another dog."

And the rest, I had no answer for. No, I didn't want to get married. I never wanted kids. But I felt that dismissing the idea completely could potentially ruin things between Henry and I. And even though I felt far from ready to make that sort of commitment, I believed Henry to be the man I was supposed to end up with. Albeit a little sooner than anticipated by the way he talked. Still, the pressure weighed on me, and I started to feel suffocated.

CHAPTER TWENTY-FOUR:

HENRY AND HIS CREW were set to finish the house the next day. I slept in, not wanting to face the world before I had to. But when two o'clock rolled around, I knew I had to get out of bed. I refused to wallow around the house in self-pity. Things had to be done, moves had to be made. I had to be a business owner.

I left the house around three o'clock, waving to Henry as he called me over. The thought of talking to him terrified me. The things he said the night before, they burdened me. I attributed it to my mind being so messy, so poisoned with horrible thoughts that I wouldn't allow myself to feel happy at the idea of being happy. Like I didn't deserve happiness. Yes, that's what it was.

I needed to de-clutter my mind, organize my life in some way. So I called Quinn and asked for a meeting, but the idea of going to the practice made me feel sick. ~~I'd been feeling sick all day, actually~~. It felt so official, so demanding of myself. And really, I just wanted to talk to someone. So Quinn told me to wait at his house. With Ella.

"Scarlett!" she said after opening the door. She pulled me into a hug. I guess now we were best friends because I decided not to sell. I remained in awe at the sight of their house. Located in one of the nicest neighborhoods in Hunter's Point, the house humbled me.

"Jesus," I said after she released me. "This house…"

Ella smiled. "It's nice, right?"

"How much am I paying Quinn? I feel like it's too much." She hesitated. "I'm kidding," I said. But not really.

The structure, made entirely of white brick, the windows, arched, the front door—some kind of real nice, thick oak. And a two-car garage. "Come on in," she said, waving me inside.

Inside, also much nicer than what I expected the couple to be able to afford. Marble floors, beige walls with crown molding and baseboards. The open layout allowed me to see into the living room, dining room, and part of the kitchen. All of their furniture seemed very classic, mostly made of wood and some fine, Victorian style fabric. All very gaudy—something Quinn must have liked. It seemed very similar to his house growing up.

A one story home, but enormous with four bedrooms and two and a half bathrooms. And each room I found to be very spacious. Much too big for two people. Perhaps they planned to have kids some day. Ugh, children. Henry wanted children.

"Would you like something to drink?" Ella offered.

"Alcohol."

The two of us sat on the back porch with a bottle of white wine. The back yard, well-maintained with short, thick, bright green grass and timed sprinklers. The porch, decorated with outdoor furniture—a table with four chairs, as well as a sofa and two arm chairs.

To the far side of the porch, a very nice stainless steel grill. I started to feel pressured about life after seeing how my peers from school were living. I still lived in a one-bedroom dump in New York City. Perhaps I stopped growing up at some point.

Ella and I conversed about nothing in the beginning, but she sensed something troubling me, and I opened up to her about Dog.

"I don't know for sure if he's dead. I mean, he could still be out there somewhere. You know?" I asked, looking for affirmation of some kind.

Ella nodded, her eyes sympathetic. "Dogs are smart. They can usually sense danger."

Her words, comforting. Her expression, not so much. I sighed and ran my hands over my face, hoping to snap myself out of the nightmare my life had become. "I dunno, I feel like I need to get out of here for a while. Take a vacation or something."

"What about the practice?" she asked.

"That's kind of what I wanted to talk to Quinn about…"

The back door slid open, and Quinn exited looking tired. "Hey ladies," he said and then leaned over to kiss Ella. He took the seat next to her, and I started to wonder why he came home so early. "What a day," he said.

"Close early?" I asked.

He shrugged. "We didn't have anymore appointments. Ever since Doctor Wilson left, scheduling has become kind of a pain in the ass. We're still figuring it out."

"Should we bring on another dentist?" I asked.

"Probably. It's your call now, boss," he said, smirking.

"Let me make you a drink," Ella said while standing. "Scarlett, you need anything?"

I shook my head, and Ella entered the house leaving Quinn and I alone to discuss business. He leaned back in his chair, still seeming rather entertained by something. "So what's up?" he asked. "You said you wanted to talk?"

I considered. "Quinn, I need you to do me a favor."

"Oh yeah?"

"I need you to sign a power of attorney. That way, you can make the decisions on my behalf..."

"I know what a power of attorney does," he interrupted. He leaned forward, his amber eyes burning into mine. "Why?"

"Why? Because I know nothing about the business, that's why. It'll only be for a little while until I get...a handle on everything."

His skeptical expression faded into concern. "Everything all right?"

"Not really. Anyway, I don't think I'm in a position to be making the big decisions. Not yet at least. I want to take some business classes, bring on another dentist...maybe a business manager. But I need you to step in for me while I do that."

He considered for a moment. "All right. But I get paid more, right?"

I rolled my eyes. “Fine, whatever.”

Ella exited and handed a glass of what I assumed to be gin and tonic or maybe some vodka soda. Typical drink for Quinn. She sat next to him, and I looked out to the horizon. The sun would be setting soon, and the idea of facing Henry made me nauseous. Like he’d want to talk about what he said last night.

“You going back to New York?” Quinn asked.

I sighed. “I don’t…know. I don’t know what to do. I feel like I should, but…I don’t know if I want to leave Henry behind. But the idea of bringing him to New York seems so…”

“Henry?” Quinn laughed. “Henry King?”

“What?” I asked.

Quinn started laughing hysterically. I almost threw my drink at him. Ella seemed unimpressed as well as she shot him a pointed glare. “Stop, Quinn,” she said while bringing her hand to his shoulder, glancing at me apologetically while she did.

“What’s so funny?” I asked, offended.

Quinn’s face started turning red. “Wait, let me get this straight. You’re dating Henry King?” he asked. “I thought you said nothing was going on.”

“Well, something started going on…”

Again, he laughed, and I grew impatient. “Jesus Christ, Scarlett…”

“Quinn…” Ella began.

“What the fuck is so funny?” I asked.

Quinn managed to contain himself for a bit. “I’m sorry, it’s just…funny. He was always such a…he was odd back in high school.”

“Quinlan,” Ella warned.

“Ugh, you sound like my mother,” he groaned.

I became confused. I went to high school with Quinn and Ella. Henry hadn’t been present. “Back in high school?” I asked.

“He was sweet,” Ella said.

What the fuck is going on? I leaned over the table, trying to wrap my brain around what they were saying. "Wait, wait…high school?"

Quinn studied me for a moment. "Yeah, you remember. That weird kid from Devil's Elbow…"

"He wasn't weird," Ella assured.

"He's not normal," Quinn interjected. "How could he be after what happened to his mom? I mean…the entire student body thought he was gonna shoot up the school one day."

I barely remembered that kid, but it wasn't Henry. I also never really knew the reason everyone seemed so afraid of him, but I steered clear. "No…" I began.

"Oh, come on, Scarlett…what did he go by back then?" Quinn asked Ella.

"Asher," she said.

Yeah, I remember that being his name. I remained unconvinced though. "I'm pretty sure Henry was homeschooled."

Quinn chuckled, but his entertainment faded. "He never said anything?"

"Why didn't you guys ever say anything?" I snapped.

Quinn scoffed. "I thought you knew, Scarlett. What, the name Henry King never rang any bells?" he asked.

"Why would it?" I snapped.

Quinn seemed astounded. "Henry King, Scarlett! The guy who freaking killed his wife in front of his kids, like…twenty years ago…"

"Enough, Quinn," Ella snapped. "You're upsetting her."

I shook my head. "I'm not upset." I felt sick. Very sick, but upset? No.

"You look pale," Ella said, concerned.

"I just, uh…I need to use the restroom," I stood abruptly, a gnawing in my stomach fighting to be freed. I felt sick all day, but it seemed now the knots in my stomach decided to ~~make an appearance and~~ work its way up my throat.

I ran into the bathroom and hunched over the toilet. Vomit immediately poured out of me into the bowl. My body jolted forward at the feeling of more coming out of me. Though purging myself gave me no relief. My eyes burned, nose burned, face grew hot, and I became lightheaded from hardly being able to breathe.

"Ugh," I groaned while lowering myself to my knees. I ran my hand over my face to remove any fluids that seeped out, but strangely, I wanted to cry. I'm not even sure why—it's not like I believed Quinn when he said we went to high school with Henry.

Or maybe I did but just didn't want to admit it to myself.

A knock came to the bathroom door. "Scarlett? Are you all right?" Ella asked.

I hesitated. "I'm…I'm fine!" I yelled, my voice shaky. I wanted to leave.

Henry called me on my way back to Devil's Elbow, but I ignored. Too confused and bewildered to have a normal conversation with him, I settled for having a drink at Dante's to clear my mind. Try and work through the information—process everything. Try and remember Asher—though I hardly knew him back then.

With hardly anyone present at the bar, I had any choice of seating. I settled for a booth at the far end of the bar, far away from anyone present. Instead of beer, I ordered whiskey. An awful drink, but one I felt completely necessary to indulge.

Henry called again, but I ignored once more. I knew I couldn't avoid him all night, but for the time being, I just wanted to be alone with my thoughts. I finished my drink, contorting my face to the awful taste and considered grabbing another.

Max entered the bar. I became frozen, expecting Henry to walk in behind him. But he never did, and when my phone started ringing again, I shut it off.

Max sat at the bar. He hadn't seen me. Perhaps a sneaky exit might be the best route.

No, I wanted to talk to him. I had to ask him about Henry. I stood and started making my way over to him, my heart pounding out of my chest with every step. The closer I got to him, the sicker I felt. An annoying voice in the back of my head kept telling me to run away, but when Max looked at me, I became committed.

"Can I buy you that drink?" I asked after Dante slid a double shot of whiskey to him.

Max stared at me, skeptical. He shrugged.

I tossed a twenty on the bar and ordered another drink for myself before taking the stool next to him, but he continued to stare, a cigarette hanging out of his mouth.

"What're we, drinking buddies now?" he asked.

"I wanted to talk to you about Henry," I said and grabbed my drink from Dante.

Max scoffed and chugged his drink. "What makes you think I'd talk to you about him?" he asked after slamming the empty glass back on the bar.

I thought for a moment, staring at his empty glass. "I'll keep your glass full the entire conversation. Drink as much as you want, I don't care. But this is important."

Max took a long drag of his cigarette, his black eyes burning into me the entire time. He considered. "All right. Dante, another one!"

The two of us sat across from each other in my original booth. As much as I loathed the sight of him, Max had valuable information about Henry. Questions I needed answering, but remained uncertain if Henry would be honest.

"I should warn you, whatever you got to say about Henry, I'm loyal to him. He's probably gonna hear all about it," he said.

"Well I appreciate you telling me that. I'll keep that in mind."

Max took a drag of a newly lit cigarette. "You know…I don't know what my brother sees in you," he said while exhaling smoke in my face.

I scowled. "Fuck you."

"You got a mouth on you, you know that?"

"You're one to talk." ~~I snapped.~~

"Your parents know what kind of person you are?" he asked.

"My parents are dead. You know that."

"That's right. Flooding accident," he said, and I shot him an evil stare. "Don't be so defensive. We've both lost our parents. We're one in the same. What's that they say? Birds of a feather?"

"I hardly think the two of us flock together." He laughed and then took another drag of his cigarette. "Henry told me…your mom was dead."

"Oh yeah?" he asked.

I hesitated, unsure if I even wanted to know the truth. But I had to know. What Quinn said, I knew I couldn't keep something like that to myself. "How'd…how'd she die?"

"He never told you that?" he asked. I shook my head. "She was murdered. Right in front of us." I stared at him, stunned by the news. "My old man came home drunk one night. He was so sure that she'd been screwing around on him. And in his drunken rage, he bashed her head in with a frying pan. Over and over again until her head was complete mush."

Oh my God, I thought, put-off by his insistence to be so crude.

"My old man took off that night. And as much as I tried, I couldn't call for help. There'd been a flood that night. Roads were out. Power was out. For two days we sat in the same house as our dead mom…"

"I know this story."

"Well, you should. It was all over the news," he said. "You were probably too young to know the details. Hell, Henry was just a little kid."

"That didn't happen to you," I snapped. "I went to school with the kid from that story."

"What was his name?" Max asked.

"Asher, his name was Asher," I said, certain in my discovery. His name had been Asher, not Henry. Not my Henry.

"Asher?" he asked, smirking, and my heart started beating faster. "Henry Asher King?" I felt sick. His goddamn middle name, Asher, and I never knew. "Yeah, he never did like going by Henry back then. But who can blame him? When he's named after the bastard who killed our mom." Max studied me for a moment, clearly noticing how unnerved I'd become at the news. "It's all coming together now, isn't it, Scarlett?"

"No. No, I would have remembered him."

"And yet you don't. I'll give it to ya, he looks a lot different. The boy grew into a man. He's changed a lot since then," Max said and then put his cigarette out in the ashtray.

The news of Henry's trauma was disconcerting. And even more so, I didn't remember him. And he never mentioned it before, which angered me.

Max finished his drink. He chuckled, and for a moment, sounded exactly like his brother. "Jesus, that boy's been in love with you since high school. And you can't even remember him."

"What?" I asked, bitter.

Max studied me for a moment. "It killed me to see him like that. Heartbroken over a girl who would never even give him the time of day. And then your parents died. And you came calling, asking him for help." Max scoffed and looked down at his drink, hateful. "He never even stood a chance. Just fell right back into you."

I grew uncomfortable. "You're lying."

"I wish I was," Max muttered. "He deserves better than you."

CHAPTER TWENTY-FIVE:

I RETURNED TO MY PARENTS' HOUSE, relieved to see that Henry's truck wasn't there. Though only a matter of time before he decided to make an appearance since I ignored one too many calls. I entered the dark, lonely house, and my heart felt heavy. With Dog gone, my parents dead, and the man I loved keeping secrets from me…dark, horrible secrets, I started feeling suffocated.

I attempted to climb the stairs to my room, but my grief overpowered me. Instead, I lowered myself on to the steps.

I remembered the night Henry came over. The night he fucked me on the stairs, something that at the time, I found sexy. His animalistic side having broke through him, taking over me, dominating me. But after what Max told me, I felt violated.

I remained seated, in a trance. Completely confounded and deeply disturbed by the information given to me. I still loved Henry. I loved him with all my heart. But I felt betrayed by him. The secrets he kept unnerved me. On one hand, I felt that he didn't trust me by not telling me about his mother. On the other hand, I felt our relationship had been based on a lie. And then, the unshakable guilt and shame I felt for not remembering him, tormented me.

Headlights shined through the viewing windows on the side of the front door, and I knew I couldn't avoid speaking to him anymore. I ignored too many of his phone calls, sending him into a panic. I knew I had to answer for my actions, and even though he had plenty to answer for himself, I felt unprepared.

I started to wonder if I should even be angry with the revelation. Henry, no matter who he had been in his past, was still Henry. The man I loved. Though my animosity and discomfort seemed unshakeable. And when Henry entered the house, his worried eyes met with mine. And I grew bitter all over again.

"Scarlett…why haven't you been answering my calls?" he asked.

I leaned my head on the banister, staring at him, studying his face, trying to find any trace of the man that had been Asher. But I saw nothing. Just my Henry. "I didn't know what to say."

He planted his hands on his hips. "What, are you mad at me for something?" I hesitated, but he grew desperate. "Baby, did…did I do something wrong?"

A lump grew in my throat, choking back my words. I wiped tears from my face, fighting hard to keep a quivering breath at bay.

Henry kneeled down in front of me and grabbed my hands. In his eyes, I saw fear. "You're scaring me, Scar." I pulled my hands away from him to wipe away more tears. "Is this…about what I said last night? About getting married? I didn't mean now, I just…"

I shook my head. "No, it's…not that."

"What is it, Scarlett?"

I looked into his eyes. The pain inside of them killed me. Like he knew I made my decision to leave him before I did. I brought my hand to his face, bringing him closer to me. Allowing me to fully examine him, look deep into his soul to find that shadow of a man I knew of so long ago. Though I hardly even knew Asher, and painting the picture seemed a trivial task.

"Are you hiding something from me, Henry?" I asked.

He broke eye contact with me. He shook his head. "Nah, I…I got nothin' to hide."

A lie. A lie so massive that I started to resent him more and more. Though I felt a cruel person to tell him my true reasons for wanting to leave. Henry couldn't help his past, but he could help lying about it. Still, I couldn't bring myself to say his secrets drove me away. I don't think he'd ever forgive himself.

I sighed and wiped more tears from my face. I managed to swallow the lump in my throat, but I had to look away from him. I felt too ashamed to watch him in that moment.

"I'm going back to New York."

The silence between us seemed to last forever, and my words seem to have stunned him more than expected. "What?"

"I have to go back. I have to get back into work or…I'll completely destroy my career."

"Screw your career!" he shouted, and I shot him a pointed glare, causing him to retreat almost instantly. "Baby, I didn't mean it like that. It's just…you can be a writer anywhere, Scar."

I shook my head. "No, I…I have established connections in New York. I need to start making money again. All the renovations, paying Doctor Wilson, it's…it's taken its toll," I said. Though not completely a lie—not like his—I was far from being poor.

"So this is about money?" he asked. "You're…leaving me because of money?"

It sounded awful coming out of his mouth. "No, it's not…"

He grabbed my hands again, pulling me closer to him. "I told you I'd take care of you. You don't have to worry about money, I…I'll start working more hours, or…find a better paying job. I think the high school is looking for caretakers, and they have benefits…"

Again, I shook my head. "You wanted to go to college. Remember? And I don't want to stay in Devil's Elbow."

"I'll come to New York with you. You know I will, Scarlett…"

"No, Henry."

Henry hung his head. After a few seconds of attempting to hold back his tears, he stood. His face, red. Eyes, glossy. "I wanna marry you, Scarlett. I wanna settle down with you, have kids with you. Grow old with you, I…I never wanted those things with anyone else. You're the love of my life, and…I know that if you walk out that door," he winced. As valiant as his attempts to keep his tears hidden, they broke through. "If you leave me, I…I don't think I'll ever be okay again."

My heart broke at his words. I no longer fought my own tears.

Henry quivered. "Please, just…tell me what I did. What I can do to keep you here…"

"You lied to me, Henry," I said sternly.

He seemed confused, though he swallowed hard. As if fearing the worst. Fearing that I figured him out in some way. "I didn't lie…"

"I talked to Max."

He hesitated. "You what?" he asked in his quiet, raspy voice.

I nodded. "He told me all about you."

"He did?" he asked, horrified.

"How could you keep that from me? What, you don't trust me?" I snapped.

"Baby, it's…it's not about trusting you. I was trying to protect you…"

"Asher?"

Henry became white as a ghost when I said it, and I felt guilty about ripping him back into the world that terrorized him into lying to me. Though as guilty as I felt, his secret—I couldn't ignore. "What did you say?" he asked.

"That's your name, right? This whole time, you've…you've been keeping that from me. What happened to your mother, that we went to school together…"

Henry turned away from me. "That's what this is about? You found out who I was?"

Yes. "No, it's…I have to go home…"

Henry punched the wall, and I became frozen. Never had I witnessed a violent outburst from him, and it seemed so out of character. Though after discovering the secret he worked so hard to keep from me, I felt as if I didn't know him at all.

"So I blew it then. That's what you're telling me?" He never faced me. I think he may have been ashamed of his pain. "Jesus Christ, I…finally get you, and…" He hung his head and let out a quivering breath. He brought one of his hands to his face, shielding his expression even though his back faced me. “You’re the only thing I ever wanted, Scarlett. Now you’re telling me I have to let you go?”

A tightness in my chest grew. I found it difficult to catch my breath. If I looked back on the two of us, I never imagined saying something so hurtful to him. And seeing him in pain because of something I said, destroyed me. But every moment I felt the need to run to him, fall into his arms, beg him to forget I ever mentioned it, I just remembered one thing. He lied to me. To my face just minutes before.

I gave myself to him completely, and he refused to be honest about his true self. And when I thought about those things, I resented him. We could have ruled the world, he and I, but he lied to me since the first day we met. A stranger stood before me. “You shouldn’t have lied, Henry.”

Henry exhaled, his breath shaky. “Yeah, I know. But I always loved you, Scar. That wasn’t a lie.”

I winced and buried my face in my hands, trying to muffle the sound of my cries.

Henry exited the house and slammed the door behind him, and as much as I wanted to call out for him, I refrained.

I booked a flight leaving from Nashville to New York in two days. The soonest I could get out of Tennessee, unless I wanted to drive eight hours to Chattanooga. The thought didn’t seem too appealing.

That evening, I spent my time packing everything I needed for New York. I threw out all the perishable food, gathered a few of my favorite photos of my parents, and sealed up my suitcase.

Even though my flight wouldn’t be leaving for another two days, I decided that I would make the drive to Nashville the following evening and stay at a hotel. The idea of staying in Devil’s Elbow longer than I needed to sickened me. ~~Another problem I tried to bury deep down inside of me, my sickness from everything.~~

The night proved to be restless. The scent of Henry in my bed made me choke up, and I had difficulty keeping him out of my mind. So I moved to the living room to attempt sleeping on the couch, but my mind wandered and kept me awake the better part of the evening. I managed to drift off into a light sleep at around five in the morning. Light enough to where I could hear a vehicle pull up in front of the house and a door close. I opened my eyes. The living room, now well-lit by the light, blue sky.

I picked my head up and looked out the window. I saw the front of Henry's truck. My heart fell into my stomach at the sight. Surely nothing good would come of our conversation.

I opened the front door and saw Henry at the foot of the steps. He stared at me for a moment, hesitating to speak. I folded my arms, waiting to hear what he came to say at seven in the morning.

"Come take a drive with me," Henry said after a long moment of hesitation—his voice quiet and timid.

Not the best idea, I told myself, but I relented. My curiosity having got the better of me.

Henry and I refrained from speaking while driving into Hunter's Point, and the tension between the two of us seemed enough to drive anyone mad~~, though Henry pretended not to notice~~. He kept his eyes forward on the road, and I noticed how tired he looked. Tired and burdened.

I looked down to a bouquet of red roses in between us. A curious thing, though I was certain they weren't for me.

When we arrived at Hunter's Point Cemetery, I became queasy. The thought of facing my parents—even though they were six feet into the ground—disgusted me. But Henry took us in a different route. I followed behind him with my arms folded, protecting myself from the chilly, spring morning.

A thin layer of dew fell over the grass and headstones. The sky remained a light blue with no colors from the sun to compliment the promise of a new day.

I heard crows. It only unnerved me. Death and depression surrounded us, the only bit of color and beauty being the roses that Henry clenched in his hand. I kept my eyes on the roses. I'd had enough of depression.

Henry stopped in front of a dirty, worn, and faded grave. I watched him, confounded by him as he kneeled down and placed the roses in front of the headstone. And when I looked to the epitaph, it all made sense.

Roslyn King
1962-1992
Remembered With Love

I became depressed at the sight of the headstone. Hardly well maintained at all. Perhaps she'd been forgotten for a while. Or perhaps too painful a memory for those who remained.

"I never told you about my mom. I should have," Henry muttered, never taking his eyes away from his mother's headstone.

"Why didn't you?"

Henry hesitated. "I didn't want you to remember me. Didn't want you to…associate me with that sort of thing." He sort of chuckled, though it seemed the sort of thing one would do when trying to hide real pain. "Truth be told, I kinda liked the way you started looking at me," he muttered, and my guilt became overwhelming.

Henry stood and faced me, his eyes seeming desperate. "When people know those kinds of things about you…that's all you become to them. Your life, everything you do, everything you want…it becomes all about that pain."

I hesitated to speak, but Henry continued. "People, when they find out that sort of thing then…I'm not a person anymore," he said, voice shaky. He looked as though he wanted to cry. "I'm just someone who saw something really fucked up when I was a kid. So to them, I must be pretty fucked up."

I understood. I understood completely, but it didn't make up for the secrets he kept from me. Secrets about having known me much longer than he led on and about his mother.

"Scarlett," he spoke while taking a step closer to me. "I know I'm not the easiest person to be around…" he started to become fidgety, almost unsure of how he should be moving at all.

"Henry…" I began, knowing that he would try and convince me to stay.

"I know that I should have opened up to you more…told you sooner about my past. And I know it don't make no difference now, but…I want you to know that I love you…" My eyes started to burn, and I forced myself to look away from him. "I always have, and I always will. And I don't want you going back to New York thinking you're alone in this world. Because you're not."

Henry forced the floodgates open with his words, and fighting my tears seemed a fool's errand. No hiding my pain, my desperation. I hated him for doing that to me, though I refused to lash out at the one person who still loved me. And when I noticed tears in his eyes, I knew I had to forgive him. He suffered more than myself.

"I'm here for you, Scarlett. Whenever you need me. You call, I come running."

I wrapped my arms around his neck and pulled him into me. The truest and sincerest form of kindness I ever had the pleasure to experience. And suddenly it seemed so much more difficult to leave him behind.

Henry wrapped his arms around me and buried his face into my neck. And there we stood upon his mother's grave, embracing each other tightly. Knowing it would be the last time we ever held each other so intimately. And when he released me, I already missed his touch.

He leaned over to pull two roses from the bouquet on his mother's grave. He handed them to me. "For your parents."

CHAPTER TWENTY-SIX:

HENRY BROUGHT ME BACK to my parents' house and then left. The two of us said nothing upon our departure. We had nothing left to say.

The house stood before me, finally completed, and I remained unsure of whether or not I wanted to sell. A decision that I would wait to make. I became hopeful that my return to New York would somehow give me clarity. That maybe I'd realize how much I wanted to be done with everything in Devil's Elbow.

But perhaps I would become convinced that the town would forever be a part of me. That Henry would forever be a part of me. Maybe I'd realize that I needed him. Something that I could only know with time.

I managed to get a few hours of sleep. At eight in the evening, I loaded my suitcases into the car. The time came for me to leave Devil's Elbow. Leave all the pain, the loneliness, the secrets, and the love behind.

The sun started to set, painting the sky in the beautiful pink and orange. The air, thick and muggy. The last rainfall of the season to appear any moment, but none of that concerned me. The Rubidoux would remain dormant until long after I left. The pain it caused, I had enough. No more, I thought. No more ever again.

While driving down Y Highway, I fell into a trance. I started feeling numb to everything, a form of self-preservation, I'm sure. I knew that if I let myself feel the pain in my heart for my parents, and Dog…and Henry…it would be impossible to survive. My sweet Henry. I missed him already, and I hated that felt the need to run away from him.

Perhaps not forever, I told myself. Perhaps not even for a day.

It started sprinkling, but I remained detached. The light rainfall, hardly enough to summon the mighty beast. Not yet at least.

I started to approach Hickman Bridge, but my phone started ringing. I'm not one to answer the phone while driving on Y Highway, though I became curious. A change in my flight perhaps.

I reached over and blindly searched my purse for my phone. I felt the thing vibrating against my fingers, but too much clutter made it difficult to grasp.

I glanced toward the inside of my purse. For a second. That's all it took. When I looked back to the road, a buck standing on Hickman Bridge sent my heart into my throat. I slammed on my brakes, but the impact seemed inevitable. I jerked my wheel to the side. I overcorrected. And when I felt the tires of my vehicle run off the road, the sound of the engine revving once in the air, I knew I screwed up.

The car smashed into the ground on the side of Hickman Bridge, but the impact was so forceful that I flew forward. My airbags deployed, smashing into my face. But with the impact, shortly after, came complete darkness.

I awoke to the feeling of icy cold water on my feet. I picked my head up from the steering wheel. Darkness consumed me. The sun had set, and I scrambled to put the events together in my head. Though my mind seemed foggy, and my forehead, sore. I touched the sore spot, smearing blood on my fingertips.

"Oh my God," I cried at the sight of the river in front of me, water already rising from the violent rainfall that started at some point during my unconsciousness.

The nose of my car, submerged by the river. Water started seeping in through the cracks of my door, soaking my feet. Soon enough, the car would be carried away completely. I started panicking, thinking of what to do. I needed to get out, obviously. I pushed on the driver's side door, but my efforts were in vain. The door seemed stuck on something.

I tried to roll down the window, but nothing happened. Either the battery died, or the water had submerged it completely, killing all power to the car. I looked to the passenger side door. No escape. My car, wedged between cement structure of Hickman Bridge and the rocky, hilly terrain leading down to the river. I chastised myself for getting a two-door, and my suitcases blocked the path to the hatchback.

I unbuckled my seatbelt and crawled into the back, tossing my suitcases aside to make it to the hatch. My efforts were straining, but I needed to get out. With the force of the downpour, I became certain I only had about twenty minutes at most.

I ripped one of my suitcases out of the way, but I became horrified at the sight of not being able to open the damn thing from the inside. And even if I could, the rocky terrain would keep it from opening completely.

"No," I cried. "No!" I screamed while kicking the window on the back, but I lacked the strength to break through. I had to call someone.

I crawled back to the front, struggling to keep my balance as I did. I planted myself back in the driver's seat and ripped open my purse to grab my phone. Full bars, thank the heavens. I dialed 911. Hopefully the roads to the Elbow could still be accessed.

"911, what is your emergency?" a woman answered.

"I need…I need help! My car, it's…trapped between Hickman Bridge on Y Highway…"

"Okay, ma'am, are you inside the vehicle?" she asked calmly.

"Yes! I…I can't get out, and…the river's rising. I don't know what to do," I cried.

"Okay, I'm sending emergency response vehicles to your location now. Is there anything in the vehicle you can use to break the window?"

"Uh…" My mind raced. I reached over to open the glove compartment, but with only a manual and temporary registration inside, I became disheartened. I slammed the thing shut. "Uh…hang on," I said while digging through my purse. Nothing. I thought of everything I packed into my suitcases, but nothing would brake through the glass.

"Shit!" I cursed. "No," I said, my breath, shaky. The river water started rising in the car—up to my calves now, and I wasn't convinced they'd reach me in time.

"Have you tried kicking the glass?" the emergency responder asked.

I had on the back, but maybe the driver's side window might give. "Hang on…" I crawled into the passenger seat, and with every bit of strength I had, I kicked the window. Over and over again, but nothing. Not even a crack.

I withdrew, my leg now in pain from the effort.

I started sobbing through the phone. The windshield maybe. I started kicking it, but once again, my efforts failed. "It's not working," I sobbed, defeated. The river came for me, and it seemed it would be victorious.

"Okay, it looks like the roads are flooded on Y Highway. We've sent a rescue boat to your location…"

"How long is that going to take?!" I yelled.

"We're doing everything we can to get to you. Is there anyone you know who might be able to help? Someone closer to your location?" she asked.

Henry. Oh God, Henry was only three miles away. I ended the call with the emergency responder and dialed his number. Henry would know what to do, he always did. Though after two rings, I started to wonder if he even wanted to talk to me. Oh God, what if he ignored me completely? It's what I deserved.

"Scarlett?" Henry answered. "I been trying to call you. I need to see you, Scar…"

"Henry, listen to me. I need your help…"

"What's wrong?" he asked.

The water reached my knees now. Any second, the car could be carried away. As much as I tried to be strong and brave in that moment, I cried like a little girl. “Henry, I’m stuck. I…I lost control on Y Highway, and…my car’s stuck…” I sobbed. “And the river’s rising, and I can’t get out!”

“What?” he asked, terror in his voice.

I cried even harder, my face becoming hot and my vision becoming obscured by the tears in my eyes. “I need your help!” I wailed.

“Where are you?” he asked.

“Hickman…” my words got stuck in my throat. “I’m at Hickman Bridge.”

“Okay, baby. I’m comin’ for you. Just…stay on the phone with me, I’ll be there in two minutes…”

But the vehicle shifted beneath the rocks, the water having devoured the front of my vehicle. I screamed at the feeling of the car jolting forward, knocking my phone from my hands and into the water along the floor of the car. “No!” I screamed.

I tried to calm myself, but the rainfall dinging on the car made it hard to focus on what I needed to do.

I tried to see the river through the windshield, but the rain obscured my vision. I thought of my parents. I wondered if they found themselves in a similar situation as myself. If they called for help, but the rescue team didn’t reach them in time.

This is where it ends, I thought. This is how I die.

I sobbed and rested my head on my steering wheel. I closed my eyes to try and find any shred of peace within my mind, but the constant coldness of the river water on my legs assured I stayed present in that moment. Fear consumed me. ~~In a matter of minutes, the car would be taken away completely.~~

Maybe I could still fight, I thought. Maybe once the river took the car, I could get the door open and swim as hard as I could to the river bank. I tried to convince myself that I hardly faced certain death. It seemed so preventable. Like something could still be done.

I screamed at the sound of someone pounding on my window.

"Henry!" I shouted when I saw his face. Though his panicked expression, far from comforting, and I started to wonder if it looked worse than what I imagined.

Henry attempted to open the door. Like I hadn't already tried that. "The door's wedged on somethin'…"

"You think?!"

"Scarlett, please don't be sarcastic right now," he said, exasperated. Though the rain made it difficult to hear him through the window. I really hoped he had a better plan. "Look, Max is gonna attach a strap to the back of your car. We're gonna…we're gonna use the truck to pull you out."

Good, good, it seemed like a full-proof plan. "Why do you look so scared?" I asked.

He shook his head. "Nah, you're…you're gonna be fine."

I hardly believed him. The water started rising to my stomach, and I started to panic. The water being so cold, it stole my breath away. "Henry, break the glass," I demanded.

"What?" he asked.

"Break the fucking glass!" I screamed.

I felt the car jolt back, and I screamed at the feeling. No, going backwards was a good thing, I told myself. Max had started pulling the car out—it all seemed fine. Still, the coldness of the water horrified me.

"Scarlett, I…I can't break the glass right now," Henry said.

"What? Why?" I whined.

He seemed like losing all control. I knew the feeling. Henry hung his head and glanced to the river before focusing back on me. "I…I gotta wait for the pressure to equalize. Otherwise, broken glass'll just shoot all over you…"

“I don’t care!” I yelled.

“It could cut you, babe,” he said, desperation in his voice. “It could hurt you real bad…”

The car went forward, though Max’s efforts kept me from going into the river completely. I heard tires screeching on the pavement from the road, and I became convinced that Henry’s truck just wouldn’t be enough. “Henry…” I cried.

“Keep trying!” he yelled to Max.

The water reached my chest now, and it felt as though my heart stopped beating. Henry repositioned himself, the water at his waist now, and I wanted to tell him to leave. The current proved to be too powerful, and I refused to let him die for me when I couldn’t be saved.

“Henry…Henry, listen to me,” I said, and he focused on me. “You need to go.”

He seemed appalled. As if the thought never even crossed his mind. He shook his head. “Nah, I’m not leaving you, Scar…”

“You’re not gonna get me out. Not before the river takes the car out.”

I felt the car being pulled back again, and I braced myself on the steering wheel and window. Braced myself for the inevitable thrust forward when Henry’s truck failed. I brought my hand to Henry’s on the window. “I love you,” I cried. “I love you so much that…some times it’s hard to breathe.” Henry leaned his forehead on the window. He started crying. Never had I seen him cry so openly before. “I won’t let you die for me.”

Henry exhaled heavily on the window, fogging up the glass. He pushed himself away from the car, struggling to move through the water. And when he disappeared from my view, I became thankful that he listened. He rarely did.

The truck continued to pull me back, but I knew the efforts were futile. Any moment, I was to become the Rubidoux’s twenty-sixth victim. I tried to find a bit of peace. A bit of comfort in my last moment. Perhaps heaven is real, I thought. And maybe I'd see my parents soon. The only comfort I had.

Henry reappeared at the window, snapping me from my daze. I looked at him, confused. He sort of staggered, almost falling over as he did. "Henry…"

He winced and looked down into the water. In his hand, I saw a hammer. "Scarlett, move back," he said. "Get…get into the passenger seat." I did as he told. "Cover your face and neck," he said, and I did. I curled into a ball, shielding my vital organs from any glass that might fly at me.

I heard the hammer smash into the window, startling me, but the glass hadn't broken. Again, the crash of the hammer, but no broken glass. Over and over again, until finally, I heard a burst. An explosion of shattered glass covered my body, and I tensed myself at the feeling. I felt a few pieces cut into my hands, and when I looked to them, they were bleeding.

Henry smashed out the remainder of the glass and tossed the hammer aside. He reached for me, leaning halfway into the car to get to me. I grabbed onto him, now thankful he hadn't listened when I told him to leave.

"I got you," he said while pulling me out of the window. He held me up until I planted my feet on the flooded ground, the water now only reaching my waist. Oh, how good it felt to stand. Though Henry remained in place.

"Come on," I said while grabbing his hand.

"Go, Scarlett. I'm right behind you," he said while pushing me toward the rocky hill.

My hands started to sting while I gripped at the rocks to pull me up the hill. After a few steps, I pulled myself out of the water completely.

Max continued to pull the car back, and it seemed my weight had been the sole offender because the car yanked back and started moving up the hill with ease.

"Max, that's enough!" Henry yelled from behind me, but Max couldn't hear.

I started waving my arms to him. "Max!" I yelled.

But the straps connecting the two vehicles snapped, the force of which made them whip toward me. I hit the ground and buried my face in my arms to shield myself.

The car raced past me, and I heard it crash into the river below. I panted, my face buried in the dirt and rocks beneath me. Jesus Christ, I thought, though I felt relieved to have not been in the car when it fell victim to the angry rapids behind me.

"Henry!" Max yelled while jumping out of the truck. "Henry!"

Max ran past me, falling to his legs to skid down the hill, and when I turned onto my back, I saw that Henry no longer stood behind me. "Henry?"

Max made his way into the river, about waist level before ducking beneath the waters. I watched the area in which he disappeared, hoping to see Henry with him when he reemerged. But Max came up for air a few seconds later, solo. He pulled himself back on land and shouted in anger. I became afraid of what he might do.

He completely ignored my existence though. And when he climbed past me, I looked back to the river, looking for any sign of Henry. "Max," I called. I stood and went to him. "Max," I said while grabbing his arm.

He shoved me away. "Get off!"

"Max, there's a rescue boat coming," I said, my voice straining from all the screaming I'd done.

He went to Henry's truck and grabbed a flashlight. He shined it to the river, and the two of us searched the area for Henry. For any sign of distress, any indication that he made it to land further up. "Henry!" Max yelled. No response.

"Henry!" I yelled.

But the rain seemed to drown out our cries for him.

The rescue boat arrived about twenty minutes later. A small little dinghy that fought hard against the current, but the light on the front seemed to shine so bright, and I became hopeful that Henry would be found. But they didn't find him.

The rescuers looked all night for Henry, but they found no sign of him being anywhere nearby. They told us that he might have swam to shore. That he might have pulled himself out a few miles up, and maybe he made his way home. Or perhaps still wandered through the darkness of the forest and thickness of the rain.

They assured us the search would continue, but encouraged us to go home and wait for him in case he showed. In case he did make it out of the river, something that seemed a real possibility because they never found his body.

CHAPTER TWENTY-SEVEN

MAX BROUGHT ME HOME IN HENRY'S TRUCK, but he never said a word. I knew he blamed me for Henry being missing. Hell, I blamed myself. But I didn't dare speak to him. I felt anything I said might set him off and that he'd probably kill me if given the chance. So I went inside.

I waited up all morning for Henry to show. I expected a knock to come to the door any minute, but that never happened. And when morning faded into night, I felt it impossible to keep my eyes open any longer. As hard as I tried, I felt exhausted, beaten, defeated. A part of me felt that if I went to sleep, when I awoke, Henry would be beside me. Not having waken me because he didn't want to disturb me, despite how worried I'd been.

I slept on the couch, fearful that if I went upstairs, I might not hear someone knocking. Someone being Henry. But the knocking never came. In fact, the only thing that ripped me from my slumber—the sound of a dog barking.

I shot upward on the couch and listened carefully—worried that perhaps I dreamt the sound. But the barking continued from outside the house.

I got up and made my way to the front door, and when I opened it, I became stunned at the sight of Dog at the bottom of the porch steps. He whimpered and lowered himself to the ground.

"Dog?" I asked, unbelieving of what my eyes were seeing.

I stepped off the porch and kneeled down next to him. I ran my hands through his coat. His fur, damp and dirty, but no visible injuries upon him.

Yes, Dog returned to me. Still very much alive and happy, it seemed. His tail wagged excitedly and he perked up to lick my face, though his whimpers led me to believe he felt sorrow in that moment. Much like myself.

I wrapped my arms around him, thrilled to have him back in my embrace, and he continued to lick my face. I almost started crying. Now, we just needed to find Henry. Then all would be right with the world.

Search and rescue teams continued to monitor the river as best they could, but the currents thwarted most of their efforts. Two days without any news, and Max and I grew anxious.

We gathered some people from Devil's Elbow. People who knew Henry, who cared about him. They gathered people as well—bringing in blood hounds to help track his scent. But I had something better. A Catahoula Cur, one that knew Henry's scent better than myself.

Dog grew antsy on his leash, and I did my best to try and keep him on track. Try and keep him in the direction in which Max sent us to check, but Dog had a plan of his own. After walking about two miles, he started pulling on his leash more aggressively, practically choking himself—coughing from the strain around his neck.

"Dog," I whined.

I trusted where he wished to take me, but keeping up with him seemed hardly possible, and I had to keep him close. Without Dog, I knew I had no chance of finding Henry.

I fought with Dog for about another mile, having to use two hands to keep him from pulling me down. The wind blew, rustling the leaves of the forest and whipping my hair in my face.

Dog started yipping while attempting to break free of his leash.

"Dog," I whined again. But my mutt grew restless—relentless. He kept pulling harder on the leash and started becoming more audible in his cries for freedom. I started running with him—to appease him.

Dog proved to be much faster than myself though. He yanked me through the forest, and I ran as fast as I could to keep up with his pace. The more we ran, the closer we got to the river. I heard the current in the near distance. The two of us in unfamiliar territory, and I grew cautious. Concerned that I knew not what lie ahead.

I started panting. I became winded, but Dog continued to pull me, barking louder and more frequently the further we went.

I needed relief. My heart pounded, I became sweaty. I felt sick, feeling the need to vomit for whatever reason. But Dog hardly allowed me to slow my pace.

Only when he yanked me down a small hill, did I trip over a rock and release his leash. I tumbled down the hill, attempting to grab something to stop myself, but I fell too fast. I hit level ground and my hands dove into the muddy river bank. The cold, muddy water stung the cuts on my hands.

I looked at my hands, muddy, wet, shaking. They felt numb. Something broke my fall though. Instead of my body hitting the rocky line of the river bank, something cushioned me, protecting me from a much more serious impact.

I felt Dog's nose on my face followed by his tongue. I pushed him away, annoyed by his behavior—ignoring his whimpers. My numb hands dug into the earth to push myself upward, and only then did I notice that I landed on a person.

I gasped and pushed myself off—horrified, panting, heart pounding. I scooted along the damp, dirty ground, never looking away from person before me. "Henry?"

The man wore the same clothes as Henry, but it hardly looked like him. His skin, much paler than usual. Kind of blue, actually.

I crawled toward him slowly, studying the man, trying to piece together what lay before me. No, it didn't look like Henry. Henry's eyes were pale blue, concentrated. The man before me, his eyes seemed hazy with a grayish-blue tint to them. Almost like a layer of film covering them completely.

Dog started whimpering. He approached the man and started licking his face, only stopping to whine a bit before continuing. Dog seemed so distressed, and I started feeling sick again, watching him lick the man before us.

"Stop," I said, but Dog kept licking his face. "Stop!" I yelled. I moved toward Dog and pushed him away. "Get off of him!" I yelled, tears burning my eyes. I leaned over the man. His lips, the same blue color of his skin.

His hands rested by his side. I grabbed one of them. His skin, cool, damp. I turned his hand over and studied his palm. I studied his palm for the longest time, not wanting to admit to myself what became so obvious in that moment.

I started crying. I brought the man's hand to my face. His touch, empty, cold, hollow. "Henry?" I asked. I touched his chest and shook him a bit. "Baby, wake up."

He never moved though. I felt no heartbeat in his chest, no rise and fall from his breaths. I shook him again, harder this time. "Wake up," I demanded, but he never moved.

His eyes remained half-open, perhaps something people's eyes do when they're in such a heavy sleep.

But in my heart, I knew better. I clenched his hand to my chest. A tightness in my core grew and rose up to my throat. I felt like I couldn't breathe, and my only relief came from screaming. "Help! Somebody help us!"

They put Henry into a body-bag and loaded him onto a stretcher. But the paramedics' efforts to get him in the ambulance proved to be difficult with Max hunched over Henry, clinging to him, wailing louder than I ever heard any man.

None of it felt real. Nothing in that moment seemed real, and I started to drift into a dreamlike state. I started feeling lightheaded, foggy. Any moment, I planned on waking up in my bedroom with Henry by my side.

"Ma'am?" a police officer spoke, breaking me of my trance. "We're gonna need you to write a statement for us."

But Max's cries distracted me. Henry being put into the ambulance made me feel sick. I felt all the blood rush from my face, and a cold sweat came over me. I felt like vomiting. Or dying, I'm not sure which.

"Ma'am?" the officer spoke again, and I barely acknowledged him. "Are you all right?"

I felt his hand on my arm, but his voice became echoed. With every passing second, I felt my life force leaving my body. Something drained from me, stealing away any energy or will to carry on I had remaining. My eyes fluttered, I hit the ground, and I entered into a world of darkness.

I awoke in the hospital a few hours later with an IV attached to my arm. My body ached and my head remained foggy. I felt as though I recently suffered a severe trauma to my body—unlike the first time I fainted after seeing my parents dead. No, this trauma seemed different—my body unable to fully recover from the blow for whatever reason.

I pushed my call-light. A nurse entered shortly after, despondent. She took a set of vital signs. Now, I don't know much about that sort of thing, but my blood pressure—eighty over forty-six—seemed a bit low. And my pulse, a little too high at 102.

The nurse sat beside my bed, and I wondered if she heard about Henry. I don't think she knew him, but perhaps she knew my reason for being there. My embarrassing display of self-preservation.

"How are you feeling?" she asked.

I shook my head. "Not good," I said quietly. "I feel really tired."

"That's normal," she said. "You'll start to regain some energy in a few days."

I don't remember that happening after my parents died. When I fainted at the sight of their bodies, my body did well to recuperate despite having a headache for a few days. No, this all seemed so different. I became curious as to why I needed IV fluids.

"What's with all the…" I asked, motioning to the IV in my arm.

The nurse hesitated. She moved forward and grabbed my hand. "We didn't know how long you'd be out for. You have a pretty bad concussion, and the doctor is gonna want to keep you overnight for observation."

I started to tune her out, and my thoughts wandered to Henry.

"Can I get you anything?" the nurse asked.

I shook my head. I just wanted to be left alone.

The hospital released me the next morning, though I still felt lethargic and burdened. I felt like I could sleep for days.

Quinn picked me up from the hospital and took me back to my parents' house. We remained silent, mostly. He asked if I was okay, if I needed anything from him, but I told him no. I wondered how much he knew—if he found out about Henry. I refused to ask. I didn't want to talk about Henry. I didn't want to think about him.

Dog waited for me on the front porch, his head perking up when Quinn stopped in front of the house. It seemed he found his way home. Perhaps he decided to stick around a bit longer—knowing that I needed a bit of comfort. But I hardly paid him any mind. My mind, my body, my soul—exhausted.

I walked into the house and immediately went upstairs. Instead of turning left into my bedroom, I went right. I opened the door to my parents' room without even having to consider.

I climbed into their bed and pulled the covers around myself, burying my face deep into one of their pillows. My mother's. I could tell by the smell.

Dog jumped on the bed with me. He rested next to me, pawing at me, whimpering a bit. Though I had no comfort to give him. I loved my mutt, and I wanted him there with me, but any bit of comfort I managed to find—it needed to be for myself. If I had any hope of carrying on, I had to find a bit of comfort for myself.

Tears burned my eyes. I became suffocated by my own turmoil, and any breath I tried to catch quivered. The massive hole in my heart devoured the rest of my body and my soul—though I felt far from empty. What I felt could be best described as being too full. Imagine having eaten too much—your stomach is bloated, and it's painful. The only way to relieve that pain is either by purging yourself or with time.

Now imagine that feeling in your heart. Only we can't purge our hearts. That kind of pain, it only goes away with time. The love I had inside of me—though rotted and decayed from Henry and my parents' absence—it filled me, completed me in some way. The discomfort in my heart from being so full made me choke up, and I began to sob into my mother's pillow.

Something within my core started to rise up in me again. An aching desire needing to be released, one that I felt incapable of letting go simply by crying.

I needed one of them back. I would take anyone of them back, it didn't matter which. My mom, my dad, Henry. If I could just have one of them—I'd even let God decide which. I'd give myself unto him completely, so long as he gave me one of them back. Because having all three of them gone, tormented me. A pain so intense that it changed me forever.

Dog rested his head on my side, whimpering still.

"Mom," I cried, as if she could hear me. "Mommy, he's gone." I winced and tried to muffle my cries, but my pain grew to be too powerful, and I felt incapable of holding it inside me any longer. "My baby's gone," I bawled.

I cried all night. I never left my parents' bed, and Dog never left my side. I managed to cry myself to sleep in the early hours of the morning. And for the remainder of that day, I lost myself to sleep. I entered a world of dreams—a far better place to be because I got to see Henry. And he looked just as I remembered him. Pale, blue eyes squinting in the sun. A scowl upon his face, though at the sight of me, he started smirking.

"I love you, Scarlett," he said in his quiet, raspy voice.

But my dreams of him—cut short by the sound of Dog growling. I picked my head up and Dog jumped off the bed. He stood on his hind legs and looked out my parents' window, barking at something. And when I looked outside, I saw Henry's truck parked outside the stables.

"Henry," I gasped and ran out of the bedroom.

CHAPTER TWENTY-EIGHT:

I walked across the yard to the stables, pulling my sweater tighter around me as the wind blew. Dog remained at my side, growling every so often. Though the realization that Henry couldn't possibly be in the stables sent a dark cloud over me. That only meant one thing.

I peered inside the stables and saw Max, scrambling to grab handfuls of money from one of the storage spaces and shove it into a black bag. I watched him for a moment, completely confused by the sight. "What are you doing?" I asked.

Max stopped. He turned to me, each hand clenching to stacks of money. He sighed. "Thought you were in the hospital," he said and started putting the money into the black bag again.

"I was released yesterday." He continued moving back and forth between the storage space and his black bag, more money being revealed to me each time. "Where'd you get all that money?" I asked. Only the beginning of my concerns.

Max laughed, though he seemed far from amused. "Been saving it for a while."

"Why is it here?"

"I felt it'd be safe here," he said and kneeled down to close up the bag.

"Why?" I asked firmly.

Max threw his arms out to his side. "What do ya wanna know, kid? That the money's stolen? That I kept it here so the cops wouldn't find it?" He laughed and dropped his hands to his side. "Why ask questions you don't wanna know the answer to?"

I felt sick. Jesus Christ, stolen money on my property. I leaned onto one of the pillars for support, feeling woozy the longer I stood. "Oh…oh, Max. You didn't. Not all those robberies, that…that wasn't you…" I begged.

"Yeah. But don't go thinkin' your beau was completely innocent in all this," he said.

I felt as though I stopped breathing in that moment. I waited for affirmation. But the sick, sadistic look in his eyes said it all. Once again, the annoying sensation of my eyes burning forced them to swell with tears. I shook my head. "No..."

Max nodded. "Yep. Though he took a bit more convincing. Only got involved a few weeks ago. You have yourself to thank for that," he said while lifting the bag onto his shoulder.

"What?" I asked. Terrified to hear the answer.

He walked toward me—headed for the exit of the stables. "That boy never thought he was good enough for you. Thought the only way he could keep you around and keep you happy was if he had money," he spat.

All of the conversations I had with Henry about money came flying back to me, and my guilt intensified. "No..." I cried, quietly.

"I tried to tell him it didn't matter. That you'd never love him..."

"I did love him!" I yelled. "I do..."

Max scoffed and walked past me. "You don't know what love is."

His words angered me. His actions, stashing stolen money on my property, berating me about my love for Henry, and then his intentions of just leaving me completely broken, confounded by the information given to me, it made me want to hurt him.

"I'll call the police..."

But Max hardly gave me the opportunity to regret my words. He dropped the bag to the ground and wrapped his hands around my neck before slamming me back into the pillar. Though far from choking me, he held onto me tight, his face inches away from mine.

Dog started barking, growling, ready to attack if he needed to, but I kept my eyes on Max, terrified of what he might do. He started shaking while holding me in place, jaw clenched so tight and eyes filled with hatred.

"You're not gonna do that, Scarlett. Because if you do, you'll only ruin that boy's good name. The name he worked so hard to clear his entire life." I tried to speak, but Max tightened his grip. "People used to fear the name Henry King. They thought of my old man—what he did to my mama. But not anymore. Because of him, when people hear the name Henry King, they'll smile. They'll remember how good he was, how hard he worked, and what he did to save you."

"Max…" I cried while bringing my hands to his fingers, trying as best I could to loosen his grip around me, though my efforts were in vain.

"You really gonna take that away from him? I think you owe him more."

I became frozen at the blood-thirst in his eyes. "You gonna kill me?"

Max sneered. "Nah. I want you to live with your guilt. I want it to eat you from the inside out. I want you to suffer every day for the rest of your life for what you did to my brother."

He shoved me away, but his words destroyed me. "I can do it myself," I cried.

"Nah, you won't. You're too much of a coward. Or maybe you just love yourself too much. I don't know which is worse," he spat.

He started to exit the stables, but I grabbed his arm. "Max, don't…you don't have to do this…" I pleaded with him. Hoping to somehow protect Henry's last living relative.

"I gotta pay for the funeral somehow!" he yelled, agony in his voice.

"I'll pay for the funeral," I cried.

Max exhaled a quivering breath. He refused to look at me. “Yeah, I bet you will. Gotta make yourself feel better somehow.” He exited the stables after that.

I leaned back into the pillar, broken, defeated, horrified by what Max told me about Henry, but feeling so overwhelmingly guilty about Henry’s death that I couldn’t even bring myself to be angry with him. I drove Henry to do those things, and the burden became mine to carry. I would carry it for him.

I slid down to the ground, my lethargy and pain having taken full control. Dog whimpered and started licking my face, but I buried my face in my arms and bawled. The only thing I had left in me.

I did pay for Henry’s funeral. I bought him a beautiful, dark blue, stainless steel casket—one that shimmered in the light. The lining, white. I bought him a new suit—the only one he owned having been worn and faded black. I arranged everything for Max, picked out the flowers, a headstone and epitaph, though I asked what he wanted—Max remained distant. Said he didn’t care and didn’t want to be bothered with anything.

I bought a new dress for the funeral. Black, of course, but classic. But the day of Henry’s funeral, I started feeling as though I shouldn’t go. That maybe those closest to him wouldn’t want me there. Max blamed me for what happened to Henry. I blamed myself. It felt wrong though, not going. I had to say goodbye to him.

One of the only things Max asked for—an open casket. Something I had reservations about, but I told myself that anything he wanted, I would give. And during the viewing, I stayed in the back of the room, leaning against one of the walls, allowing those closest to him to say goodbye first.

It broke my heart to see that hardly anyone showed to Henry’s funeral. Only a few of those closest to him. Joe and his family, Nate, a few other friends of Henry’s I never met. The Miller’s were there too along with a few older couples from the

Elbow that he must have done work for over the years. Still, the amount of people in comparison to my parents' funeral saddened me. Though I became certain that if I died, no one would show. So at least he had that.

Perhaps none of that matters. I resented more than half the people at my parents' funeral simply because I knew they hardly cared. But everyone there, they cared. I could tell by the way they cried for him.

I remained in place, leaning against the wall, staring at the memorial photo of Henry. His Senior photo from high school. And after so many failed attempts to try and place his face in the halls of Hunter's Point High School, I looked away in shame.

When the line of mourners started to die down, I convinced myself to go see him. My last opportunity to do so. I felt insecure while approaching his casket, feeling the eyes of his mourners on me. And even though I became certain that my paranoia got the better of me, I felt as though my presence there seemed disrespectful.

I stopped in front of his casket, and the sight of him made that fullness in my heart pour over into the rest of my body. He looked just as I remembered him, only sleeping. So peaceful, just how he looked whenever he slept next to me, and I stayed awake, admiring him.

"Henry," I whispered.

I reached my hand to his, shaking. In my hand, I clenched a red ribbon. One I wore in my hair practically every day in high school. I gripped his hand—no warmth in his touch, no tenderness to give. All the love came from me now, and I left a part of it with him. In his hand, I left my ribbon for him to keep forever.

"Scarlett?"

I turned to see Ally staring at me, and I became insecure. Unsure of what she felt she needed to say in that moment. Her eyes, red and swollen. For a moment, it looked as though she wanted to comfort me. But when her eyes went to Henry, she became hateful.

"It should have been you," she said through clenched teeth.

"What?" I asked, hurt. Astounded that I could be hurt by someone I never knew.

"It should have been you!" she cried and then shoved me.

I fell back into Henry's casket, the weight of him destroying me. And at the sound of the lid slamming shut, my heart fell into my stomach. I turned to face him, uncaring of Ally's screams and cries in that moment.

A closed casket—a much more traumatizing sight. Soon, Henry would be in the ground, never to be seen again.

Ally screamed and fell to her knees, and Max aided her as best he could. Comforted her. Something he never did with me. Something he probably never dreamt of doing. He looked at me. I noticed that everyone, other than Ally, looked at me.

Again, I felt my presence to be disrespectful. No one wanted me there. I saw it in their eyes. So I dismissed myself from the funeral home—though not to retire completely.

I remained outside until the end of the ceremony, and when the pallbearers emerged carrying Henry's casket, I fought the urge to break down and cry. I refused to make the day about me though. The day belonged to Henry.

At the burial sight, I stood by my new rental and watched the burial from afar. I found myself to be unworthy of their presence—his friends and family. They never hurt him. They never made him cry, they never disappointed him, not like I had. They never let him down, not like I did. And even though I told Henry how much I loved him the night he died, I couldn't shake the thought that he died feeling unloved. That he remained heartbroken from my decision to leave him. That thought alone devastated me.

After the burial when all his loved ones left, I stayed behind and watched the caretakers pour mounds of dirt onto him. And only when they were finished did I choose to approach him. There he rest, next to his mama. His headstone, a far grander sight than her own, and I started to feel guilty about that.

I kneeled down in front of him, reaching my hands to the fresh dirt that covered him. I grabbed a handful and held it out over him before letting it fall from my fingers on top of him. I never imagined burying him, and I started to choke up at the sight. It became difficult for me to catch my breath, and I bit my knuckles to somehow distract myself from the pain.

"I like the epitaph you chose," Max said, ripping me from my thoughts. Practically startling me. I knew I couldn't handle being berated anymore.

I looked to Henry's epitaph.

Rest Is Thine And Sweet Remembrance Ours

Max chuckled. "Hell, I probably woulda just wrote…rest in peace or some shit."

I became confused by his presence. He stood over me, and for the first time since being near him, I felt no hatred toward me. He handed me a flask.

"What's in it?" I asked.

"Does it matter?"

No. Not at all. I took it from him and sipped the contents, contorting my face to the awful taste of whiskey.

Max kneeled down next to me, and I handed him the flask. "Take some more, kid. You look like you could use it."

So I took another drink and handed it back to him, perplexed by his kindness toward me. He kept his eyes on Henry's headstone while he drank. "Why are you being nice to me?" I asked.

Max shrugged. "Am I? I hadn't realized." I felt no motivation to play his game. I wanted to be alone. With Henry. "I dunno, maybe

I don't see no sense in kickin' you when you're down," he said. "You got enough of that back at the funeral home."

My, my, Max does have a heart. "She was right, you know. It should have been me."

Max took another drink and nodded. "Yeah, probably. But I don't think it woulda made much difference," he said, confounding me.

"What do you mean?" I asked.

He took another drink and handed me the flask. "Hell, if you woulda died that night, I don't think that boy woulda ever forgave himself. He'd carry that burden around the rest of his life, and I think it woulda killed him. Either that, or turned him into me." Max chuckled. "I don't know which is worse." I took a drink of the whiskey and handed it back to him. "I'd rather you carry that burden than him."

Max left me after that, but his words resonated with me. Henry's death became my burden to bare, but I refused to let it kill me. Even though I longed for the peace in which death brings. I longed to be with Henry and my parents again, even if the idea of the afterlife still seemed too far-fetched. I longed to be one with him, in some way. But I knew I had to carry on somehow. My pain I refused to let it kill me because then Henry died for nothing. I refused to let his death be in vain.

Something needed to be done.

CHAPTER TWENTY-NINE:

I RETURNED TO MY PARENTS' THAT NIGHT, immediately greeted by my mutt. Dog wagged his tail a bit, still seeming in somewhat of a funk. I knew the feeling.

I slept in my parents' room again that night, though most of the evening I spent tossing and turning, my mind racing with ideas, possible solutions, plans—anything that could possibly prevent this sort of tragedy from happening again. Though it seemed a fool's errand—I am but one person.

Still, I felt I needed to try something. So the next morning when I awoke, I started writing. I wrote all day, about nothing at first. Mostly just getting my feelings out, venting to my computer as it seemed I no longer had anyone to talk to. But through my pain and my grief, a story started to emerge.

I wrote about myself. About how I'd always had a plan for my life, always had ambition to grow up and be a music journalist in New York City. I wrote about my success, but when a terrible tragedy struck, I wrote that everything that once mattered to me no longer had meaning.

I wrote about my parents. How losing them to the waters of the Rubidoux changed my life forever. How it made me weak and vulnerable, but in doing so, I became open to love.

I wrote about Henry. I wrote that he managed to take all the pain away and give me hope in something again. How he managed to make me feel things I never thought myself capable of feeling. I wrote about how he changed my world forever and about the sacrifice he made in order to save my life from the waters that killed my parents.

And finally, I wrote about Devil's Elbow. The dangers that we as inhabitants face every day. I wrote about the Rubidoux—how it now claimed twenty-six lives. I wrote about the poorly maintained roads and bridges. I spent a week straight writing these things, rearranging my words, editing non-stop throughout.

I added in memories of my parents and of Henry. And in the end, I asked for help. My writings went from being a form of catharsis to a plea for help—some form of absolution for the residents of Devil's Elbow.

The next week—when I became confident enough in my words and assembly—I sent the story off to newspapers all around New York and Tennessee. The state of Tennessee needing a wakeup call, and New York hopefully being the flame under our asses to get something done.

I used a few of my established connections in New York to get editors to read the story. Small towns in Tennessee published it without a second thought.

And within a few week's time, the news of Devil's Elbow spread like wildfire throughout the state of Tennessee. "The Forgotten Community," is what the headlines referred to us as. A colleague of mine even sent a newspaper from the city that published the story, though they became more focused on the tragic love story than anything else.

Even with that, people seemed up in arms about our ordeal, and within a month's time, The Department of City Planning contacted me, assuring me that they planned to do something about Y Highway and access to the community. Whether they needed to set-up emergency response in the community itself or to rebuild the bridges leading to us, they assured me something would be done.

I offered myself to them, whatever they needed. I told them I had over a million dollars, ready, to invest in their efforts—to which they seemed grateful.

Even though it seemed something positive would come of my efforts, every night, I cried for Henry. I started sleeping in my own room again, and the scent of him remained on my pillow. Some times I awoke in the middle of the night reaching for him, only to realize that he would never be there to comfort me again. The shock of which only sent me into a fit of tears, leaving my sweet mutt to have to tend to me.

The nights haunted me, though my days became easier.

Quinn signed the power of attorney, relinquishing all control of the practice unto him. Something I felt eternally grateful for, though I decided to stay in Devil's Elbow. New York lost all its allure, and even with the constant reminder of Henry and my parents being gone, I felt closer to them while in Devil's Elbow. Something I think I needed to survive.

One morning while making coffee, I heard a familiar sound outside the house. Henry's beat-up, old truck pulled up out front, and I became interested in what Max wanted from me. I hadn't spoken with him since the funeral.

I walked onto the porch and Dog picked his head up at the sight of Max exiting Henry's truck. He growled a bit, but I shushed him. "What are you doing here?" I asked.

"I brought you something," he said while opening the truck bed. He removed a large box and carried it to the porch. When he set it down at my feet, I kneeled to look inside.

"What is this?" I asked, bewildered.

"Few of Henry's things. I was just gonna throw 'em out. Figured you might wanna look through 'em first," he said.

"You're getting rid of his things?"

He spit a bit of chaw, some dribbling on his chin. "Nah, not everything."

I reached into the box and pulled out a few shirts. They smelled like him, and I wanted to cry at Max's kind gesture. Though I knew he'd never admit to it being so. Simply just tossing some old things out. I looked deeper in the box and pulled out a copy of *"Of Mice and Men"* by John Steinbeck. A curious thing. Max nodded when I held it up to him.

"Yeah, that was his favorite book. Always tried reading it to me when we was kids. I swear, he must've read that book a million times."

I never knew that about Henry. Though I've read the book before, I decided to read it again, now in a new appreciation. I placed the book back in the box. A pair of white, lacy panties caught my eye. I held them up, studying them. "Wow."

"Figured you might want those back," he muttered, uncomfortable. "They are yours, right?" he asked.

An awkward laugh escaped me. "Uh, yeah…from our day at Crybaby Hollow…"

"I don't need to know the damn details," he said. "There's, uh…a few notebooks in there too. He liked to draw a lot. And write. I think there may be some stuff about you in some of them," he said, and I pulled a few composition books from the box.

"Thank you, Max. This is all…very kind," I said, overwhelmed.

"Uh huh," he muttered and started making his way back to the truck. "By the way, I read that article you wrote," he said.

I stood and folded my arms, amused. "What'd you think?"

"It read like a damn romance novel to me."

I smirked. "It's called pathos."

"Yeah, whatever," he scoffed. Though it looked as if he still had something on his mind. He hesitated. "I, uh…heard a rumor that they're gonna do something about the bridges." I nodded. "That because of you?" he asked.

"I think it's because of Henry."

He climbed inside Henry's truck and said nothing else before driving away, disappearing into the woods surrounding the dirt driveway.

I sighed and looked down at the box. I sat on the top step and started looking through his composition books. Drawings filled the pages, mostly of animals. I became impressed with him and his talent, something I also never knew about him.

I started flipping through more of his composition books, but when I stumbled upon his writings, I became emotional. I hardly read a few sentences and my eyes swelled with tears. I closed the book and set it aside. For another time, I thought. I will read everything he ever wrote another time.

Dog started licking my face, and I smiled at the feeling. He whined a bit and placed his paw on the box of Henry's things. "What?" I asked. He tried to speak, poor little guy, his voice becoming high-pitched at his attempts. I laughed and reached into the box. "Okay," I said and pulled out the copy of *"Of Mice and Men."* The book seemed to be falling apart, the pages crinkled, having been read many times.

I opened to the first page and started reading out loud to Dog. I think he just enjoyed the sound of my voice. He rested his head on the porch as I continued to read to him.

We stayed out there all day, the two of us, and I became lost in the pages of Henry's favorite book. A book I longed for him to have read to me, but this would have to do. Me reading aloud to myself on the porch. Just me and Dog.

Proof

49
115
226
317

Made in the USA
Charleston, SC
11 September 2016